AN INFINITE PULL

An Infinite Pull

TAYLOR SIMONDS

Library of Congress Cataloging-in-Publication Data
Names; Simonds, Taylor, author.
Title: An Infinite Pull / Taylor Simonds.
ISBN: 9798218376895
Cover illustration by Kelsey Soderstrom
Cover design by Rena Violet
Interior formatting by Rena Violet

*For anyone lost—
keep looking.*

A Story

This is a story about a monster, and a girl who wandered too far.
It starts like this.

Once there were creatures who swam between stars, but now, they are gone.

Luminous beings, spun from the ether itself. Hair of moondust, eyes like opals. Their voices could turn a cold heart warm and kind; their music wove illusions lovely and powerful enough to paint over reality in watercolor.

They came from a world at the very center of the ever-expanding universe, a kingdom cloaked beneath an atmosphere of frothy waves. Medyssia, it was called, and though it was beautiful and peaceful and serene, it could not measure against a stronger beauty: the endless sky that shimmered above, and the impossible melody it sang.

Come out, it whispered, *come out, come away.*

The melody filled their veins, as impossible to resist as choosing not to breathe.

Come away, it called, and they went.

Restless and curious they roamed, painting their light in streaks across the stars, learning the shapes of all the creatures of the ether until they could wear any form like the finest of robes. They wandered, and they learned, and they collected, endlessly fascinated and hungry for every bit of magic the limitless universe held.

But there was something else in the world above, and it hungered too.

A beast. A predator.

A monster.

From the depths of space it crawled, ravenous and cruel. It had no face to mimic, no heart to warm. It cared not for the wonders of the universe. It was a soulless, empty thing, no more than tentacles and teeth, and it existed only to devour.

They called it the Shadow. And when it first tasted the stardust in Medyssian veins, a craving planted itself somewhere ineradicable; a call to blood that would not silence until it had hunted them all to the ends of their universe.

Every.

Last.

One.

The Medyssians knew well how to hide. They hid upon the planets they had made their new homes and they hid in their ships and they hid inside their own illusions, wearing hundreds of faces as masks, thousands of bodies as cloaks.

And yet, the Shadow found them all. No matter where they fled, the ghost ship it used as its lair was never far behind—sails of smoke rippling, prow baring its teeth. It smiled as it tore them apart; it feasted upon screams and blood alike. And before the remains of its prey could even dissolve, its tentacles would unfurl, hungry again.

No more could the Medyssians swim through the stars. No choice did they have, the few who remained, but to flee back to their home at the core of the universe. And there, together, they created one last illusion.

A barrier. An invisible shield cradling the planet itself. It swept Medyssia into its impenetrable folds and hid it from

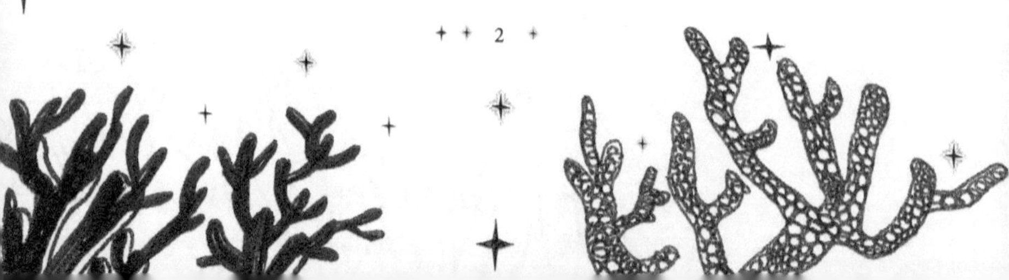

the outside world they had once loved so fiercely, never to be broken until the Shadow was gone. Until it was safe.

And so, the lost kingdom slept as if enchanted, forgotten by time. Waiting as long as it took, standing guard over every restless soul that remained. Souls that were once ethereal and inquisitive and swam between stars, but now are gone.

Well.

All but one.

A girl.

A girl who could resist the pull of the stars even less than the rest of her kind. A girl who wandered too far, who did not hear when she was called to return.

A girl who was left behind.

When she realized her mistake, she pounded against a door that didn't exist, screamed into a void that didn't answer back. She searched and searched, desperate for a sign of her home.

She searched and searched, and found nothing but an infinite darkness.

She was abandoned, alone in the expanse. The last. The lost.

I'll find you, became the desperate melody in her head as she wandered, as every star in the empty reaches of space blurred into an endless streak. *I'll find you.*

But the Shadow was out there too, and when the night went dark and still, she could sometimes hear it approaching, a ghostly echo behind her no matter how far she ran.

And its silent, hungry voice sang the same melody.

I'll find you.

I'll find you.

I'll find you.

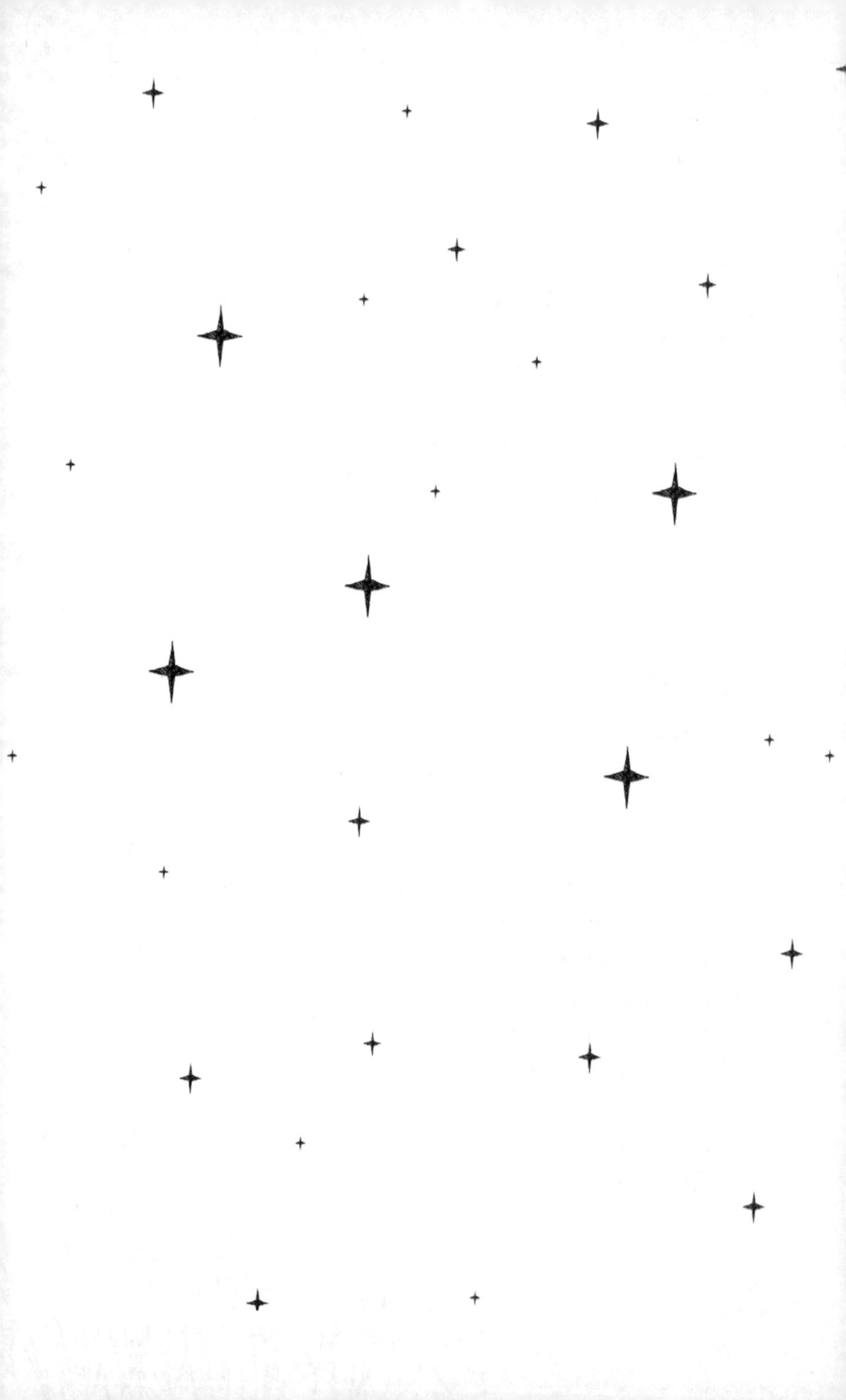

CHAPTER 1

Aren

THE void of space unfurls like liquid smoke, and the only sign of life is the flying ship in the clouds.

Its prow cuts in and out of the fog, a fortress in the emptiness poised to attack or defend. The sleek sides of it are studded with enough cannons to carry the silent threat of both, even without the thousand-strong crew that prowls its belly—counting coin, cleaning weapons, laughing or boasting or sleeping off their latest bounty—but its upper decks are near-empty. The shields armoring the ship are guardians themselves, and if any of the unknowable creatures that roam the deep exist out there, instinct keeps them subdued, teeth and tentacles and all.

There's only one silhouette standing guard from the mast. Skinny, boy-shaped. Unused blaster at his hip, spyglass secure in position. Symmetry: the ship watches over the void, and the boy watches over the ship. At least, he's meant to.

But his left eye keeps malfunctioning.

"*Oh, come on.*"

I lean over the mess of my worktable and slap the side of the crackling holographic projector, meant to be sending me a live feed of the decoy-Aren's view from the outlook. For a second, it returns—the deck of the *Starsaviour*, the fog, the star-drained void. Then it dies again.

I lean farther, flipping the projector around to reach the console as I mutter curses under my breath. This is what I get for handing off watch duty to a training dummy outfitted in one of my old jackets and a modified pair of night-specs. But in my defense, keeping watch ranks somewhere below mopping the blood off the infirmary floor in terms of pointlessness. Two things are fact, aboard the *Starsaviour*: the infirmary floor will never not be bloody, and you'd have to be an idiot with a death wish to attack us.

I fiddle with the wiring until the screen hums to life between my fingers. A bright, smaller-scale recreation of the void washes back over the worktable's corner, bathing discarded blueprints and the glass-shard remains of my last few prototypes in pale gold light. I scan the holographic deck, the sails, the shields, the space beyond. No breaches. No threats. As always.

And yet it still smells like something is on *fire*—

I yelp and leap back from the table edge. I've been leaning directly on top of a welder, still active, and its tiny flame has been calmly and merrily burning through my leather apron.

I grapple for the release on the extinguishing lever nailed precariously to the wall, beating out the worst of the fire with my free hand. An explosion of powdery steam, a hiss of sparks recoiling into ash, and soon nothing is left but the familiar smell of curdling smoke. I lift my visor, coughing into the glorified storage chamber I use as a workshop, then hastily snatch my latest prototype from the chaos and scan it for damage. No cracks in the glass shell, no breakage in the wires sprouting from the connection point of its activation switch like roots. Light refracts off the intricate weaving of conduits and gears, all still perfectly intact.

I exhale. I don't have time to start this over again, not when I need to finish a working model before the captain gets back from her latest mission. This is the closest I've gotten yet to the designs scrawled on the pages littering my worktable: a device that will scan and analyze genetic material, then create a holographic model of the person it came from. Something that could be used on the kind of nauseating remnants— blood, hair, fingernails—that get left behind by scavengers and rogues, ones the Celestial Company bounty hunters have a harder time catching if they don't have a face to match to the warrant. The crew, potentially even the captain herself, is going to be so impressed with a device like this.

Once I get it to work.

I lay the orb next to its two-dimensional counterpart, sketched roughly on an ancient blueprint, and search for inevitable flaws. The original design model was a mess beyond its original concept, and so were my first fifteen-or-so rounds of modifications. But this one, apart from a few leftover smudges of ash, looks . . . functional. It hasn't melted, like prototype twelve, or collapsed in on itself, like prototype six, or turned its own mechanism into a propeller that nearly sliced my fingers off, like prototype eight. The liquid weaving through the tubing is a clear, viscous blue instead of the puce-colored sludge of prototype three, or the mess that evaporated when exposed to artificial oxygen, like protoype seven. This one will do what it's meant to.

I just need to test it.

I spin my chair to glance up at the endless bronze storage towers walling me in on all sides but one—the last belongs to the churning gears and steam-exhaling pipes of the engine room. The precariously tilting shelves are a chaos of forgotten tech, half-finished blueprints, broken weapons, and boxed-up spoils. This is where the long-neglected remnants of the Celestial Company's innovative endeavors go to die. Everything in this room has been deemed worthless: broken, useless, incomplete. It's also the only place where no one will demand to know what I'm up to, which is usually a rhetorical question that ends with me having to clean something.

I heft the retractable ladder compressed under my table out, then flip on the hypermagnetic teeth of the gears I've rigged to its outermost rungs. The steadily-moving chain of the clockwork engine guard churns past my worktable's platform, disappearing in a spiral between the storage towers. I brace myself for the whiplash, edge close enough for the ladder's teeth to catch, and wait for the grating *clank*—

—and I'm lifted up, ladder swinging like a pendulum.

The towers glide past, and I angle myself away from the lone porthole as the chain curves in front of it, scanning the shelves.

"Biomaterial," I mutter to myself, squinting ahead. *Where are you?*

I can easily imagine the number of knives that would get drawn on me if I asked any of the crew for a blood sample, and I've fainted at the sight of needles enough times to know that using my own isn't an option. But I hid a case of vials in cryo up here, out of the blast range; I just have to remember where—

"*—ha!*"

I pull hard on the crank, and the gears churning the platform along grind to a stop, disconnecting and reconnecting to the metal of the tower instead of the chain. The bronze case juts haphazardly out from beneath a massive caricature of a blaster, sides riddled with cracked gauges and gears. I wrestle it flat one-handed, unlatch it with a hiss, and peer into frost-steaming rows of rust-red fluid. They belong to someone who mattered as little as the rest of this abandoned chamber. Disgusting. Perfect.

I've never been able to find the right words to explain to the rest of the crew what it is that draws me to tinker with things everyone else has dismissed as junk. Technology is artistry and science all rolled into one; it's learning to speak languages that will fry your fingers or fill your lungs with ash if you get the translation wrong. It's messy and infuriating.

When it works, it's almost magic.

But the Celestial Company tends to prioritize the blasters-and-swords sort of artistry. It's easier to outsource tech design and leave the crew to just pull the expertly-crafted triggers. There's something of a gap when it comes to in-house design.

I would fill it, if they'd let me.

I jam a few vials in my pocket and punch a fist to the side of the ladder. With a half-hiss, half-screech, it careens back down.

One more glance at the porthole, at the hologram of the prow. Clear skies. No threats in sight.

"Okay. Prototype uh… seventeen? Eighteen?" I squint at the opaque support column scribbled over with formulas and calculations and scratch a quick note on it. "Eighteen." *Come on. Come on.* I pry a canister open, fish a dropper out of my toolbelt, and hunch over to carefully, carefully lower a few drops of blood into the tubing. Seal it, fingers shaking, and lower my thumb to the activation switch. This is the one. It'll happen this time. A whirring of gears. A beam of light. A stranger's face materializing on the other side.

"Come on," I pray under my breath. "Please. This time,

please."

Sparks explode across my workshop.

I throw my arm in front of my head just before they hit me. But when I emerge panting, there aren't any flames—not on my arm, not on the floor, not spewing from a blackened prototype. The entire room is untouched.

It takes too many precious, confused seconds to realize what that means: the blast came from the hologram.

No. *No.* The orb rolls benignly away as I fumble through the chaos for my communicator, which has somehow burrowed itself under a stack of calculations.

"Hey, uh, Havelock?" I stammer into the buzzing static. "I mean, Lieutenant? Um, small problem."

A pause long enough for me to worry that I'm out of range, and then a clipped, even: "Define small."

"There's a—" I scan the frenetic projection for the piece that's wrong, and a dormant spark reasserts itself helpfully. "—hole in the shields. Uh, midship. Starboard—" *Wait.* I hold my hands out in front of me, forefinger and thumb splayed in an L, and mutter the mnemonic under my breath. "Port side."

"Dimensions?"

"Um . . . problem . . . sized?"

"Cause?"

"I don't know, I—I didn't see."

Another pause, and I know this one is being filled by my training commander pinching the bridge of her nose hard enough to bruise if she weren't more bronze than flesh. "Any breaches?"

"No." I tap the side of the projector, and the hologram flickers out, then in again. This time, a set of wriggling, fanged curves appear on the other side of the hole. "Potentially. Um. They sort of look like worms with teeth—?"

"Devouring eels. We must have hit a hive. Don't engage. We'll meet you up there."

And with that, the line whirs closed.

I exhale, lowering the communicator. What in the void is a *devouring eel?*

Something that isn't my problem, I guess. I did my job. The decoy worked perfectly. I caught the breach. They're gonna meet me up there.

Oh. They're gonna meet me up there.

My chair clatters over as I lunge. Stuff the prototype in my pocket, grapple for the worn leather of my night-specs, pat myself down—specs, blaster, tool belt, pants, okay, I'm wearing pants—then dive into the passageway leading back to my quarters.

It only takes a few steps for something worse than adrenaline to start pumping through my veins, reminding me exactly what I'm running toward. I can see the breach and its cause in every shadowy corner, hear it in every moaning overhead pipe: that piece of the shields crackling and sucked away, the monsters—*devouring eels, why is it never, like, sightseeing eels*—that are now seeping through. I consider, not for the first time, whether I could get away with taking a blaster to the foot as an excuse to stay in my workshop, leave what's waiting for me on the top deck to anyone else.

Knowing Havelock, she'd make me finish the job with a limp.

Knowing me, my shot would probably miss, anyway.

By the time I stumble through the sliding panel in my bedroom wall and pull it shut behind me, impatient footsteps are already thundering down the hall outside. I get the door open just in time to catch a glimpse of a pair of pink topknots, both speared through with a slim blade, and ears that taper into a sharp, gold-scaled point. Cassiope. Two years older and always two steps ahead.

"Havelock said we've got eels!" she shrieks, turning to race backward. Her reflection darts ahead of her against the mirror-polished walls, as if even it's eager to outrun me. "Whoever kills the most wins!"

I try and fail to match pace with her. "No way Havelock said that."

Her fanglike incisors catch the blinking red lights overhead with a mischievous gleam. "I'll win anyway."

"Nobody's challenging—*hey!*"

Something yanks hard on the back of my specs, choking me to a clumsy halt in the center of the hallway.

"And you won't be winning anything unless you put a suit on," I hear, and then a metal clip pinches painfully into my ear.

"*Ow*—Felix!" I clap a hand over the throbbing cartilage. Starwalking suit activator. Once it's triggered, it'll encase my body in a permeable, flexible layer of oxygen and regulated pressure. It's exactly as claustrophobic as it sounds.

I wince up at Cas's twin brother, identical in every sharp detail down to the gold-edged scales outlining his cheekbones, apart from his hair and skin—luminous teal instead of pink. "What are my odds regarding *not* participating in an eel-killing challenge?"

"You mean ignoring a defense call without the captain keelhauling you? Zero." Felix herds me toward the hydraulic lift that'll take us to the top deck. Cas is already holding the grate open, tapping the curling-vine heel of her boot impatiently. "And weren't you supposed to be up on deck already? Aren't you on watch?"

"N—no. I mean ... I forgot my blaster." I don't know why I bother lying. I have the universe's most obvious tell—my hand is already leaping up to scratch at the two overlapping crescent moons tattooed at the base of my neck. "Assuming blasters even work on devouring eels. Probably has an impenetrable hide, or eats cannons."

"Everything has a weakness." Cas slides the grate shut with a flourish, and the lift shudders upward. "We'll figure it out."

It'd sound like a bluff on anyone else, but "we'll figure it out" is extremely literal when it comes to Cas and Felix. That's their thing, after all: Felix can look at anything and instantly understand how it works. Ship blueprints, building layouts, the anatomy of every species imaginable—it's all in his head. One look, and he knows exactly where the weak points are.

Then he tells Cas, and she stabs them.

Lieutenant Havelock is in the anteroom when the doors open, white pixie-cut gleaming in the slivers of starlight escaping from the open hatch, brow furrowed irritably over her telescopic eye. An arsenal case gleams open at her side.

"You need to be ten seconds faster on response," she barks, unloading a matching set of long-rage blasters. "You know what to do. Try to keep the deck clean, would you? That hole will need to be cleared before Aren can—" She frowns when the twins move forward to take their weapons, leaving me in her sightline. "What are you doing down here?"

"Um." I evade both the lie and the unavoidable twitch that would give it away with a shrug. "Getting . . . orders?"

"Your orders are to fix the breach." Havelock unhooks a crackling energy diffuser from her holster and shoves it into my chest, where I fumble for the deactivation switch before any skin gets fried. "You like tech, don't you?"

Not this kind. Using a diffuser to manually patch the shields is about as techy as repainting a door is artistic. Worse, it's going to put me right next to the hole the eels are leaking through.

"Actually, could I maybe—"

"It's a *stick*, Aren." Havelock scowls, adjusting the rod so it's pointed right-side-up. "You pull it from one end of the hole to the other, and you fill in the gaps. It's the easiest possible task."

"But—"

"Is that too much for you to handle? Would scraping filth from the hull be more to your liking?"

"*No.*" I don't remember deciding to move, but suddenly my feet are on the first rung of the ladder. "No, I'll fix it."

"That's what I thought." Havelock's eye contracts, and she grasps the rim of the hatch and pulls herself through in one swift motion.

Cas and Felix scutter up after her, but I'm still frozen, clutching the diffuser.

It's a stick, Aren. I repeat Havelock's words in my head, teeth gritted, because she's right. *The easiest possible task.*

I pull my specs up and fumble for the color-correcting knobs, squinting against a view that suddenly turns sharply, painfully fluorescent. Brown glows yellow and white goes searing and the black filter of space seeping through the hatch becomes an intense, vivid blue. No one else's specs have lenses like these; I had to modify them myself. It's headache-inducing, but the knot in my stomach unclenches slightly as soon as my eyes adjust.

Because the truth is, the layer of panic tightening around me like a shell casing has nothing to do with devouring eels. And the real reason I skived off watch wasn't just so I could finish the genetic scanner.

I force myself upward until I'm overcast by a lattice of deep mahogany rigging and rippling solar sails and dangling gold ropes, all catching the light of the thousands and thousands of stars echoing out into forever. Even with my specs turning the infinite black into a peaceful ocean, I can barely stand to look at it.

No, I'm not afraid of the monsters that crawl through the space between stars. I'm afraid of space itself.

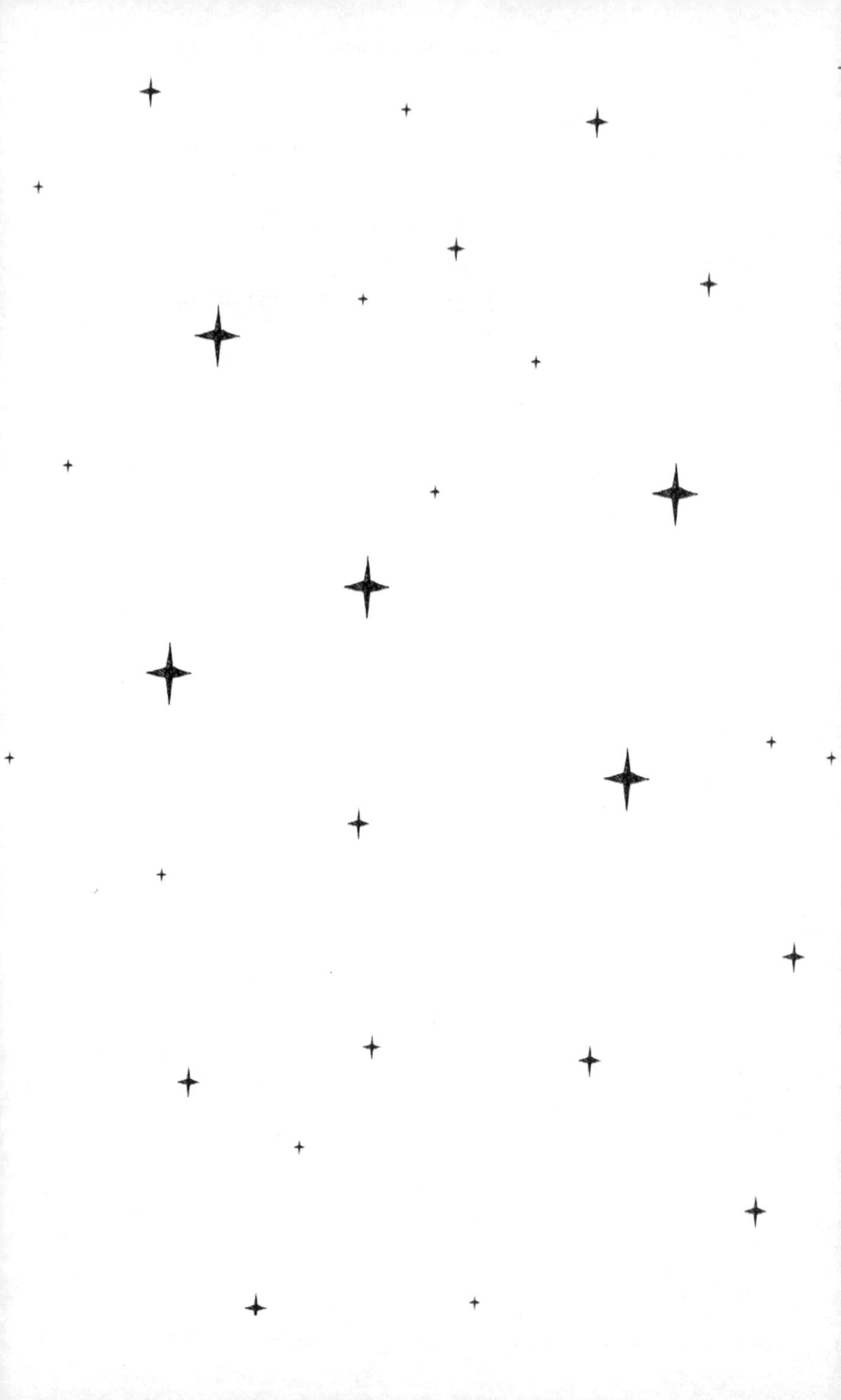

CHAPTER 2

Aren

THE crew of the *Starsaviour* has a lot to say about the void. Deep, poetic things. The kind of thing that must only come to you while leaning out over the bow, wind in your hair, starlight glinting in your eyes. They say it's the beginning and end of all existence. That our souls return out into the essence of the universe when we die. That it can be a vicious tempest or a restless mistress or any manner of other nonsensically deep, poetic metaphors. I know what they all see when they look into its black depths: adventure, glory, mystery. This is a crew of fighters and bounty hunters, smugglers and sailors, and the void is their home. And as for me—I was raised on this ship, born into that void. How can I be afraid of it?

It's an excellent question. It's a question I have never been able to answer.

All I know is that the void is a beast looming over and around and beneath me, desperate to wrap me in its fist and squeeze. It wants to drown me in its silent, airless depths, billions of ghostly eyes leering as I suffocate. It's always there, cold fingers clawing at the cracks of anything I invent to keep it out.

But the only thing that can match the terror I feel when

I think about space is the thought of anyone else finding out about it.

The Celestial Company is full of the ghosts of crew members who couldn't keep up, who showed weakness, who fell behind and were left behind. Marooned in that void, permanently. Lost, tetherless, swallowed by the dark. Everyone else forgets their names, but I remember them all. Baen Frakes, who sang like an out-of-tune horn. Keira Locke, who liked to swear she could steal the nose from a man's face without him noticing.

One man who doesn't even have a name, banished personally by the captain so long ago that everything about his memory has been annihilated like the worst of her enemies. A man who is only ever mentioned in vague, peripheral whispers too inconsistent to make sense of, extinguished like a dying candle before the captain can overhear. *He panicked. He cracked under pressure. He let something big get away. Someone almost died. Someone* did *die.*

I think about him most. That shapeless, formless stain on the *Starsaviour's* history. What he must have done, how he must have failed, to be so worth erasing.

What I can do to make sure I never follow in his path.

My fingers twitch toward the orb in my pocket as I force myself through the hatch, and in that distracted instant, I get my first glimpse of a devouring eel.

It's a slithering nightmare, at least three meters long and completely disregarding the entire concept of artificial gravity. It dives through the air straight toward me in a slimy blur of ink-dark hide and bulging eyes, and then its permanent grin unhooks and its jaw stretches large enough to inhale me whole.

I let out a yell and fumble to aim the diffuser even though

it hardly counts as a weapon, but as the eel's gaping mouth closes in, there's a loud *crack*, and its body is thrown sideways. It drops to the deck and rolls to a limp stop, at least six other corpses littering the stretch behind it.

"Margot, guard your own quadrant!" snaps a gruff voice.

"Maybe if your aim were better, I wouldn't have to guard us both!"

I scan the deck and catch a glimpse of the rest of the crew Havelock must have ordered up to assist—Osgood, a just-recruited fighter pilot, with his jovial, bombastic shooting technique; Margot, who names all our engines like pets; and Jori, a communications expert who speaks almost every known language in the galaxy.

"They're hungry!" Jori shouts, launching a harpoon that connects with one of the eels and drags it writhing to the deck. I guess "eel" is one of his languages. "Hear that hissing pattern? That panel needs to get fixed before they frenzy!"

"You don't say," Havelock snarls, leveling her own harpoon gun and striking another black ribbon out of the sky. I watch it drop behind her as she wheels impatiently toward me. "Are you waiting for the shields to extend a personal invitation, Master Aren?"

The shields in question crackle in a wide sphere over the *Starsaviour's* netted rigging, encasing the ship in its own atmosphere. I swallow, scanning the thousands upon thousands of perfect gold hexagons for the one weak link that's ruining my life today. I hope it's close to the railing. "No, Lieutenant."

"Then get—" Havelock lunges for my collar, and her telescopic eye whirs toward the apex of the dome. "—*up* there."

"Up" does not bode well.

And there it is—the damaged panel. It's past the top of the highest foremast, hundreds of feet above me. Nowhere near the rigging; nowhere close enough to the mast for me to work with my feet still clinging to any form of solid ground.

I'm going to die.

"There?" I choke out. "Up *there?*"

"Cassiope, Felix, cover," Havelock orders, then storms back into the fray, wrenching her harpoon free of the downed eel.

I peer up at the hole, at what's on the other side of it. It's small, not nearly formidable enough to win a fight against the *Starsaviour's* gravity cores. Am I imagining it, then, the way the ropes beneath the sails seem to strain like they're already caught in invisible teeth?

"Watch this." Cas unsheathes a ruby-hilted knife from somewhere beneath the deep V of her billowing shirt's collar, aims at a creature reduced to a wriggling worm by distance, and flicks her wrist. The flash of silver not only slices through the first eel, but boomerangs off and guts a second. Her victorious smirk consumes her face. "Two-zero."

Felix thwacks at one of Cas's topknots. "No one else is counting, you halfwit. Aren—wait for us to clear out the swarm around the breach before you move in, okay?"

I'm *really* going to die. I clench the diffuser. "You know, I hear patching shields is even more impressive than shooting down eels. Last chance to trade."

Cas gives my forehead a mocking flick. "If you get eaten, I call your room." Then she runs for the main mast without even bothering to tether in and vanishes up into the rigging. "*Three-zero!*"

"Still not counting!" Felix rotates a blaster over his shoulder and fells another eel in one soundless, precise shot, then takes off after his sister.

"Show-offs," I mutter, but I'd do the same if I could, with

Havelock watching. She's the one they need to impress, after all—the one all three of us need to impress if we ever want to get out of training and be sent on real missions. Cas and Felix, at least, must be close by now. Unlike me, they weren't raised on this ship from infancy. They were nine and they were orphans on Vitalari, and they stole a jeweled compass right out of the captain's pocket.

And she didn't realize it was gone for three hours.

Then she tracked them down, and they'd already sold it for food. "Get it back," she ordered. And they did. From the locked inside vault of a shop guarded by two armed sentinels.

In six minutes.

Obviously, she recruited them.

Youngest recruits to the Celestial Company ever, actually. They don't forget it, and neither do I. The day Cas and Felix came aboard was the day I realized I could be replaced.

"Today, Aren!"

"Sorry!" I haul a line of tether away from its anchor and clip in, then start maneuvering my way up the foremast, diffuser hooked securely to my belt. *You are safe,* I order my frantic pulse as I climb, *you are fine. It won't pull you out.*

Maybe an eel will bite through your tether, the other voice in my head whispers sadistically, and I press my knees to the mizzen.

I don't realize I've reached the gaff rig until I run out of wood to cling to. The rest of the way up is all solar sails, impossible to grip without interfering with the ship's trajectory. The wide expanse of the deck spreads out below me, eels coiling and uncoiling like streaks of oil on its surface. I can see the rest of the swarm through the damaged panel—maybe two dozen of them on the other side, writhing against one another to get in. Whenever one gets close, unharnessed energy sparks out from the edges, frying its hide and sending it back hissing.

And all I can see is that hole yawning wide as a squid's maw the second I approach it, of eel tails lashing around my wrists and dragging me into that infinite darkness, of the shields falling away behind me as the universe swallows me whole.

Havelock said the patch rod was nothing but a stick, and that's never felt more accurate. I clutch it like the most useless kind of sword, numbness starting to give way to desperation. I'm not the only crew member who's ever had to crawl up to the line between safety and oblivion, one tether malfunction or rabid predator or calculation error from being sucked into the void. My own fear aside, there's got to be a better way to complete a patch job.

A streak of black slithers into my vision, but just as its carnivorous eyes turn toward me, a cannonball flies toward it and expands into a staticky net, dragging its shrieking form out of sight.

"*Taste that!*" Osgood bellows somewhere beneath me.

It's unfair, really, that I'm even up here. If I were a better shot, I could be back on deck with everyone else, with nothing to do but aim and release instead of... of...

Hmm.

Half an idea takes murky shape.

I glance up at the panel I'm supposed to be patching, then carefully feel around for my blaster; unscrew the base of the diffuser and rummage through my belt for a wire threader and an ammo pod. The tide of anxiety starts to ebb as I blur everything but the tools into white noise. White noise, and everything I can remember about how the coil of raw energy inside the rod is looped, how it fuses with the shields, how the ammo charge reacts to a firing mechanism. Tiny boxes in my head cracked open and reassembled, configuring into something new.

When it's done and not combusting, I cram the pod into my blaster and stare directly at the stars, heartbeat thundering in my ears. *Breathe in. Aim.* The hole is a fixed point, impossible to miss the way I constantly miss moving targets. *Breathe out. Release.*

I stay my hand. Is this a bad idea? No. No, the worst thing that could happen is that my shot goes wide, that the altered charge does nothing, that I end up exactly where I already was. I at least ought to try.

This will work. It will.

Release. RELEASE.

I fire.

And I miss.

Of course, I miss.

But somehow, the mechanism works anyway.

The shot collides with the shields three feet to the left of the missing panel, but then it ripples—traces the network of crackling gold panels right to the edge and erupts into a net of pure energy that attaches itself seamlessly coil by coil, inch by inch, until the hole is filled, the gap is closed, the shields are fixed.

The shields are *fixed.*

As if hungry to test it, a soulless flesh-puppet of a face strays toward the net, only for a burst of energy to sear against its hide, throwing it back with a screech.

I let out a noise that's somewhere between choke and laugh, between victory and disbelief.

"Did you *see that*—" I wheel to face the deck, but no one is watching—too busy dealing with the last straggling remains of our invaders. It doesn't matter. I made something practical, something useful, something that will help the entire crew. It worked, it—

Something stings the back of my hair, and I only recognize it as a sharp burst of heat when it doesn't let up.

I tilt back toward the shields with a frown, only to find an erratic spark of orange crosshatching the center of the re-placed panel. When it flares out, I have to adjust the focus on my specs because they must have gotten bumped; they must be malfunctioning; the light is refracting wrong. There can't be a missing spot in the center.

The spot spreads.

It spreads like someone's taken a match to it, eating away at the net thread by thread until the entire panel crumbles away.

And it doesn't stop there.

The burning continues, out and out and out, two panels, four panels, nine, growing and growing until there's not a hole in the shields, but a crater.

No. *No.*

"Uh… Lieutenant?" The voice that comes out doesn't sound like mine. "Lieutenant!"

"*What*, Ar—" Havelock doesn't even finish my name. The last two letters turn into a gasp, and then she's shouting something that might be commands or expletives or just *What did you do, what did you do?* but whatever it is, I can't hear it anymore.

Frenzy, Jori warned, and frenzy is how the remaining eels descend.

They fall through the cavity in an avalanche of serpentine bodies, not two dozen individual creatures but one writhing mass with two dozen heads. They swarm straight past me, and three horrible noises follow.

A howl like the first wind before a storm.

The crack of two dozen jaws unhinging as one.

And then the screams from below.

I don't remember moving—there's no way I would, could never look at the shrieking cyclone of teeth and tails and gunfire blooming over the deck below and not want to stay as far away as possible—but somehow, I do. I seize hold of my own tether and haul myself back to the deck, boots pounding like a second heartbeat against wood, like I can *fix this, I have to fix this* if I only reach the ground fast enough.

But Havelock is yelling, and Osgood is shooting with reckless abandon, taking splintered chunks out of the railing, and Cas and Felix are picking eels off one by one from somewhere in the rigging, and all the sound in the universe has been replaced by the clanging pulse of an alarm.

All hands is the subtext it bellows, *all hands, all hands—*

I hit the deck in a crumple of limbs as the first wave of crew spills through the hatch. Some shoeless, some stained with the blood and sweat of a just-completed mission, all passionately committed to the *shoot first, ask questions later* code this alarm demands. Charges sizzle past my ears, and I should help, have to help, because every inch of this is my fault, and—

And somewhere in the swarm, Osgood is roaring at Margot for commandeering his harpoon gun, and there's an eel lunging straight for them, and—

I fumble for my blaster, aim at the shrieking beast, and—

Nothing. There's not even a charge emission to go wide. The trigger jams in my hand, the insides fried by my failed experiment.

The eel's tail lashes out, catching Osgood in the chest.

And then it throws him up and over the side of the ship.

Osgood is a cannon of a person, bulky and stalwart and

solid, and he should never be able to move like a leaf caught in the wind, but he does. He's not wearing a tether, and his stalwart, solid limbs go limp and flailing, his eyes wide with shock.

The crater in the shields is a whirlpool, and it seizes him, and I can't do anything but watch as he shrinks through my lenses like a star being reclaimed by that endless black.

"Man overboard!" someone cries, and then Margot's over the side too, her own tether streaming behind her. But as she reaches for Osgood, she slams to a stop like she's hit a wall, a jaw clamped around the base of the tether. The eel worries her like a fish caught on a line and then snaps—

"Margot!"

I don't know how I manage to catch the rope before it slithers out into the current, but I do, and then I can't do anything else. The ship's railing practically cuts me in half at the waist trying to wrench me over the side, rope burn dragging its way through my palms.

"Hold on!" I gasp, and I don't know if I'm talking to Margot or myself, because I can't move, and the pull of the void is a monster I will never match. "Hold on, hold on—"

My pulse spikes through my wrists. My arms shake.

The rope wrenches itself out of my hands.

And Osgood drops to the deck.

He splinters the floorboards as he lands, a cannonball with enough force to knock over the crew members closest to him. Slick black hide pins him down, nothing but sturdy boots and his ruddy face visible. My stomach heaves as the sawdust settles and the eel slithers to the side, ready for a view of mauled flesh and bloodied stumps for limbs and lips blue-frosted from his brief exposure to the void. But the eel doesn't feed. It's motionless—*no.*

It's the one who's been mauled.

A clean slash vivisects it from skull to tail in one swift line. The pasty curve of its spine gleams in the moonlight. Osgood finishes pushing it away, groans, and rubs the back of his head.

Another cleanly slaughtered creature crashes down beside it.

A third. A fourth. A fifth. Each finished with one thin, surgical line.

I scan the storm above me, a different kind of fear beginning to bleed through my veins. The Celestial Company crew is ruthless, unbeatable. But only one of us works with this kind of finesse.

"Cease fire!" someone bellows, "Back—clear a path—" Weapons lower, bare feet pound a retreat beneath the sails. But the eels continue to rain down bloodlessly, effortlessly, one pair of dead eyes after another.

A hand clamps down on my shoulder. "Better get out of her way."

My heartbeat short-circuits. Margot leaps down from the railing—she must have hauled herself back in while I was anchoring the loose end. Relief flutters weakly in my veins. That's one thing I did right, then.

I doubt it'll matter much. Not to the phantom slaughtering eels above us.

It's an invisible blur—the only way I can track it is through the path it cuts through the mass of beasts, now scattered and fleeing and never fast enough to escape. And in the offbeat of that steadily droning alarm, I hear the familiar slash of a sword through flesh, a metallic whisper slicing through each eel one by one, until finally—

Whump.

The last monstrous corpse slams down to the deck before me, spattering me with gore and throwing me to the ground.

The decoy-Aren spills from its mouth, stomach torn to ribbons and cracked night-specs hanging by threads from its broken neck. I fight the urge to gag as I scramble away from it, and then—

Whump.

A sleek pair of boots lands beside it. The silence that follows rings in my ears—enough to make me think for a second that the shields have failed completely, that the soundless vacuum of space is pouring in. But no. It's just *her.*

The captain of the *Starsaviour.*

Leader of all one thousand members of the Celestial Company. Untouchable, invincible. The closest thing the space between stars has to a queen.

Valyra Vanthal.

The trailing ends of her ivory coat settle in the dust; her sword leaks blood like an open wound. Stray flecks of fire settle in her long, dark hair and turn to ash.

I don't even have to look at her to know which blend of fury and rage is caught in her face; it's radiating off her like smoke. But I swallow and look up anyway, until I find the bronze pin at her collar—two large crescent moons, one light, one dark, just like the tattoo on the back of my neck—and stare at it instead, unable to make eye contact.

"Hey, Mom," I whisper.

CHAPTER 3

Aren

H ERE's a better story than mine.

Once, there was a girl. Seventeen, same as I am now. An orphan, her only family the one she had chosen for herself. Depending on who tells it, she was either ruthlessly beautiful or beautifully ruthless, but everyone agrees on this: she was a girl with a sword, and she wielded it like it had chosen her. She was only seventeen, but she had enough fire in her blood to burn down a planet.

And there was an emperor. The cruel, bloodthirsty kind who loves to crop up in weak pockets of space, who had amassed enough power to draw half the galaxy under his control and slaughter the rest. Worlds fell beneath his heel. When he killed her parents, she could have run and hidden like everyone else, but she had a sword, and she had her loyal friends, and she had a spirit that didn't know how to rest without justice. She trained and trained, and then she came for him.

They say he laughed at her. He called her a little girl.

She used that sword, and she annihilated him.

After, when his prisoners found her, they held her blood-stained hands and cried on her dirt-stained clothes and called her a savior. And she could have rested after that—her family avenged, her people freed—but then she learned about a beast hunting children in a distant star system.

Maybe some people can stop being a savior, once they've started. Maybe they can go retire on a farm somewhere. But it woke something up that day, in my mom, and she realized she couldn't stop.

She has never stopped. Valyra's ship might be called the *Starsaviour*, but the title is hers, through and through. Twenty years, one thousand loyal crew members, and an uncountable number of missions later, she is still that woman with the sword, smoke combed through her hair, grinning dauntlessly at her next adversary.

She's not grinning now.

I force myself to look right into the weight of her cold stare and see everything I hate about myself reflected back. Our eyes are the same gray-blue, our hair the same dark navy—like it was dipped in ink, people say. I don't know when she grew into the sharp angles of her face, but I'm really, really hoping it was post-seventeen, because I don't know if I can handle looking this malnourished forever.

"Mom," I begin, stumbling to my feet. "I—"

"*So.*" Her voice is velvet lined with razor blades. "I leave for one night to bring aid to the Idri rebellion, and the ship falls to ruin."

She turns away, surveying the damage. Splintering ribbons of torn wood curl away from the masts; rotting corpses cling to the deck like leeches. Half a dozen tethers are tangled in a knot around their anchor, the one severed unit leaking depressurized oxygen with a miserable hiss. And then there's this small fraction of the crew—two hundred coughing, disheveled, irritable mercenaries dusting blaster refuse from their clothes and eel guts from their hands.

I should have picked scrubbing the filth from the hull when I had the chance.

Valyra flexes her fingers around the hilt of her sword. "Is someone going to seal that breach? Or must I handle that for you as well?"

A green-scaled engineer disconnects from the crowd and scuttles up the mast, another sealant rod clenched nervously in his teeth.

"Now." Valyra rakes her gaze over the rest of the crew, her tall boots *click-click*ing gently against the floor. "What. *Happened?*"

Havelock's white hair emerges like a lit candle from the shadows. "There was a shield malfunction. We hit a nest of—"

"Yes, that I gathered, Lieutenant. What I'd like to know is who is responsible for *this*." Her gloved hand winds in and out of her coat, and then a cracked bronze pod with tentacle-strands of disconnected wiring glints in her palm. My failed invention. It must have caught on the fried edges of the breach.

"What," Valyra asks quietly, "would you presume this to be?"

Havelock's telescopic eye twitches wide, then flashes laser-red in my direction. My legs turn to water.

"Oh." Valyra's hand curls around the still-smoking device. Something terrifying brims under the surface of her gaze. "Of course."

"It—it was an accident." At least four hundred eyes—some of the crew has more than two—snap toward me. There's no chance I'll talk my way out of this, but I can't stop. "I was just trying to—okay, right now, if the shields fail, they have to be patched manually, right?" Valyra steps closer and closer with every word, the broken invention still crackling in her fist. I back away instinctively and grip the railing, the still-hungry winds plucking at my hair. "And there's tethers and the floating and the rod and—and I had this idea, that maybe there was a way the hole could be patched safely from right here on deck, if…" I swallow, glancing around at the peripheral crew. Havelock looks murderous. Margot looks disappointed. Bayless, the chief surgeon, and Skoenig, a three-headed gargoyle of a galley cook, look like they're considering carving me up and cooking me into a stew, respectively. And worse than the ones staring at me are the ones who aren't. Pockets of crew members are already turning away and trudging back to the hatch, muttering resignedly to each other. I swear, I even catch the gold glint of money being exchanged, like someone just lost a bet on exactly how badly I'd screw up.

"If, you know—" I finish in a mutter, shame heating my neck. "If it worked."

"Yes." Valyra stops a breath away from me, cold fury rippling off her in waves. "Yes, *if it worked.* That's always the problem, isn't it?"

"But I—"

"Two crew members were almost lost because of you. Do you understand that? Was it worth it, for an *experiment?*"

"No. *No*, Captain."

"Is this how you expect to lead this crew someday—as though no life matters but your own?"

"You know I don't," I say helplessly. Over Valyra's shoulder, Havelock's eye contracts, quivering with the untold promise of later punishment for humiliating her so incredibly. I can't bring myself to glance at the rest of the crew—I know what they think of me. That I'm the Celestial Company's weakest link. That if I weren't the captain's son, I wouldn't belong here at all. That maybe I don't belong here anyway.

"You're not a child anymore, Aren. And every year, I think, well, he still has time. He could be like me, if he tries. But I don't know how much longer you expect me to have patience with you, with this *trash*." The broken device is thrust hard against my chest. I scramble to catch it before it falls to the ground, but she doesn't remove her hand. Instead, she leans in and says something even worse.

"Do you want to end up like him?" she murmurs, gentle venom quiet enough for only me to hear. "Is that the path you want?"

Him.

Acid settles in my stomach.

No other context is needed; I know who she's talking about. The marooned man; the ghost. Nameless, banished. The one erased by time and shame and her own orders.

The one who was my father, once, before that was stripped away too.

How? I want to scream, though she never speaks of it and never will. *How did he fail you so irredeemably? What did he do? Tell me, and I'll be anything else you want.*

I used to ask. I used to beg for scraps of him like a starving animal. I know better now.

"No," I whisper instead. "No. I'm not like him."

"Then prove it," she hisses. "You will clean every inch of this deck. And then… then we will decide what to do with you. Am I understood?"

My heartbeat pounds in my ears, fear and humiliation fighting for dominance. I'm dead, so dead. It'll be merciful if keelhauling is all I get.

"Yes, Captain," I whisper. "I just… I'm so, so sorry."

Valyra strides toward the opening in the semi-circle,

pausing only to hand off her bloody, grime-spattered sword to Havelock.

"No, you're not," she says. "Not yet."

I'm GOING TO be scrubbing the deck for the rest of my life.

In a way, it's a relief. I don't know what's waiting for me on the other side of this, but the fact that Valyra was too furious to even tell me isn't a good sign. Maybe I should be thankful for the amount of time I've spent scraping eel guts from the floorboards.

I scour furiously at a congealed stain, imagining the hard lines that disappointment has etched into her face. *You're not a child anymore,* she said, and she's right. She would never leave a child behind, but I'm almost eighteen. Old enough that if I can't keep up with the crew… if she thinks I'm holding them back—

"You're gonna take off a whole layer of varnish like that."

The teasing drawl startles me enough to make my sander jerk out of its careful path, carving a line in the floor. "Leave me alone, Cas. Please."

"I'd love to." She's up in the rigging, one leg dangling as she chews on something spiky. "Unfortunately, not allowed to leave until the deck is unruined. Havelock's orders."

I look for Felix and find him just before he disappears down the hatch with a mass of perfectly coiled tethers. "You're not even cleaning."

"I'm supervising." She takes another liberal bite. "Are you gonna report me? Order me to clean up *your mess,* star-prince?"

"No." I exhale bitterly, trying to smooth the scuff from the deck with the edge of my shirt. "I'm sorry. You're right, this isn't your problem."

Cas drops airily down onto the deck and throws the core of her fruit over the railing. "If you're going to apologize for something, apologize for taking up all the attention. No one even noticed all the eels I murdered." She swipes a kick at something through the shadows. "Missed a spot."

I lunge as soon as I hear the tinkle of glass. The orb—it must have fallen out of my pocket.

"Hey, careful, that's my—" I bite down on the end of my words and search the device for scratches, which proves difficult given the black sludge coating the external gears, seeping into the mechanism. Disappointment, just as rancid, trickles through my chest. Ruined. It's ruined.

"No, no, finish the sentence." Cas's grin is incredulous, eyes glittering. "You were really about to say, 'my invention,' weren't you? After everything that just happened? Do you know what the word 'destructive' means?"

"It's not destructive."

"I was referring to you, actually. And what's this one for? Firing your blaster for you?"

"*No*. It's—" I press my tongue to the side of my cheek, pretending to think past the *danger* signs flashing through my head. If I start telling Cas what it is, she might ask me follow-up questions, and I won't be able to lie.

I might find myself telling her that it was never just about impressing the crew, designing a device that could pull a face from a drop of blood. That the marooned man left something else behind, other than the cautionary tale of his rotting legacy.

I might tell her how little I could believe it when I stumbled across the blood samples in a forgotten corner of my workshop, buried and discarded like the rest of him, and how the most pitifully desperate of ideas took hold of me and refused to let go. I'll have to explain something I don't fully understand myself, which is why I want to see the face of my banished father at all.

I'd have to explain how painful it feels, the way Valyra refuses to tell me what he did so wrong that he was practically wiped from existence. That with every mistake, every accident, every time I succumb to my fears or lose control of my inventions, I feel like our fates are getting more and more intertwined.

That I had this desperate hope that if I can just look into his eyes once, I'll be able to find something in them that finally tells me what makes a person worthy of being erased.

And then, I can finally make sure the same thing doesn't happen to me.

"It's just an old holographic projector I'm modifying," I say instead. "That's all."

Cas narrows her eyes skeptically, but my tell doesn't give itself away. I was close to the truth, after all.

"Boring," she says airily. "Better get rid of it before it explodes, too."

And with that, she vanishes, likely to hunt down a better source of entertainment.

When it's just me and the night again, I tug the hem of my shirt out to combat the eel-blood dripping onto my pants. A small hairline crack mars the surface, but the only thing left of my father is still somehow humming gently beneath it, winding its methodical way through the glass veins. No internal bleeding, as far as machines go. Maybe it can be salvaged; maybe it doesn't even *need* salvaging—

I tip my head up into the dark and shut my eyes. I can't bear to watch this failure, if it comes. My usual prayer leaves my lips, but this time it's so desperate it tastes like acid. A wish for the stars that laugh down at me. *Please. Please, please, please.*

I let the activator slide upward beneath my thumb.

Nothing.

I'm alone on the deck, beneath stars that have never cared for anyone's wishes.

What was I even expecting? Even if the mechanism weren't damaged, seeing the marooned inventor's face wouldn't change anything. It wouldn't give me the answers I crave. It would just fill the hole with even more questions.

Useless, just like everything else, I think sullenly, and I take one last vicious scrub at the side, harsh enough to nearly crack the activator in half.

And a beam of light bursts against my eyelids.

Blinding, searing, pulsing like it's alive. I have just enough instinct to clamp the orb against my chest like an active bomb, too startled to even yell. Dim, broken fractals seep out through my fingers.

There's no way.

I've inhaled too many cleaning solvent fumes. It's a fluke that's about to either sputter out or explode completely. After everything, it can't have actually *worked.*

Warm light pulses against my palms. I peer around the empty deck to make sure no one else is watching. Then, without exhaling, I carefully, carefully, peel away my grip.

Luminous fragments float back together, and I wait for it to resolve, to form a torso and legs and a face. *Dad.* The words are already rushing to my mouth before the image can even appear. *It's you.*

But no ghost appears.

Instead, the hologram contracts, sharpens, straightens, until it's a dense, silvery-blue line bursting in front of me. It doesn't move. It certainly doesn't speak. It's nothing that could be considered even remotely human-shaped. Just one unvaried, uninteresting thread.

It didn't work, after all. This invention was a failure, too.

But just as a familiar disappointment pools inside me, I see something else. Tiny words etched into the tiny cannister feeding into the orb.

Match: found.

I frown, rub the grime away from the display.

Match. Match found. What does that even mean?

I run through the list of tech I dissected and re-harvested into this device, hunting for an explanation. Genetic extractor I poached from the tech lab, holographic recording device used to make training room simulations, the light-diffracting projector off an outdated navigator—

Wait.

The beacon doesn't just trail off into nothingness; it charges straight through the repaired shields, charting a path somewhere into the abyss. *Exactly* like a navigator. I can't make out the end of it from here, but those tiny words keep blinking insistently. *Match found. Match found.*

Blood match found.

This prototype has failed, just like the rest. I didn't find a way to draw a holographic memory of my father out of his blood.

I think I might have created a path directly to him instead.

Heart pounding, I slowly work myself to my feet, take three steps to the left. The beacon tracks the entire journey, adjusting itself as the orb moves. I can feel it humming in my hands, the way two magnets forced to the edges of their field will struggle to get back to each other. Like it wants to be reconnected with this distant *match, found.*

Impossible.

It's too much to even consider—the chance of finding

the real him, of asking him what happened all those years ago. Finally learning the exact shape of the last line, the final straw—the thing so unforgivable that it ended in my mother banishing the person she once loved most in the world. My imagination runs wild with it.

And I can't even feel a shred of happiness about it, because the only way that imagining becomes real is if I go out there. Into the void. On my own.

The thought makes me want to lean over the rail and throw the orb as far into the abyss as it will go.

Instead, I edge forward, the hum of the beacon chilling and coaxing all at once. The void, with its flickering eyes and its breathless weight, is an endless cave curving around the path the map creates. But sailers have walls and shields and auto-navigation, don't they? It's not like I would really be lost in the deep. Not like I'd be stepping off the side of the ship, walking out into nothingness.

No, I can't. I *can't.* What if there's no one at the end after all? What if I can't find my way back?

I should just destroy it. Stay here, and…

Stay here, and wait to be banished yourself. A cold, practical voice in my head. *End up exactly like him anyway.*

It doesn't take any effort, that thought. Fear is easy, comfortable. I hate the way it feels, but at least I know what to expect. More terrifying is the prickle I feel beneath it, something sharp and tugging.

Because I let myself imagine it—that was my mistake. Not just meeting him, this person whose flaws I've absorbed without meaning to, but finally finding out exactly how to avoid meeting his fate. And the knowledge that if I don't do this now, I might never get the chance again.

For the first time, the idea of stifling that chance feels like a worse kind of darkness than even the void.

Before I can change my mind, even as every self-preserving nerve in my body screams *no, no, no, what are you doing,* I slip the orb's chain around my neck. I can do this. I have to. I'll find him, wherever he drifts.

And I'll make sure my story doesn't end like his if it's the last thing I do.

CHAPTER 4

Nym

*T*HIS *is a story about a monster, and a girl*
who wandered too far.
Shall I tell you? It's a secret. It can be your secret too,
if you listen.

My audience is not listening.

The small girl burbles, her pale green cheeks dimpling, and then she tugs at one of the vines trailing from my head and trips away. Her brother, equally small and equally uninterested in stories of girls and monsters, tips a spiky mushroom into my lap and runs to uproot another. There was another child too, but she's run into a moss-covered dome to fetch someone I'm hoping is either the astrarium-keeper or knows where I can find him.

"Pretty." The girl circles back around; one pudgy hand grapples to reach the branchlike horns protruding just above my ears. I tilt my head so she can reach a white flower blooming from the base and let her pluck it off. *Pretty.* I thought the same thing when I first saw the girl whose appearance I've borrowed on the outskirts of the Cosalian marketplace. Those elfin cheekbones, that curling vine-hair, the wings falling like a cape from her shoulders. I heard the music in her veins when

I brushed against her—the gentle humming of reeds caught in a summer wind—and I mimicked that hum until all the colors and shapes of my body mirrored hers too. So pretty, so gentle, so delicate. The sort of person who can ask odd questions without arousing suspicion. My favorite sort of form to take.

"Everything here is pretty," I reply, picking off another flower and tucking it behind the boy's ear so he can match his sister. "But mine is only pretend, because I am from somewhere else. Isn't that strange?"

The boy blinks at me, and then he dumps another mushroom into my collection.

"Would you like to hear the story? It starts like this." I am sure now that these children cannot understand what I'm saying and will forget as soon as I've said it, which makes them perfect listeners. It's good to let someone listen, every once in a while. It helps me not forget. "Once, there were creatures who swam between stars…"

"*Enek!* Leave our visitor alone!" A Cosalian bursts through the wooden door and scoops up the boy, sending a rainfall of mushrooms and leaves and stones flying from his little fists. "So sorry… bent on uprooting the entire garden, this one…" He shakes his head apologetically, then throws the giggling boy over his shoulder and tickles him. His face is cracked as bark, but his hazel eyes are bright and jovial and warm. It awakens something hollow inside of me, which isn't fair at all, because I have been to hundreds of planets and seen thousands of families across the universe, and meeting one more shouldn't come with such a twinge of longing.

And yet.

"—needed help with something?" I've stared too long without speaking; the man has the beginnings of polite discomfort written across his face.

"If you please." My panlingual tongue latches onto his dialect with ease as I scramble to my feet, sweeping my skirt free. "I'm looking for the astrarium-keeper. Are you him?"

"You are? That is—" The man frowns as though I am the first visitor to have ever sought him out. Perhaps it has something to do with the fact that, as I am just now noticing, the telescope jutting out of his domed roof looks like it's been cobbled together by one of the children: a monstrosity of bark and vines zig-zagging back up to the surface. "Why?"

His bewilderment would act as a warning if I didn't understand its source. When the villagers pointed me toward the astrarium-keeper in response to my questions about strangers visiting from outside Cosalia long, long ago, it was not because they thought him an expert on the world outside their planet.

You sound like Sirafen, they said with distaste. *All this talk of unnatural creatures from beyond the atmosphere. There is nothing beyond. Take your madness to the tower with him, and keep it there.*

Which is how I learned of a man who fell in love with the stars no one else in this quiet, underground planet even believes exist.

His unnatural creature may not be the kind I am searching for. He may be mad, it's true. Or... *or.*

"I've heard a story," I say, "from the village. About someone you saw, years ago. Someone from outside."

The distrust in his gaze reshapes into a sad, resigned twinkle. He smiles the smile of a man who has found a comfortable peace within his own loneliness. "If you've come to laugh at me, I'm afraid I'm not feeling quite up for it today."

"No! Please. I—I believe in them too. That is..." I remember I ought to be a girl who has never known a view beyond twisted roots and moss filled with fireflies. "I'd like to believe in them."

The keeper pats the girl's verdant curls, and she chases her brother through the astrarium's draping curtain. "Believe in what, exactly?"

You know what, I want to cry. *I know you remember. You must.* But I must be gentle, delicate, oh-so-pretty with my smile and my words.

"I believe there is life beyond the surface," I say. "I believe you met someone. From the stars. All I want is to hear the story."

And that resigned twinkle flickers, and his brow arches down as if he's never seen anything quite like me before. I pinch the rough pads of my fingers together to remind myself that I am still, as far he knows, Cosalian. Friend, ally, just like him.

"Yes," he finally says, and my hearts leap. "I—yes. Alright, then. Come in, come in."

The interior of the astrarium is far more promising than the slapdash exterior. The rounded walls are lined with shelves upon shelves of leathery books and scrolls, and a curving staircase leading to the base of the telescope sprouts from the center of the room. Nestled inside its coils is a glass cylinder filled with untethered globes, which rotate without direction around the largest sphere of them all. Its gold paint is an optimistic reflection of the dull yellow fog surrounding Cosalia.

The man stops at the root of the staircase. His wings form a shield, but I can see even more books arching beneath the stairs, through the cracks. "I warn you, this story…it will sound impossible."

I smile softly. "That's my favorite kind."

He sighs with resignation and doesn't turn around. "When I was a boy, just about your age," he begins, "a girl came to my window in the night. Her name was—" My heart leaps, but the shadow of a frown tugs at the edge of his still-turned head. "It always slips away from me. I suppose it doesn't matter. When I was a boy, I had a friend. Anyone else will tell you I made her up, that she never existed. They'll say I only dreamed her. But she was real—that much I remember. She had green skin like mine, green hair like mine, but her eyes were something otherworldly. She told me stories, though I can't remember what about, and took me on adventures, though I can't recall where. But I can still hear her laugh, the way she would hum when she was pleased by some new trinket. I cannot forget it, just as one can never truly forget a song they once knew.

"And then one day, she told me she had a secret, one I must swear never to tell anyone. She knew she could trust me, and it must have been true, because this memory was the only one I've ever been able to keep whole. She—" Finally, he turns, wariness etched into his forehead. "You did say you weren't here to laugh at me."

I have moved away from the door without realizing, reeled in by his memories. "What was the secret?"

"She was..." The astrarium-keeper sighs, and his next words release like a long-restrained tide finally reaching its shore. "...something else. From somewhere else. She wasn't... like us. She took me out there; she showed me." He runs a hand over the base of the pitiful telescope. "So many other worlds, just on the other side of the surface. Not endless fog, as we'd all thought. Like ashflies trapped against canvas."

I lower myself to the lens, hearts hammering. I'm foolish to even dare expect the view on the other side will be a perfect still of a ringed celestial body, swirling with purple clouds. Instead, a dark blanket settles before my eyes. A familiar universe, muffled by fog and distance and poor craftsmanship. "Which one was hers?" I ask, not even caring how desperate I sound. "Where did she come from? Can you see it from here?"

"Oh, dear girl. I don't remember."

No. I straighten. "You must. Oh, please, you must."

He tilts the telescope away from me, looking somewhat perturbed. "I never got a perfect look. We were only up there for a few moments, and then… then something else came. I don't… my *memory*…" He frowns, visibly straining. "I remember screaming and smoke and a blow to my head, and nothing else. And then, she was gone. My heart was hers, and she left me behind. I woke back in my bed without knowing how I got there."

No, she didn't leave. I can pen the final chapter of this story myself. A tentacle unfurling from the deep. The ghostly outline of a decaying ship veiling the moon. The not-Cosalian, from-somewhere-else girl pushing the young astrarium-keeper back to the safety of his planet before he even realized there was danger.

"Is that the end of the story?" I force myself to ask. "Is there nothing else you remember?"

He smiles bitterly. "I told you it would sound impossible. You see now, why no one believes me. Sometimes I think it would be easier to pretend I dreamed her into existence. But this… this won't let me forget."

He reaches up into the cradle of his branchlike antlers, runs his fingers through the twigs. A cord unravels from above his scalp, like a single thread being plucked from the center of a bolt of cloth. Something at the end of it glints through the thin leaves, outlining every green vein, and my dismal heartbeat quickens once again. A map? A key? A message?

Finally, he lowers his hands, cups whatever he has kept hidden away close to his chest. "I don't even know what it is," he says, "but when I woke again after she was gone, back on

Cosalia, this was in my hand."

His fingers part. I cannot mask my face from falling. The only thing clutched there is a strange little object—narrow and crystalline, opaquely white, with something like a pointed spindle at either end. Something between vial and stone.

And I do not recognize it. It means nothing to me.

It must have been important to her, I remind myself, even as despair begins to weave its familiar cloak. It had to mean something to her, for it to be the only trinket she left of herself.

I glance up. "May I hold it?"

"I… I suppose. But be gentle."

I must have one bare shred of hope left, enough to be disappointed yet again when the trinket does nothing in my grasp. It does not twist like a compass toward home, does not whisper clues to me in a Medyssian voice. It only lies there, an empty reminder of a girl like me who once swam to this shore.

But a powerful reminder, if it has allowed the astrarium-keeper to hold on to her ghost for this long when it ought to have melted away. And the only reminder of home I have found in so long. The rest of my trails have ended in stories just like his, faded memories drawn back to the surface with glazed-over expressions. *I met someone strange once, but then they were gone.*

"Careful!"

I don't even realize I'm squeezing until the brittle glass begins to chip beneath my fingers. "Oh—I'm sorry—"

"Clumsy child." He snatches the relic back, and his face, once so kind and open, goes fraught with distrust. "Who did you say you were, again?"

"I…" I swallow. I had wanted to explore the astrarium just a bit more, maybe peer through the telescope and imagine I could tell which of the countless stars winking back might be mine. I could weave a vision that would make him forget the last few moments, that would replace the damaged relic with a perfect one until I am gone. But I don't suppose there's a point. Instead, I look him in the eyes. I turn my voice soft and gentle as a spell.

"I'm no one. I don't exist," I whisper, my vision blurring, and I ease the glass gently out of his hands. *I'm sorry. I'm sorry. I need this so much more than you.* "I was never here."

The words are strong enough to wrap me in a gauzy mist of invisibility. The man blinks, and I can see his memories rewriting themselves over his eyes, faithfully obeying the illusion I've woven. It's almost strong enough to take me too, if I listened to it, so I close my fist around the odd little stone and focus only on the way the spindle pricks my skin. It is enough to puncture the haze falling over my own mind. *I do exist. I am here.*

I am still lost.

"Goodbye," I tell the astrarium-keeper, the distant sound of squealing children, the library of stars that don't belong to me. And I slip away, leaving only the echo behind.

CHAPTER 5

Nym

WHERE are you?

I wait until I've reached the planet's smog-ridden atmosphere before shedding the Cosalian girl's face. The surface is barren and unlivable, with no one to see me. No one to hear me quietly begin to sing my own transformation.

My voice is the most familiar part of myself, a power more precious and personal than my own name. More familiar still is the melody buried in my veins—a light string of notes, soft and wistful, circling up and down and up again without resolving. With each note, I'm guided out of the Cosalian cloak I wear and back into my true form.

It dissolves the horns, the wings, the shades of mossy green. My legs dematerialize into nothing until I'm left floating in my own body, pale lavender umbra rippling gently beneath me.

"Where are you, House?" I call softly, tucking silver-gold hair behind my ear. "Are you hiding?"

I hum five more notes, the beginning of a song I remember from long, long ago. Something someone used to sing to me, a blanket of stars above us.

Come out, come away…

The melody winds through the smog until it finds what it's looking for, and an echo returns the song back to me.

"There you are," I whisper, and swim for home.

It doesn't take long for the shape of it to weave itself together. It's just smoke at first, but then I see it all—the glass-windowed basket, the lofty canvas dome. My sanctuary. Warmth cocoons me as I dive inside, onto the cozy nest burying most of the floor.

"Hello, House," I greet my home, flopping onto my back until I can see through the opening in the ceiling, all the way up to the apex beyond. On the other side of my semblance of a skylight, the curving dome is painted in swirling purples and golds. Constellations that move if I squint my eyes, curlicues of galaxies, twinkling objects hanging from string. A map of every place I've been, and every place I still have yet to go. "Did you miss me?"

The ropes holding the entire configuration together strain against their anchor, emitting a dim, affirmative sigh.

"Brought back a treasure." I finger the spindle, twist the simple chain. The canvas ripples, and the pieces of my collection chime against one another. I begrudgingly lift myself off the comfort of my nest to float up into the folds, scanning the painted whorls until I find a sphere painted dull, smoky yellow.

I reach for a dangling pot containing a meager supply of pins and string, puncture the center of Cosalia, then tie a knot around the trinket and let it hang between its neighbors—crystals of ice that never melt, dried flowers, shards of mirror-glass.

I draw an invisible circle around the yellow sphere, tracing to the southern tip. Then, I twist upside-down. The stars on my map invert into painted constellations I know so well—a lonely beast, an oblong whirlpool, a star-woven prince chasing a wild-haired girl across the night sky.

She showed me where she came from. That's what the astrarium-keeper said. This angle, the view from here—this could be the slice of sky where Medyssia hides.

I used to feel true joy when I came across this sort of lantern in the darkness. Now, I know better.

I have narrowed my family down to one pocket of the universe, but in that pocket there are still a hundred planets. A thousand stars. A trillion individual strands of ether, waiting for me to unravel.

And my family is not even on one of those hundreds of worlds, thousands of stars.

I move my finger an inch to the right, where it meets the rich indigo that stands for uncharted space.

For every planet, every star, every celestial object I've charted that has a form and a size and a trackable place in the sky, there's too much of *this*.

The unknown. The unseen.

And it's so much more tremendous than I could possibly replicate with paint and canvas. It stretches out infinitely, and it's getting bigger every second, and I'm just one small speck in that endless, ever-expanding ocean.

Somewhere on my map, somewhere in that violet in-between, there's an invisible planet that doesn't want to be found.

I worry I'm forgetting it sometimes. I worry that the colors of my own home are fading from my memory, that I'm twining my scraps of it into other places I've visited—like the way the trees floated above the ground, or the fish swam through the air. I worry I'll forget the number of sisters I had the way I've already forgotten their faces.

I worry it never existed at all, that I'm searching for a dream that crept inside me one night and quietly planted its haunting seeds. That the stories I chase through the universe aren't about my family at all, but the pitiful fantasies of souls even more lost than I.

But it *did* exist. And I'm not supposed to; it's dangerous, but maybe… maybe if I just let myself see a bit of it…

One faint layer of an illusion. That's enough.

The fog around me transforms as I sink down to the basket, dragging every desperate shred I can out of the depths of my thoughts.

I pour my memories into the smoky yellow air until it turns the purple-blue of bioluminescence. Vibrant green plants tangle their way out of the ground in long, fluttering ribbons. A cluster of fish, their glowing bones shining straight through translucent skin, meanders above me. And there's a pearly house nestled in the curving branches of a floating tree, and there are people inside, though all I can see of them is the sway of the tendrils under their umbra, and all I can hear is a tinkle of laughter that sounds like music.

I press my hand to the window, watch the way my reflection creates its own sort of illusion: that I'm out there, weaving between the flowers, just a few pulses from home. Home, where I never should have left.

It's just an illusion. I could touch it and sense it and live in it if I wanted to, but it's not real. Which is why I *won't* touch it—I won't lose myself in a fantasy. I won't become more lost than I already am.

I won't stop until I find the real thing.

I let it begin to fade, let dull reality start to stain the vision yellow, but the longing doesn't drain away as easily. My collection twinkles above me, and I float back up to the thousands of imaginary arrows leading in every direction, drawing possibilities across my map.

"So," I whisper, "where to next?"

House shifts, the basket creaking gently, and I know that it too is impatient to be anywhere but the ground. That the stars on the other side of this impenetrable fog are singing its name just as they sing my own.

"Good idea." I unlock the anchor weighing my home down. It releases with a relieved exhale, and the ground sets us free from its gravity like a fist uncurling from around a bird. "Anywhere that calls to us."

And as the last remnants of the Medyssia I've lost wither below, we slip quietly up into the beckoning unknown.

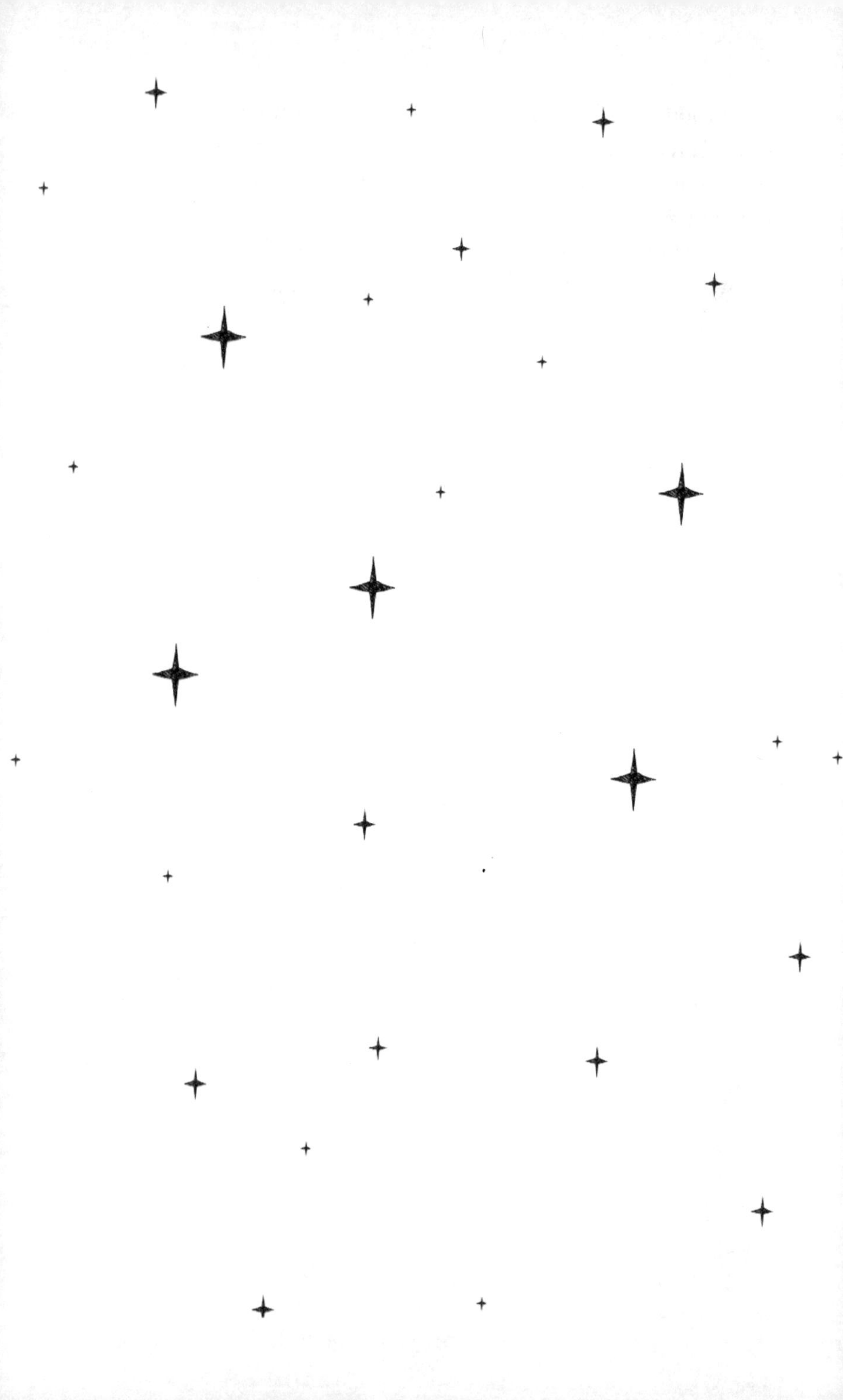

CHAPTER 6

Aren

"Hi. I'm your son. I have some answers that you're gonna question—I mean, questions that I—"

Hmm.

I frown at my reflection in the viewport's sleek glass and try rearranging my face into something more confident. "Hello. I'm Aren. You made me."

Worse. I give up. How do I greet the person who gifted me his worst qualities and then disappeared? *Hey, thanks for nothing? Can you take the coward half of my genes back, please?*

The abyss stretches before me, around me, beneath me. It's the same void the *Starsaviour* has sailed through my entire life, so I don't know why it feels like I've wandered into an alternate dimension. I never realized how loud it was back home, how much the clank of the engine or the bustle of footsteps or the constant sound of laughing and fighting and shouting chased out the true sounds of the universe. I would kill to hear the ripple of wind through the solar sails. I'd kill twice to hear Havelock telling me off. Because instead, when the imaginary conversations I've been attempting with my faceless father dissolve, I have nothing left but treacherous silence roaring in my ears.

The beginning of the path has been gone for hours. I watched the gold lights of the *Starsaviour* until the darkness swallowed them, and since then, it's just been me and the beacon, charting a ravine through space. The void breathes around me; with every inhale, I'm swallowed deeper.

"Hey, Dad." I push my hair back the way Felix does and try for a smirk. Hand on my blaster, head tilted to expose my tattoo. "Surprise."

Oh, yeah, sure. Let him think I'm a Celestial Company assassin come to finish the job.

Maybe practicing is pointless. It's been hours, and I'm the only life left in the void. What did I think would happen? That I'd just pop out to find a man who's been missing for seventeen years and be back in time for breakfast?

And let's say I actually find him—what if he won't help me? I am half of him, but I'm also half of *her*. The person who banished him. Maybe when he sees me, all he'll see is an opportunity for revenge. I didn't think of that at all.

I'm Aren Vanthal, I remind my intrusive thoughts. *Heir to the Celestial Company, son of Valyra. I will be worthy of that title. This will work. This has to work.*

And I'm so good at it, concentrating on how much this has to work, that it takes me far longer than it should to realize the beacon is gone.

I pull the anchor as fast as I can, almost throwing myself straight through the viewport. And on the other side of it, no light. No path.

"No. No, come on—" I tap the orb wired into the console. Thin specks of crystallized light still trail out of the projector; they're just no longer connected to anything. The map is completely gone. Vanished. And in its place, nothing but the unfeeling blackness of a starless void.

My temporarily evicted panic stampedes back into its home.

I've lost the path. I've lost *myself*.

Don't—my last shred of level-headedness orders, but it's too late. The suffocating tendrils of my astrophobia unwind inside me, tightening invisible cords across my chest. The void reverses direction until it's not a vast ocean, but a cocoon shrinking around me.

I grapple for my specs and pull them up over my face, leather burning against my cheek. And as the oversaturation bleeds into my vision, my pulse jolts. I'm not lost in a vacant emptiness at all.

I'm nose to nose with a nebulous storm.

Crimson and green gases swirl in a furious vortex in front of me, forming a cloud so thick that it eats the sky. If any sound could pierce the vacuum, it would be roaring, untamed, heartless. And the only bright spot—literally—is that the beacon isn't gone. Its light has just been crushed to dull powder within the winds. The tail cuts straight through, faint and distant.

My father is on the other side of this storm.

I breathe in until it feels like my lungs have eclipsed all my other organs. Celestial Company ships are sturdy, built to withstand way worse than this. I refuse to imagine myself swept away and battered against the shores of space. It's only wind. I can make it through.

"This," I mutter, "is the worst idea I've ever had."

I turn the thrusters back on.

But the clouds don't try to break me apart. Instead, they seem to split and fold around me as I cross the threshold. The nose of the sailer slices through the tornado as though it's nothing but thin fog. I follow the light until all the angry colors of the storm begin to fade too, and the air is once again clear and calm.

And in the center of that calm, with the end of the beacon leaking right into its glistening stomach, there's a devouring eel.

For a second, my own stomach forgets how to curdle. Instead, I feel nothing but numbness.

Ah, I think vaguely, *you're not my dad.*

The eel circles the thinning clouds just as easily as the ones that breached the *Starsaviour,* and I understand in a way that makes me want to dissolve into hysterics. That even though I thought I cleaned the orb, eel blood must have gotten inside the scanning mechanism, and the map must have read *it* somehow, but that still doesn't make any sense. The eel that blood came from was dead. Why would the beacon lead me to this one?

The predator unhinges its jaw and hisses at the light bisecting it, its silhouette identical to the eel that tried to attack me before it was harpooned down. The two beasts could be twins. They could—

I look down at the navigator clipped innocently to the console, at the scanner that was supposed to have read my father's blood and turned it into a map.

That's right.

Genetic material can be shared.

The scream the nebula ought to be making roars in my head, and I can't move, can't do anything but watch as the eel's jaw unhinges. A snaggletooth drips down from its gums. *Go away,* I will it. *I didn't mean to follow you. Please, please, just go away.*

The eel hisses once again, but then it curls in on itself, light reflecting off its smooth hide as it ripples off. I don't release my breath yet; I feel like I might have forgotten how to take another one. It's going to turn around. It's just giving itself more room to streak toward me. It's coming back.

But it slithers off into the fog, the beacon's light curling up after it, and it doesn't come back. The mist enfolds it until it might never have existed at all, leaving me alone in the eye of the storm.

And then, I'm not alone at all.

I don't see the thing that takes the eel's place at first. At first, it's nothing but another roiling cloud. But slowly, slowly, its dim edges sharpen, until another beast emerges from the shadows. No, not a beast.

A ship.

Gray as smoke. Gray as the veneer of a dream.

It's abandoned, that much is clear—the wreckage of a long-ago disaster, lost to the void. It doesn't just take up space; it *eats* it, big as a gaseous planet. Dark gray sails, slashed with frayed holes; dark gray rope anchoring lopsided gray masts in place, like they'd snap in half and drift away otherwise. Gray like death, like rot, like if this glass weren't between us I'd smell the sour sharpness of maggots and mold. So gray and bleak that I might not even have seen it at all if it not for what's on the bow, angled straight at me, gleaming ivory.

The ship has teeth.

Teeth.

Hundreds of them, jagged and uneven, like barbed harpoons poised to fire. And behind them, a cavernous mouth opens straight into the belly, deeper and more endless than the blackest of black holes. It gapes wide, like an unhinged jaw.

The eel finishes its long, winding journey and vanishes into the unending cavity of that mouth, but as I watch, another takes its place. Then another. And another. Ten. Fifty. A hundred. Too many to even think of counting. They slither out and drape themselves over those terrible, impossible teeth like thin, slimy tongues. Two hundred sets of eyes leer back at me, bulbous and yellow in the gloom.

I can't tear my own away. The ship takes my astrophobia and chokes it, smothers it. Every nightmare I've ever had about what might be waiting out in the universe turns to sand. The invisible cords across my chest tighten, flatten my airway.

And I know one thing, as I stare up at this monster of a ship. Real fear isn't caustic, isn't a pounding heart and shaking hands and jittering nerves. It's numb. It's cold. It drags you outside of your own body, saps you into a shell.

It's what I feel now.

Blood matches. That's the one clear thought that breaks through. *I have a navigator that follows blood matches.*

That means it should lead me back to my mother, too.

I reach for both the orb and the knife sheathed to my belt slowly, like any sudden movements will set the eels to strike. I don't even feel it when I slice a shallow gash through my palm, don't hear the knife clatter to the ground. I squeeze my fist above the drained navigation canister until three crimson drops pool at the bottom. *You worked once. Do it again.*

I twist the tiny knob, and that same explosion of blue bursts into my vision, and—

Wham.

Without warning, without anything but the sensation of being rammed into by a comet, the entire sailer convulses.

The navigator launches itself out of my hands as I'm thrown from my chair, and the hard metal of the back hatch is what catches me. I gasp, pain sending electric bursts up my spine. The viewport is now my ceiling, and I'm staring straight up at the nightmare ship as it quivers in the center of the rounded glass like an iris.

And it's moving. Toward me.

The clouds swirl around it in an angry vortex, and it's getting larger, its gaping mouth wider, all of its illogical pieces creeping closer and closer as I watch.

And then I hear a quiet, skittering scrape against the hull, like nails being dragged over metal. Louder and louder, like an icy wind. Then a long, viscous body with dead eyes and a protrusion of needle-thin fangs slithers over the glass, and I realize the nightmare ship isn't the one moving. I am.

The eels are dragging me in.

When the next convulsion wracks through my sailer, thrusting it into a barrel-roll, I throw myself into it. The walls and floor have switched places, but I have to get back to the console, have to—

I fumble for the starwalking suit trigger at my ear, feel my only defense shimmer into place. The view through the port is just a windstorm of gray and silver streaks without form, but every few seconds I get a glimpse of the gaping, rotting mouth sucking me in, its teeth glinting. It gets closer every turn. A hundred meters. Seventy. Fifty.

And by the time the seam where console meets window is latched under my fingernails, it's too late.

The sailer smashes to a halt against something that crunches around us like snapping bones. I'm thrown backward again as the sailer falls into a steady, horrible sort of sawing motion—forward, back, forward, back, in a sadistic cycle, and there's no more "closer." There's no more hungry pull.

There's only the teeth, bared sharp and gnawing through the window, and I can finally see enough of them to realize they're not quite teeth after all.

They're wreckage.

Jagged shards of scrap metal and driftwood. Remnants of

all the ships already shredded between the eels and this gaping jaw, left behind to pierce through that ghostly gray bow in perpetual warning.

And my own ship will join them.

Skreeeich. Clang.

Skreeich. Clang.

Skreeeich. Clang.

The wall is tearing open. I can hear it, the snap of the bronze paneling ripping from the outside in, molecule by molecule. Without my starwalking suit, the change in pressure once the crack breaches completely might be enough to kill me. Maybe not. Felix would know.

Skreeeich. Clang.

Felix. I'll never see him again.

Skreeeeeich. Clang.

Skreeeeeeich. Clang.

Cas was the last person I talked to. What will she tell the crew?

Skreeeeeich. Clang.

My mother is going to think I ran away.

A bolt of ice down my spine.

They're not even going to look for me. I left in the middle of the night. I didn't tell anyone where I was going. I knew I was going to be punished.

I will die a deserter.

No. I won't. I can't.

I rip my gaze away from the steadily darkening crack—no, *cracks*, now, four in an uneven vertical row, the metal curling away from the openings like an infected wound. The console is a language I have never mastered, but I splay my fingers wide over the countless rows of knobs and slam down on as many as I can reach at once.

One of them has to be the distress call.

The inside of the ship turns pure white, then yellow. Something rumbles beneath my feet, something like the grating of gears or the turning of valves. And the wall finally gives up.

The narrow line splinters and bursts, and the pale, writhing front halves of the eels rush to fill the opening, jaws impossibly wide, unblinking eyes flashing hungrily. That movement alone is what saves me. They act like a stopper, keeping the vacuum from becoming strong enough to suck me right into their waiting mouths. Nausea pounds at my consciousness, threatening to pull me under, but—

Come on. My shaking hands grapple against the console, as much to brace myself as to search desperately for my only hope at rescue. *Come on—*

But the angular head of one of the eels is already tearing through the opening, splintered metal snagging through flesh. A hanging flap of exposed muscle drips from its cheek, but it doesn't stop driving forward, blind to anything but its own hunger even as it carves the ribbon of its own flesh deeper. Its yellow eye meets mine. Turns *red*.

A reflection from the console, where the last button I've pressed has gone crimson and flashing.

Distress call. I actually found it.

And there's no time to feel even a second of relief. A second eel head writhes through, and as it's red-yellow-red eyes and fangs angle toward me, I realize I only have one choice left, if I want to give the Celestial Company any opportunity to find something other than my corpse.

"Please," I gasp to whoever might be receiving, even as my mind and fingers and stomach scream at me to pick something else, anything else. But it's too late. This is all that's left.

"Please, please, come find me."

The lever that opens the emergency hatch is one of the few I can recognize.

The door slams open. The vacuum of space explodes in.

And still, I can't stop the instinct that makes me claw for the edge of the console. Bronze rips under my nails, but space wraps tentacles around my legs and waist and mouth and pulls like a beast dragging its prey back to its lair. *Let go*, it howls, *let go let go let go LET GO*—

My eyes water. My nerves scream.

Please find me, I beg to whoever's listening, the universe blurred into an ocean of red. And metal shrieks, and the eels thrash, and the void orders me to *LET GO*, and I couldn't choose anything else even if I wanted to.

I let go.

I let go, and the wind takes me, drags me out.

Empty space rises to catch me.

Please.

The ship and its smoky sails fall away above me. I can't hear anymore, but I can see, see the sailer grinding between teeth, the metal flaking away in orange sparks, see it finally lose its pathetic battle against the eels. The mindless things don't even know I'm gone; I can only pray they won't until they've torn through the entire hull from bow to stern. Time. That's all I need. Time.

Help. Whoever's out there.

Please.

I fall and fall and keep falling.

Weightless. Tetherless.

I spiral into a sea made blue and clear by my specs, and the numbness starts to return. But this time, it's coming from the outside in. Through my skin. Inside my ears.

Am I dying? Is it killing me? No. Not yet. My starwalking suit is both a life raft and a cage, and this death will be slow. Like falling asleep.

Like drowning.

I close my eyes.

Please.

Somebody.

Come find me.

CHAPTER 7

Nym

I WAKE to the sound of screaming.

It does not startle me. It is a common sort of awakening. Howls of pain flit in and out of my dreams like winged predators: the memory of my own, when I realized I was lost; the voices of my family, imagined a thousand times over; the haunting cries of the rest my kind, the last sound they made before they were swallowed into the dark. They are their own sort of music, by now. And so, when this scream wakes me, even when I find it is not coming from inside my own head, I merely turn drowsily.

"House?" I murmur. "Was that you?"

The floorboards hum indignantly.

I tilt my head away from the window I've nestled in. No, only a dream. Or a star at the end of its life somewhere distant, its once-perfect song rattling into the endless gasp of a black hole.

But then it comes again, louder. A sound no star has ever made, like shrill, forceful agony.

I frown and glide through the window, catch myself on a straining rope to listen. Most think there's no sound in the ether; this I know. That it's a vacuum, or a void, one that crumples and stifles everything it grasps into blank nothing. But that has never been true for Medyssians. For us, the universe is filled with the endless melody of a thousand million unknown voices. Caressing, coaxing, inspiring. It is what first called me to the stars all those years ago.

And there it is again: a new sound twisting an arm out through the inky purple of space, outstretched and prying. It winds itself through my ears, skewering me on a hook.

This time, I know I did not imagine it. But I also know its source is not out there, the helpless cry of another lost soul. No. The scream is *inside my ship*.

The relic.

I streak upward, into the violet-painted night of my star-map. It is a matter of moments to find the little spindle, even amidst the hundreds of glittering treasures. But it is silent and still, just as I left it. I linger at a cautious distance, braced to protect my ears should it once again cry out. But nothing, and nothing, and nothing.

And then, it *moves*.

It strains and rattles against its weak tether, casting a starfly-swarm of light baubles across the shadowy backdrop before it jerks to the side, colliding with a vial of sand that cracks open and dissolves into a murky cloud. When I reach for it, coughing through stained air, it skitters from my hand and throws itself against the wall. A hairline fracture splits the side, enough to rent but not wound. And then, again. It *screams.*

Something is inside. Something that wants to be set free. Something *alive.*

The only thing she left behind.

The astrarium-keeper's words blur vivid across my mind. I should have known she'd left it for a reason; I should have known it could be more than a trinket.

After all this time . . . can it *be* . . . ?

Whatever has been locked away inside of the spindle's armor howls again, agonized and pleading.

I do not hesitate; I do not know how, but I am strong enough to split the metal casing, sealed shut by rust and time. The glass crumbles; the chain snaps and slithers lifelessly off the pin. Eggshell pieces are suddenly littering my palms, which tremble and tremor away the dust that remains. I hold my breath in the silence, dizzy with the worst kind of hope: baseless, weak, all but imagined. I wait for the moment that I realize I have destroyed the only thing left of my world for nothing.

But then, the dust stirs.

A feathery rustle passes over my palm. The broken glass sifts, shakes free, and out of it crawls… a *creature*.

A thin V of a body, a ridged back, no face and two slim antennae. It lifts itself to the space above my hand, hovering on tiny, frenetic wings like a moth born from dust itself. Iridescent, luminous. A wisp of a thing; a sentient bit of stardust.

"You're alive," I whisper, desperate for and fearful of its response. "Have you been in there all this time?"

The dustmoth creature settles before my face, the glimmer beneath its translucent edges casts a pale tinge against my skin.

"You came from Medyssia, didn't you?"

Slowly, delicately, it flutters upward, then down, then up again. Like a head nodding *yes*.

"Are you lost, like me?" I feel untethered, as though I am caught between two forms and my body cannot settle. "Do you… do you know how to find home?"

Its tiny face peers up at mine. Featureless, immobile.

Then, it turns and blurs toward the window.

"Wait!" I catch the ledge just as it begins to vanish. "You can understand me, can't you? Is this—that is—you *do* know the path?"

The creature's edges sharpen as it hovers upward. Its faceless form turns toward me.

Come out, I hear within its vibrations. *Come away.*

My grip on the rope slackens. That melody. My sister's voice echoing in a cavern, my mother's arms holding me tight. A blanket of stars, whispering my name. A pull in my chest, splitting it in two, coaxing me in opposite directions. A song that belongs only to Medyssians.

Come away, come away.

The dustmoth answers its own call, its tiny body already reabsorbing into the stars.

"House. House, I think she left it for him on purpose," I say breathlessly, urgently. "Didn't she? The Medyssian the astrarium knew. To help him find her again, only he didn't know how to listen. And now—now—"

It is ready to go home.

I wait for House to twist against me, tell me I am wrong, anchor itself in this corner of the universe until the dustmoth has vanished completely. It has always known how to keep me from harm. But it shifts instead, basket creaking curiously.

The dustmoth is still vanishing upward. In moment, I will lose it. Perhaps I *should* lose it—I should not follow strange creatures with stranger voices into the ether like a child lured into a wood.

But, "Wait," I find myself crying, and its own voice murmurs a seductive echo. "Wait for me. I'm coming."

I HAVE NEVER feared interstellar cyclones.

Quite the opposite. I love their violent beauty, how they look like a thousand different shades of sunset colliding with one another. How they send out long spikes of blue lightning, drawing lines through the nearest constellations. They're loud and volatile and light up their corners of the universe in a way that says, *I'm here, I'm here.*

But I've never been too close to one before. House is sturdy, but I always imagined those angry winds tearing through the cabin, shattering glass, ripping my carefully preserved memories from their strings. I have seen the terrible wreckage that drifts in their wake. Bodies that I cannot bear to witness, scraps of once-majestic ships torn down to nothing but driftwood caught in a tide. It never seemed worth the risk.

I am close to one now.

House bobs at the periphery, at the edge of the path the dustmoth has trailed. We have followed it for—well, I'm never quite good at measuring time, but long enough to hover near something even more dangerous than what swirls before us.

Hope. The impossible possibility that I could be moving toward a place where I might no longer be the lone, the last, the only. My guide has yet to falter, yet to stray. And now, it has brought us here.

It would be easy to consider it all a mistake. To call the creature I have followed thoughtless, purposeless, incapable of knowing where it travels or leads. But there is a truth in this place it has brought me, so obvious that it is painful to realize I never thought of it myself: that nebulas are wild, fierce, often unbreachable, and mine is far from the only ship that doesn't dare enter their folds. To enter is to risk never re-emerging.

What better hiding place could there be, for a creature afraid of being found? For a *planet* of such creatures?

"House, we have to follow," I urge, leaning halfway out the window in my rush. The dustmoth has not ceased its movement; already it is difficult to find against the rippling canvas of color and sound. "Please. It's just a cloud. It only looks bad from here."

For the first time, the rope under my hand creaks, pulling in the opposite direction.

"*House.*"

It strains until it goes taut.

"Fine!" *It is only a storm. Only a storm.* I push myself outside, giving House one last reassuring stroke. "Stay here, then. I'm just going to see if… just stay here."

I ignore its nervous groan, letting it fade away as the sky folds me in its arms. My tendrils unfurl beneath me; my umbra balloons out like the frothy layers of a skirt, then contracts, propelling me forward. Ahead, lightning sets the sky on fire, and cold tongues of smoke drag themselves over my arms.

"You're sure, aren't you?" I call softly. The dustmoth's glow fades and brightens as the unfurling clouds pass over it. "This is truly the way to—to wherever we're going?" The dustmoth hasn't ceased moving since I set it free, but now, it finally turns. Its smooth face seems to take mine in, and it tilts to one side, like a tiny head being cocked in curiosity.

Come, it offers, but then one quiet consonant changes shape.

Come home, it says. *Come home.*

My pulse stammers. "What?"

Come. Home.

I glide forward to peer into the swirling winds. There is nothing behind them; no shadow of a lost planet, no whisper of waves against a forgotten shore. But I breathe in this corner of the universe, absorb the only thing that has ever kept me going. The belief that *home* is still a thing I could find if I searched hard enough; a pull I could never resist.

"Alright. Just a bit farther."

But as I poise to swim again, I see something strange.

An inky blot in the near distance. It hovers just out of reach of the nebula's seeking tongues, suspended without moving. Its faded shades of brown are dull enough to belong to debris, but the shape of it is wrong. It could be another creature of the ether, swimming without direction, but it simply floats there. Something too solid to be a mirage, too still to be alive.

No. Not a something at all. A *someone*.

A boy.

His arms and legs are splayed out wide, his muscles frozen by the devastating weight. Inky blue hair, the vibrant shade of a starless sky, floats away from his pale, angular face. His irisless eyes are blank and unseeing, just two bronze cylinders above his cheekbones. No pulse tremors in his throat. No breath passes his lips.

It *was* a boy at one point.

But now, I think he might be dead.

I scan the space surrounding him for a rope, a companion, a bit of wreckage. Nothing. Only the quiet fury of the storm. It must have taken his ship as I feared it would House. He must be all that is left.

"Do you see—" I turn toward the dustmoth and find only the whirlwind of color roiling off the nebula. I scan frantically until a paler flicker flits through the streaks of yellow.

"Wait!" I blur to catch it, but it dissolves like mist through my fingers. "You were speaking before. Somewhat. Can't you understand 'wait'?"

The dustmoth hums. Its voice, so weak and otherworldly before, has developed a thin layer of urgency. *Come,* it calls, stronger, *Come home.*

"I am," I beg. We're close enough to the nebula now that I can feel it curling through my hair, but the floating boy darkens the corner of my vision. "But can't we, for a moment—suppose he needs help?"

The dustmoth quickens its pace.

"Obstinate thing." I swim after it, closing the distance, but just as its within my reach again, I feel a fierce sort of plucking in my chest. Guilt? No, I know what guilt feels like. This is different.

I peer back at the floating boy.

"Hello?" I call softly. "Are you alive?"

He doesn't speak, doesn't twitch. The ether has preserved his body like an insect trapped in ice. I wonder if his ship was reduced to splinters, his crew reduced to ash.

I wonder if they survived, but they didn't come back for him. If he will wake alone and afraid and wonder where they've gone.

Nails clench unbidden around my heart.

I turn from the boy, try to shake the feeling free. This is foolish. There is no choice here. The dustmoth will not wait for me. The boy is a bottle tossed to a storm, and the fact that I am another such bottle does not mean I owe him anything. He is likely already dead. What good would it do, to lose myself again for someone who is already lost?

My only hope of home ascends into the darkness, devoured by clouds.

I have no choice but to follow it.

CHAPTER 8

Aren

I'm

still here

I

can't be sure

still

alive

but I

wish

I

weren't

And I

have to

Have to

No, no, I can't—

Breathe.
No, *no*—
Breathe.
I gasp for it.

It comes in shallow, first my lungs, then my brain.

It tastes like desperate relief, like guilt and panic.

A full-strength starwalking suit can last up to twelve hours in the void; a basic suit only lasts one. Three guesses which kind Felix clipped to my ear for eel duty. It's not his fault—I should have checked before I ran away. But now, there's nothing left of the oxygen but the gaseous equivalent of a few drops of water left at the bottom of a bottle. And I'm supposed to be making it last, making *me* last, but it's getting harder and harder to pace myself.

I'm dying.

My limbs were the first to go once the suit began to give up against the stifling pressure of the universe. The nerves at the end of my fingers prickled like static, and by the time I realized the prickling was moving up my body like a grid blacking out one square at a time, it was too late to do anything but drown in it.

Drown, and keep drowning, here where I can't feel or hear or move or—

Breathe.
No, no, I can't.
And even though I'm

Fading

I can't

Be weak

Black stains keep creeping in, and I

Should fight them off, but I

'm tired, so tired and

I must be somewhere in between

Somewhere in between awake and asleep because my thoughts become more solid, and so does one of the stains, until it forms the outline of a person. A woman in an ivory coat with dark, gold-threaded hair.

She came for me. She found me.

She walks right across the sky like the constellations are her staircase. I reach for her wildly, legs thrashing, but she doesn't reach back. She stops in front of me, just out of my grasp, and folds her arms behind her back.

"Just like him," Valyra says, her voice low and melodic. "To the end."

"No." Every word is a painful gasp, like I'm choking on shards of glass. "Help me . . . *please* . . ."

Valyra sighs and steps closer. "It would always have ended like this for you, darling."

I wake myself back up screaming without sound, hunting for air that no longer exists.

Oh, no, I realize as my gulp feels like sucking through a thin straw, *no, no—*

How long did I go unconscious for? How long did I spend wasting my last remaining moments on a nightmare?

It doesn't matter. It's all gone.

My lungs convulse, but there's nothing for them to hold

onto. The weight of the sky presses down from every angle; I swear I can hear my own blood vessels bursting in my head. The stars are swallowing me, like I always knew they would.

Someone. Even focusing on the word is difficult. My head is all buzzing terror. *Please, some—*

And without any warning that I've been dragged back under, my hallucinations return.

This time, it looks like—

Like—

Well, *jellyfish* is the only word that makes any sense—not that I've ever seen one, outside the pages of books from obsolete worlds. Like a half-girl, half-jellyfish. Like a girl wearing a jellyfish as a skirt. She floats from her distance, the legless lower part of her rippling like waves against the shallows. Beside her is something like a tiny, pulsing star, detached from its canvas. She watches as it darts away, glances back at me. A look of resolve crosses her face.

And she swims after it.

No, I think desperately, *no, please, come back—*

But I can't even keep my eyes open to watch her abandon me. The vacuum presses down on my neck, my jaw, my eyelids. It forces its way down my throat. *Let go,* the universe croons, just as before. *Let go, let go.*

Let—

"…hello?"

I try to force my eyes back open, but a bare slit is all I can manage.

On the other side is a blurry silhouette. A halo of silvery light, wide opal eyes staring me through. Lavender skin so pale it's almost translucent. The girl. She came back.

Hello? her mouth shapes, her other hand waving gently in front of my face. *Are you dead?*

I choke for air that doesn't exist anymore. *No*, I try to say, *no, please, help*—but all I manage is a final gasp that brings nothing but empty space into my lungs, and then the darkness drags me down for the last time.

CHAPTER 9

Nym

"No... *no, please.* Come back. Come *back.*"

I flit in a circle through the violet sea, scanning the stars. One must move. One must cry out to me in that unfamiliar voice. But I turn and turn, and the gentle melody of the universe is the only response I get. The storm has moved on. The dustmoth has gone with it. It left me, and in doing so took the first real chance I've had in memory of finding my way home.

My eyes sting. I swallow furiously as I retreat to House's sanctuary, still searching through the blur. But I reach the ropes, and there is nothing. Only me and a ship and a dying-maybe-dead boy.

I perch on the edge of the basket and frown at him, this creature I lost my thread home to save. He's sprawled on one of the upper beams branching from House's gravity core, his head tipped back, his hair collapsing in an exhausted rumple over his forehead. I've seen humans before. Slender fingers to curl around the weapons they use to fight back the rest of the ether; smooth, scaleless skin half-concealed with coarse fabric and worn leather. But the eyes on this one are strange—round and metallic and bottomless as tiny pools. Not human at all.

He stirs, and my heart leaps with panic, relief, curiosity,

until I realize he is not responsible for the movement. The branch beneath him agitates again, slivers of wood rattling as though disturbed creatures are burrowing beneath the surface. One side of the boy's unconscious body begins to slip off.

"Oh, stop." I slide down and set an irritated hand against the column. "I know he's a stranger. But we can't just throw him back out."

The door beneath me creaks on its hinge, then tips open.

"*No.* You know that's not what I mean." I blur down to catch it, and a mumbling sort of groan tremors through the floorboards. "Don't be difficult. It's only until he wakes up. Then it'll be just us two again."

And besides, is the selfish truth I don't say aloud, *he can't die, or I'll have lost the path for nothing.* It's hard not to feel selfish, though. Selfish and bitter. Maybe the dustmoth was nothing but a memory with wings; maybe it was never leading anywhere at all. But maybe it was. I will never know.

So the least this boy can do in return for what he cost me is *wake.*

I float back up to him and trace all the places a pulse might live—the hollow of his neck, the inside of his wrist, the heart buried in his chest. The music in his veins is a soft, weak whisper of a melody, but I've no idea how to make it louder. And then there are the eyes, so dull and unnatural.

I lean in and brush one curiously with my finger, but find a smooth, manufactured sheen under my touch. *Glass?* I trace down the curved side until I find the seam where bronze meets skin. The gap becomes apparent when I push gently against his cheekbone. *Oh.* They're not eyes—they're some kind of tool.

I lift the thing off his face tentatively, then hold it up to peer through the lenses. The view is dizzyingly vibrant, each color too loud and sharp, each thread of the universe outlined in its purest hue. I slide the straps on to get a better look and crinkle my nose under the pinch of the metal bridge, squinting around at the walls. My plants turn sickly green; my glittering trinkets send piercing stabs of whiter-than-white through my eyes. It's truly a headache of a sensation. *Fascinating.*

My gaze settles back on the maybe-dead boy. I might not have noticed it without the glass eyes, but with everything in such vivid focus, a pinprick of brilliant yellow stands out against the cerulean backdrop of his hair. I push the lenses up and see something pierced through the cartilage of his ear, something that lets out a dangerous-looking red flash.

It's sharp and stiff beneath my fingers, and there's a light crusting of dried blood around its base. A near-invisible hole is a millimeter away from it; whoever clipped the device in missed the mark by a painful hair. It doesn't look very nice, whatever it is.

"Please don't be the only thing keeping him alive," I mutter, and I pull the piercing free.

A network of gold veins ripples over the boy's entire body, and then he spasms into a choking gasp.

I flinch back in terror, but after a few more hoarse coughs, his breathing steadies and smooths. He's not dead, though he came earnestly close.

Alarm quickly replaces my relief as the nightmare behind his eyes fades and his lashes start to flutter. He cannot see me, not as a Medyssian. That's the only thing that keeps me safe until I can get back home: no one must know what I actually am, or I'll be hunted the way everyone else was.

Instinctively, I press my hand to the quiet song beating through his heart. Something about its gentle descending notes, underscored with the earnest tick of gears, feels unusually familiar, but there is no time to listen. Only to mimic it in my own voice. The luminescence fades from my hair and spins it pale yellow; the silver-lilac of my skin loses its luster; my umbra turns to something opaque and silk-spun. My ears and fingertips shrink and round and smooth away. The colors of both myself and the world around me change through the prism of my new eyes. I am like him, now—a human, an ally. A more familiar stranger.

And right as I finish shifting, right as I kick human legs free from the bell of my umbra and lose my weightlessness entirely and crash in surprise to the floor, his eyes snap open.

CHAPTER 10

Aren

I AM dreaming, still drowning, and the girl watches me.

The stars loom overhead, and my limbs are heavy and unyielding, and she is here, for one more brief flash. Moonlight hair and opal eyes and clouds and clouds of something light and shimmering. And then, she's gone. She came back, but only to watch me die.

But I take a shuddering gasp, and it doesn't get trapped. The air goes all the way down until it feels like my lungs might cramp, and then I exhale, and I do it again. I can breathe. I'm not drowning. Not even dreaming.

I'm… alive.

How am I alive?

I somehow manage to prop myself up on my elbows with a groan, the inside of my head ringing and foggy. A hard, solid surface is beneath me. Wood. I'm on a ship. I'm in—

I rub the spots from my vision with the heel of my hand, certain I'm still hallucinating. I'm in a cocoon of—there's really no better word for it—*junk*. Ten feet beneath me, a sea of shimmery periwinkle fabric ripples over the rounded floor, fraying ends trapped under stacks of yellow-brown papers and pots of paint. The windows walling in the basket from every side are hidden behind a chaotic display of cooking utensils hung from wires, lopsided shelves of empty bottles with peeling labels, hanging planters of dead-looking greenery.

I tilt my head back enough to see that my ledge is protruding from a bronze gravity core that looks ripped from an entirely different ship and unceremoniously replanted. A length of wire strung with gears and softly blinking lights winds around its whorled branches, over the oxygen valve. An even more bizarre collection of objects is crammed into the cracks between panels—crumpled scrolls, brass coils that don't connect to anything, gilded horns, something that looks like a leathery wing. The apex of the core disappears somewhere through a skylight.

Skylight. That's why I thought I was still in the void: there really are what looks like a thousand miles of stars hanging straight above me. But it's a *tapestry*—someone's painted the inside of the domed ceiling a dozen shades of violet and lilac and gold.

"Hello?" My tongue feels like sandpaper, like I swallowed every dust particle the universe has to offer and don't know how to spit them out. "Is anyone here?"

I think one of the unidentifiable piles below shifts, but then a whistle comes from somewhere above my head. I peer through the skylight again. Something glimmers in the dome.

"Hello?"

The whistle doesn't repeat. There's someone up there, though; I heard them. My arms are still sore from remembering how to be arms, but I stretch for the next-closest beam. The unmistakable sound of breathing pulses from the other side of the canvas, which scrapes against my hair as I kick my way up to the opening.

"I can hear you. Is someone—" But when I straighten, my

words fall away. It's not just a tapestry, up here. Not just stars. I'm in a painted recreation of space itself.

It balloons over me in an unending kaleidoscope, swirling lilac and silver and gold. I step up and across the beam, no idea where to look first. Carefully curlicued names I recognize leap out from circles that must represent planets—Idri, where the Celestial Company has been sending supplies to rebels. Andanere, whose imperial reach spread to every rock in its orbit until my mother put a stop to it. Vorescan, almost wiped out by a plague until she found a way to run medicine through its viciously impenetrable atmosphere. Ceres, which would have been decimated by ice volcanos without her aid. And the places I haven't seen myself, I recognize from stories, from past missions, from holographic terrain recreations used in the training room. I can't even calculate how long it must have taken to paint it.

It makes me a different kind of breathless, looking at it all. It doesn't make any sense. This place. This *stuff*. There's a collection up here, too, but it's not chaos. It's perfect and meticulous, with a single ornament hanging from every painstakingly drawn planet. A pressed flower with a spiky stem. A coin strung through its center. A jagged mirror shard clear enough to reach into.

I've seen people brought into the crew who could chart the universe in this kind of detail. Valyra always finds them, recruits them as navigators or strategists. But this is beyond anything even the Celestial Company could produce.

My heartbeat quickens, as if desperate to make up for all the time it wasn't working. I've heard of scavengers who are beyond recruitment, too, who don't care about anything except roaming the universe for parts—machine or body. I find myself reaching for the mirror shard without thinking, certain I saw a face that wasn't mine on the other side. What's this collection for? Where did it all come from?

Who dragged me from the void, and why?

The beam creaks behind me.

I wheel so fast, I almost fall off the slope. The shard is in my hand before I realize I've grabbed it, too many years of Celestial Company defensive training wired into my reflexes.

But it's not a threat. At least, I don't think it is. I lower the glass.

"You," I tell the silhouette on the other end of this microcosm. "It's you."

The girl from the void.

Her feet are bare, her skirts billowing as if caught in a tide I can't see. It must be the same girl—there's no way it isn't—but the details I remember from before are all wrong. The halo around her head is only hair, pale gold and rippling in gravity-rejecting waves to just below her chin, and her eyes are clear blue, not prismatic opals embedded in her skin. *Opals? Halo?* Who even talks like that? I must have been completely out of it.

And what I distinctly remember thinking was a jellyfish, of all things, is just a dress. Frothy and ethereal as the rest of her, all layers upon layers of fluttery material that shifts from lilac to silver to dusty blue with the light, but definitely a dress. She doesn't fit with the rest of the void I know—cold, static, desolate—and neither does her hoarder's paradise of a ship.

She's the only reason I'm still alive.

"It was you, wasn't it?" I lower the mirror-shard. "You saved me."

The girl doesn't respond. Just stands in the center of the dome, her odd collection orbiting her.

"I—" *Thank you* isn't even close to enough. "Who are you?"

I find myself blurting out instead. "What is this place?"

She is silent. She does nothing but tilt her head, light glancing off her hair.

"Can you speak?" I take a tentative step closer, then another when she doesn't back away. "I thought you did before, when you—" The light refracting from her forehead changes direction, and I squint against the sudden glare of starlight hitting glass.

My glass.

My free fingers jump to my neck and meet nothing but worn cotton. She took my specs. And glinting in her hand— that's my starwalking suit activator. My two most important weapons against the crushing darkness, and she's taken them from me. The warning in my head reactivates. *Scavenger, scavenger.*

I swallow, try to keep my voice steady. "That's mine."

The girl's eyes widen, then narrow. "That's *mine*," she echoes.

"Can I... have that back?"

"Can I have *that* back?"

Can she only mimic other sounds?

"The activator. The specs." I gesture forcefully. "*Give me—*"

"Do you often threaten to stab people with their own things?" she demands.

I look down. She wasn't mimicking me—I forgot all about the mirror I absolutely stole from her wall.

I tilt the glass smooth-side first, jagged tip sheathed in my palm. "I'll trade you, okay?"

Her hand ventures tentatively out, then detours toward my specs. I try not to buckle with relief the second she exchanges the glass I'm clutching for worn leather.

"I was just trying them on," she says softly, indignantly.

"You weren't breathing. I didn't know what was causing it."

I want to stab *myself*. "I'm sorry. Really. The specs, I just need—"I bite my tongue. The Celestial Company would wring my neck—you never give away your weaknesses to strangers. "Let's start over, okay? Thank you. For saving me."

The girl slides past me, nearly edging me off the narrow beam.

"*Hey.*" I juggle my tech against my shirt, and by the time I find my balance, she's already by the sloping wall, carefully re-fastening the mirror to a loose bit of string. I squint at her bare feet and dare myself to imagine fluttering lavender ribbons in their stead. "When I saw you out there… you didn't even have a tether. How did you—"

"Why were you out there at all?" she interrupts. "Were you attacked?"

Attacked. The memories assault me. That ghostly ship with its graveyard of teeth, the cyclone of eels, the way it felt when the storm captured me in its claws. I was lost. I should have been permanently.

"I… I was looking for someone," I say. "But I went to the wrong place, and then—" I bite my cheek, hoping the silence says *and then I was thrown into the yawning cavity of unbridled space,* so I don't have to say it out loud. "—you know."

The girl turns, arms crossed. "You're dreadful at telling stories."

"Okay, well, you're not great at answering questions. Can you at least tell me who you are?"

Silence. Her head cocks, reproachful.

"Look, I'll go first. I'm Aren."

"Aren." She sounds out every letter as if inspecting them; I've never heard anyone stretch four letters out that much before. Then, she blinks up at the canopy, brow furrowed in concentration.

"Alright," she finally says, once I've started wondering whether the answer is written somewhere up there, between the painted constellations. "I suppose it would be no harm. Nym. My name is Nym."

"Nym," I repeat. It sounds made-up. It sounds like someone humming the beginning of a song they'd forgotten to finish; it sounds exactly right for a girl in a shimmering dress in a balloon in the middle of the void. "Nym. Okay. Listen, I know I don't deserve to ask anything more of you, but I have to get back to my crew. They'll be looking for me."

"Your crew is…" For the first time, something like pain flashes across her face. She chews the edge of her lip, frees it as she turns from me. "They are all gone, Aren."

"What?" The static beneath my skin reignites. Walled in from the void, I am suddenly once again drowning in it. "No. That's impossible."

"It was a very powerful storm. You… you were the only one I could pull from it."

The static smooths away quick as it came. "*Oh*. No—they weren't with me. I went alone."

"Oh." That flash of pain gives way to something sharper, more brittle. "That was very foolish of you, don't you think? Going off on your own, without your family?"

I bristle. "You're alone, aren't you?"

"I am never. I have House." She runs a hand over the side of the canopy, and it seems to expand like lungs. "I suppose you know how to find your way home, then? Where do you belong?"

"Um…" *Here we go.* "Celestial Company," I mutter, tilting my head and lifting the back of my hair to show her my tattoo. "See?" I wait for her uninterested gaze to fill with recognition as she finally realizes whose features I share. She could prob-ably demand enough reward money to buy herself an airship twice as big as this one, or at least a good storage unit. Maybe some cabinets. Assuming they'd even pay to get me back.

Nym nods once. "Okay." Then, she breezes past me and drops right through the mouth of the balloon.

"Please don't—wait, what?" The phrase *please don't ransom me* is already halfway out of my mouth before I realize what she's said.

Okay.

That's all.

Does she… not know what the Celestial Company is? Impossible. Everyone knows the name—Valyra's made it her life's purpose. Is it really possible I've managed to be saved by the only person, then, who just doesn't care?

I peer down, watching her hop from one bar to the next, arms outstretched like a dancer. "That's… that's the problem. They're kind of elusive unless they want to be found. I sent out a distress signal before I—you know, so if it's not too much trouble to go back near the wreck, I might be close enough to—"

Oh, no.

The wreck. The signal I left.

Both of the signals I left.

Nym's basket seems to turn itself sideways. I can see it: my modified navigator with its screaming beacon, the one I was so relieved had finally worked. I see it exactly where I left it onboard my sailer, turned on and activated. That beacon, and the brilliant line it's drawing straight through space, back to wherever the *Starsaviour* currently is.

A perfect map for anyone in the universe who stumbles across it and decides to see where it leads. Rival crews.

Monsters drawn to the light. Every enemy my mother might have.

"Do me a favor," I say weakly, "and just throw me back into space."

The ship's tilt makes the door below clank against its lock, as if backing me up.

Nym plants her hands on her waist. "Now, *really*."

"They're going to kill me," I gasp, tripping over myself to clamber down after her. "My crew. I screwed up." Why—*why* did I put my blood in the navigator? I should have waited. If I hadn't panicked, if I'd just sped my sailer out of the nebula before turning it on… This takes every other mistake I've ever made in my life and crushes it into dust, and this, *this* is what's going to get me left behind for good.

"I made this navigator, this thing that can follow blood matches to their source, and I left it… I left it…" Saying the words out loud only makes it worse, more real. I don't even realize how far down the mast I've stumbled until I feel hands on my collar, pulling me back up to the lowest crooked branch. Nym squats on the narrow ledge.

"What," she asks, and *opal* is once again the only right word for her wide, flashing eyes, "did you just say?"

I tap her wrist irritably. "Hi. Choking."

"The navigator. Blood matches. What did you mean?"

"Um." Between my self-inflicted breakdown and the way she's managed to make a noose out of my collar, breathing is getting extremely difficult. "You put blood in it. And then it draws a path to the input's closest genetic match, I guess. I don't know. It's not what I meant it to do."

"But it works?"

"Yes. Yes, it works."

Nym lets go. My muscles disregard every moment I've

ever spent in the training room; I lose grip on the bar and go plummeting down the last ten feet into a mountain of fabric.

"*Ow,*" I groan once I extricate myself. "What was that?"

"A *blood navigator!*" Something wild and effervescent has taken over her face, turning her into a completely different girl from the wary, guarded one I met ten minutes ago. She doesn't leap down beside me so much as float, landing on the only inch of floor not covered by uncategorized trash. "Why didn't I ever think—of course, the ether must recognize which of its souls belong together—"

"You might be a little too excited about something I just told you is going to make my crew *kill me.*" I straighten my crooked specs. "You don't get it—they're in danger, they have enemies that'll use this—"

"Show me." She whirls and yanks on one of the objects hanging from her ceiling, something that must be part of the ship and not part of her collection, because the next thing I know we're *flying.* Straight up, like we're trying to break through the atmosphere of a planet that doesn't exist. I have to roll out of the way as crates come tumbling down from their uneven stacks. "You must show me."

"Nym, what—"

"The light I saw—that was yours, then. That's what you're saying? Not lightning. A map between souls." She flits faster than I can track, pulling levers, leaping to readjust ropes. Her rippling skirt hits me in the face. "I'll take you back, and you'll show me. Flip the compressor, would you? No, never mind, I can do it." Another swoosh of skirt as she lunges on her tiptoes somewhere above my head.

"Are you serious?" I stagger away from the avalanche of fabric. "Did I mention the hundreds of carnivorous eels?"

"I'm not afraid of eels."

"Well, you should be!" The stars outside are a thousand identical streaks of silver; I have to grab the railing to hold on. "Okay, just—just stop for a second!" I finally yell, and miraculously, she does. The ship doesn't stop moving, but she hangs from one of the pulleys on her toes.

"What? You did say you wanted to go back, didn't you?"

"What's your deal?" I demand. "Don't you dare say you just want to help. No one is that selfless. I have to know what's in this for you, or I'm going to lose my mind."

She releases one hand from its grip to tuck her hair back. "You truly have such a map? And it works as you say? You swear it. You *swear* it."

I was pretty sure we'd covered this part. "Yes. Yes, I swear it."

She inhales and holds it, refusing to look at me. Three words finally stumble out, in a tone that sounds like a confession.

"I need it."

I frown. "The navigator? For what?" I shouldn't bother asking, when she hasn't even told me why she owns the world's largest dead plant emporium.

"Can I borrow it?" she pleads, instead of explaining. "If I help you get it back? Just once?"

Borrow it? For what, though? The question still bats around in my head, but as I look at the earnest glimmer in her eyes, I can see the vague outline of a different kind of map being drawn. She needs a device that would guide her to someone that shares her blood. She's not a scavenger. She lives alone, even though she can't be any older than me, with nothing but a star chart and a basket of junk.

Who are you? I want to ask. *Who are you looking for?*

But it doesn't matter, because there it is. She doesn't care about me; she just wants the map for herself. And I know that kind of deal well—it's the kind the Celestial Company lives for. *No mission without a commission,* I heard a pilot say once, deep in his cups, with the air of someone reciting poetry. Why should this stranger be any different?

"You help me get the navigator back," I tell her, "and you can *have* it."

CHAPTER 11

Nym

*I*T *may not work.*

It may be gone.

It may not be real.

Hope is a dangerous, heady thing. I take it in small doses. I never give myself enough for it to hurt me when it fades. I have already given too much to the dustmoth, more than I ought. I should not make that mistake again.

It may be destroyed.

It may have been taken by someone else.

But maybe it is because of the dustmoth that I want so badly to trust in the map this boy claims is out there. I've met so many dead ends, painted every one of them across my sky to remind me to keep looking for one more, one more. But today was the first time I let one slip through my fingers. I want it back, if there's a chance. I will take it back.

Human eyes take in color differently, so the sky is black as pitch as I watch our journey through the window. The stars' luster is faint, the streaks of dust and debris painted gray against that pitch backdrop. But it's beautiful nevertheless, stained with a promise that might at last, at last bring me home.

Did the dustmoth know, all this time? Could it sense it? Is this where it was always trying to lead me?

I'm coming, I'm coming. I'll find you.

"You're coming up with a plan over there, right?"

I drag my gaze away from the window. Aren's been crouched over the clip I took out of his ear since we turned around, performing some sort of strange surgery on the mechanism. Now, he looks up, a pointed tool stuck between his teeth.

"A plan? For what?"

"For—for not getting eaten by a hive of devouring eels?"

I had forgotten all about the eels. Even now, I don't feel any terror—creatures of the deep have always seen me as a friend. "The plan is we go back, get this map, and leave."

"Oh, okay. So, the plan is to let them eat us."

I swing my legs down to face him. "What could be so scary about these particular eels, exactly?"

"Have you ever seen one? With the—the teeth, and the eyes, and the—*ow.*" A spark zings out of the device's wiring. Aren dislodges the tool between his teeth and replaces it with his finger, sucking on the burn. "Hold on. I'll show you."

He unfolds a yellowing bit of paper from one of his belt's many holsters and traces out a few curving strokes. But when he hands it over, I accidentally let out a laugh.

"What?" He frowns. "It's a decent sketch."

It's true; he's rather good—sharp and precise, like a blueprint—but I'm not laughing at his skill.

"I *have* met these!" I cry in delight. "They're allovores." He must have been terrified when they tore into his ship, but it was never him they were after. "They eat metal! Bronze, brass, gold."

"Oh, good, great. Nym, what's your ship made of?"

"House?" The outside is all glass and canvas, but there's quite a lot of bronze around the console, I suppose. "Hmm. We can just swim down to the wreck, then."

What color was left in Aren's pale face bleeds dry. "We can what, now?"

I pull myself back up the branches of the mast. "If it's just us down there, the eels won't attack. Oh, there's got to be a rope—*yes!*" The coil crashes down to the deck. "Found it."

"I—sure. Flawless plan." I had no idea someone's voice could crack so much on just four words. Aren swallows, staring at the tangled heap of rope, but I can suddenly feel something else not being said, can see it in the stiff muscles in his face. He's scared of that wreck even knowing the eels are practically harmless, and he doesn't want to tell me.

"Or," I suggest carefully, swinging back down, "you stay and guard House, and I'll find the map."

Aren cocks an eyebrow. "Aren't you worried I'll commandeer your ship?"

I suppress a laugh and peer up into the dome. "I hear that, House? He thinks you would move an inch with someone else at the helm." The floorboards grate mockingly, and a rope flicks Aren's hair. But his eyes flit somewhere behind my head, then widen.

"We're here," he says quietly. "We're back."

All thoughts of what Aren might be hiding vanish as I flatten myself against the glass.

"Oh, *wow.*" With human eyes, the end of the beacon cuts an even more brilliant path through the dullness of the sky. It's not one solid burst of lightning after all, but a hundred, a thousand, all wrapped in one luminous artery.

"You're really sure about this?" Aren doesn't look at the beacon as though it's beautiful; he looks at it as though it's the ugliest thing he's ever seen. "If you change your mind… I mean, you can change your mind."

"I haven't. I won't." *I'll find you. I'll find you.* I am a breath away. "House, take us up above the eye of the storm, okay?" I pat the railing and go back for the rope, gathering its bulky mass in my arms. I've never swum through space on human legs before, but I don't suppose the mechanics should be hard. Kicking and wriggling and the like. I just need to—

And then, as I heave the rope over to the edge of the basket, I find I can't remember what I need to do at all. I look down into the gaping abyss, and I see exactly what attacked Aren for the first time.

A ship.

A *beast*.

Gray sails, gray wood, gray mast. A ship of smoke and ash, of crumbling bones and rusting bloodstains.

Not *a* ship. *The* ship.

And the end of the beacon is singing from somewhere in its depthless cavity.

Once, there was a—

No.

a ship, ghostly and dark.

Not now. Not after all this time.

and inside its heart lived a monster.

It can't be. It can't be here, beneath me, not when I've spent so much time being careful and hidden and

and when the night went dark and still, you could sometimes hear it approaching, always behind you no matter how far you ran

The rope tumbles out of my arms.

"Nym?" I can hear Aren somewhere distant, wading closer. "I know. It's like a nightmare come to life. It's—"

"The Ghost Ship."

"What?"

I've never, never said it aloud. The name always felt like a summoning, like it could track me through the sound alone. But that doesn't matter anymore. It's *here.*

"That's what it's called," I whisper. "The Ghost Ship." Aren swallows. His heartbeat is

drumming a warning

loud and percussive, an echo of my own terror.

"I thought you said the eels were harmless," he says. "What's wrong?"

I'll find you. I'll find you. It found me. "It's not the eels. There's… something… *else* on that ship. A hunter. It's—" I try to keep my voice steady. I try to keep the truth—*it's hunting me*—buried. "It eats—" *Medyssians.* "—anything in its path. It's a monster, Aren—" I hold onto the railing, the legs that don't belong to me threatening to crumple. This isn't fair. I was careful, so careful, so *close.*

Aren is silent. We float there on the edge of the abyss, the Ghost Ship yawning beneath us, and I know what he's thinking. It's not worth it. Maybe it's what I *want* him to be thinking. My longing for home aches inside me, but for the first time, something else fights back.

"So," Aren finally says, "it's alive, whatever's in there? Sentient?"

I nod.

"It could use the map itself, then. It could follow it back to the Celestial Company and attack them."

It could. The Shadow takes what it wants. It just always wanted Medyssians most.

I nod a second time.

"And you're going down there anyway?"

Am I? *No,* I want to scream, as the skymap above me

morphs into something mocking and cruel. But I have been fooling myself with leads that led to nothing forever. This is a lead that could actually work. I cannot let go of that.

"Yes," I whisper, "I suppose I am."

"Okay." He lets out a forceful exhale, then pulls his glass eyes down. "I'll go first."

CHAPTER 12
Aren

*I*LL GO *first?*

I'll go first?

What's wrong with me?

I've been possessed. Mind-wiped. I should have said, *Good idea, Nym. Forget the navigator. Let's just run.* If anything counts as going way too overboard trying to fix my own mistakes, this is it.

Because I'm literally overboard.

The tether trails behind me as I swim, one end looped tight to my belt. And my specs, typically so good at turning dark colors light, have only made the Ghost Ship's grayness come into sharper focus. I can see every rotting hole in its mast as I dive, every rusted edge of the shards that make up its teeth. There aren't any eels, not right now, but that's somehow worse. It means they're waiting somewhere in the deep, prowling and creeping and biding their time.

The tether tugs gently around my waist, the only sign that Nym is descending behind me. I can't bring myself to turn around and look, see how far we've strayed from the safety of her ship. Balloon. House. Whatever it is. So instead, all I can do is look forward, watching the mouth I'm about to feed myself to open wider and wider.

Something is down there. Something worse than eels.

A hunter, she said. *A monster.*

I try to imagine it, to give it a shape. This lurking, insatiable beast. But all I can get are flashes of ideas—a set of fangs, a blazing crimson eye, a claw tearing ribbons in the rotting floor. A dozen terrors, assembled crudely together without form.

Or maybe it's invisible, untouchable. Maybe it slips through your pores and rots you from the inside, leaving your skin behind as a shell. Or maybe the ship, with its gaping mouth and jagged teeth, is the monster all on its own.

I am the son of Captain Valyra Vanthal, I think to myself. An order. A prayer. *I survived the thing I feared most. I will do it again. I will.*

I will not die here.

One of the teeth protrudes close enough to reach, and I haul myself in on shaking hands, try to touch down against the crumbling wood. My feet slide out immediately. Right. No crew. No gravity. Which also explains what I see looming inside the mouth once I find my balance, what turns my already-cold blood frigid.

It's a graveyard for shipwrecks.

The teeth are just the gate. The teeth are for the shards lucky enough to find something to latch to, giving whatever crew might have been lost in their attack a permanent headstone. The rest float without direction, reanimated corpses wandering the cave of the Ghost Ship's stomach forever. Wood and metal, torn sails and dull wings. Ropes drifting like dead snakes. Wires chewed off and sparking. Every vessel the Ghost Ship has ever crossed, and all that remained after the beast inside it had finished. I can't even see the end of the labyrinth; there's no pattern to the way the wreckage swirls around itself, no way to see how far up or down or back it goes. How are we going to find one sailer among thousands?

"Oh." I didn't hear Nym finish coming down behind me, but suddenly she's leaning in from the shard next to mine, eyes wide. "You don't see your ship, do you? Very, very close to the edge?"

The nearest ship, one that looks miraculously whole, drifts past until it crunches against a rusted engine and turns, revealing a starboard side that's been gnawed away to nothing. The exposed interior leaks three stories of crumbling rust. I watch the invisible current sweep the half-eaten carcass back into the depths until it's gone.

"No." I swallow. "But let me see if maybe…"

I adjust the knobs on my specs and wait for the gray ships to saturate. Instead, my entire vision goes black, like my eyelids have been sewn shut. I frown and reposition, but no matter how much I twist or which direction I face, the view in front of me is completely colorless.

"It's like it eats light," I mutter, "like it… *wait—*"

I push the settings back a hair. There was a blue flicker somewhere in there; I swear I saw it. One thread of color hidden in all that black. I stare and stare, and the flicker returns.

"There's a light. It's faint, but I think it's back there."

Nym points fifteen degrees in the wrong direction. "That way?"

"There." I angle Nym's shoulder slightly to the left, then tap my lenses. "It's the only spot even showing up, after the color distortion. The beacon's gotta end there."

Nym lowers her arm. "The debris is in constant motion. Would—would the current bring it closer, maybe, if we stayed here?"

Everything in me screams to say yes. I can think of at

least twelve different ways to die in there, and that doesn't even include the monster hiding somewhere in the spiraling wreckage. But I managed to reset my starwalking suit by siphoning oxygen out of the core on Nym's ship, and I could run out my remaining hour just sitting here, waiting for my sailer to be washed in.

I refocus the settings. I think the light might actually be getting *fainter*. Or maybe I'm about to pass out again. "I don't think it's a good risk. I think we should—" We should *what*? This is the part where someone higher ranked gives me directions, but there's no one else here. Just me and this strange girl and the knowledge that we both need the map, but she's even more afraid to go after it than I am.

Maybe that's why I swam down first. Maybe that's why I'm about to step off this ledge. I've never known how to be brave for myself, but maybe I can figure it out for someone else.

"We should follow the light. Staying near the top, where there's not as much wreckage," I hear myself saying. My skin crawls with discomfort; I don't give orders to people. "That way, if it moves, we'll be able to track it. And—and we should tie ourselves together, so we don't get separated in there. One facing front, the other back, to cover any attack points. Does that make sense?"

If Nym clocks me as an imposter who's never strategized a mission in my life, she doesn't give it away. All she does is nod. "Good idea."

When it's done, when House is anchored to the ledge and Nym and I are knotted loosely together by our waists, I can't come up with any more reasons to delay going in there. Already, the display on my wrist cuff tells me I'm down to forty-nine minutes—if we waste any more time, I won't have enough air to swim back out.

I take a deep, stale breath and watch the broken whirlpool swirl by. "I'm going to be completely honest. I may need you to push me."

Nym lets out a sound halfway between laugh and choke, then flexes her grip against the shrapnel.

"I think it's my turn to go first, actually," she says, and then, with the resolved, fearful expression of a person jumping out of an airlock for the first time, she lets go.

I have exactly enough time to half-consider untying myself before I'm dragged in after her.

It only takes a few moments to regret being the one who got stuck facing backward. It means I have a permanent view of not just the shipwrecks circling us like predators, but also of the only exit, shrinking mockingly as we move away from it. My blaster feels like a toy in my hands—I only have six or seven charges, enough to miss whatever attacks us six or seven times. Can't wait.

I'd prepared myself for a vacuum to fill my ears as soon as we crossed the line into the ship's stomach, but it's almost worse. I can hear... *things* in the dark. The painful groan of metal as shards grate against each other. Whispers, like all the people who must have died in here are warning me to turn around. A glint stabs through the corner of my specs, and I turn in time to see the bloodstained grin of an eel peering out from behind a crumbling grate. The slow current carries it away, unblinking eyes locked on mine.

"So." I thought my throat couldn't get any drier, but I underestimated myself. "This monster you mentioned. The shadow. Can you tell me anything else about it? What it looks like, maybe? You know, so I know what to shoot at when it tries to eat me."

Silence. I reach behind me and tug the rope to make sure she's still there. "Nym?"

"I've never seen it." Her voice is somehow even quieter than my own. "Only heard its story."

"Maybe it's not real, then. Maybe it's just a story."

"This isn't that kind of story."

I reposition the blaster, certain I saw something moving in the corner of my eye. But no, it's just my full-to-bursting paranoia. Nym's voice is the only anchor keeping me from spiraling. "So, tell it to me."

Silence once again.

"Or don't, if you'd rather just—"

"Alright," Nym interrupts warily. "Once… once there were creatures who swam between stars, but now they are gone."

"Oh, so it's a fairy tale."

"It's—do you want to hear it or not?"

"Yes. Sorry."

"There were these creatures, and they—" Another pause. "Some say they were made of the light that formed at the beginning of the universe. Pure matter, able to transform into anything they touched. They had a home, and it was beautiful, but they were restless. And curious. So they wandered. All over the universe, everywhere there was life, just… exploring."

"That sounds nice." I consider the difference between that sort of wandering and the kind the Celestial Company does. "Peaceful."

I can hear Nym's face light up through her voice. "Peaceful, yes—they'd never hurt anyone. But when these creatures were born, something else grew from the cavity. A being of dark matter. And because the creatures were made of pure light, of joy and curiosity and hope, this monster was made of the opposite. Fear. Rage. Hunger. They called it the Shadow, and they say it could split itself into pieces small enough to hunt the—the creatures down one at a time, wherever they were, snuffing them out like stars behind a cloud. And then it would drag their souls back in its teeth, and—" She stops, and I know it's because this part doesn't need to be described. I've *seen* the teeth. I'm *in* the teeth. "They didn't know how to fight back. And each time it killed and fed, it got stronger and hungrier, until there was nothing left for it to feed on. So then… then it started hungering for everything else. Swallowing all of the light in the universe."

A shiver skates from my neck down my spine. "Wait, nothing left? It ate all of them?"

Nym doesn't answer.

I'm supposed to keep my gaze firmly on my own semi-circle, but I risk turning over my shoulder. Nym's own head is turned enough for me to see an indiscernible shadow of her own stretched across her face. A flicker in her expression, sad and deep as the void itself. Fear, terror—those reactions make sense for a legend like this. Sadness doesn't fit. Sadness is personal.

"Who told you that story?" I ask.

"What?" Her expression contorts toward confusion. "I don't—what do you mean?"

"I mean it had to come from somewhere. How do you know it's real?"

She laughs mirthlessly. "It's real."

I know that tone—certain beyond certain, the kind that eviscerates protest. I've heard it in Valyra's voice too often not to recognize it now. But how can she have so much faith in what sounds like nothing but a ghost story, a warning for children? *Stay at home, where it is safe. Don't go too far, or the monster will get you.* I believe there's *something* on this ship, but star-swimming shapeshifters aren't—

Hello? Are you dead?

Something sizzles in my veins—a trigger, a memory I'd carelessly buried. That otherworldly girl who saved me from the void, her prismatic eyes, the way her lower half rippled in formless ribbons. No. No way. It was just a hallucination—my half-drowned mind smashing itself to pieces, turning Nym's hair and dress and face into nonsense.

Pure matter. Transformed into anything they touched.

I look back at Nym again, her *humanness*. Human legs, like mine, kicking their way gracefully through this mixture of corpse-dust and rust shavings. Those same ribbons I saw in the void stitched together into a skirt, still shimmering. "That story. Is it—"

"Forget the story," she says. The rope around my waist tugs under my ribcage as she picks up speed. "It's not important. The Shadow is real, and it's dangerous—that's all that matters. Just forget everything else."

Creatures who swam between stars. Hunted down, one by one. "But… Nym, are you—"

I frown.

My thoughts slip away like water cupped in my hands, seeping out through the cracks until all that's left is damp and intangible. What was I about to say? Something about Nym. Something about creatures who… who…

I shake my head, press my free fingers to my temples. The Shadow is the only part that matters. I should forget the story.

I *have* forgotten the story.

It wasn't important.

No. *No*, that's not right either. "Was I—I was about to ask you something, right?"

"I think—" Nym's voice cracks. Probably just scared of the

Shadow, still—the only thing that matters. "I think you saw something in the wreckage, but it was nothing."

"Oh." I saw something in the wreckage. It was nothing. "Yeah, we're fine. Sorry. Keep watching your section."

But as I settle back into my watch, I can't help poking at my mind like a tongue prods the gap of a missing tooth. Something about her was in there, I think. Something important.

"Nym—" I say, and then a tentacle closes over my mouth.

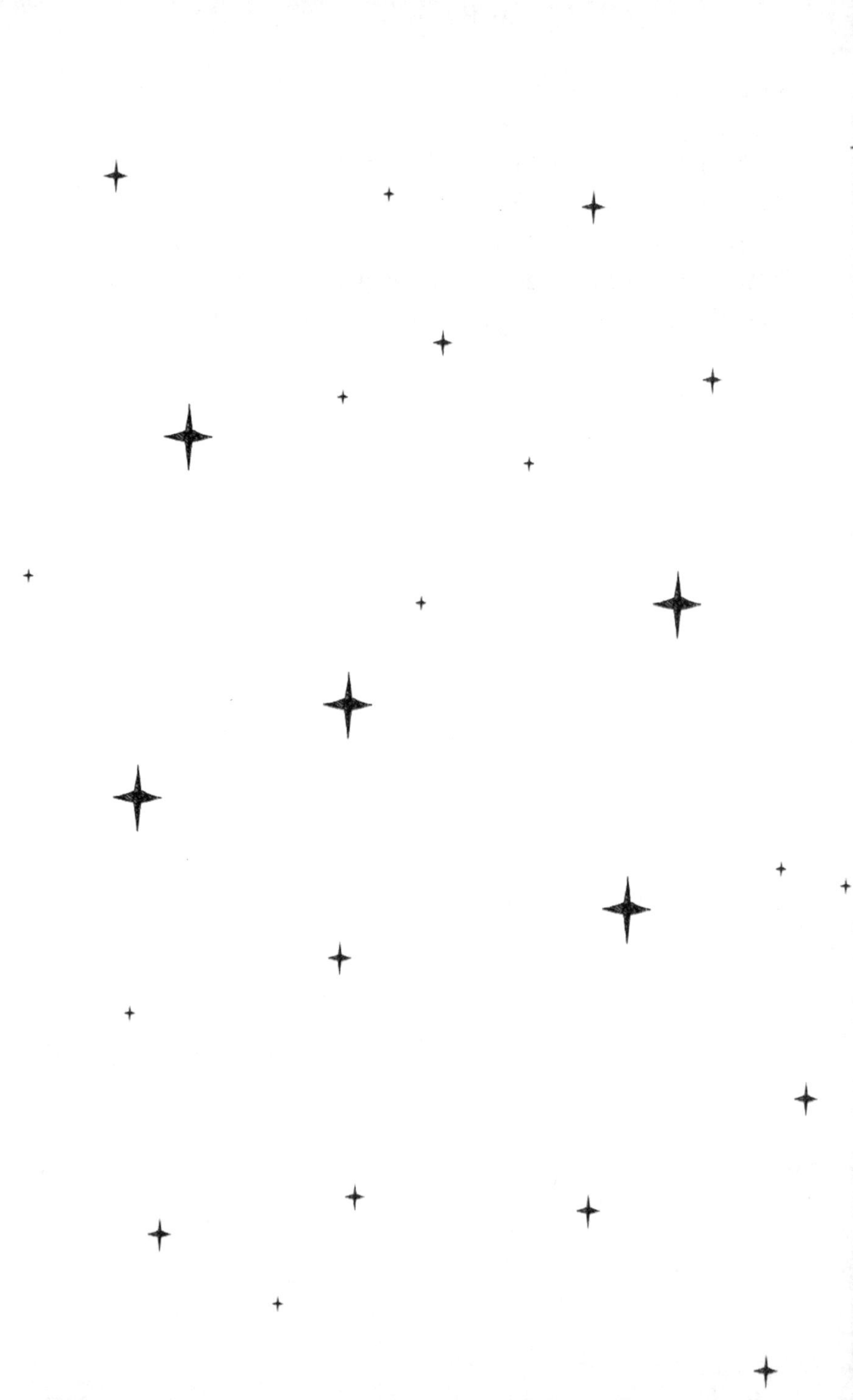

CHAPTER 13

Nym

The only warning I get that Aren has been taken is the yank at my waist.

It rips me backward, too startling for me to even remember how to scream. The momentum spins me around completely, and I catch myself on a rope that now leads to nothing at all.

"Aren?" I grapple against the unseen nothingness, panic seizing me. *"Aren?"*

I order these useless human eyes to adjust the way they've yet to, to create sharper shapes out of the darkness. And I pull myself hand over hand up the length of the tether, closing the distance between me and whatever's at the end of it, until—

Wild, terrified eyes glow in the dark. Aren's glass lenses are the only visible part of him. The wall has grown tentacles—no, *vines*, somehow hungry and alive and wriggling like worms—and they all latch onto his struggling body. Slick ropes curl around his wrists, his ankles, his neck, his mouth. One leg kicks free desperately, and two more coils slither up its length in an instant.

"Hang on—" I gasp, seizing beneath his arms and hauling backward with all my might. "Give him—*back*—"

A gap forms between Aren and the wall, vines stretched

rigid between them. They're not long enough to reach much farther. I dig my nails into Aren's shirt, waiting for a leafy *snap*. Almost there, almost—

One lashes around his neck and pulls tight.

"No!" I lunge under Aren's arm, into the swarm. The vines writhe in hungry confusion, distracted by the possibility of new prey. Half of Aren's bonds release him, clinging to me instead, and it's enough for us both to fight back. Together, we kick and claw, thrashing too desperately for them to latch again, until finally we're spiraling free.

I grip Aren's arm like a life raft, both of us panting heavily. Slimy residue still clings to his skin, his clothes. A line of red collars his neck.

"Are you okay?" I gasp. "Did it hurt you?"

He rips the final seeking rope away from its mouth. "Was—was that it?" He's shaking. No, that's me. "Was that the Shadow?" I watch the grasping things settle back into place, waiting for whatever strays too close next. And now that I'm looking closer, I can see they aren't just confined to this panel. They coat the walls as far into the darkness as I can see, like the acidic lining of a stomach.

"No." I can't seem to let go of his arm, like something will snatch him away again if I do. "It's not the Shadow. But this place… it's alive."

Aren massages his throat. "Guess staying near the edge won't work after all."

I glance back at the innocently hanging vines, horror and guilt simmering in my chest. They didn't attack us before—not until I used my illusions, however barely, to write over Aren's memory, make him forget what I'd told him. They must be symbiotic with the Shadow itself, something that traps its prey for it. I must have triggered something. If I hadn't drawn their attention… if I had been a moment later reaching Aren…

I should never have used the illusion in the first place. It was instinctual, whispering a lie that would take my story back. I'm so used to living in fear that even letting him suspect my true form felt dangerous. And it almost killed him.

He could have died in here, I realize with a jolt. I've never had to look out for anyone but myself, be concerned with anything but my own survival. I thought I was the only one in danger, that Aren could escape if it took me. But humans are so vulnerable, born as they are without claws or fangs or even lungs that can accept anything but pure oxygen. Already, the cuff counting down to his suffocation reads thirty-eight instead of sixty. *If he dies in here, it will be my fault.*

"No more facing backward. We'll be faster if we just keep moving." Aren's weapon spiraled away when he was attacked, and now he nudges us forward to untangle it from the loose netting it's caught in. "Together, okay?"

"Yes. Together." Away from the wall, there is nothing to guard us against the unpredictable whirlpool of ghost ships within ghost ships. Metal whines and lost spirits whisper, and the only sound that doesn't feel like a threat is the one pulsing up from beneath his skin. "I'll watch out for you better this time."

It is a promise I don't know if I can keep, as the floating steps of a once-grand staircase arc over our heads, and we are swallowed up yet again.

Silent minutes blur together as we drift through the broken remnants of more ships than even I can recognize. I wonder how many corners of the universe the Ghost Ship has seen. *Terrorized.* Gnawed wires erupt from consoles like upside-down roots, threatening to shoot electrifying sparks into the stale air around us. Scraps of stained fabric float by;

gauzy things I have a terrible fear are shreds of Medyssian umbra stick to my legs. And the labyrinthine current stretches on and on, and every surface is a trap the Shadow might be hiding behind. Watching us. Playing with us.

I see you. The words pound an eerie melody in my head, replacing the one the phantom voice of the Shadow usually haunts me with. *I see you, I see you, I FOUND YOU.*

Maybe it moved on, I dare to hope, as though thinking it will make it true. *Maybe it found a new lair. Who would choose to live in a den this rotting?*

I couldn't. I cannot find a shred of beauty in this place, and worse than that, I cannot *hear* one either. I have never strayed anywhere too far to hear the song of the universe, even when no other soul is in sight. But here, I can hear nothing. The Shadow's lair devours the call of the stars just as it devours their light. The emptiness crawls inside of me, hollows me out, fills my head with an unbearable silence. I wonder what might have happened to me if I'd come alone—would I have wandered through ghosts until my own mind slipped silently away from me, never even noticing the loss?

I am too afraid to speak again, terrified of triggering another of the Shadow's traps. Aren is the first to break, while we cross the deck of a vessel whose cannon-lined length wasn't enough to save it. Somewhere in the center, he lets out a faint *"No,"* and stops moving.

"What is it?" I ask as he fiddles with the knobs on his glass eyes, head tilted toward the place a ceiling might be were it not clouded by wreckage. "What's wrong?"

Aren twists in a circle, the rope knotting around his waist. "Don't panic," he says in a voice that demands the opposite. "But I can't see the beacon anymore."

An invisible floor cracks beneath me, plunging me into ice.

I fight for the surface, reminding myself this is a complication we knew might be coming. We knew the wreckage would get in the way; we knew it would be harder to see when we left the wall. "It's okay. It's—it's probably just blocked by something."

We turn in a slow circle, kicking against nothing. The graveyard mimics us, spinning in counter. There, a splintered mast stabs through a ripped canvas like a broken bone. There, an exoskeleton turned gray and shriveled, caught on the prow of a sailer. There, the gleeful rustle of the carnivorous vines on the starboard wall—no, the port wall. Or is it the ceiling? Beyond the very nearest bits of driftwood, everything is black, black, black.

"How much time do you have left?" My own voice feels as far from me as the ether.

Aren swallows. "Twenty-seven."

Over half his air is gone. We have minutes left to search before Aren toes the edge of not having enough to get back out. Assuming we can even find the way.

"Does anything look familiar to you? Anything at all?"

"Sure." His tone pitches upward, his spine rigid. "Those are the weeds that tried to kill me. That's one of the eels that tried to kill me. There's a ship that—" His breath catches.

"Don't panic," I remind us both firmly. "You said not to panic."

"No, it's—that ship. *I think I see my ship.*"

"What?"

I swivel. "Where?"

In response, he lets go of me and *kicks*, the tether connecting us the only thing that allows me to keep up with him. A glass viewport, spiderweb-cracked and dusty, looms before us, and on the other side, a distorted gray mass hovers. I can make out no details but one: a pair of crescent moons, just like the tattoo on the back of Aren's neck. My heart leaps.

Aren climbs the glass until the uneven weight tips us both over, and then we're cradled in its curve, the ship just feet from us. As I look at it up close, horror blooms in my chest.

It is an ugly, angry thing, its prow bleeding rust, its underbelly grown over with rocky pustules. It has only been lost for hours, but it has deteriorated into a corpse so quickly that I would not believe it to be Aren's ship if it did not share that clear, unmistakable symbol. Its shape is somewhere between shark and arrowhead, something between hunter and weapon. It does not match the boy beside me.

And no blue glow radiates from its stomach. The map is gone. It must have broken free of the console and been sucked into the current.

"Should we search inside?" I squeak. "Just to make sure?"

"No. It's not in there." When I look at Aren's face, he's gone pallid and ill-looking.

"How can you be sure?" I reach for the hatch's grimy handle. "We're running out of time. We have to at least check."

"No." Aren grabs my wrist before it can make contact and lowers it slowly. "It's not my sailer." His thumb twitches. "I think it's my dad's."

CHAPTER 14

Nym

"Your—your father?" The decades of pustules clinging to the hull suddenly don't seem quite so impossible. But this isn't right. I'm the one who was supposed to find taunting remnants of the past I've run from down here. "Are you sure?"

He doesn't cry out as he looks at the tomb, as I would have. He only wipes the dust from those ancient moons, glassy-eyed and stoic. "I know this sailer. I've seen its twin. My—the captain has the same one. They started the Celestial Company together, before—" His grip loosens around my wrist, but I don't pull away. "This is what I was looking for. When you found me. I was looking for him."

I feel dizzy. He did say he was looking for something, but I thought that meant *scouting*. Not the same sort of searching as me. "He's part of your crew? Did you get separated on a mission?"

"No. He… he went missing." Aren massages the back of his neck, then runs his tongue over his teeth, wincing. "That's a lie. He got banished. Forever ago, and I've never known why. I thought the map was going to lead me to him, and I guess it did after all. He's—" His arms wrap around himself, a pathetic shield against a freshly discovered monster. "His … *body* …

must be here somewhere."

He lost his family too.

The strands of Aren's story I haven't touched since I first saw him out in the ether, abandoned and forgotten, weave together. He had a father he was searching for, just as I search for mine.

They are not the same, our losses. He still had people who chose to keep him. He still had a home. But that clenching around my heart reasserts itself anyway. It may not be the same, but he has spent as long as I have, looking out into the ether and feeling a pull toward a person who shares his blood, with no way to find its source.

"I'm so sorry, Aren." It's all I can say.

"I feel like it should hurt more. I never even knew him. But I just—" Aren laughs, bitter and hollow. "I thought he was still out there, you know? Isn't that stupid? I thought he was just wherever he'd been marooned, growing old and regretful. But he—he must have crossed the Ghost Ship's path, like I did. And he didn't have you to save him."

Guilt is an anchor in the pit of my stomach. I haven't saved him. Not really. I might have plucked him from the stars, but it would have been better if anyone else had. Because it was me, he is in this ship now, with prying vines and lurking eyes surrounding him, no guarantee he will ever reemerge. Because it was me, he now has to live with the truth that he will never find his missing family. People always say it's worse, not knowing, but they're wrong. Sometimes not knowing is the only hope that keeps you in motion.

And though every instinct in me screams to stop, that the only way I have ever survived is by never giving a shred of myself to someone else, I realize that I want him to know just a little of a truth about me, too. To know that we have this one thing in common.

"I'm lost." And now that I've unstoppered myself, the rest pours out. "I lost my family too. That's why I need your map. I've been lost for a very, very long time, and I don't know how to find my way back home. I'm… I'm scared that I never will. I'm even more scared that if I do, no one will be there waiting for me. So I know how you're feeling, Aren, and it doesn't help, but you are not alone in it."

Aren turns, and his face is everything I might fear and envy about being a human. Too open, too expressive. There could be no secrets, no hiding, when a look alone cries out *I'm sorry* so loudly. He says nothing at all, only reaches for my hand and squeezes. We float there, staring at the moons, and I realize that it does help, maybe. Not being alone in it.

Ripped sails float above us like clothes washed from dead bodies. Boards glance off each other and spin away, and no flash of light spears through. *This is wrong,* I suddenly think. I was wrong to come down here, wrong to let Aren come with me just because I was afraid. I don't want his body to join his father's, as it will in—*eighteen*—as his wrist flashes. The beacon is gone. Maybe an eel chewed it up; maybe it simply faded away. We could glide in circles along with the rest of this wreckage until we become part of it ourselves.

"Maybe we should go back out." I say quietly. "Recharge your suit. Come up with a better plan."

Come out.

"There has to be another way to get the map."

Come away.

"We could—" I frown. "Sorry, did you hear that?"

Come out. Come away.

Aren reaches for his blaster tentatively. "Did I hear what?"

"That *voice.*" I press my ear to the forgotten sailer's door and hear it again. A tinkling, bell-like hum.

I grasp the rusted handle, but it sticks with the cement of age. "Help me."

Aren and I push together, straining against the door's stiff joints. Finally, like a branch snapped from a tree, it rips free. A dim light explodes from the cavity, and it might as well be the most fiery sun.

"You!" I cry, while Aren scrambles back with a startled yelp.

"What *is* that?"

The dustmoth circles my head, and I laugh in surprise until it settles back into my hand. "A friend, sort of. I lost it when I saved you. But you found me again, didn't you?"

The creature has no face to smile, but its wings flutter happily. It lifts away and blurs out a few feet, then turns. *Come out.*

"You heard that, right?" Aren adjusts the knobs on his glass eyes as if attempting to reconstruct the dustmoth into something more logical. "Did it just say—"

The dustmoth bobs up and down and repeats its melody. Then, it turns and arcs over a disconnected pipe, back into the whirlpool.

"It's trying to lead us," I say. "Come on."

The way out is ever so much smoother than the way in. The dustmoth seems to know instinctively how to avoid the shards that angle toward us like harpoons and the planks that crumble into disorienting streams of sawdust upon impact, all without straying back into the grasp of the weeds. Simply having a guide beyond the fragile glimmer in Aren's lenses makes the maze feel smaller, less endless. When we cut under a balloon like House's, deflated and sagging to one end, the wreckage on the other side is suddenly overlaid in a less-gray mist than I've become used to. *Light.*

The crowded shards of metal begin to melt apart. I feel as though I am kicking my way up to the shallows after diving into a very deep cave, and when the dustmoth beckons us through a hole in a ship so vast it must span from one distant wall to the other, I feel as Aren must have when he took his first gulp of air after drowning. The mist on the other side clears, and I never thought I would be glad to see those sprouting teeth.

Come out, the dustmoth whispers, as though I have forgotten the words. It bobs in the cavity, waiting for us. Its luminous wings sharpen brighter.

We are swimming so fervently that I only have a moment to react when the view clears. I manage to brace us inside the hole at the last second, before we tumble over the edge. Aren is not as fast; I snatch his shirt and yank him back, his feet scrabbling for traction against the dead boards.

Behind the dustmoth, there are no teeth. No escape.

Just as the Ghost Ship was the axis the raging nebula spun around, I know instinctively that the mass floating before us is the core of the Ghost Ship. No, core is the wrong word. I look at the misshapen sphere, and the right one pummels my mind.

Heart.

All the most dreadful pieces of devoured wreckage have fused together, created their own planet. The sharpest prows, the most lethal-looking machinery. Figureheads shaped like creatures with tentacles, fins, flowing hair, serpentine bodies. Protruding wires spark. Limp pipes hang like severed veins.

And there, in the outer shell, is an orb with a glittering spotlight of a beacon, broken and redistributed by the burgeoning ash clouds. The map. It perches between two dark figureheads, blinking innocently. Its fractured light stains the air a sickly blue-green, which bleeds over the rest of the floating metal heart.

"We found it," I whisper. The dustmoth brought me to the path home, just as I thought it might. "*We found it.*"

Aren grasps the frayed end of his tether. "S—stay here. I'll go get it."

"No, wait." The core is only metal and wood, just like the rest of the ship, but something about it stirs fear in my gut. A strange sort of creaking ripples out from its edges. *Crrk. Crrrk.* "What… what does that look like to you?"

"I don't know, an engine?"

No, that's not it. Besides, it isn't connected to anything. It just hovers there, pulsing like a heart, but reminding me of… of…

Crrrk. I stay Aren's arm. *Crrrk.*

One of the figureheads moves.

And in the same instant, I realize what the heart-core-engine-mass the orb clings to looks like, with all its artlessly assembled bits of shrapnel. A *nest.*

I drag Aren into the shadows, pressing his back to the wall.

He pushes his glass eyes up with one hand. "*What are you—*"

I raise a finger to my mouth and shake my head, and he goes silent. And then we both peer into the chamber—him searching for an explanation, me watching for another quiver of movement.

A pale stab of yellow zig-zags through the green, halfway to the heart.

"Wait—*no!*" I was too focused on Aren, and the dustmoth has no instinct for terror. Its light flits toward the mangled sphere, still humming lithe nonsense. I wonder wildly for a moment if it's strong enough to lift the orb, if it's small and insignificant enough to escape detection and bring the map back to us.

The figurehead's clawed hand snaps out and clamps around it.

A cry escapes me. Aren clamps his palm over my mouth.

Something unfurls from the root of the statue, dark and snakelike. Its tip tapers into a glinting, barbed hook that scrapes serenely against metal as it slithers free, carving up ribbons. A second dark something uncoils beside the first. Then a third. A fourth. Out and out, one after another, until there's ten, twelve, fourteen, slithering free from the center of that sick mass as though hatching.

The rest of the figurehead leans forward, its fist still closed around the dustmoth, and I see a coarse, hunched body, the stomach concaved with malnourishment, a lethal spike protruding out of the knob of each spinal ridge. A second arm wrenches from its side like a naked bone being ripped free. Both are the pasty-white of an animal that's never seen sunlight, the hand ending in seven dagger-sharp claws. Skeleton arms. Dead branches sewn stiffly to its shoulders.

The Shadow.

My Shadow, caught up to me at last.

It moves into the light cast by the beacon, and I don't want to look at it. I don't want to see its face. Once it has a face, the scars of seeing it will never leave me. It will appear everywhere I look, behind my eyelids when I sleep, inside my nightmares.

I can't look.

I can't look away.

But when the creature turns, I realize I shouldn't have worried about seeing its face at all.

It doesn't have one.

Where its features should be carved, there is nothing but

the bare, fleshy head of a maggot—no hair, no eyes, no mouth. Angular skull aching to slice out of its skin. A neck with the flesh clawed away in a perfect V, a clear view to the vertebrae on the other side.

Aren's inhale is sharp in my ear.

The Shadow's closed hand lifts the struggling dustmoth. Aren's grip around me tightens, though I'm not sure if it's a horrified reflex or an attempt to keep me from diving to its rescue. But I catch one final glimpse of frantic wings, and then the creature disappears into the Shadow's throat. Gone. Devoured.

I choke on my sob. It *ate it*. Like it was nothing. It—

"It absorbed it," Aren whispers, all numb shock. "Did you see?"

I can't see anything else. "It… it just swallowed it whole, like—"

"No," Aren repeats urgently, "it *absorbed it*."

I frown and lean as far forward as I dare. What difference does it make? The Shadow saw a shred of Medyssia, and it destroyed it.

But its claw travels down from its throat, and something odd pulses in its place. A spot of gold, pinned to the surface. I can no longer see the skeleton on the other side. Where that vacant triangle once rested, the dustmoth now perches, its wings fused perfectly to the decaying skin around it.

The featureless moon of the Shadow's face snaps toward me.

Come out, the creature in its throat mocks, its once seductive voice now sinister. *Come away*.

Understanding trails a cold finger down my spine.

The only thing left behind. The dustmoth was not planted on Cosalia by a Medyssian. It was never a guide.

It was a lure.

And I followed its call, like a fool.

The serrated tip of one finger climbs the creature's cheek and punctures straight through, the skin around the hole flaking off like ash. It drags down the curve of its own jaw, then up the other side, leaving a wide, leering gash that leaks blackened blood in its wake. A painted smile. A *mouth*.

"Aren," I breathe, "*run*."

And as the monster lunges toward us, I do something very, very reckless.

I rip the rope around my waist free, and I lunge too. I lunge *toward it*.

Because I will not die with my back turned, I will not let it get me from behind, closing in on me in the dark like I always feared it would. I will not let it win, won't let it devour me laughing the way it did the rest of my kind.

The map blinks at me tauntingly, fifteen feet away, ten, within reach—

A tentacle crashes through the center of the shrapnel heart, slicing it in half with a splintering crunch. The map wrenches free like an eye being plucked from its socket. Its glowing atmosphere goes dark, and then it vanishes into the current surrounding us, sucked away in an instant.

"No!" I lunge forward and am thrown back immediately by the force of another monstrous tentacle. Suddenly, my back is pressed against the crumbling ship, and the Shadow rises on its coils, that serene, bloody smile widening as it looms above me, and I have no plan.

Do something, my brain screams, *do something do something,* and as those glistening tentacles draw back to strike, I have a bizarre, awful idea.

The whip slices toward me, and I clench my fists and

prepare to absorb its touch, and—

Something else dives in front of me. A crack resounds, with no pain to accompany it.

"No—*no!*"

Aren hovers between me and the Shadow, face a carved mask of dazed shock, like he can't remember how he got there. A violent gash runs through shirt and skin from collarbone to abdomen, the seams around it torn and the fabric wilting from his shoulders.

"That," he gasps, "hurt so much more than I thought it would."

And then he passes out.

I leap to catch him, tensing for a second sting, but when I turn, the Shadow's head is tilted, and it's drawing the pale tentacle painted with the wrong victim's blood back and back, up to its black mouth. A single droplet falls from the tip, and then it sucks through its teeth on its own oily appendage, sucks Aren's blood right through its maw and down its skeletal throat. And then… then it *shimmers.* Its pasty skin seems to ripple as though it's made of a thousand insects struggling to tear free, and when it settles back into place, I swear one layer of the crumbling, ashen cracks in its flesh has shrunken. Its grin elongates. All of its tentacles draw up in a disturbed, rattling nest.

One drop, and it's already stronger.

This time, its entire body charges. This time, that face streaks toward me in a white blur, and I have no other ideas, no choice but the only thing that might stun it long enough for us to get away, and I scream in its voice and I

Change

Into

It.

The shift doesn't come easy the way it normally does, like sliding into a clear pool.

My consciousness doesn't slide into its new body so much as crash unwillingly, fighting me every step as though it's being forced into a too-small container. But I demand it change anyway, until I'm a perfect mirror of my greatest enemy and longest fear, and suddenly I'm

I'm

only barely me

every molecule torn in half

every particle howling

that endless scream a magnified echo in every nerve

inside my bones inside my veins inside my mind crawling inside me like worms

a scream that has teeth like the ship, that gnaws and craves and doesn't stop

and a hunger like a tumultuous sea—

No. No, no, no, I scream inside my own head, but the pain is a rope tightening around my neck, and my consciousness falters again, and—

And Aren's unconscious body is at my feet—no, tentacles—and I

want

want him drowned, destroyed, torn to pieces, and

"NO!"

The tentacles that don't belong to me lash out in an explosive arc and I change back, fall into my body like one falls into wakefulness after a nightmare. My real body—shimmering, translucent Medyssian. I have no strength left for anything else.

But the Shadow does not attack.

A gash identical to the one searing across Aren's chest

splits its pale body, too. I must have struck it by accident.

Its chin tilts down with something like curiosity, and it dips a long finger in its own black blood, then brings the tip up to its expressionless face. Can it even feel pain?

I don't wait to find out. With the fabric of my consciousness splitting, I snatch Aren up, and I flee.

CHAPTER 15

Aren

I'M getting a little tired of this. This whole being-unconscious thing.

I see only in bursts. A ripple of murky water. A grasping curtain of weeds, reaching for my face. A searing pain in my chest.

Pick one, I order myself drowsily as the darkness starts to flood back in. *Either be dead or not; pick one.*

The next flash brings a familiar angle—so familiar that I think it's a dream at first. *A girl with opal eyes and starlight hair. A girl who rescued me.*

Nym. She's rescuing me again.

We've gotta stop meeting like this, I try to say, but all that comes out is a groan. I feel like I'm at the bottom of a bag, and my ability to concentrate is the light shining through the hole in the top. I grasp at the edges of that hole and force my way through until everything snaps back into sharp focus.

And then I wish I were unconscious again.

We're flying against the wall, the weeds lashing out wildly. The sting of them is hot and sticky against my arms and legs, but they can't get a solid grip. We're moving too fast. And Nym's carrying me, and—how? How can she be moving this fast?

I tilt my head up, gritting my teeth against the pain.

And then I *yell.*

She's—

She's.

"Don't freak out!" she orders, and she looks so manic and determined that I obey.

So manic and determined and so, so not human.

"You're—"

"I said don't freak out!"

I can't. The Shadow is closing in behind us, and Nym is flying—no, *swimming,* swimming through air like it's water, a thousand times faster than the labored kicks that brought us here. We corkscrew out of the way just as a tentacle cracks behind us, and she *glows lavender* and her ears are like small, spiky fins and her dress isn't a dress at all but a jellyfish; I wasn't just drowning, half of her is an actual jellyfish, and what is she? *Who* is she? A memory splits my skull like a needle puncturing fabric. Nonsensically strange, inexplicably familiar. *Once, there were creatures who—*

We veer sideways, and I decide to put a pin in whatever's going on with Nym, for now.

Broken shards of shrapnel after shrapnel, mast after mast, speed by. Wood explodes up in volcanic bursts; the monster is *under* us, using its hooks to peel away at every decaying inch that keeps us separate. I grapple for my blaster, then twist over Nym's shoulder and fire just as the Shadow erupts into full view. The shot goes wide, as expected.

Four whips crack down at once, and Nym dodges them like they're the heads of a hydra. "I'm going to… try something…" she pants. Her lower half is starting to flutter in agitation, like we're moving against a current. "Don't freak out."

"You already said tha—"

The ship behind us bursts into flames. Then the one next to us. A wall of fire, blocking us in.

I freak out. Appropriately.

"It's not—real!" Nym gasps. "Illusion—look at me, not at it, okay?"

"It's—*what?*" The heat of a dying star blossoms over me, creeping up the hair on my arms, and I can't stop yelling, as though my voice is connected to an automatic trigger somewhere too far away for me to turn off. The fire is a wicked blue tongue snaking from ship to ship and apparently *not real, illusion,* but how? "What do you mean, it's just an illusion? How are you doing that?"

"I said don't freak—"

"Yeah, don't freak out; I remember!" I shout, but this is impossible. Illusion magic doesn't exist. It's something out of a fairy tale.

Then again, so was the monster chasing us.

I glance back to where it's trapped on the other side of the flames, its gash of a smile glowing in terrifying pleasure. Did Nym actually stop it?

I don't know if it matters. The wreckage spiraling around us is thick as the cyclone outside—I can't even see the mouth of the ship. We could be swimming in the wrong direction, for all I know. We'll go in desperate circles until the last of Nym's strength and impossible abilities are gone, and then we'll become another set of bones in this graveyard.

The creature pauses for three more too-fast seconds, considering the fire, and then it crawls through it. No burns. No crackling sound of smoldering flesh. It really is an illusion.

"It's still coming!"

"I don't know what to do!" Nym cries. "I don't know where I'm going—I can't—"

"Wait—can you do *us*? With your illusion-thing?" I don't know how her powers work; I didn't even know she had powers until five seconds ago. But my head is full of the image of those very, very realistic flames she drew out of her imagination, and it's the only solution I can come up with. "Can you make it follow that instead?"

"What?" As Nym looks down at me, a leaking gravity core juts out and clips her shoulder. My stomach inverts as she loses her grip and I fall, tumbling through a split metal hull and crashing into the layer of wood shards below.

Nym dives in after me, pulling the two halves shut behind her like the jaws of a clam snapping closed. Something lands with a slippery thump on the outside and begins to scrabble against the slick metal, but the closure holds. I drag my crooked specs back into place as claustrophobia sets in, willing my lungs to keep working. *Be scared of the squid monster, Aren, not the darkness. Prioritize.*

"Are you okay?" Nym gasps.

"Yeah. Yeah, I'm fine." I am not. I wince, one hand pressed to the worst of the gash, right below my shoulder. "But can you do it? Make a fake version of us for that thing to chase, while the real us finds some way out of here?"

Nym shakes her head, lavender skin blanched near-white. "No. No, I won't."

"You can't?'"

"I can, but I won't."

A tortured scraping sound rains down from above— the Shadow, still trying to claw its way through. "Um… why?"

"Because it's… I might…" A crash, followed by a cacophony of hissing. The eels. Were they feeling left out? Are they joining the hunt too, now? Wonderful.

"They trick you. They make you forget what's real," Nym

says, and at first I think it's just a distortion in my specs, but no, her eyes are beginning to well. "That's how they work. The illusions. Whatever I make, the more believable I make it, the more *I* believe it's real too."

"Meaning what? The illusion, like… takes over your mind? So, you'd think the fake you was the real you?"

"Only if I let it get too strong."

"Okay, so what if you didn't?"

"I—I don't know if I can—"

Rust shaves off the hull, and a tentacle slices through our makeshift ceiling. Nym and I spring away from it with a yell as it writhes like a worm on a hook, grappling at the space between us.

My wound erupts with a fresh burst of pain at just the sight of those wickedly curving tentacles; one more slash, and I might not wake up again until nine minutes from now, when I'll be dead, according to my timer.

No. Make that eight minutes.

"Okay," I pant, scanning the underbelly of the hull. "I can try to… um…" There's wires, rusted gears, an engine leaking fuel. I yank a few pieces loose with no plan for what I'm going to do with them. I've never had to do anything under this kind of pressure before, alone with no backup, no experienced crew members to lean on or ask what to do. If I try to make something functional, I'm positive it'll just explode, as usual.

Oh, wait. That's *exactly* what I need.

"I think I have an idea. A half-idea," I tell Nym, pulling more wires away from the engine and smashing them back into places they're not meant to go. "Just give me like, three solid minutes—" A third tentacle slices through, and now there's a skeletal claw tearing through the slit, stripping it away in pieces. Nym screams and flattens herself against the wall.

"*One* solid minute?" I yelp desperately, but even I know there's a difference between optimism and delusion. It's going to be way less than a minute before it gets us.

"Alright. One."

"Huh?" I tear my focus away from the engine. Nym's face has turned into something both determined and terrified.

"Don't look at it." She grits her teeth. "No matter what, promise me you won't look at it." And then, before I can ask what she means, something lavender and fluttering and clutching a mass of angular limbs streaks through the opening in the hull. *Us.* A perfect illusion.

There's a starved roar, and then the tentacles vanish, just suck themselves upward like the crack is a drain. It actually worked. The creature is following us—them—it. It thinks the illusion is real, but if I'm understanding Nym right, that means I only have so long before she starts thinking the same thing.

Nym dives upward and hovers there, watching. Her jellyfish half trembles overhead.

"Just for a minute!" I repeat weakly. "Don't lose control!" I adjust the saturation on my specs until everything is outlined in a different primary color, then get back to work with the vague sensation that I'm putting together a puzzle and I don't know what the end is supposed to look like. Hopefully, it looks like an us-sized hole in the wall.

I wrap both hands around the coiled ends of the engine and pull with all my might, forcing myself not to cry out even as the effort rips my skin open even more. My tattered shirt drenches itself in fresh blood and sweat, but I finally manage to get the bulky engine away from the meager pull of the gravity core. Its weight drains out of it like a leaking bucket. I shake my arms out, panting, then kick the device toward the wall. Just as I'd hoped, the already-roused vines lash onto it hungrily, dragging it back into their fold until all I can see is a pulsing crosshatch of green. Steam singes the leaves and turns the air smoky; whatever I've done to its insides has angered it, if nothing else. Hopefully all it needs now is a spark.

"Keep holding it, Nym, it's almost there," I say, kicking myself away from my makeshift bomb. Half an airlock door floats by, and I position it like a shield in front of us, then fumble to line my blaster up the way the captain taught me. One eye shut, long breath in and out. *Practice shot. It's okay to miss.*

I fire, and—

And it lands.

Right in the center of the bomb. A bullseye. A perfect shot. The first and only one I've ever made, and no one is here to see it. No one will believe me when I tell them.

And then it explodes, just as it was supposed to. In one shot.

Well.

Kind of.

It explodes inward, self-contained. It decimates the vines until they hang in a wilted curtain. And in its place is an opening the same size the device was to begin with, like a sad, tiny porthole. Too small for any human. The darkness of space is just barely visible through it, a grate of barely-hanging-on stripes of wood separating us from the outside.

Five, blinks my cuff.

"Oh, *come on*—" I rush forward to pry the smoldering remnants of the bomb loose and begin to hack at the hole surrounding it with a nearby board. "The one time I actually want to destroy something—"

"No, no," Nym whimpers faintly, "not now…"

"Almost there, hold on," I gasp, sawing and slashing

with all my might. I'm so close, so close; I could put my arm through the hole and be met with the cold fingertips of the void. I've never wanted it to draw me out before; if we survive, I never will again.

"Aren—"

The air is full of wood splinters; the gash in my chest is on searing fire. I drop the board and switch to my hands, ripping whole chunks of rotting crust out one by one until my palms go numb.

And then, finally, the hole in the side of the ship is wide enough.

"Nym." I sound unhinged, like my voice belongs to someone else. "I got it, come on—"

She doesn't respond.

"Nym?"

I half-drag, half-clamber over the mangled organs of the metal carcass, until I'm high enough to see what she sees.

Don't look, she ordered me, and now I know why.

The Shadow has caught us, the fake us, cornered against a gray-rotted sailer. The eels are there too, drawn to the Shadow as if it's their leader, and they weren't supposed to feed on flesh but they're attacking my body anyway, long teeth slicing through skin like an oar through water, and my eyes are wide and dead and my mouth is full of blood, and—

I clamp my hand over my own mouth, resisting the urge to vomit. *They make you forget what's real,* she said, and she's right. I'm not convinced that's not me up there, that all I am now is a soul thrown from its body in death. She pushed the boundaries too far, just like she was afraid she might, and this is the result.

And the fake-Nym is wrapped in the Shadow's clutches, and a hook punctures a hole in her chest, begins to carve—

Both the fake-Nym and the real one beside me scream in unison, and I finally turn to look, ill at what I'm going to find.

The color is gone from her face. Her eyes are completely opaque, clouded over with a thick black fog. The edges of her body have gone distorted and hazy, as though she's fading away from the outside in.

She's gone, lost in a reality that doesn't exist, and I have no idea how to even begin to bring her back.

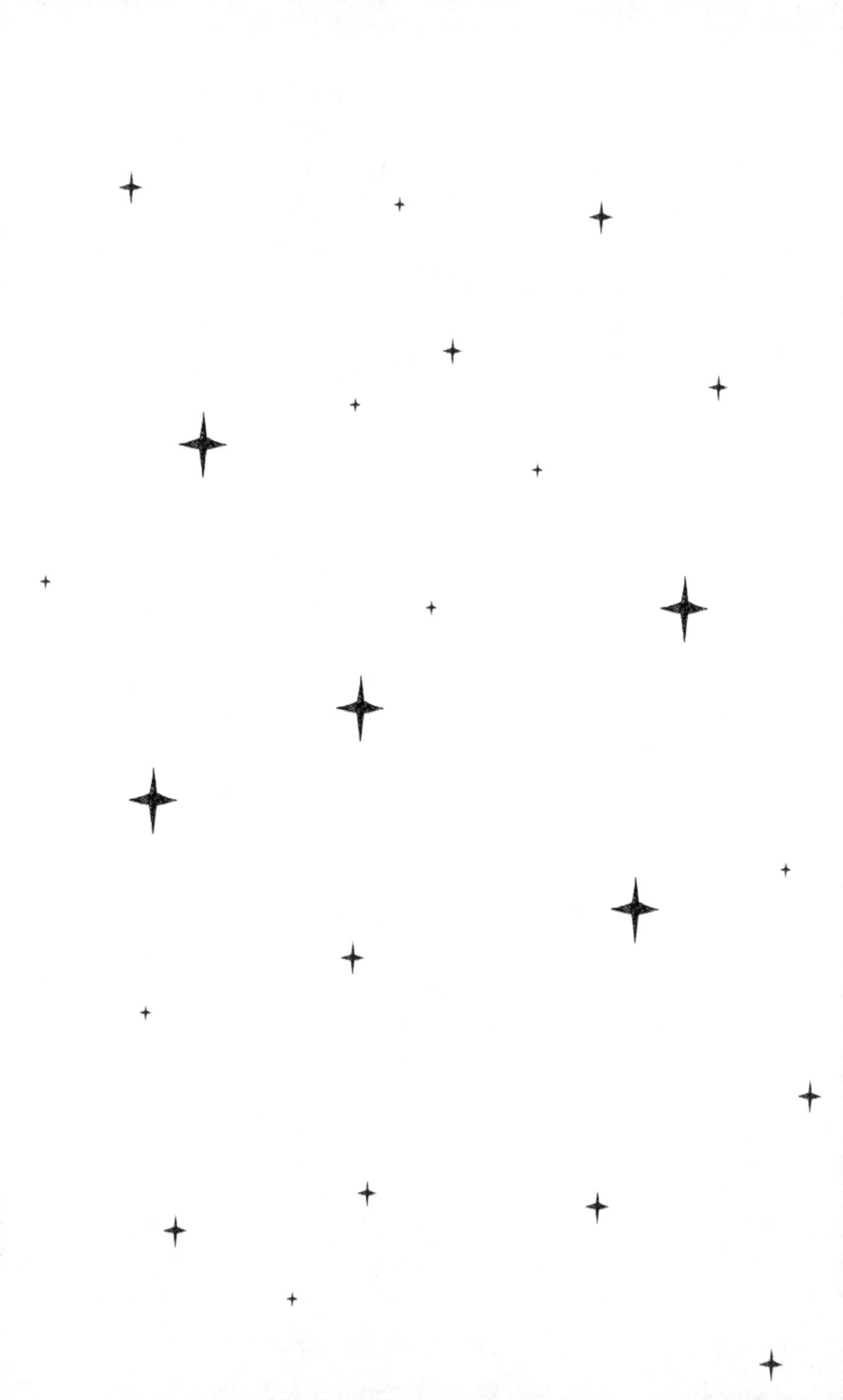

CHAPTER 16

Nym

THE Shadow has me.

And it doesn't.

I'm wrapped in its tentacles, and I'm cowering by the wall fifty yards away.

My head is ripped in half, each eye feeding me something different. Caught, free. An inch from death, a mile from it. And like two different-colored lenses layered on top of each other, I can only switch back and forth between the two halves for so long before they start to blend inseparably.

I don't know what's real. The dim thought should save me. If I'm still alert enough to know the illusion has gotten out of control, I should be able to reign it back. But the problem is that when you don't know what's real, everything is.

The Shadow leers. It's so happy to see me. It can't remember the last time it felt happiness like this—happiness at all. It was so lonely, so starved. But now I'm here. I can help. All I have to do is give myself to it.

"Nym!"

A boy is suddenly in front of me. There's blood everywhere, dripping from his hands, staining his tattered shirt. The eels did this. They saw him as I do, all the clockwork gears and gadgets of his mind, and they're ripping him apart.

"No, no, you can't do this." He grabs me by the shoulder, and he also lies dead, a slithering eel-body feeding on his exposed neck. "I'm the real one. Come back. We have to *go*."

Go? Go where? The Shadow needs me. It's been waiting for me, all this time. And now it has me; now I can give it what it wants.

"Okay, this worked once today," the boy mutters, and he draws his blaster, points out into the graveyard. I can see him out of the corner of my vision, too, as a small pinprick on the other side of the room. A pinprick that fires straight toward me and—

The shot collides with the Shadow's arm, and it whirls, hissing in a voice only I can hear. When it sees the smoking blaster in the boy's hand, it drops me.

No. Drops *it*. Because the Shadow knows which one of us is real, and that means I can too.

The illusion I've created crackles into nothing. I gasp for reality, drinking it in like nectar. I'm real. *I'm real*—and I'm here on the wall, not dead on the floor, and Aren is alive and pulling me toward a narrow hole with starlight leaking through it.

"*Twice!*" he's crowing. "No one will ever believe me—come on!"

When the Shadow's piercing wail comes again, it's not like before. It sounds… *sad*. It's begging. Pleading. It wants me to stay. It wants it with a desire so great, it doesn't remember how to feel anything else. It wants to take apart everything that makes me Medyssian particle by particle. Don't I want that too? Doesn't it *deserve* that?

It launches itself at us, and its face is a scream.

Don't I want to help it? Don't I? *Don't I?*

"Jump!" I shriek when Aren's first step inside the hole in the wall is tentative, arms braced to either side. His cuff's screen has multiplied back to forty-five—seconds now, not minutes. I push us both through with all my might, cannonballing us into an ether that scoops us into its arms as soon as we make contact. Even outside, that *thing's* voice still pounds in my ears, louder than the thrum of my heartbeat. And it's found a new word to call out in my head. A mimic it's stolen from Aren.

Come. Back. Come back.

I seize Aren and plummet toward the mouth of the ship, but hooked tentacles spear through the walls, tracking us as we flee. When I shriek, the ether sucks it away.

Come back.

The bow approaches—I know, because I see the gently waving tether before I see any of the teeth. *Ten,* croons Aren's wrist when I dare to look down.

"Almost there!" I speed toward the rope, up, up, up, until I can see the swaying basket of House right where we left it.

Come back.

Up and up and up, my eyes blurring and my grip on Aren painful, until I hurl us both inside. *Two, one*—his wrist flashes and goes dead. He nearly rips a line through his ear as he tears the suit activator off, gasping for the oxygen valve I've never been so glad to have collected. I throw open the door, and as I slash the tether loose and let the broken end flutter lazily away, I look down and I see it.

A white smear against all that gray. It stands between two of the ship's teeth, one razored hand clinging to the edges. Swirling tentacles, foul red grin.

Come back, the Shadow wheedles one last time. *Come back.*

The words alone are pitiful, but I know they're missing an unspoken second act.

Come back.

Come back, or I will come to you.

House erupts into the sky, and the Ghost Ship begins to sink into the nebula like a dissolving dream. This is not an ending; just an interlude. But for this one moment, I've won. I've done what no other Medyssian ever has. I escaped the Shadow with my life.

For now.

I slam the door shut and collapse next to Aren.

CHAPTER 17

Nym

I AM unable to move for some time, panting in wide-eyed disbelief toward the ceiling. Terror has a way of electrifying a person. When the spark is gone, it leaves you withered. And the truth of our escape does not feel real, quite yet. Maybe I am afraid to move; maybe I am terrified that I will find a crack in the world that will prove this is the illusion, that my real self is back with the Shadow still. Or even if we did escape…

I'll find you. I'll find you. The Shadow's silent threat. How long until it catches up to us again?

Aren suddenly spasms beside me, and concern chases all the spiraling fear from my veins. His injury—the wound that ought to have been mine. I'd forgotten all about it. One arm, sleeve torn to ribbons, is thrown over his face; his other limbs are splayed out wide. He's shaking—no, convulsing.

"Aren? What's wrong?"

He continues to shake wordlessly. But then the sleeve moves and his mouth opens and a rasping breath comes out. He's laughing. *Laughing.*

"We survived," he gasps, and all thoughts of the uncertain future subside. Before I know what's happening, I'm somehow laughing too, hands pressed to my face. *We survived.* We did, didn't we? It's impossible.

"Did you see that thing?" Aren clutches his side. "How are we not—*ow*—dead?"

"I don't know!" I gulp down tears. "I can't believe you jumped in front of it like that."

He flushes. "Guess that was pretty useless. I didn't know what else to do."

"I would call it rather brave, actually. Most of what you did in there was."

"Oh, yeah. That's me—Aren, the dauntless. Behold him, as he bleeds out all over the floor. *Quiver in fear as he faints—*"

"You're not going to bleed out all over the floor." I carefully peel his shirt from the line of congealed blood bisecting his chest, and his smirk turns to a wince. "Is it bad?" Aren pulls his collar out to look, then rolls his eyes back up to the ceiling with a shudder. "Oh, that's bad."

He leans stiffly forward to tug his tattered hem up over the wound. I stifle a sharp inhale; 'bad' doesn't begin to cover it. It's clotted and sticky, the edges of his skin puckering away from a frozen-over black river. A pale green tinge creeps at the edges, teasing a promise of infection. Aren peels the shirt up as far as it will go, seams straining, but the gash carves up into his shoulder.

"It's not poisoned, is it?"

"I don't think so." Still, that green color can't mean anything good. "But I think I've got a medicinal potion somewhere."

I flit through the chaos of baskets and strings hanging from the walls until I find it: a crystalline bottle of purple liquid which fills the air with the eye-wateringly bitter, pungent scent of medicine when I uncork it. "This should be it. Shouldn't make it worse, right?"

Aren doesn't respond.

"Aren?" I turn in mid-air and realize he's staring up at me. The bloody shirt lies next to him in a rumpled heap; the curve of the gash looks like the leering smile of the Shadow, as though the monster has branded his chest. I'm suddenly very self-conscious of the space between me and the floor, of my billowing umbra, of the thousands of differences between the way he looked at me when I was human and the way he looks at me now.

"Is this," he says quietly, "an okay time to freak out?"

I sink back down, the bottle clutched in my hands, and hold it out hopefully. "Don't you want to make sure you're not poisoned?"

Aren places one hand over the stopper. "You set ships on fire with your mind. You can make illusions so powerful you don't even know what's real anymore. You're not *human*, Nym."

There are a million implied questions in that statement, and I don't know how to answer any of them. *Who are you? What are you? Where did you come from?*

Why did you lie to me?

They're questions I'm not prepared for because I never dreamed I would reach this point with anyone. My instinct is to not answer, or to answer incompletely.

But the Shadow already found me. The worst thing that could possibly happen already has. So maybe, after all this time, I don't risk anything by showing someone who I really am.

Or maybe I risk things I didn't imagine.

"You…" Aren says, realization dawning across his face, "… you're one of those creatures, aren't you? From the story. The ones the Shadow ate."

The story. The illusion must have fractured when he saw

me as I really am.

"Medyssians," I whisper.

"What?"

"That's what we're called." I haven't said the word out loud in so long that it feels made-up on my tongue. I douse a scrap of fabric with the potion and lower it carefully to his hip. "Medyssians."

"You said—*mm.*" His teeth grit together as the rag makes contact. "You said they were all gone. Are… are you the last one?"

"No." Oh, how I wish I were sometimes. It would be easier. It would be a different kind of loneliness, and maybe it would hurt less. I don't know. "I didn't tell you everything. The Medyssians aren't really *gone,* just… hiding."

"Hiding? Where? *Ah*—" He sucks in another sharp breath as I move the cloth to his collarbone. "Shouldn't someone have found them by now—run into one like I ran into you?"

"They're not hiding out here. The whole planet is hiding. It's invisible, cloaked in illusions from every angle. You could be an inch from its atmosphere and feel nothing."

"So when you said you got lost and couldn't find your family…"

Something catches in my throat, but even after I swallow it, I can't bring myself to finish his sentence.

"Nym?" Aren glances at the painted ceiling above us. The relics hanging from strings, the kaleidoscope of purple and gold tracking my history. His voice goes soft. "How… how long have you been lost?"

It's the worst question he could possibly ask. *Ask me anything else*, I want to say; ask me how many planets I've searched for clues; ask me how many faces I've worn while hiding. Don't ask about time.

"I don't know."

"You haven't kept track?"

"It's not that." I should just agree with him. It would be easier. But he already saw the way I lost control back on the Ghost Ship, and he deserves to know why. There are secrets I keep from others; there are secrets I keep from myself, too. "Back with the Shadow, when I forgot what was real. It's… it's not the first time that's happened."

"What do you mean?"

I can do this. I can talk about it without losing control again. "Once. Sometime after I got lost, I… started to give up. It had been so long, and I'd found too many dead ends, and I was lonely and scared and I missed my family, and so I… I made them. I imagined I had found my way back, and I imagined it so hard that I made my own Medyssia." I don't have many details to draw forth anymore; I locked them all away when I escaped from my mind to make sure it would never happen again. But the few that are left crash forth even as I try to push them back, and I can remember what it felt like, that world I lived in until I forgot what I was missing. Arms hugging me from behind. Laughter chasing me through a forest of weeds. A voice welcoming me home over and over and over again. A dream that only ended when House crashed into a drifting mass of rock, and I woke up to splintered wood and torn sails and no idea where I was. I was stranded there for an eternity, mending all the tears and sobbing out apologies and mourning what I'd lost twice now.

"I wanted to go home. I wanted it so badly that I thought I could make home come to me, and it would be the same, and it *was*. That's the problem. I don't know how long I lived in it, and that's why I don't know how long I've been gone. And why I didn't want to use my illusions back there with the

Shadow. I can't… lose myself that way again."

Aren doesn't respond. My vision clouds over until I can't see the painted sky or him or anything else, so I can't see whether his face is crumpled with pity, or horror, or just more confusion. But then a light pressure settles over the hand still holding the rag to his chest and stays there. "I'll make you another one." The pressure squeezes. I can feel the flutter of his heartbeat right under my palm, through the cloth. "The map. I swear. I'll help get you back to them."

I swallow. I do not believe in people. I do not make alliances or bonds; I do not put my faith in anyone but myself and my House, and that is how I've survived. But *I swear*, he says, and he means it. I trust him, and there's so little effort required that it terrifies me. Somehow, I have slipped into it the way I slip into a new body. The version of myself who feels safe for the first time because of a boy she hardly knows—this form feels like mine.

Aren leans back against the pillows. "Can I ask you one more thing?"

I nod. It is oddly freeing, depleted of secrets, relieved of my walls.

"How do you do it? The illusions."

I furrow my brow, hunting for any untreated edges of the wound. It's the obvious question to ask, but I've never tried to explain it to someone else before. "Everything in the universe has a… a melody. Creating an illusion is just like… like asking the universe to compose something new."

"Is that how you made yourself look human?"

I shake my head. "No, changing myself is different. It's a true change, not just a mask. It runs deeper. I have to touch someone, so I can hear what their essence is made of. And if I mimic it, singing it in my own voice …"

"You can mimic them, too," Aren says, awe dawning across his face. "What… what was mine?"

"Yours? Yours was…" I shift one thumb away from the rag, and the gentle strings of Aren's heartbeat tiptoe back into my mind. I match each note for note, humming with my eyes closed. Soft descending strings, a clockwork ticking I can't replicate. The notes tumble over each other, then leap earnestly upward, ready to fall again. Just as my umbra begins to transform into legs, I switch easily into my own song, drawing myself back toward Medyssian. Then, watching the way Aren's breath catches, his again. His and then mine and then his, until they're strung together into one continuous melody. I glow into Medyssian and fade to human and back again, the outer shell of me reshaping itself around the song.

They are the same notes, I realize, in a different order. That's why his melody felt so familiar to me, when I borrowed his form. The first note of each resolving the final note of the last. How strange.

"Aren." I open my eyes to tell him, but now his are closed, his chest moving steadily beneath the rag. He is falling asleep to the sound of his own soul.

"Sorry," he murmurs the moment I let my humming fade away. "I'm awake. Not dead."

I draw a blanket over his shoulders. "You should rest. I'll keep watch. When you wake up, your chest won't hurt anymore, and the Ghost Ship will feel like a dream. Trust me."

"I do…" Aren exhales, then does as I say, all the gears of his face beginning to relax. "… trust you."

I bite my lip and tug on the edges of the blanket until they form a curtain over the gash. The green edges have already melted away, and I've managed to clear the worst of the leaking blood. He's going to be alright. I'll make sure of it.

I trust you.

Has anyone ever trusted me before? Have I ever even wanted anyone to? It feels wonderful and frightening at the same time, knowing what that small word means.

I don't know if I deserve it yet, but oh, how I would like to.

When I wake up an unknowable stretch of time later, not realizing until a violent turbulence throws me from my dreams that I'd even fallen asleep at all, I wake with the sickening knowledge that I've somehow already managed to betray that trust.

Because I didn't keep watch, and something has House.

Something is pulling us in.

CHAPTER 18

Nym

THE ropes strain against an invisible pull; the canvas above us flaps wildly, threatening to rip free. We're in a vortex, doing whatever the opposite of plummeting is—being dragged up and up by something massive.

"What's—" Aren wakes in a panicked flurry of limbs. "What's happening?"

"I fell asleep!" I cry, leaping for the window. The railing tremors like a pipe about to burst. "I'm so sorry, I didn't mean to—"

"What is it?" Aren tries to stumble to his feet, but the basket's movement is too frenetic. "Is it the Ghost Ship?"

"I don't know—" It can't be, can it? Can it really have found us again so quickly? The more likely and no less terrifying option is this: that space is vast, and any of a thousand things could have caught us while I was failing to keep watch. Pirates. A black hole. An ice kraken.

I lean out as far as I dare, but meet only wind and chaos. Black squalls tear at my vision, no semblance of color or form or shape. But then, the clouds begin to thin. A light made of something other than stars peeks through.

"There's something up there—" I gasp, and when the sound carries in a way that doesn't remind me of an endless tunnel, I realize the swirling wind has begun to die down too. "It's…"

Not the Shadow. Definitely not. But as I catch a clearer glimpse of its underbelly, I see that it's a very different kind of beast.

A ship. A *titan*. Its hull is all mahogany and bronze, lanterns gleaming from the bow like jewels in a crown. Masts sweep into the sky like turrets, shadowed by rippling carnelian sails. The portholes, too many to count, watch the night glide past imperiously.

The ship cuts a line smooth as a stone through still water—there's a crystalline globe around it all, a gold web that disintegrates every obstacle in its path. As I watch, a meteorite strays too close and erupts in a shower of glitter. But just as we approach it, the vortex pulls the seams of the shield apart enough for House to slip through, then stitches back up beneath us.

It's a floating city. A floating *kingdom*.

And it's beautiful. The most beautiful ship I've ever seen. Too majestic to be pirates, too regal for a cargo junker. What could it possibly want with us?

"It's not the Shadow," I say breathlessly. "I don't know what it is. It's got this great, golden shield and it's *massive…*"

Aren's eyes go wide as they fix on the shimmering atmosphere sliding past us. "Oh, no."

"Who are they?" Is it pirates after all? Is all of this opulence stolen? "Are we in trouble?"

"Um… you're not. I think I might be."

What does that mean? House rattles to a halt, ropes moaning, and the sunlight-brilliant glow of the lanterns melts away.

Wood panels slide down around the windows, trapping us somewhere that smells like sawdust and gunpowder.

"Nym," Aren hisses, lunging for his discarded shirt and pulling it on backwards. "Do you want anyone else knowing about you?"

What? "I don't—I—"

"*Hurry!*"

"No!" Something in his face scares me. "No, I'm not supposed to."

"Then hide. Quick. All of it."

"Why? What's coming?" Then, I hear something. The click of boots on polished wood, a swish of heavy fabric. Aren tenses beside me, and I suddenly feel a spark of uncertainty. Perhaps I ought to be more afraid.

"*This is the ship Aren was lost in,*" I whisper to House, and the illusion layers itself over all my beloved treasures. The door becomes a sleek hatch, my collection whitewashes away into unadorned, sloping panels, and a sharp arrowhead of a console plunges through the wall. *Not real,* I croon, stroking the wood I can still feel under the polished mask, and House creaks. *I know you're still under there. I won't forget about you.*

I shroud myself in invisibility just as the door bursts open and a statuesque figure steps through.

The dim light draws her together in fractals. An ivory coat with a high collar and leather boots. An avalanche of hair so dark blue it's almost black trailing down to her waist, a spider's web of braids threaded with gold. A sword she holds like an extension of herself. Her cheekbones are high and regal; her blue eyes feel familiar in a way I can't immediately place. She steps slowly, carefully, over the threshold and into my ship.

She's as beautiful and imposing as her own vessel, power cloaking her like perfume. Who is she? What does she want with us?

Then, I notice one last detail. A bronze pin at her collar. Two overlapping crescent moons, one light, one dark. Two Cs, just like Aren's tattoo.

The Celestial Company.

His crew.

His *captain.*

A thrill of understanding shivers up my spine. This is Aren's ship, his home. This isn't an attack at all, but a rescue.

But then, why can I hear his heartbeat pounding through his skin? Why did he make me hide?

But before I can ask, he pushes off the wall and staggers into the light.

"Captain," he says, "I can explain."

The woman's face doesn't betray a thing in response. She sheathes her sword back into her belt, then reaches for Aren's chin and tilts his head from one side to the other, examining the thin scratch through his eyebrow and the dusting of blood matted to his hairline. Then, without warning, her beautiful face hardens, and she raises her other hand.

Aren flinches in anticipation, but his posture doesn't slacken. Like he's used to it. Like he is expecting it.

I leap forward instinctively, veins filled with fire. But the moment of hardness has already fled the woman; all that's left is something raw and betrayed. The sharp lines of her brows soften and her mouth curves down like she's about to cry. Her hand fists, then lowers. And as I look at the way her eyes have gone glossy and hurt, I finally realize what's familiar about them.

They're *his* eyes.

"So," she says quietly, "my son returns."

CHAPTER 19

Nym

S ON.
Son.

For a moment, I don't think I've heard her right. Aren's family is gone; he is lost like me. We found his father's ship. He told me—no. What *did* he tell me? He never spoke of his mother at all. I filled my own head with stories, decided we were the same because it felt so warm to recognize myself in someone else.

Son. He's not an apprentice or a cabin boy of the Celestial Company; he's the *captain's son.* This floating kingdom belongs to him.

"Mom." Aren's gaze twitches in my direction, but he doesn't dare let it linger. "Captain. I—really, I can explain."

"You ran away." Her voice is at a complicated place between hiss and shout. "How could you do this to me? To your crew?"

"I—I didn't, I would never, I—"

"I only came after you because if you're going to defect, you should do it in person." Even the gold thread in her hair seems to crackle. "Go on. Tell your own mother she means nothing to you. Tell me everything I've built, everything I've devoted every second of my life trying to train you to inherit, didn't matter."

"I didn't run away!"

It's difficult to tell who looks more surprised at Aren's outburst: his mother, or Aren himself. He looks as though considering swallowing his own tongue, but presses on, "I know what it looks like, but I didn't. I just made a mistake, and then I got lost, and attacked, but I was trying to find my way back. I swear. I would never leave you like that. Never."

Something harsh and aching sprouts inside me. I cannot place its source. And before Aren's mother can find her voice again, the silence is drowned out by a cough somewhere out-side the door. The noise makes all three of us turn.

"Shut up, Cas!"

"Keep that rat pelt you call a scarf away from me, then—"

"Cassiope," the captain snaps. "You're supposed to be in the kitchens."

"Beg your pardon, your excellency, your majesty, Captain Valyra." A girl drops straight into the doorframe from above. Her shell-pink hair is thrown artfully into a coil across her crown; a few loose curls frame a face dusted with rose-gold scales. She has elfin slants for ears and emerald eyes and a smirk that could cut through a person as easily as one of the knives lining her belt loops. "I just thought, seeing as we were only sent to the kitchens for failing to keep an eye on the star-prince—I mean, Aren—his return might eliminate the need." She peers around at Aren himself. "Welcome back. We thought you were dead."

"Cas thought you were dead." The owner of this voice is a taller identical of the girl, sharp and beautiful, but with teal hair and paler gold scales trailing across his cheeks and down his neck. He's cleaning a fork on the edge of his jacket, as if to prove to the captain that he, at least, can follow orders and break them at the same time. "I thought you were only near-dead."

"Well, as you can see, he is neither." Valyra turns and considers her son. "You're telling me the truth." It's a warning, not a question.

Aren nods. "You'd know if I wasn't."

"Yes." Valyra's gaze flicks to Aren's neck. "I suppose I would." And then she does something startling, given her demeanor up to this point: she strides forward, jerks him by the shoulders, and hugs him tightly.

Aren stiffens, his eyes wide. "Mom?"

"Do you know what it felt like to be told you were gone?" she says. "You will *never* do something like this again. Never. Do you understand me?"

"Never." The noise Aren makes is half-laugh, half-choke. "I promise."

Suddenly, the source of the twinge inside me is clear.

I thought you'd run away.

I didn't mean to. It was an accident. I've been trying to come back to you ever since.

Those are the words I want to say. This is the plea I send out into the night that no one ever answers.

The twinge thrums again—something like heartache, something like envy.

"Don't think I've forgotten about your disaster with the shields. We will still—" Valyra cuts herself short with a frown and glances down. She steps back to examine a large crimson streak above her stomach, tinging the lining of her coat with rust. "What...?"

She wheels on Aren, brows slanted once again, and rips

his shirt wide from collar to navel. He jolts as if electrocuted and tries to cover himself, but the gash is far too thick. Fresh blood leaks below his ribs—it must have stained through his own clothes and onto Valyra's when she embraced him.

"You win, Felix," Cassiope mutters. "Near-death."

The teal-haired boy cocks his head. "Funny. It doesn't *look* like he did this one to himself."

"I'm okay." Aren shivers in the cold air. "Really, I swear."

"What attacked you?" Valyra breathes, but there's something hungry and sparkling in her eyes. "What did you fight off?"

I tense. Is he going to tell her? Does it make any difference? This is his family. If I can trust him, I suppose I should trust them.

I take a hovering step back and reach for his melody in the shallows of my mind—I know it by heart now. I'll reemerge as a human, so I won't startle anyone, and then we can try to begin to explain.

"You're going to tell me everything." Valyra pushes Aren toward the door, and my quiet hum dissolves into nothing. "After the infirmary. One of you—"This to the glittering twins silhouetted in the doorway—"if you're going to be somewhere you weren't ordered, then be useful and alert Bayless. The other—"

With no further instruction, Felix swings Aren off the ground.

"No—oh *no*, come on, I can walk—" Aren protests, but the other boy is already striding back toward the ramp, while Cas springs into the rafters.

Valyra flanks them, and I rush to catch the door before she can slam it, then slip invisible out the other side. All have disappeared down the ramp and through a massive archway backlit by lanterns, thousands of them, just like the ones we saw from the outside of the ship. They illuminate red-brown shafts with golden grates, a dozen sailers with gleaming hulls, pilots in fitted white uniforms laughing and lounging and unloading crates. It was a docking bay House was hauled into, then, and it pulses with a comfortable vivacity. It feels like drums and tambourines, like rollicking fiddles and pipes. This—this is his home. He has a home. He has a mother and friends. People who noticed he was gone. People who will worry over him and bandage his wounds far better than I.

I crouch down in the darkness of the hold and blink away the mesmerizing shine, scanning for a glimpse of deep blue hair. But Aren has disappeared into the crowd, enfolded easily back into the place he belongs.

And I, as I have always been, am alone with my House in a sea of color, the one shade that doesn't fit.

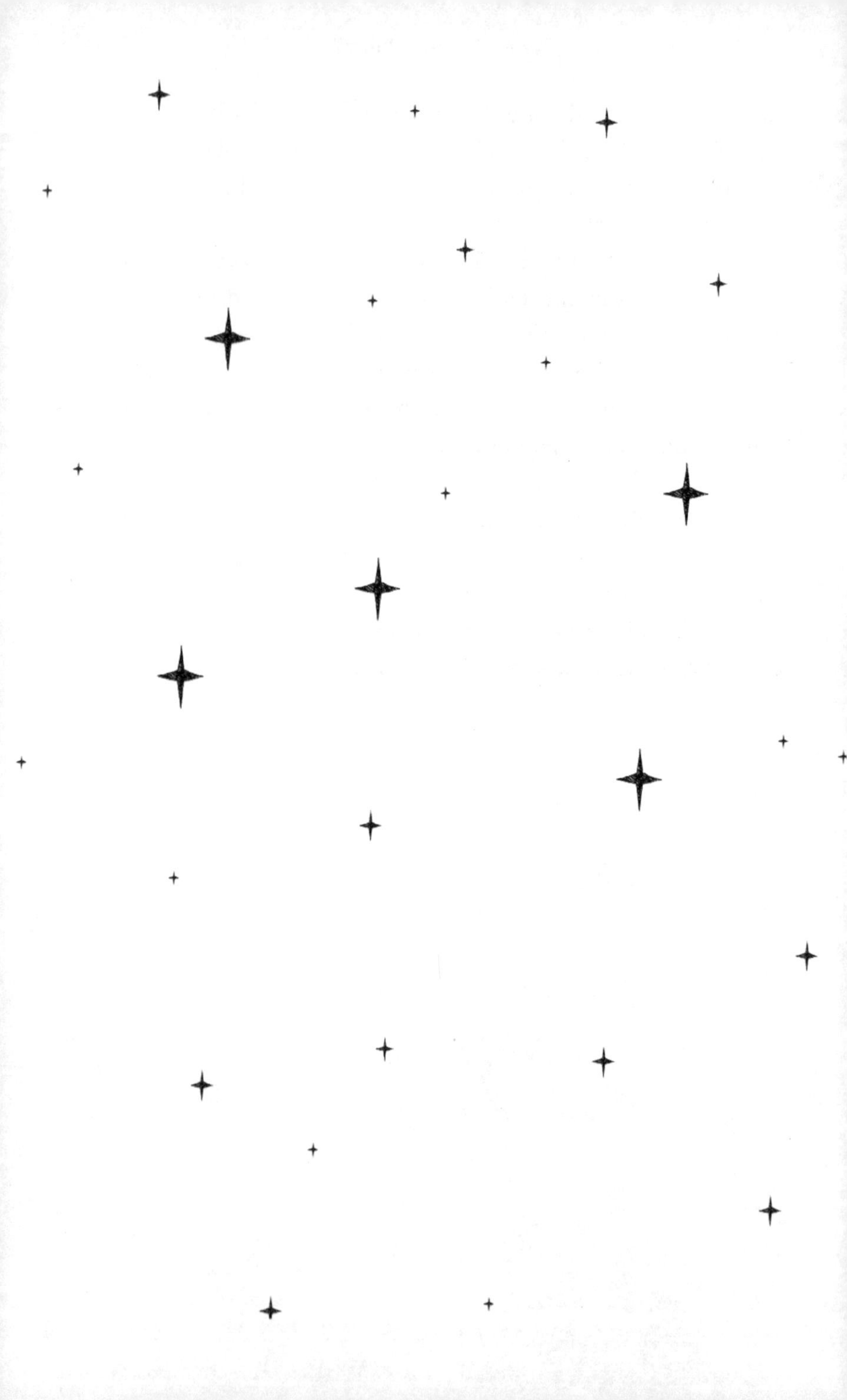

CHAPTER 20

Aren

Cas thought I was dead, and Felix thought I was near-dead, and right now I'd prefer either.

I've been dragged away to the infirmary bleeding more times than I can count, but the journey has never felt this miserable before. Between all the sweat and blood and grime, I feel like I've been coated in salt. But worse, much worse, is knowing what Nym must be thinking, now that she knows who I really am. I should have just told her. When we found my dad's ship, I should have told her everything, not just the parts that didn't humiliate me. What if she thinks I'm lying about other things, like whether the map even works?

I have to get back there before someone else finds her—or worse, she decides to leave.

Wham. The infirmary door flies open, Cas gliding out from the other side. "Bayless says he's busy."

"He doesn't get to be busy." Valyra shoulders through, setting the chaos inside free.

A loaded syringe whizzes past and embeds itself in the wood of the doorframe. A roll of gauze arcs over a drawn curtain, then hits the floor and starts rolling under the nearest cot. Every bed in the massive chamber is full, and so is all the space in between—people complaining loudly with strips of cloth pressed to limbs, biting down on sticks as medics heal burns, yelling for pain suppressants or bandages or ale. I think a mission or two might have just gotten back. Or eight.

Valyra reaches up without looking and wrenches the syringe out of the door. By the time her boot takes its first clicking step inside the infirmary, the noise has been cut in half. By the second, it fades into a dull, nervous buzz.

"Where, uh—where should I put him?" Felix asks, shifting his hold. "Looking pretty full in here."

"Put me nowhere." I wriggle in an unsuccessful break for freedom. "Put me *down*—"

"Everyone, quiet." Valyra pinches the bridge of her nose, eyes closed. "Aren, I have temporarily replaced my vexation with concern; do not push your luck. Felix, you know Aren's cot is reserved, kindly deposit him there. And Cassiope, I asked you to do one thing and you've already done it, so go be underfoot somewhere else."

A pout flashes across Cas's face, but she stalks away.

Maybe my mother isn't in quite as forgiving a mood as I thought.

"Bayless, my sweet, light of my life," she drawls as we approach the cot I've laid permanent claim to after over a decade of accidents. Felix dumps me on the starched sheets.

Bayless emerges from under a pile of rumpled linens on the opposite cot, one crusty eyelid cracked open to reveal three overlapping irises, all full of murder. "Go away."

"I pay you to look after my crew. That includes my son."

The linens burrow back into place. "I've been performing surgeries on *your crew* for ten hours. I'm on break."

"Bayless, I swear—"

I sink onto my back with a groan. Bayless has always

lacked that blend of fear and awe that keeps everyone else from ever questioning the captain, and for good reason—he has irises that can see through bone, an eidetic understanding of anatomy that makes Felix look like a child learning to spell, and the natural ability to produce an odorless gas that doubles as anesthetic. This makes him completely irreplaceable as a medic, and therefore completely immune to Valyra's wrath. And that means this argument will go on until Valyra either irritates him into getting up or he irritates her into leaving him alone. Neither bodes well for me.

I don't open my eyes until something cold and gelatinous brushes against the outline of my wound, freezing it and wiping away all sensation in the same breath.

"This should have been infecting already," Felix says, screwing the cap back on the numbing agent and then giving the wound a calculated prod I don't feel.

"Yeah." I demand all thoughts of Nym pressing a rag to my chest to leave my head, just in case Felix can read minds, as I've always suspected. "Got lucky."

"You always do." He wheels toward the counter. "It might be your strongest skill."

"Luck? Hardly."

"You're still here, aren't you?" Felix holds one of the needles up to the light and gives it a quick polish, then darts a glance toward Valyra, who's still alternating between chewing Bayless out and trying to wheedle him into cooperating. He leans in and lowers his voice. "Do you want to know what your weakest skill is? Secrets. You're terrible at them."

Fear flicks on a warning light in my brain. *He knows*, it says, *He knows, he knows.*

But knows *what*? Which secret is he talking about? There's so many now. The Shadow. The map, still lost on that ship. Nym herself.

"I'm not keeping a secret." My tattoo prickles, begging me to scratch it, but my arms are too heavy at my sides. *Ha*, I have time to think before my neck spasms reactively against my pillow.

Felix leans back in his chair, a self-satisfied smirk tugging at his mouth.

"That sailer you came back in. It's not yours," he says. "And there's someone else onboard."

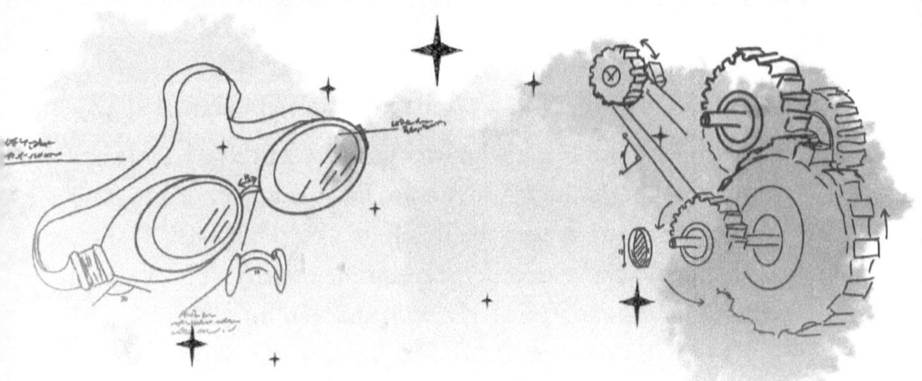

CHAPTER 21

Aren

"WHAT are you talking about?" I instantly regret speaking.

You really can't get much more guilty-sounding than *'What are you talking about?'* "What do you mean, it's not my sailer?" I'm making it worse, I think.

"The proportions are wrong. Windows too big, doorway too narrow. And it doesn't smell right—like salt and dirt instead of leather. There was something wrong with the walls, too. A whole corner that was just a little bit blurry. Some kind of camouflaging creature blending into it, I'm assuming. Like a synanceia, or a mimetic."

I don't know what angle to play this. Trying to lie again. Twisting Felix's camouflage guess into something close to the truth but far from Nym. Staying silent completely.

I take too long deciding, and Felix moves on without me, and it all becomes a million times worse.

"You didn't notice, did you? We should tell the captain, then, in case it's something dangerous." And he stands and takes the first of the ten steps that'll lead him to my mother.

"Wait!" I hiss, and throw a pillow at him instinctively.

He catches it one-handed with a vague combination of surprise and irritation, but he stops walking.

"Sorry. Just please, please, Felix, don't tell her. I did know, okay? But it's not a… a whatever you said. It's a girl, and she's in trouble. I'm gonna tell my mom, I swear, but I need to do it in a way that guarantees she'll help me keep her safe."

He doesn't take another step, but he doesn't sit back down either. "That's a new level of bad idea. Even for you."

"She's not dangerous." Surely the fact that I'm not messing with my tattoo has to be enough for him to believe me. "I swear. She's just a girl, and she needs help. You have to trust me."

He doesn't say anything. He just stares, probably searching for a telltale flicker of dishonesty.

And before he can tell me what he finds, Valyra is back.

"I would maroon him—" My mother sweeps the curtain around my cot shut with a flourish. "—if I didn't know how bloody thrilled he would be to get away from me."

"I could help," Felix offers. "It's just a suture, isn't it? I've been practicing."

"Fine." Valyra scowls, waving her hand. "Impress me."

The discomfort in my gut twists into something much worse. "Wait—you're going to let him—I mean, you want him to do my—*what?*" I choke out.

Valyra retrieves a fresh set of gloves from the cabinet and hands them to Felix. "Darling, if you could escape from whatever did that to you by yourself, surely you can manage a few stitches."

Sure it is, until Felix decides to tell my mother what I'm hiding mid-surgery, and I end up with more than one scar.

"Now"—Valyra drags a chair over with a grating scrape—"you can distract yourself by telling me exactly what happened to you."

"Um… right." I don't even know where to begin. From

the beginning? Impossible. The worst thing I could do is tell her I left because I was looking for my father. She'd never understand. Her interest in the rest of the story would evaporate, replaced with pure fury.

Felix lines the suturing rod up at my hip, and I dig my fingers into the cot to keep myself from shuddering. He's going to thread this needle through my body and weave me into a state I'm already dangerously close to, one where I'm so overwhelmed that I blurt out the entire truth and ruin everything.

"Aren, I'm *waiting*."

And as the first incision pricks through my numbed flesh, I realize I can't do this. I can't keep hiding something this dangerous.

"There's a monster out there. That's what happened. That's the only part that matters." I should have done this the moment we stepped aboard. "And it might be coming for us."

I don't know what I expect—for the needle to grind to a dramatic halt, for Valyra to leap from her chair and race to alert the rest of the crew to battle stations. But her expression doesn't change, nor does her position in her chair. Of course. "It's coming for us" is hardly a worthy alarm. We're the Celestial Company. Something's always coming for us.

"Most of the time," Valyra says coolly, "I like my stories told linearly."

I shake my head. "Not this time. You ever hear of something called the Shadow?"

I swear I see something flicker in her eyes. Then, her hand glides up to support her tilted chin. "Shadow?"

"It's…" What word is there, other than *monster*? "It's hungry. It's this faceless thing with tentacles and teeth and it glides around this old shipwreck like a ghost, and—" I'm not explaining it well, I know I'm not, but it's only because my head is filled with the memory of a rotting mouth leering wide, hooked tentacles slashing and beckoning and *seeking*. "It was—I don't know, *hibernating* or something, but it woke up. It won't stop until it feeds."

"A hungry monster." Valyra's voice is straddling the line between soothing and impatient. "I've seen a fair few monsters in my time, Aren, and most looked like men. You'll have to be a bit more specific."

"Fine. I'll show you." I reach for the roll of gauze beside the cot—"Watch it, do you want me to stab you?" Felix snaps—and twist to pull a nub of charcoal from my grimy belt. I can't explain it right, so I'll show her. The oval head, the painted smile. The thin, sunken body, the grasping hands. And dozens of snaking curves for its tentacles, billowing out from around it. For all my other faults, I know I'm fair at sketching, and when I finally hold the sheet up, the figure contains all the ominous promise of movement that the real Shadow did. The tentacles feel poised to ripple; the shading around it suggests it's slithering out of something dark and everlasting, the same way it did when we first saw it. The negative space of its mouth leers through the paper.

"That's it." I hand the image to Valyra. "That's what I found out there."

Felix's last stitch folds itself next to my collarbone.

Valyra holds the paper up to the light, traces the lines with her gaze, and frowns. I steel myself for another insistence that I'm worried about nothing, or that she still doesn't know what I'm trying to tell her.

"Oh," she says, "it's back."

CHAPTER 22

Aren

*B*ACK. Of course, Valyra's encountered the Shadow before. She's encountered everything. She's the queen of the stars. And if she's seen it, she'll be able to protect us from it, just like I thought she would. That's the half-second of relief I get, before it deteriorates.

Because if she's seen it before, if it's *back*, it's because she couldn't kill it the first time.

It means the first time Valyra Vanthal went up against the Shadow, she lost.

"What do you mean, 'back?'" Impossible. Valyra doesn't lose. Valyra doesn't let things escape. The Shadow must have been weakened beyond belief for someone like me to be able to get away from it alive—what must it have been like at full strength, for the queen of the stars to have had the same experience? I have to know. I have to know we have this one thing in common. "When did you fight it? What happened?"

Her jaw hitches as she swallows, and I wait for a story, an explanation, anything.

"Bandage that," she commands, dropping the rest of the gauze on my chest. Then she crushes her fist around the drawing, gets up, and walks away.

"Wait!" I roll off the cot and stumble after her, only managing to catch up as she bursts out the swinging doors.

"You can't just—just *say* something like that and then leave," I pant. It takes three strides to match one of hers. "What do you mean, back? How do you know what the Shadow is?"

"Get back in that cot, Aren," she orders in the kind of voice that annihilates protest. "You need that wound covered."

"I'm *fine.*" I start winding the roll into a coil around myself as proof, though jogging and winding at the same time proves massively disorienting. "I want to know what's going on. You can't just—"

"Aren, I swear, if you don't keep your voice down, I'll—" Valyra pulls ferociously on the crank to call the hydraulic lift, and oh, good, I've broken her—she's so irritated she can't even remember how to threaten me properly. "Just go back to the medical bay."

"I found his ship there, Mom."

How weird. *Yes, captain* is what I meant to say, like usual, and yet here we are. Somewhere in my skull, my brain is writing a negative performance review for my mouth. But Valyra wheels, her jaw half-open in disbelief.

"You what?"

"I found Dad's ship," I continue in a rush, before she can channel whatever she's feeling about the Shadow into rage. And as I'm saying it, what started out as a last-second ploy to get her attention by any means possible clicks into something else. I should have seen it before. I should have known as soon as I saw the look on her face when she recognized the creature in the drawing. It's so obvious it hurts. My dad didn't cross the Shadow *after* he was marooned.

"That was his final mission, wasn't it? The one he ruined."

I'm stupid, so stupid. "The one that got him banished."

Her eyelids have forgotten how to blink; a muscle twitches in her jaw. And just when I'm certain I'm about to get the worst verbal thrashing of my entire life, "You were looking for him," she says, in a low enough voice to terrify me under any other circumstance. "That's why you left."

My body aches to cower. Bow my head, hunch my shoulders, tell her I'm sorry. Muscle memory knows exactly what my next line is. But I survived the void. I escaped the Shadow. I can speak to my own mother.

"I was looking for him," I echo, fists clenched tight. "But only so I could finally figure out how to stop myself from *becoming* him. So you have to tell me what happened. You *have* to, so I can make sure it doesn't happen again."

Valyra doesn't respond. The lift stutters to a stop, the crank of gears squealing through the acidic silence. She pulls the grate open, then glares coldly over her shoulder.

"In. Now."

I practically dive in headfirst.

The grate creaks shut behind me, and the lift begins its ascension. As we disappear into the space between floors, just as the glow of the infirmary halls melts away into nothing, I hear the metallic whisper of a sword being unsheathed. Before I have time to react, Valyra's sword is flashing through the air. I flinch on instinct, then stumble with a yelp as the floor slams to a halt. When my eyes adjust, I can see the dim shape of the sword caught between the curling vines of the lift and the teeth of the cogs behind it. Darkness washes over us like a shroud.

"You've seen the beast," she says quietly, "and it's clear you won't leave me alone until you know how your father was involved, so I'll tell you. But we are never speaking of him again. Do you understand?"

"Yes," I reply quickly. "Of course. You can trust me."

"I…" She laughs then, with no real mirth behind it. "That thing you saw, that *monster*. It's the only one that's ever gotten away from me. I always hoped it had crawled off somewhere and died, but I've never been sure, and now…" I hear the soft rustle of gauze, then a faint tear from inside her fist. "The last time this… this *Shadow*, as you call it, menaced the universe, I'd only just begun building my crew. People knew who I was, of course, but I was still proving myself as someone who could be relied upon. Back then, you'd hear *guns for hire* or *mercenary* and think of ruthless cutthroats who would stab you in the back at the first opportunity. But I wanted us to be a crew of integrity, of honor. I wanted people to hear my name and know without a flicker of doubt that we would always come to help."

"Starsaviours," I whisper, and she nods.

"It's what we were becoming. We had a solid crew, we had perfectly executed mission after mission under our belts, we'd hunted so many monsters across the stars that people weren't even afraid of them anymore, because they all knew we'd be coming right behind them. And then, this… *thing*. Hungrier and wilder and more slippery than the rest, worse than anything I'd ever seen before. I knew once we killed it, no one would ever doubt us again.

"We went together. Me and—and your father. We had a weapon we'd built, the only thing strong enough to weaken it enough to destroy. Something that could strip it of its strongest method of attack. But when the moment came, your father looked at that creature, and he *dropped* it. Ran away like a coward, abandoning me. He was supposed to be my partner, and he…" Her teeth grit together, and she looks away. "I wasn't strong enough to take it down alone. I barely got away with my life, but it got away too. The shame would have killed me, if I'd told its intended prey what had happened."

Medyssians. My heart rate quickens—what if she knows where they went? "You never told them you failed?"

"I didn't get the chance. It killed them."

No. The lift itself seems to gasp, hydraulic pressure letting out the stifled moan of a punctured lung.

"So. No one outside of the crew knew what your father had done, but I couldn't trust him anymore. The crew couldn't trust him anymore. And if I'd forgiven him, even though what he did almost killed me… if I'd let the crew, the *universe* believe this was a ship of people who would turn tail, break promises, abandon their own…" She closes her eyes again, combs her hair back. "I loved him, you know. But I had no choice but to banish him. I did not deserve to lose everything because of his cowardice."

My stomach contorts. If this is really her greatest fear— that one mistake could ruin her—then suddenly, every reprimand, every scolding, every punishment makes sense. I always thought I was the only one terrified I would become the crack in the Celestial Company's perfect reputation, but maybe that isn't true. "Could one mistake… I mean, could it really do that much damage?"

Valyra's lip curls in a bitter smile. "He had a chance to kill a monster that had nearly run an entire species to extinction. He did not, and today, it almost killed his son. You tell me how much damage it caused."

My head rings, my understanding of both my parents writing over itself. "Why didn't you tell me any of this before?"

"Because he doesn't deserve to be remembered," she says crisply. "Because that creature slipped into oblivion, and it took my greatest betrayal along with it. Is it so wrong that I wanted to forget them both?"

You still could have told me, I think. But she's telling me now, and I guess that's what matters most.

"It's become weak," I say. "It's been starving. It's still, you know, the scariest thing I've ever seen, but it might not be as threatening as it was before. I think that's the only reason w—I was able to get away."

"It's weaker than it was, and I'm much, much stronger." Valyra wrenches her sword from the wall, and the lift bursts upward like a drowning victim finding the surface. "It won't get away from me this time. I'll finish what I meant to."

"I want to face it with you." I can't believe what I've blurted out until the words echo back to me in the narrow shaft, shaky and rattling as we reach our destination floor. But it's true. I ran from the Shadow the first time because I didn't have a choice. This time, I'll stand my ground beside the captain. This time, I can prove forever that I'm someone who can fight, not flee.

Valyra brushes past me to slide the grate open, and I follow her out and end up in a velvet-carpeted hallway lined with identical brass doors. Upper-deck sleeping quarters. I'd assumed we were going to the throne room, or the weapons chamber, or a secret storage facility full of Shadow-hunting equipment. "Captain?"

She strides ahead of me to the end of the hallway and turns the knob to my room. "We'll see."

"We'll *see?*" I halt in disbelief, the hall stretched between us. "How can you say that? After everything you just told me? He abandoned you last time. But I won't. I—I wounded it just like you did, I built a bomb to escape that actually worked for once. You would have been—" *Impressed? Proud?* That's optimistic. "—surprised. Let me help you."

Finally, Valyra turns away from the door.

"That means everything to me, Aren. Truly," she says, and my heart soars, then plummets just as fast. "It just might not be safe for you."

"Since when has that mattered? It's not exactly safe for anyone, is it?"

She sighs and lets go of the knob. "I didn't want to alarm you. And I don't fault you for it. In fact, it's going to be rather useful for snaring that thing as soon as possible."

"Wait, what's useful?" The word only makes me more nervous, somehow. "What are you not faulting me for, exactly?"

"That creature is a bloodstalker, darling." She brushes a matted streak of hair off my forehead. "One drop, one taste is enough."

The floor goes liquid beneath my feet. "Enough for what?"

Her touch moves down to my shoulder, settling with gentle firmness next to my wound. "We don't have to hunt it down. It's already hunting *you*."

CHAPTER 23

Aren

I don't notice the bathtub is overflowing until water hits my feet.

I don't even remember filling it. I remember being herded into my room with orders to *don't let it concern you, darling* and *maybe get yourself cleaned up, hmm?* and then I remember the door shutting behind me, leaving me drenched and bleeding all over my rug. All of the moments in between were done by a sleepwalker.

I look down at my rippling, bloody reflection in the bathwater. I think about undressing, about how many individual movements it will take to handle buttons and clasps and cloth, then clamber right in with my clothes still on and sink down to my neck. I force myself to stare at the ceiling and practice a shaky inhale.

The gash through my chest is a black spot. Why was it so important to give the Shadow another title—*bloodstalker?* "Shadow" was enough. *Bloodstalker* draws an invisible chain between us that it's going to follow until it finds me.

This must be how Nym feels all the time.

Nym. Everything in me begs to run back to the hold, to not waste another second in finding her again. But if I go traipsing around the ship covered in gore, people are going to have questions I'm not sure I'm allowed to answer. I just need to soak myself out of looking like a walking corpse, and then we'll go figure out how to deal with the fact that we're both being hunted by the same monster now.

"Were you going to tell me when to stop hiding at any point, or am I meant to stay invisible forever?"

I swear, if the layer of dried blood coating me were a second skin, I might jump right out of it. Instead, I flounder beneath the water and resurface sputtering, nose full of soap. She's *here*, hanging off my ceiling like a silvery moth emerging from a cocoon. "Nym, for the love of—"

"You left." She crosses her arms upside-down. "I was scared you'd forget about me."

"I think you'd have to surgically remove my brain for me to forget about you." Even though I'm still coughing soap out of my esophagus, just the fact that she's here is the emotional equivalent of dropping a magnet into a bowl of nails. All my loud, jumbled, fearful thoughts find their anchor and settle. "Were you with me the whole time?"

"Yes." Nym flips right-side-up and lowers herself onto the other end of the tub sheepishly. "Your mother is… formidable."

The pit of my stomach contorts. "I'm sorry. I never wanted to lie to you, I just thought… I thought it would change everything, if you knew who I was."

"What would it have changed?" She's so gentle with it. Like she's not upset, just curious. It makes me feel worse.

"I don't know." I spool water over the back of my neck. "Yes, I do. Look, the first thing anyone ever knows about me is that I'm Captain Valyra Vanthal's son. They expect me to be exactly like her, and then they're disappointed when I'm not. And I guess I thought that if you didn't expect anything of me, I couldn't let you down the way I let down everybody else. It was like… you looked at me, and you weren't looking for somebody fearless, and you weren't looking for someone on the edge of screwing up. And I think I… I was scared to let go of that."

"Hmm." Nym's jellyfish half folds upward, and she rests her chin on the crease. "It was kind of nice, in that moment, thinking we were lost in the same way. But having a home doesn't mean you don't know what loneliness feels like. And I'm glad you have a family, that you didn't lose your only parent to the Shadow. I wouldn't want that for anyone."

"So, you forgive me?"

"There's nothing to forgive. I understand wanting to feel like someone else." She tilts her head, and a tendril of her umbra nudges me gently underwater. "But for the record…I wouldn't have been disappointed by you."

"Then you'd be the first," I say. "But I'll hold you to that, when the Shadow comes back."

Her fingers trail over the bottles lining the wall. "That's the thing, actually." She won't meet my eye. "I was thinking that maybe… maybe I should go. Back to it."

"*What?*" I swipe my sopping hair out of my face. "I'm sorry, I think my ears are full of water."

"Aren."

"No, it's a great idea. Should we gift-wrap you, or send you over on a salad?"

"It's *following* you," she says fiercely. "Don't you under-stand what that means? It wants you, but it has always wanted Medyssians more. If I go to it first, it will switch targets, and then you'll be safe."

"What? *No*, no way!"

"No, listen." She twists her mouth to one side. "While

you were unconscious, I—I shapeshifted into it, tried to attack it with its own form. It didn't work the first time because it was hard, and painful, and I wasn't expecting that, but I think—I *know* what it feels like now. I can be in control this time. And—and the other map is still there, so if I survived, I could use that one to get home. Right?"

"No. Not right." Leaping to my feet is a thrashing endeavor that ends with water all over the floor. "Absolutely not."

"But—"

"You heard the captain. She *wants* the Shadow to come here. She wants to kill it the way she couldn't the first time. The only way I'm letting you leave is if you're running as far away as possible. Actually—" The way forward suddenly illuminates, and it's so obvious that I'm furious I didn't think of it sooner. "I'm making you a new map. Now. Before the Shadow catches up to us. By the time Valyra kills it, you'll be long gone. Okay? Everybody wins."

Nym frowns, and I can practically see her stretching the plan into a thin bubble, searching for a good place to puncture. "And what happens if Valyra can't kill it?"

"Look, when Valyra says she's going to do something, it's sort of an inevitability." I wring out the pockets of my pants and take a soggy step back onto the marble floor. "You're staying. So. Do you want some clothes that aren't covered in Ghost Ship?"

"I—that's not—"

"Do I *have* any clothes that aren't covered in Ghost Ship?" My closet is barren, everything I own in a bloodstained pile I keep forgetting to take down to laundering. All that's left is the scratchy, gold-and-white nightmare my mother expects me to wear on formal occasions. "The espionage wardrobe is going to ban me," I mutter as I lift out the jacket and use it to dry my hair.

"I won't let you—wait. What's…" Nym's voice goes tentative. "What's an espionage wardrobe?"

"It's—" I freeze, head still wrapped in wool. A collection, is what it is. Walls and walls and walls of clothes for every purpose, for every mission. A million kinds of masks, more than Nym herself has likely ever worn. It would put the hoarder's worth of clutter coating House to shame. And that's just one of the rooms on this ship—I think of all the others, ones I'm so used to that they've become drab and uninteresting. The engine room, the armory, the vivarium, the galley. She'd *love* the galley.

And that's it. If I can't make her stay myself, I know what can.

"You know what?" I hide my grin. "Why don't I show you?"

CHAPTER 24

Nym

"**This** is low."

"I don't know what you're talking about."

"*Low*, Aren. I know exactly what you're doing."

"What? I thought you might be hungry."

My hunger is irrelevant. Aren can pretend all he wants, the same way he pretended that visiting something called an "espionage wardrobe," an absolute labyrinth of fabric I could have stayed lost in forever, was simply so he could change out of his wet clothes. But I know the truth. He's trying to distract me with beautiful, wonderful things to give himself time to build a new map.

And it's working.

The smell of the *Starsaviour's* galley washes over me, and I get a hint of something garlicky sautéing over a flaming pan. No, cinnamon-sugary and warm, straight out of the oven. No, the salty smokiness of roasted meat. I don't know where to look first—the clawed sous chef julienning spiky purple vegetables with his own pincers, the tower of white pastries being frosted on a table that rotates steadily on its own, the open pantry of dried spices from every corner of the galaxy. A baker with six arms flambéing four pans at once. A carving station where a scaly creature ensnared from the ether is being elegantly butterflied.

Aren, now dressed in a soft brown shirt and olive trousers and a belt clunky with map-crafting tools, snags a berry and offers it to me. "Don't say you don't like it."

"*Like* it?" I put the berry between my teeth, then sweep a handful more into the pocket of the simple green dress Aren claimed would help me blend in as a cabin girl. "Of course, I like it. *Look* at it. That doesn't mean—" I finally bite down so my words will un-muffle, and oh, does it taste like magic. When I close my eyes to chew, swirls of color firework behind the lids. "I'm so furious with you. I cannot believe you're doing this."

"I'm giving you a tour of my home. It's polite."

"This is clearly a diversion, not a tour," I mumble as I gaze at the whirlwind of people filling the kitchen. It's the strangest thing. I know these species, these forms. I've worn the cerulean-tipped feathers of the Friisian dicing spiky fruit into triangles. That Rengulor melting a slab of marbled cheese over coals—I know how difficult it is to maneuver with those long, curving claws. A girl with four legs and a pearly shell scuttles a tray from one open flame to another, and I remember borrowing a body just like hers on a nomadic colony of metal traders. I *know* them. I know what their souls sound like. Every one. Little living bits of planets and places I thought I would never see again, but they're all here. I've spent my life collecting scraps of the universe. Aren got to grow up with the entire universe contained in one place.

"How did they all end up here?" I ask.

"Hmm? Oh." Aren looks up from the skeleton of wires he's been twisting into a sphere, tilts his head. "I think my mom likes collecting as much as you do."

I pause mid-reach for another handful of berries. "She collects people?"

"She *recruits* people. Anyone who's the best at what they do. Sharpshooters, pilots, analytics. Chefs, obviously. Anybody skilled enough to make a name for themselves and smart enough to take orders." The wire lowers, and he looks me up and down. "She'd probably try to collect you, if she knew what you were."

"Me? Why?"

"Why? Are you kidding?" Aren's volume halves under the din. "You're a shapeshifting illusion-caster with personal knowledge of almost every inhabited planet in existence. If that's not stealth mission material, I don't know what is. She'd want you for sure."

I've never thought of using my voice for such a thing, though I suppose it's true. Another good reason to steer clear of the captain. I may be enamored with the colors and the smells and the seductive melodies of this place, but I cannot be distracted into thinking of anything but home, home, home, just as always.

I tilt my head toward a three-headed cook who looks as though he was carved out of a single slab of stone. "What is he the best of?"

"Skoenig? His hands are self-heating. He can cook an entire cut of meat perfectly without even touching a stove. Or fry an enemy's head, if the ship gets attacked. Also, one-man vocal trio. Each head can sing in a different key. Sometimes he gets sent to the hold to torture prisoners."

"*No.*"

"Not creative enough to make that up."

I stifle a giggle, then point toward a bald-headed, violet-skinned person with two swords strapped to their back, leaning through the open porthole between the galley and what must be the dining hall. "Alright, what about them?"

"Fera Thronn. Took down the Empire almost singlehandedly."

"Which empire?"

"I don't even remember."

I marvel as we pass through the swinging doors into—yes, it *is* a dining hall, lined with long black tables overflowing with crew members who lounge and bicker and arm-wrestle, eating dazzlingly plated food and drinking great flagons of something that turns the air sour.

"And them?" I glance at the nearest table, around which clusters a dozen or so people all wearing shiny, tight-fitting gray clothes, all with hair shaved identically at the sides.

"Oh, the Mori gang. They were almost as fearsome a crew as the Celestial Company until the captain absorbed them. They cheat at cards like you wouldn't believe." He's grinning now, fully committed to the game. "Go on, ask another."

"Okay." I scan the hall, settling on a broad-shouldered figure with short, pure white hair and a gold lens settled over her eye. She's striding stiffly in our direction. "What about her?"

"Who?" Aren turns, but when he sees the person I'm staring at, he grabs my arm and wheels us both around just as fast, eyes alarmingly wide. He curses below his breath, scrambling to stuff the beginnings of the map into his trousers and herd me toward the bustle of the galley at the same time. "Come on—"

"Master Aren," a voice snaps coldly from behind us. "And who is this?"

CHAPTER 25

Aren

WELL, it was a nice twenty minutes of peace.

"Lieutenant Havelock!" I rotate, a painfully unconvincing grin plastered to my face. "Good to see you. Sorry about the eels. Again. You'll be pleased to hear the top deck has never been cleaner."

"I'm very pleased." Havelock does not sound it. "Answer the question."

I swallow. "Which question?"

"The one where you explain *who this stranger is.*"

"Ah. Of course." I steal a glance at Nym. What can I say that's close enough to the truth to not set off my tell? "She's, um… new. I'm showing her around."

Havelock's telescopic eye contracts as she looks Nym up and down. "I've been told nothing of new recruits."

"It… it wasn't planned," I stammer. "She—she, uh—"

"She saved his life." A smooth voice says above my shoulder, and it's all I can do not to jump. I didn't even hear Felix approach, but there he is. He takes a casual bite out of a hunk of bread and steps on the toe of my boot in a play-along-if-you-know-what's-good-for-you sort of way. "When he disappeared. We're *all* showing her around—the captain thought she'd like a tour from people her own age."

"That's right." Cas materializes on my other side. She flashes an innocent grin and loops her arm through Nym's. "It'd be kind of rude to just send her on her way, right?"

My heart is pounding so loudly in my ears that I can hardly hear anything else. It strikes me that I should be giving Nym some kind of unspoken signal, letting her know she should mimic the twins' easy lies, but I don't trust myself to even change my expression without giving the whole thing away. But I don't have to signal anything—her mouth tilts into a virtuous smile that's much more believable than Cas's, and she nods shyly.

Havelock sniffs, eyes the three of them.

And then they all look at me.

"Is this true, Master Aren?"

No. My tattoo starts prickling proactively, and I clench my fists at my sides. I did a lot of things I didn't think I could today—maybe I can do another. I focus on the parts of the lie that aren't lies at all, searing the words *she saved his life* into my mind until they're the only thing taking up space.

"Yes," I say firmly. "Of course." *She saved his life. She saved his life. She saved* my *life.*

My hands remain where they are, far away from my neck.

I don't even dare breathe. *She saved my life, saved my life, saved my life. This is the truth.*

There's a long, painful pause, but finally, Havelock's eye emits a dull buzz and refocuses. She gives us all one last long-suffering glare.

"See that you stay out of the crew's way, then," she snaps, and then, unbelievably, she stalks away.

Now, I breathe.

"What are you doing?" I hiss, whirling on the twins. "Why

are you helping me? I thought you were suspicious."

Felix lopes an arm around both my neck and Nym's, then begins strolling us toward the wide double doors leading out to the rest of the ship. "I am suspicious," he says lazily. "That's part of it. And I was right, wasn't I? There *was* something hiding on the ship you came back on."

"I'm not suspicious," says Cas. "Just bored. And this is probably the most reckless thing you've ever done, so I want to see what happens."

I scowl. "If you want to watch me get in trouble, why didn't you just let Havelock catch us?"

"We don't want you to get in trouble." Felix herds us to the wall, guarded from eavesdropping by the ramble of the dining hall. "The opposite, actually."

"He's always so paranoid, our star-prince." Cas leans against the doorframe beside Nym, tilting her neck conspiratorially. "Look at him. He thinks everything is out to get him."

"I do not." And even if I did, I'm usually right. "Are you going to tell us why you're helping, or not?"

"We—"

"He's desperately curious. That's why."

Felix turns his cool gaze to Nym as if surprised she can speak. "Excuse me?"

Nym juts her chin out. "I heard what you said before. In the medical bay. You think I'm a stowaway, but you don't know how I hid. You heard the beginning of the story about the Shadow, but don't know why it bothered your captain so much. You don't like not having answers."

I gape. Cas stifles a snort. Felix arches one scaled eyebrow.

"So, the stowaway is observant *and* stealthy," he chuckles. "You'd fit right in here. Fine, you're right—that's part of it. So, how were you hiding? I have to assume it's what helped Aren escape whatever you found out there."

"What makes you think I always need help?" I interject.

Cas directs an openly pointed look at Havelock.

My tattoo prickles again, and I slap a hand over it. "I'm not going to mess anything up again. I swear."

"Yes," says Felix. "We'll make sure of that." He turns his attention back to Nym. "And maybe in exchange, you'll tell us the truth. How *did* you cloak yourself? And what exactly happened to you two?"

Nym's eyes meet mine before she answers, and though I can't be sure, I swear there's something distinctly Cas-like in her expression for a second. A sharpness in her pupils, a flash of green somewhere in the blue. "Maybe I'll tell you before I leave," she says, crossing her arms smoothly. "*After* you've kept us from getting caught."

Definitely a very Cas-like thing to say. Fast learner, this girl.

Cas's incisors flash mirthfully. "Oh, I like her. We're gonna have fun."

Unbelievable. She's only been around the twins for a few minutes, and she already knows exactly how to communicate with them. Felix is right—she *would* fit in well here.

Cas is already pulling Nym through the door, asking her whether she's seen the armory yet, but Nym turns and catches my eye. Hers isn't just Cas-like in expression, anymore—she's transformed the left corner of her face into an identically smirking match, from the emerald slit of an iris to the scales dotting her pale pink face. She flashes a caricature of a grin, copycat-incisors caught comically on her bottom lip.

I snort, sparing a cautious glance at Felix to make sure he's not looking. *Stop,* I mouth back. She stifles a laugh, and the scales and extra teeth vanish just as she does, under the arch.

I trail after, listening to Cas's chatter and Felix's questions, watching as Nym folds into their stride as though she's always belonged there. And as I begin to carefully test the conductivity on the half-finished wiring, I find I can't stop thinking about what Felix said. Something pointless, as I stand here literally making her a device that will send her as far away as possible. Something that's undeniably true, anyway.

She'd fit in here.

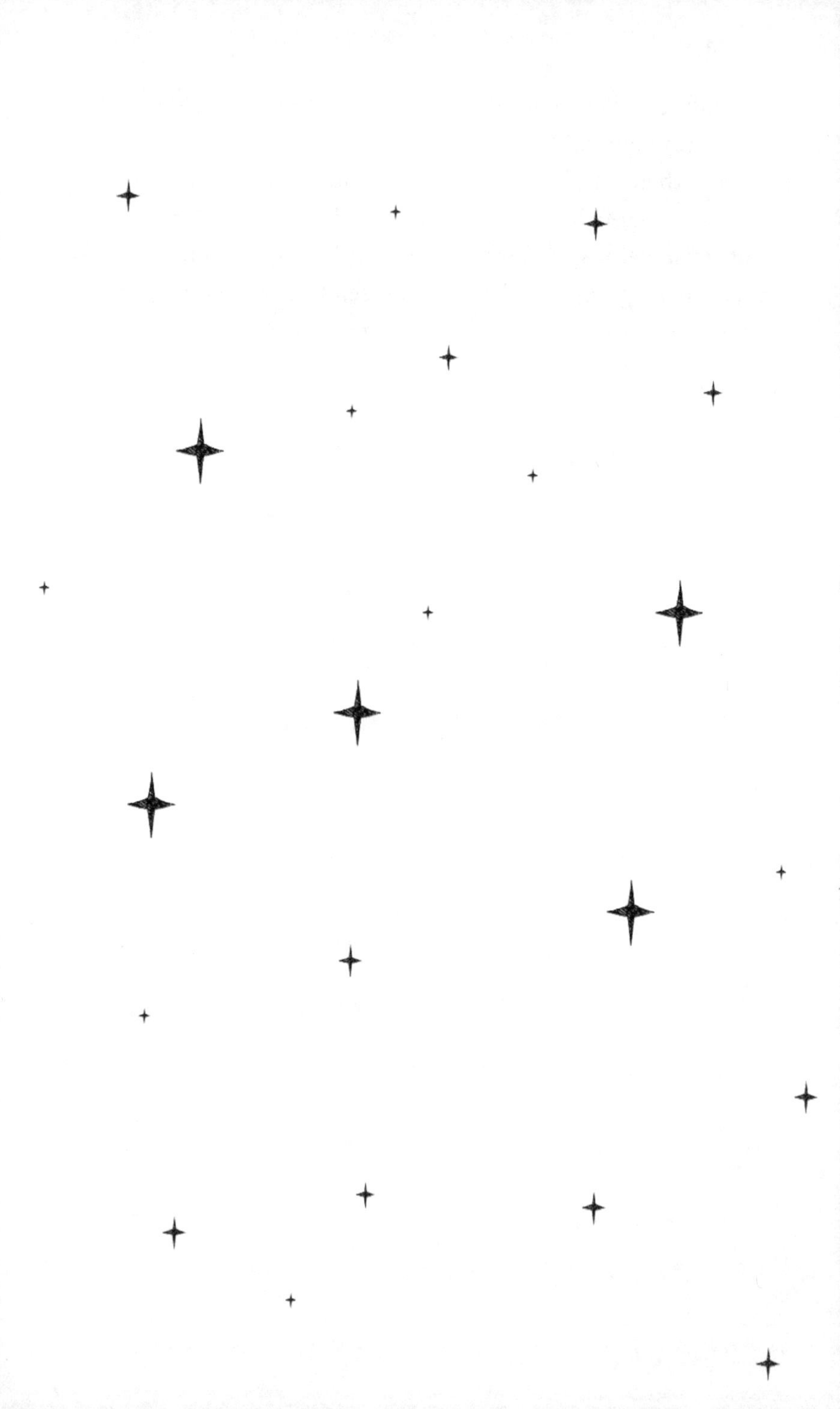

<h1 style="text-align:center">CHAPTER 26</h1>

<h1 style="text-align:center">Nym</h1>

I'm betraying House.

I don't mean to, not at all. From dozens of decks up, I can imagine that it's rumbling somewhere beneath me, sending envious pulses through the floorboards in response to being left behind. *I still love you best,* I think in its unknown direction, and it's true. House is my home, my sanctuary, my best friend. But the *Starsaviour* is… something else. Something magical.

My head is cluttered with fresh memories I'm struggling to catalogue. How Cas led us sprinting to the armory, shouting that the last one there had to be target practice; how she chased Aren up and down the gleaming aisles after he lost, wielding a puffy training dummy as a lance. The herbs in the white-walled vivarium, which put my own meager collection of plants to shame. A cozy barracks, a crystalline pool. My pockets are already full to bursting with souvenirs from every room we've visited—pastries and plants and hypermagnetic cuffs—and somehow there is still more to see, more to collect.

Aren's device was a seed when he first began, but now, cogs and wires blossom from its core, twining about into the shell of a sphere. He must be so close to finished. I have wasted so much time, letting myself be distracted. I should—

"Wait, what was in there?" I crane over my shoulder for a fleeting glimpse through a red velvet curtain, behind which beckons a chamber of wall-to-wall books. "Was that a—"

"Library's boring," Cas says airily, dragging me toward a staircase by the sleeve. "Observatory is better."

"No," Aren interjects from behind us. "No observatory. We've observed enough of the void today already."

Felix yawns and inhales half of a powdered cake I could have sworn was deep in my pocket. "So, what—rigging? Training room? Barracks?"

"We're not going to the—*oh*." Aren maneuvers something glassy and faintly smoking between his fingers, then tucks a spent matchstick behind his ear. "Okay, no. Training room next. Definitely."

"You hate the training room," Cas says.

"I'd argue the training room hates me. But she'll love it. I don't have to participate."

My head spins, still trying to catch up from *observatory*. "Training for what?"

"Celestial Company missions. Heists, rescues, jailbreaks— anything, anywhere that might show up. It's—we're—well, you'll see." Aren chuckles under his breath. "I don't know why I didn't think to take you there first. Come on."

One more stop, I order myself ferociously. *Just one more.*

When we reach the bottom of the stairs, I nearly crash into a massive white door. There is no hallway on this level, only a narrow strip of carpet between the next staircase and this wooden monstrosity, as though whatever's inside has absorbed territory from the rest of the deck by force. The groan of shifting joints ripples out from the other side, then a sound like a bag of sand being dropped from a height. My head fills with visions of beams and bars, sleek racks of swords, wall-to-wall mirror-glass.

"Training room," Cas announces grandly, then kicks the door open.

There is nothing on the other side. Nothing at all.

I blink against blinding darkness. The chamber is black as its door was white, as though I have found the edge of the universe itself and stepped off. A cavity where the *Starsaviour's* heart might have been. And without any hint of the seams where walls must meet floor, it's impossible to tell how far the sheer emptiness goes on. There is nothing inside which looks suitable for training—there is nothing inside at all.

I squint back into the now-searing light of the stair, but Aren has his lenses back on and the orb held up to his face.

"Just wait," he says.

"Right." Felix swings around the inside of the doorframe and cocks the side of his head toward the only drop of light the chamber has allowed: the faintly glowing outline of two crescent moons embedded into the wall. A matching set winks behind his ear. As the tattoo lines up, a faint bell chimes, and he grins. "Where should we train?"

And the abyss… *changes.*

Pale, transparent globes materialize out of nothing, like foamy bubbles brimming to the surface of a dark lake. They shimmer in iridescent shades—green and blue, invisibly gray, harsh red. They circle us with twice the determination of the wreckage on the Ghost Ship and none of the predatory threat. One curves close enough to pass through my chest, and I see ridged grooves painted on its face. *Planets,* I realize with an incredulous jolt. That's what they are. Thousands of them. Maybe even *all* of them, every celestial object ever charted.

If we were on the precipice of the universe before, it's as though we've turned away from it, turned back around to see the ether splayed before us. Stars and moons and suns and more, more, more, a sea in every direction. My starmap is put to shame. It turns to something flat and pitiful in my memory, compared to this living, breathing recreation. The entirety of the ether, contained in one shifting pocket dimension.

"Is that—"I cup the nearest sphere, my hand passing right through its jagged, uneven rings.

"Euurestal? If you're up for it." Cas holds her own hand up, and the planet seems to recognize the crescent moons tattooed to her wrist. It shimmers once; I blink away from the flash.

I blink, and in that tiny span, the room shapeshifts yet again.

I'm perched on a platform what feels like miles above a city, so far that it disappears into a grid. A curdled layer of smoke turns people and streetsailers and homes into identical squares of burnt orange. The air smells of metal and salt and adventure; the wind gnaws at my hair and my skirt. My stomach tremors with a thrill of recognition. I am on the Starsaviour, with Aren and Cas and Felix beside me, but I have *been here.* I know this tower, and if I turn just there…

Yes. I toe to the edge, and the slope of the platform falls off into empty air, with a gray sea below. Humidity sticks to my skin, and the thin air siphons away at my human lungs, and I have been here. I have known this. I have scanned those streets from this height, searching for a sign of a clue. There is the voluminous tent of the market I passed through, filching a piece of fruit, seeking out a heartbeat that sounded like the chirp of a machine and slipping into a body that was hard and slate. There is the cave by the sea where I hid House until I was ready to leave. I could not create a more powerful memory with my own illusions. If I tried, I would be lost in it forever.

I thought I was overwhelmed before, and I was wrong. I could not feel any more weightless and disoriented if I let myself fall from this height. "How is this—what is this—"

Cas grins. There is a harness crossing her chest that wasn't there before, a tether that came from nowhere trailing from the end of it. "Do you want to scale this wall, or not?"

"*Not.*" Aren rolls his eyes, and I realize he's wearing a harness too. As am I. "We're not doing Eurestaal. This course takes five hours."

My mind spins, words like *wormhole* and *portal* coursing through it. "How can we be here?"

"Holograms. Room's full of platforms that rearrange themselves to match the course. Heist, in this case." Felix tests the straps on his own harness. "Anytime the Celestial Company goes anywhere, it gets multidimensionally mapped. That way, the rest of the crew can learn a new terrain, practice skills, find more efficient ways to complete missions. And since there's a thousand of us… we've sort of been everywhere."

I can't make his words register. I am overwhelmed with the sensation of being on Eurestaal, the knowledge that I could repeat this sensation on any of the thousands of globes floating just out of sight.

"Do you have to stick to the course?" I ask breathlessly. "Or can you move around in it?"

"Stick to the course." Cas hooks her thumbs under the straps below her shoulders. "No escape until you beat the—"

Felix flicks the end of her braid loose. "*No.* You can go wherever you want. Anywhere that's been mapped."

"And if you want to be done and go somewhere else, you just say—*ugh,* I never do it, but—" Cas glares at the ceiling. "*I yield.*"

The tower beneath us vanishes, blown away on an unseen

wind. The sea between worlds returns. I realize I'm shaking, overcome. I thought I would have a hard time choosing my favorite part of the *Starsaviour*, which bit I would take with me and hang from my ceiling if I could, but there is no longer any competition.

"So. Training room." Aren nudges my shoulder. "Where do you want to go?"

Cas and Felix are not watching me. If they were, I do not know that I would be able to hide it from them—the way something shatters in the face I have given myself, leaking out through the cracks of the mask for just a moment. It is there in the silence when I look at Aren: a question, *the* question, yearning and hopeful as it always is. I know the answer. But I cannot help begging for it anyway.

And the answer comes, just as silent. The soft downturn of Aren's mouth. The way his head twitches in a way that would look like nothing at all to anyone else, but to me is a full, aching sentence. *No.*

No. It would not be here. They would have had to visit it themselves, felt the ripple of fins gliding past their faces, breathed in salt and sand. And Medyssia's great gift to itself and curse to me is how well and completely it has hidden. I will not find it here.

In its certain absence, the prismatic universe expands wider than it ever has before.

Where do I want to go, if not Medyssia?

Celestial baubles twirl around me teasingly, and I find I don't know how to answer. I've never been asked, not in this sense. I have already seen so much of the world. I have followed clues. I have chased dead ends. I have gone anywhere I thought there might be a whisper of home. So where would I go if that focused was broadened, if I could go anywhere? See anything? Just for myself, and nothing else?

Everywhere is the only answer, because that's exactly where I *could* go. Everywhere, as often as I liked. Never running. Never lost.

"Andanere," I breathe, thinking of a field of pink-frosted roses beneath a pastel-hued sky. "No—Feldnown." There was a permanent festival buried in the roots beneath a swamp; I heard its fiddles long ago. If it was there already when the planet was mapped…"Wait, no—have you seen—oh, there's this cluster of moons in constant eclipse of one another, never colliding—"

"You're giving me motion sickness," Felix observes dryly, and I realize the baubles have been spinning toward us and away in response to my requests.

"I'm sorry." I expel something between a laugh and a gasp and let the sea calm. I could drown in my own euphoria. *Everywhere, everywhere* dances in my head. "I can't choose. Where do you like to go?"

Cas's eyes glint, and she catches a flash of orange in her fist. "Usually someplace a little more dangerous."

She presses the captured celestial object to her wrist, and the floor leaves us.

My euphoria is left behind along with my stomach.

Something sharp and painful spears through my ear; a phantom rope catches me by the waist and drags me up until my back is pressed against a bronze wall, its cracks spewing smoke. I can hear the explosive cry of fire behind my head, as though it's a beast desperate to break free of the ship caging it. Above me, solar sails flap unrestrained, brilliant flashes blinding me with every chaotic spasm. And before me, a nothingness wider and hungrier than the form the training room first took, as though something has taken a bite out of the sky. A black hole. It *roars*, invisible teeth gnawing at my hair and my dress. There isn't a trace of color in the sky darkening its edges—this ether is hideous and rabid. I am powerless to swim against its pull.

A roiling sky howls in every direction; the soul has been sucked from the universe I have always seen as a friend. The panels below my fingertips rattle like scales being ripped from the back of a fish, and the one just to my left wrenches free and goes careening off in a shower of sparks. The ship in this hologram is dying, and we are chained to its sinking corpse.

I don't like this one. Not at all.

"It's a repair challenge!" Cas yells over the storm. *"To practice for emergencies! It's fun—come on, you can do the sails!"* She swings herself upward, where Felix already appears to be passively knitting a rope to the railing.

I try to steady my breathing and find I cannot. Every gulp is stale and compressed, as though I'm trapped in a tank only slightly larger than my own body. That pinch I felt in my ear—the simulator has put me in the kind of suit Aren must wear in order to survive the ether. It's horrible, suffocating. I scrabble at my ear and can't get a grip on the tiny clip—it is only real enough to do what the simulation orders it to do, just like the rest of the hologram. I cannot even use the music of the stars as an anchor. These stars are not mine. They do not sing; they only watch with the hungry eyes of a beast I've never seen before. My skin feels too tight, my lungs too weak.

Flames from the failing ship lick at my back, and the tether anchoring me suddenly seems so fragile, a few threads from snapping, and is this what Aren felt, when I found him? Is this how he drowned?

One glance confirms it. He has not followed Cas and Felix to the sails, even though I'm positive he has the skill to fix them. His eyes are clamped shut, his fingers shaking against the knobs of his glass lenses. The sailer jolts, and his face contorts, teeth gritted. This is not a simulation to him, but something entirely too real. All that's missing is the eels.

Yield, I remember, with the uncomfortable realization that I have never considered the ether something to need to yield to. "I yield!"

I have just enough time to fear it won't respond to anything without a Celestial Company brand before the black hole vanishes. The wicked stars level out. We are returned to the loveliness of the in-between, and I have to look down in terror to make sure I'm still human because I cannot feel my legs. Beside me, Aren sinks to the ground, jaw tight.

Cas slides down from a platform gone opaque. "Too much for you?"

It's a repulsive understatement. How can she be so calm? "You *enjoy* that one?" I touch my throat. It feels as though freed from a tight coil. "You go there on purpose?"

"It's not real, though. It's just an exercise." Her nose crinkles. "Don't tell me you're afraid of space, too."

It felt real. It was real to Aren. "No, but that was—" Suddenly, her word choice sticks like a thorn. "'Too'? You are afraid of space?" I suppose you would have to be, if it looked like *that*. I hunt for a reason she would want to expose herself to such an awful reincarnation of it. "Does that sort of exercise help one cope with the fear?"

To my surprise, Cas snorts. "Oh, sweetheart, I'm not afraid of anything. But sure, maybe that's what it does." She looks down at Aren. "What do you think, star-prince?"

The little color left drains from Aren's face. "What—why are you asking me?"

"Oh, come on." She rolls her eyes back to me. "Nym, you

know what I mean. You were with him out there all day. Right? You know he's terrified of the void."

"He's… wait, what?" My human heartbeat is still pounding in my ears—this body feels everything so much more strongly, I can't stand it. "What are you talking about? That's not true at all."

"Sure it is. You put him anywhere near space, and he just—" Her fingers splay wide, her nails sharp as arrows. "—freezes. Like somebody's shot him with an immobilizer. Look, he's doing it now."

"Why would you say that?" Confusion and defensiveness spark inside me, made sharper by my own residual panic. Cas has been so fun, so playful up until now—why is she being cruel? "When we had to leave my ship, he swam out first. Tell her, Aren."

But when I look at him, his lenses are off, the nearly finished navigator tremoring. "You know?" he asks with quiet, confirming horror. "You all know?"

Felix raises an eyebrow, leaning against another invisible platform. "You thought we didn't? We've seen your specs, you know."

The specs. The way they stain over the color of the universe. Is that what they're for? It rewrites every second we've spent together, if it's true. It turns every moment on the Ghost Ship into an act of rebellion. Why did he come with me? Did I pressure him into submerging himself in a fear I was too selfish to notice?

The smirk falls from Cas's face, an awkward layer of guilt replacing it. "Wait, did you seriously think it was a secret? I wasn't trying to embarrass you. I thought she knew. I thought *you* knew we knew."

"I—" Aren's gaze darts between the three of us, cornered

prey backed against a tree. "Okay. I have to go."

"Aren?" I reach for his arm. I still don't understand Cas's tone, like a fear of the reality we just visited is something to be ashamed of, or his stricken expression, like he *is* ashamed of it. Anyone would be afraid of that simulation. It's the ether at its worst and most carnivorous, a form I've never seen it take before. And if that's the way he sees it all the time, who wouldn't want to hide from it, press yourself under your bed as it prowled outside your window, hoping it wouldn't come in? "Wait—"

"I'm fine. I have to finish the map." He backs away from me, the orb jammed into his pocket. "You guys have fun."

And without another word, he flees the training room.

CHAPTER 27

Aren

IF there's one thing I've learned from the Celestial Company, it's that when something scares you, you're supposed to fight it, not run away.

And yet, here I am, running.

He's terrified of the void.

You thought we didn't know?

This isn't happening.

"Aren?" Nym's caught up already—of course she has; she's faster than me, just like Cas and Felix, just like all of them—but I can't talk to her because I can't breathe, can't breathe, *can't breathe,* until I find myself somehow back in my room. Nym's footsteps trail behind me as I head for my bed and let the finished orb thump onto the stiffly tucked blanket.

"So." The word is a stone I have to force out of my throat. "The orb is done, actually. I don't know why I said—anyway. I need your blood. I mean, your hand. For the blood." My mouth feels like a disconnected tap. I'm somewhere far away, five minutes ago and three decks up, listening to Cas say *What do you think, star-prince?* over and over in a mocking loop. Who else knows? Havelock? Bayless? My mother herself? Has everyone been laughing at me behind my back all this time, while I clambered around in my useless tech?

"Aren, *answer* me."

I lift my head. "What?"

"Is it true?"

I swallow. "Um, is what true?"

"Aren."

This time, I'm not a tap, but a burst pipe. "Well, what kind of freak is afraid of space, Nym?" I yank my specs off as I slump onto my mattress. I might as well paint *coward* on the sides. "That's what these are for, okay? They're not so I can see in the dark. They're so I can exist without having a panic attack as soon as I step out on deck."

"But you... the Ghost Ship. You went down first."

"Yeah, well—" My face heats fiercely. "It was for you, okay? I thought you were afraid, and it made me want to fight through it."

Nym sinks hesitantly onto the rumpled blanket next to me. "I *was* afraid. But you should have told me. I never would have—I would have told you to stay—"

"I've never told anyone. I mean, we *live in it*, Nym. There's nothing out there that isn't touched by the void. Being afraid of it? It's a joke."

"It's not. Neither are you." She turns to consider the curtains cloaking the porthole I hate so much, keeping the void at bay so it won't bleed into my nightmares. "How... how long have you had to live like this?"

"What do you mean, how long? Always. I can't remember a time when I didn't." I've never tried to dissect the root of my fear before. It just is. I let myself fall back until my only view is of the drab ceiling. "I don't know what's out there, so my head has always filled it with monsters, all waiting to drag me out and drown me. To me, the void is nothing but emptiness, and loneliness, and…" I pause, suddenly wary and agitated, the same feeling I get when it's time to train and I know I've forgotten something important. The words are right, but a piece is missing.

Because that's not true. Not completely. It's one part of it, but there's another layer that molded to the first until they became inseparable. I push past the way my chest tightens just thinking about the void and look for the source. And there it is, because it always comes back to this, doesn't it? Of course, it's him. It's always him. My own Shadow.

I pass a hand over my eyes. "She marooned him in it, okay? My dad." The word tastes like sand. "After he let the Shadow get away. Broke the tether binding him to us, to this ship. And for all I know, he could have just been left on a distant planet somewhere, but for some reason, I guess that in my head, not belonging here has always looked like—"

"Like being lost in a void," Nym says. "Like being alone in the dark."

"I know it doesn't make any sense."

"Of course, it does." Cautious fingers touch my arm. "And you think she'd do the same thing to you?"

I can't bear to say yes. I've set a lot of secrets free with Nym already, but this one is one too many. Speaking it into existence would be a curse.

"What if I never get over it?" I ask instead. "What if I'm afraid forever?"

"Then you'll be a person who has already spent his life fighting something he fears instead of letting it defeat him, and that makes you stronger than most. But Aren, that version of the universe, as something dark and hungry… it isn't like that. It doesn't want to swallow you. It's…" She trails off, but just as suddenly, there's a loud rustle of fabric and then the startling intrusion of her hand jutting straight down at my face.

"Up," she says. "I know what to do. I want to show you something."

"Show me what?" The curtains shielding my porthole window come into focus—they're thrown wide, the stars beyond leering through the glass. I flinch away reflexively. "No. No, thanks. Anyway, the map—we have to test it. You have to get home before the Shadow shows up."

"It won't take long," she insists, palm still outstretched.

"Nym. I'm—I'll be fine. Really."

"Aren," she says firmly, "I'm not going to leave you without at least trying this. Otherwise, I'll always remember you this way."

"As what, a whiny coward?"

"No. As someone I left alone in the dark."

I glance at the map again. "*Nym.*"

She nudges it away with her foot. "You need my blood to make it work. I'm not giving you any unless you trust me."

This will never work. What am I doing? I'm putting my hand in hers; I'm letting her pull me to my feet, up to the windowsill.

"Okay," I say, heart pounding in my ears. "I trust you."

CHAPTER 28

Aren

"CLOSE your eyes."

"Nym, I really don't think I can do this." My fingernails are in the crack between window and wood, my palms clammy and cold. In every direction, the void ripples like a fathomless black pool. "Don't make me let go."

"I won't." Nym leans back, heels against the side of the *Starsaviour.* "We're not going anywhere. I just want to show you something. Close your eyes."

"How am I supposed to see with my eyes closed?"

"Aren."

"Fine." Nothing changes. The inside of my eyelids is the same shade of infinite nothing as space itself. "If you push me out, I swear—"

"Did you know human eyes only have three color receptors?" she interrupts. "I found it terribly dull at first. I didn't ever consider that it might be scary."

Is she trying to distract me? "Okay, how many do you have?"

"Sixteen."

"So…" I try to fathom having thirteen more receptors in my eyes and physically can't. "…you can see more colors than me?"

"More colors, yes. And more light. More depth."

"Meaning what?"

"Meaning to Medyssians, the sky looks… different." A breath. The feel of her sleeve brushing mine as she leans in, her voice a gentle whisper. "Alright. Open your eyes."

I grind down an entire layer of fingernails drilling them into the side of the ship and keep my eyes firmly shut. "Maybe you could just describe it."

"You said you trusted me."

I did. I do. *I can't believe I'm doing this.* I open my eyes.

And nothing. The sky is still dark. Maybe whatever she did won't work on me; maybe my fear is a barrier not even she can breach.

But then I see a spot of pink on the horizon. Its edges crackle, turn gold, and expand.

I grip her hand. "Nym?"

"Shh." Her chin tilts toward the pink in a way that makes me certain she's controlling it.

The edges keep uncurling outward, like all the darkness of space was just a paper veil being burned away. A splash of lilac mingles into the pink. A trace of gold after that. They swirl together, filling the void with trails of glittering stardust and far-off planets that glow like floating silver lanterns. Back and back those dark edges burn, until the entire universe, as far as the limits of Nym's power can reach, is nothing but a dome of softness and light. And I realize I've seen it before, this pale purple and gold sky. It's the map on the ceiling of her ship. It wasn't an artistic choice. This is what the world really looks like to her.

It's not real is my automatic reaction. *It's just an illusion.* But it's different this time. My human eyes feed me a universe that's cold and dark; hers feed her one that's brilliant and ethereal. Does that make her version less true than mine?

It's not real, insists every tremulous bone in my body anyway, but there's something else fighting against it, soothing and persuasive, and I have just enough of an understanding of how Nym's illusions work to recognize their side effects. They make you believe in them, down to your core, the stronger they are. *It is real,* this vision of the sky tells me. *It is.*

"Something's missing." A frown twists across Nym's face. "It looks right, but—oh!" She tilts her head until it settles right under mine, and when I look down, startled, she starts humming something both strange and eerily familiar. Again and again, five bare notes under my ear.

And this time, it echoes across my new sky, into every star and every planet and every inch of the blanket of space. A melody repeating; a thousand humming voices like Nym's calling back to us. *Come out,* it sounds like it's saying, soft and loving. *Come away.*

The same song the Shadow stole to lure her in. It should have ruined it forever, turned it into something sick and haunting. But now, I can hear how shriveled and weak its mimic was in comparison to the real thing. This is what she saw, that first time she left her planet. This is what she heard, what she always hears.

"It called to you," I say. "The ether. It's still calling to you, even though you want to go home."

Her head lifts. The iridescent universe reflects in her eyes, shining with longing even now.

"How could I ever resist?" she whispers.

She couldn't. No one could, if they saw the ether take this shape. It's a million glittering pathways promising adventure and light. A hypnotic melody I feel strange about hearing, like I'm intruding on something that's supposed to be Nym's. It drowns out the one that's usually in my head, warning me to *Stay back, stay away.*

And she never even got to enjoy it, this thing she gave up her entire home for. She spent all the freedom she'd gained overcome with guilt that she left her family behind, constantly beckoned out to see more and having to resist. What a beautiful loneliness.

"Aren, you don't have to."

What? I realize I'm leaning out, that I look like I'm about to dive into the dusty pink cloud beneath us. Am I? It looks so solid, like I could walk right into the sky.

"I want to," I reply, hardly believing I'm the one saying it. "I want to try." *I want to have a better memory of this. I want something to keep after you leave.*

"Well, hold onto me, so you don't drift off. It'll be just like dancing." Nym steps into the air in front of me, walking on a pale gold sea. Her voice softens. "It's alright if you're still afraid."

Just like dancing. "I am," I reply, just as quiet.

She reaches for me, pauses. "Wait. One last thing that might help." And suddenly, her hands are gentle at my waist, cool through my shirt. "We are the same," she whispers, and I recognize the delicate cadence of an illusion in her voice. "You belong out here, just as I do."

I don't understand at all, until I look down and see what she's done.

My legs are gone.

No, my legs are replaced.

Pale tendrils of translucent umbra, like hers. Narrower, dusky blue instead of lavender, but just like her. It blends seamlessly into my chest. When I lift my arms, the skin is ethereal blue too, with paper-thin fins sprouting from wrist to elbow.

She's made me Medyssian. No, she's made me *feel* Medyssian, that's all. But out here, with her kind of magic, they're one and the same.

I carefully push off from the wall, and the umbra responds the way a real Medyssian's would. It lifts me up; it contracts the tendrils and explodes them in a starburst around me; it turns me into something weightless and free. I can't find the words to capture the feeling. I would need an entire symphony to try.

"I can change it back," Nym says hurriedly. She's shifted herself too, and now she's like me—no, I'm like her. Two luminous creatures. "If it's too strange, I can change it back. I was just thinking—"

"Nym." My voice is hoarse when I remember how to speak again. "Don't you dare."

And when I move again, it's free, weightless. Like dancing.

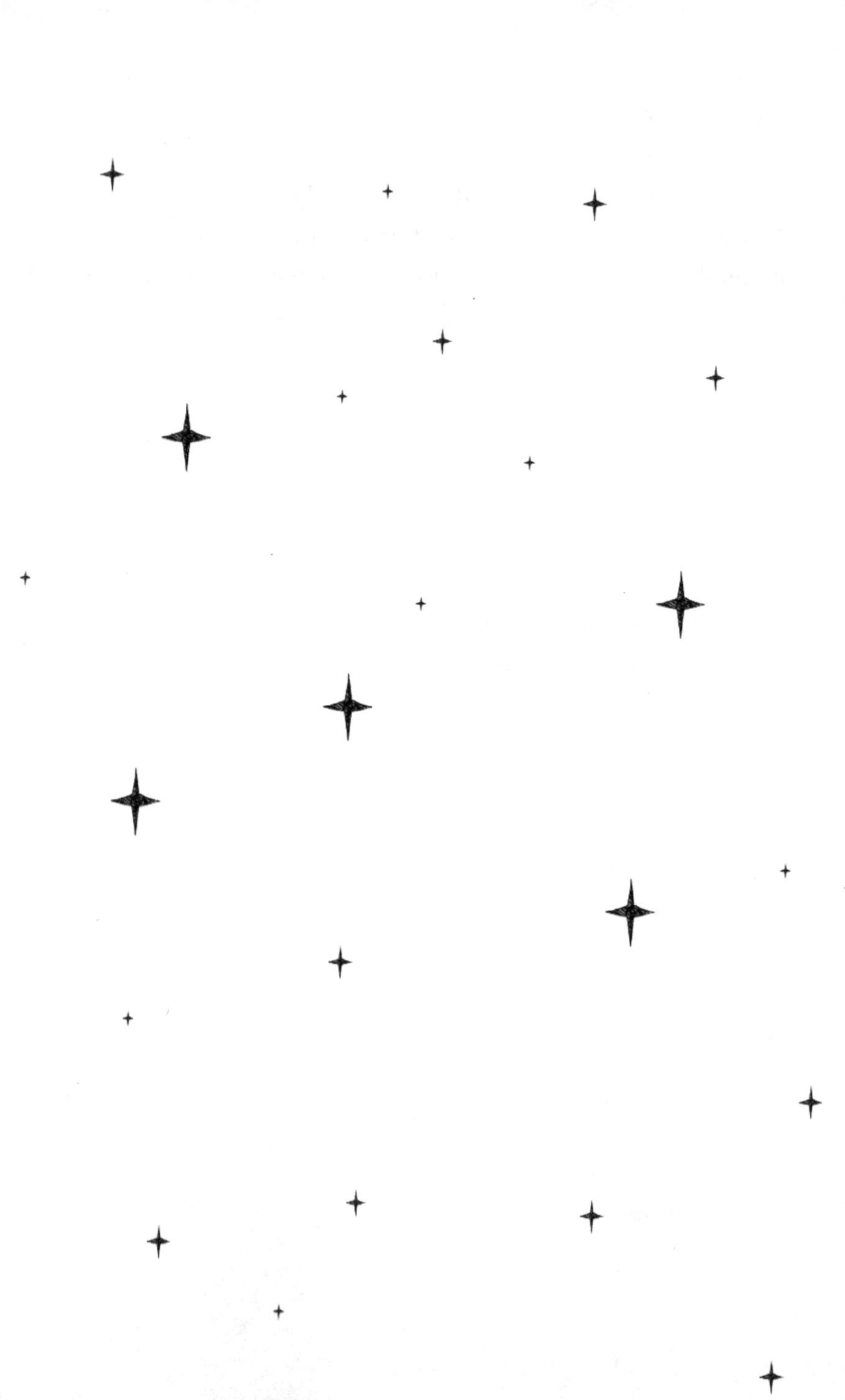

CHAPTER 29

Nym

JUST like dancing.

The clouds are our floor, the stars our chandelier. And am I imagining it, that Aren looks more comfortable in his own skin as a Medyssian than he ever has as a human? His deep blue hair melds seamlessly with the periwinkle of his illusion-skin; his illusion-umbra holds none of his legs' clumsiness.

It's wrong, I know. I've given him too much, and if I leave it, I could forget. We both could. Already, I can see from the way his fear has stifled itself like a dying candle—the illusion is seeping right into his veins, making him believe he's as safe out here as I am.

But is that so bad?

He has a starwalking suit. He has me. He could be safe out here forever, his hand in mine.

Come away with me.

The words rise on their own like a tidal wave. The same words the universe has always sung to me, now in a different key with a different meaning.

Come away.

He could. I could keep this illusion masking him when I go home. I could tell my family I found another lost

Medyssian on the way. All his fear of the dark, all the worries and insecurities that plague him, gone.

He spins me out again, and I catch his gaze on the way back. His irises are full of galaxies; his grin is a sun. We could be happy. We could be together.

Come away with me.

And do what, though?

Stay on Medyssia for the rest of his life, trapped on a hidden world with false memories of who he is and how he got there? Collect him like one of the trinkets on my ceiling? Never.

You could ask. A smaller but no less persistent wave. *The worst he could do is tell you he won't.*

We spin as one, our own solar system, and though he might be fearless now, I am not.

CHAPTER 30

Aren

WE dance until I forget I ever belonged anywhere else. I let Nym lead, pulling me through a pastel mosaic I never imagined of the sky. It feels like I could drag a hand through each passing comet and leave a trail of stardust in its wake. And the song of the universe keeps on, soft and beckoning.

There's something I want to tell her, I think, with my fears gone. Something I want to ask before she turns me back into my weaker self.

"Nym." I kick against air until we glide to a stop. "I…" My words cut short. There's something growing over the sky—thick ribbons of seaweed, blooming strange purple flowers with long, rippling petals. Even the air looks different, distorted somehow, like we're underwater. "Wait, what's going on?"

"What?" She peers around us and covers her mouth. "Oh, no. I was thinking about home, and I guess I—"

"This?" There are shadowy shapes behind the seaweed, ghostly versions of Nym flitting in and out of caverns that leak bioluminescence. "This is what your home looks like?"

"Something like it. I never let myself go much farther. It's too dangerous."

"It's incredible." I trail my hand through one ribbon and can almost feel its slippery smoothness. "Nym, listen—"

But it ripples like the surface of a pond under my fingertips, only solidifying when I pull back. This is all she has left of home. A mirage.

This is what she wants, all she's been talking about since we met. Her map is waiting for us back in my room, and she's going home, and that'll be the end. I'll never see her again, never again feel this lightness I get just from being around her, and that has to be okay. I promised I'd get her home. I *promised.*

"What is it?" I suddenly realize Nym is still waiting for me to finish my sentence, but she looks distracted. She reaches for the same ribbon of seaweed and presses a finger to it. And instead of rippling into nothing, it solidifies and turns a brilliant, opaque silver, then dissolves into a flurry of hundreds and hundreds of fish with tiny moonlight scales. They circle us in a whirlwind, their fins streaming behind them like veils, until they vanish completely. She sighs wistfully and removes her hand, and its edges begin to fade. "What were you going to say?"

I glance at the scenery, at the way her underwater kingdom is fading back to limitless purple and gold. Every hidden corner of the universe is out there, and I want her to show me all of it. *Stay with me.* That's what I was going to say, that terrible, selfish thing. *Don't go. Stay here with me.*

"Just… thank you. For all of this." I rub the back of my neck and offer her a half-smile. "But I think it's time we get you back to your real home. No more illusions."

Nym nods. "Home," she repeats, but something about her smile feels like an illusion, too.

The sky fades behind us as we glide toward the *Starsaviour*, as the magic pours back into Nym. The path ahead is still golden, but I can see the dark veil closing at the edges.

And then there's no path at all, just us back where we started, beneath my open window. Two Medyssians, floating above my bed.

I reach down to lift the map. "Ready?" I ask, even though I'm not at all.

Nym cups the orb along with me, and with the movement, my Medyssian form fades like a dream until I'm human again. Ordinary, uninteresting human, the way I'll be forever. "I'm ready."

She doesn't wince when I prick her finger with the spindle protruding from the mechanism. She doesn't watch when her silvery blood traces its way through the coiling and into the heart of the orb. I can feel her eyes on me instead, only looking down when I straighten.

Stay, stay, stay. It's a roaring in my ears; if I let it continue even a moment longer, it might drag me under.

"Together," I say, guiding both our thumbs to the trigger. "One. Two… Three."

Click.

I order myself not to shut my eyes against that familiar blue light, even though I hate what it means. I won't be selfish. And maybe this won't even be goodbye. Maybe my mother will kill the Shadow, just as she's promised, and then it'll be my turn to search for an invisible planet. I'll find her again. I will.

But I don't have to shut my eyes against anything, because no light appears.

I frown. *Click.*

Maybe the mechanism got jammed. Maybe I turned the

switch wrong.

Click. Click click click.

"Aren?" Nym says, a note of fear polluting her voice, and I have nothing to say for myself.

The map doesn't work.

Like always, I've failed.

CHAPTER 31

Nym

I am not going home.

I am no stranger to dead ends. The sensation of finding a string in the darkness, of following it to its fraying threads and finding nothing there, is one I know well. I could almost see the end of this string—I could see the beacon flickering to life, could see my home rising out of the clouds in the distance. But there is nothing. *It* is nothing, just a ball of glass and copper.

I close my eyes and wait for disappointment, my oldest friend, to press its full weight upon me. For my heart to break, for my spirit to shatter. I am not going home. Not this way. And I feel... I feel...

What is this, this unclenching in my stomach? What is it, this flutter in my heartbeat? It's unallowable, that I should feel glad I don't have to say goodbye quite yet. My head splits with something screaming and furious—the sound of guilt. I press into my temples to quiet it, but the noise is just as familiar as disappointment and just as reluctant to leave. The shriek fades out, then in again.

I lower my hands and turn toward the window.

"I'll figure something out," Aren is stammering. "I'll fix it. I—Nym?"

The scream is not coming from inside of me.

Come back. Come back. COME.

"Nym." Aren shakes my shoulder; his fingers grip harder when I don't turn. "No. Don't you dare tell me you hear it."

I don't want to. I want the wailing to have grown from inside me, rooted in my heart and blossoming in my skull, but it's not true. It's the Shadow, and it's not the miserable, desperate scream it released when we fled. It's fierce and rabid, dripping with hunger. The Shadow has gotten stronger, just as I feared it would.

Come back to me.

"We're out of time," I whisper.

"No. No, we're not." Aren yanks the curtains shut. "How far? How long until it gets here?"

"I don't know. It's in my head—*why is it in my head*—"

"Stop. Listen—*listen* to me." Aren drops the useless map onto his bed and whirls me away from the window. "It was always going to come here, hunting me, and my mother was always going to slaughter it. This doesn't change anything. All we have to do is keep you hidden. When the Shadow is dead, we'll go back to the Ghost Ship and find the other map. Okay?"

Hidden. I'm always hiding, aren't I?

"And what about you?" I demand. "What about everyone else?" The chefs, the medics, the pilots. Everyone who calls this place home. I can see them all dead, torn apart. Cas and Felix, their eyes unseeing and their limbs mangled. Aren, his gash reopened and his heart torn out, slumped against the wall.

"*Nym!*"

I meet Aren's eyes and gasp, wrenching myself out of his grip. The irises are rolled all the way back, his gash reopened, his hair crimson with his own blood. He jerks backward, taking in the room. They're here—all the terrifying visions in my head. His floor is covered with the phantom bodies of his crew.

"It's not real," he says firmly, and takes me by the shoulders again. "It's not going to happen like this. It's not real. It's not real."

I shut my eyes against the illusions, against the distant call of the Shadow, against everything but his voice. *Not real. Not real. Not like this.*

When I open my eyes again, the bloody overlay has vanished, but I'm trembling beneath Aren's grip.

"Hide with me," I beg. "Please. Don't face it. I will hide, but only if you come too."

"I—Nym, my mom… I have to…" Aren falters, but I don't let him pull away. I know him now. He is a boy who has been taught all his life that he cannot be brave unless he's running toward danger. I will not let him die because of me, convinced that is bravery.

"Please," I repeat, my voice small and unyielding.

"I'll…okay." He massages the back of his neck. "I'll stay with you."

I take my first steady breath in minutes. He will hate me for this, but he will be alive to feel hatred. "I know where to go."

CHAPTER 32

Aren

"THIS is good, actually. The hangars are all soundproof," I say as Nym boards the ramp out of the launch bay and back into House's dock. The muscles in her face are already beginning to relax a little; she must have missed her home. I turn the wheel that controls the wide hangar doors, and they slide closed with a sleek hum. All the bustle and chaos of the ship vanishes behind the wall. "Are you okay?"

"Yes." Nym unwraps one of her arms and caresses the railing absentmindedly. "I'm sorry about before. I don't know what's wrong with me."

"It can't be the terrifying predator hunting us down."

She smiles reluctantly. "No, that can't be it."

But then her expression twists into horror, and I look down before I can stop myself. My shirt is slashed to ribbons, the white fabric brown-red. The nearly invisible lines of my stitches have been replaced by sinewy black threads, hanging loose like I'm a rag doll being torn in half. *Not real,* I shove into my mind, but I can taste blood in my mouth. I can *feel it,* the phantom slice of the Shadow's whip against my skin, the stitches pulling me apart.

"No—stop—*stop*—" Nym's hands shake as she flattens

them against the wounds. The illusions melt away from her touch.

"This is my last clean shirt, you know." I force down the tremor in my voice. "I don't know why you're so bent on ruining it."

Nym doesn't laugh as she backs away from me. "I'm losing control."

"Don't do that. You're not losing control."

"I *am*. Don't let me look at you." She stumbles around House's gravity core, hiding herself behind the column. "I'm not even using words anymore; I'm just *thinking* it, and it's there. It's not supposed to—it never—"

"Hey. Listen to me. We already escaped from the Shadow once, right? And that was when it was just the two of us. We'll protect you. I'll..." I lean against the other side of the core, the bronze separating us warm against my neck. "Think of something happy instead. Think of after. You'll be free."

I can hear the frown in Nym's response. "Free?"

"The Shadow will be gone. The Medyssians won't have to hide anymore, right?"

She inhales sharp and surprised. "I didn't even think of that. I've only been thinking of going home. But if the Shadow were killed... it's true. The barrier could come down."

"Exactly." My heart hammers in my throat. *Say it, coward.* "And I've been thinking... well, maybe..." She'll say no. She'll say no and it'll crush me, but only for a moment. If I don't say anything at all, living in the nebulous what-if will crush me forever.

"Stay here," I blurt out. "After. Stay here with us. With... with me."

House's balloon is the only thing that breathes.

"Aren," Nym says. "I can't. My family—"

"Bring them," I reply quickly. "Bring everyone. You can all stay here; it's not like we don't have room. And if they're anything like you, they'll fit in perfectly—you know they will. You can all explore the universe the way you used to, and…" I swallow. "Well, what do you think?"

She says nothing. I wonder if the gears are at work inside her head; I wonder if she's seeing the same imagined future as I am. Maybe she doesn't want it. Maybe even if I figured out the right way to tell her she's the only thing that's ever made me feel safe in this world, she wouldn't feel the same.

Forget it, I'm about to say. *I'm sorry. Just forget it.* But then—

"I want that," she says, "more than anything."

My heart leaps. "Then—"

"I want it," she continues, "but not at this cost."

"But there's not going to be a—"

"Listen to me!" Nym cries, and suddenly she's in front of me, eyes sparking, jaw tight. "You think this is going to end without blood just because you want it to. It's gotten stronger, Aren. *Someone* is going to die."

"They're not. You've never seen the Celestial Company fight—you'll see. You will," I snap stubbornly. "What other choice do you have, anyway?"

The second the words are out of my mouth, I realize my mistake. Because there is another choice. One I already talked her out of. But that was hours ago, before I knew my map wouldn't work. Before the sound of the Shadow approaching crept into Nym's mind, filling her with the kind of fear that turns my crew into ghosts. And now—

"Don't." I seize her wrists. "I know what you're thinking. Don't. I won't let you."

She looks down at our hands like they're a species she

doesn't recognize. "You know, it would have been a nice dream," she whispers, "staying here forever."

I don't realize what's happening until it's over. I don't hear any kind of warning *clink* of metal; I hardly even feel the movement. All I know is that one moment, Nym's pulse is caught in my hands, my heartbeat an out-of-practice drum pounding accompaniment.

And in the next, her hands are wrenched free, and I'm pushed back against the gravity core, my own pinned behind me. Something cold and sharp and tight clamps around my wrists.

"What—" I twist in numb shock. My wrists are bound together by a set of hypermagnetic cuffs, the kind that seek each other and fuse automatically the moment they touch skin. I strain, but they don't give a millimeter. "Did you just—"

"I'm sorry." The whites of Nym's eyes glisten. "I can't let anyone get hurt because of me. Especially you."

"What is this, another illusion? Turn it off. *Now.*"

"It's not an illusion. They're from the armory."

"They're…" I strain against the cuffs, but they bite into flesh, unyielding. "Are you *kidding me?*"

"I transformed into it once, and I can do it again. I can fight it."

"You're going to get yourself killed!"

"Better me than any of you!" Nym cries. "I never should have let you come with me into the Ghost Ship. I was selfish. I've always been selfish. I won't be again."

"You—" I will the chains to be an illusion. That's what they do—they trick you, make you feel things that aren't there. But the chains don't dissolve no matter how hard I struggle; they just cut deeper. "My mother is getting ready to fight," I pant. "This is what the Celestial Company does. They *fight.*

They never fail."

"But Captain Valyra did fail. She fought the Shadow before, and it got away."

"She was younger then," I snap dismissively. "She *wants* this fight, she thinks she's making up for the one failure that haunts her. You're not doing her a favor by leaving. You don't have to do this."

"And what about everyone else? How can I ask you to risk any part of your family just so I can get back to mine?"

I don't care. I don't know what's more of a knife in my gut: her challenge, or my reaction to it. *I don't care.* The knife twists deeper. Because of course I care. I do. They're my family, my crew, the only home I've ever known. And yet, I would still let the Shadow come for us all if it meant protecting her. What does that mean? What does that say about me?

I stop struggling against the cuffs and sag against the gravity core. "Don't do this," I say quietly. "Please. Don't go. At least let me come with you."

"Take care of House. Take care of each other." Nym takes a step forward, close enough to touch if I could. This is wrong, all wrong. I don't want to remember her this way, with tears in her eyes and a human skin she's trapped herself in, gliding straight toward death. I want to remember her the way we were out in space, both of us free and blissful, with starlight in her hair and a whirlwind of fish behind her.

I wish I'd never met her. I wish I'd known her my entire life.

She reaches down, and for a breathless moment I think she's changed her mind, that she's going to let me go. But instead, she unclasps my belt and pulls it free. Every tool I have, every chance I might have had to fight against the mechanism binding me here, clatters to the floor.

"Goodbye, Aren," Nym whispers, and then I'm alone in the dark.

CHAPTER 33

Nym

*T*HIS *is a story about a monster, and a girl who wandered too far. It starts like this.*

Once there were creatures who swam between stars, but now they are gone.

Well. All except one.

It's cold out in the void. It's never felt cold to me before. It's never felt like anything but a thousand strings tugging me infinitely in every direction, begging me to follow.

But now it's cold, and all the strings are gone but one, and it has a voice I know well.

I'll find you, it seems to croon. *I'll find you.*

Well, I'm coming to find it first.

I should be afraid, as I swim into that purple sky, but I'm not. Even if the Shadow does take me, it will sink back into hibernation once I'm gone. It will sleep for a thousand years; it will starve, just as it was already starving. And one day, when it's safe, the barrier will open and the rest of my family will swim between stars again.

And Aren… Aren will be safe, too. I will blink out of his universe, and his life will go on. By the end of it, I will be one small, half-forgotten adventure in a whole tapestry full of them.

The nebula rolls in like a gray fog above a lake.

I pull up short just to look at it, just to watch the way it blossoms into view, eating the sky.

It has grown. Lightning rips free of it in crackling spears. It was a sunburst the first time I saw it, but now it's been poisoned. There's not a single color left, nothing but gray and black, like all the smoke of the Ghost Ship has spilled out and tainted it. Even as I watch, the storm seems to exhale, its cloudy edges unfurling. Reaching for me. That dismal wail crawls from its depths.

I'll find you.

Another spiderweb of lightning shudders across the sky, and in it I see the dim shape of the beast the storm conceals. I see sails and a mast and a bow like an unhinged jaw, jagged teeth exposed. Tentacles spill from its sides, great rotting worms feeding on the wood. The lightning fades, and so does the mirage, leaving nothing but smoke.

"You've found me," I tell the twisted voice of the Shadow before it can repeat its persistent threat. I've been running away from this moment for my entire life, but I'm not running anymore.

Another flash of lightning; another flash of tentacles.

"Come out," I call to the depths. "Come out, come away."

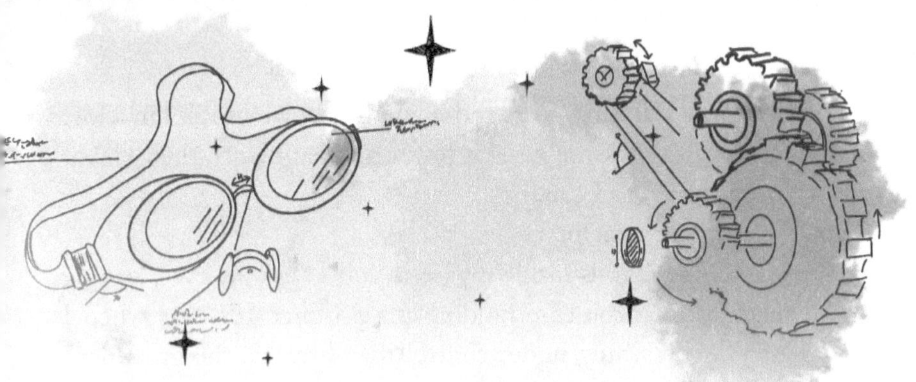

CHAPTER 34

Aren

"Come on—come on—*no*—"

I let out a hoarse cry as my tool belt slips away from my boot for what feels like the eightieth time. My voice is barely a rasp now; extinguished from too long spent calling for someone, anyone to hear me from inside a soundproof vacuum. My arms are on fire, my wrists slick with sweat.

This isn't working. And I'm running out of time.

There's an easy choice here. There's one that says, *Good, fine, go then. I don't care.* There's a choice that lets her be a martyr, that knows bravely sacrificing yourself for the good of an entire crew is the right—the only right—thing to do.

I don't care. I know with a certainty I've never felt before that I will never be a worthy enough captain, and it won't be because I'm weak or anxious or wear specs to chase away darkness. It'll be because in this moment, even if it puts the *Starsaviour* and everyone inside it in danger, even if it gets me killed instead, I can't just let her go.

The next time I try to loop the belt back over my foot, it skitters out of reach instead.

Panic turns my thoughts red. I pull against the chains as I try to *think, think, come on*, but they refuse to yield. Another guttural yell rips free, and I shuffle down until I'm close enough to kick the nearest tower of alien plants, then kick it over as hard as I can.

It doesn't help.

A groan roils inside my head, and I shut my eyes, leaning back against the core holding me prisoner. It's only when I get my breathing under control that I realize the groan isn't coming from me.

I open my eyes a crack, squint up at the ceiling. The balloon is wavering, ropes rustling softly, like a creature emerging from a deep slumber. I must have stirred the engine into power.

The ropes whine again, the sound somehow more urgent. Accusing, almost. I frown. Ropes can't sound accusing. The ropes shouldn't be moving at all.

I focus in on them, searching for the optical illusion. But no, they're straining against the basket, and the balloon is shuddering, and we're in a vacuum. We're inside a hold with no wind or movement, and House is moving despondently. On its own.

My frown deepens.

House might be Nym's home, but it's just a ship. It can't be anything but just a ship.

But she always talked to it, about it, like it was sentient. Like it could somehow understand her.

"House," I say. I can't believe I'm doing this—I really must be out of ideas. "I don't know if you can hear me or understand me, or whatever. But if you can, you have to help me. You have to let me go."

With the smallest hint of a creak, the basket rotates to the left. Then back to the right. Like a head shaking no.

My breath catches in my throat. I thought Nym was just lonely and desperate for something to talk to, but was it more than that? Is there something in this core that's *alive?* She's made of something strange and magical. Maybe her ship is too.

"I know why she left me behind. But if I don't get out of here soon, she'll die. And if you…" *Can ships care? Do they feel?* "…have any kind of bond with her, you have to let me go bring her back. Don't you care what happens to her?"

The ropes creak furiously again, and this time, there can be no mistake as to what it means.

"Just let me save her." I clench my fingers behind my back, nails biting into my palms. "Let me bring her back, and you can both go home." I wait for another groan, another whine. "House? I know you can hear me. *Answer* me."

But nothing comes. No creaks from the floor, no straining of the ropes. Just my own ragged breathing.

I sigh and tip my head back. I don't know what I expected. It's still just a ship, and it's as trapped in this hold as I am.

Something tremors against my spine.

Like an engine, or a heartbeat.

I tilt forward again. It's in the floor, the walls, the column behind me. An earthquake coursing through every fiber of wood. The ropes shudder; the canvas flaps in an invisible wind.

"House?"

A howl bursts from somewhere under the floorboards and up through the gravity core. The tall pillar sways violently against its harness, fighting like a caged animal. Fabric and string rip free from its branches. A thick slit rents its way through Nym's painted map.

"House, what are you doing?" I try to shout, but my voice is too hoarse and the wind is too loud.

An avalanche of wood erupts above my head, burying tiny chips in my hair.

The core. It's tearing itself in half. Even as I watch, the ropes strain and pull, deepening the cut even further. And the canvas map, caught in the tug of war between veins and spine, fractures in three, five, twelve more places. Trinkets rain down around me; careful recreations of planets and stars disappear in long strips. All the remnants of Nym's journey, destroyed.

And then, with a bone-shattering moan, the last sinewy strands of wood holding it together snap free.

I turn and duck just in time, pulling my knees in as much as I can. But I hear the pillar crash through the side of the balloon behind me, hear the rest of the map come tumbling to the floor. Sawdust falls like snow; glass sinks pinprick nails into my neck.

And then, finally, silence. No soothing exhale of the balloon. No otherworldly heartbeat in the floorboards. And when I do resurface, I'm in a canvas ocean. The map lies around me in lifeless folds, paint peeling from its edges.

I stumble to my feet and feel my bound arms thud against my back. I'm free.

The core has been cleaved through just a few feet from the base, like a felled tree. A flicker of starlight winks through the breach it's made in the wall.

House let me go, and it destroyed itself to do it.

"I'm so sorry," I say, even as I make for my tool belt and rummage through it behind my back. "I'll—I'll come back. I'll fix you." It's a promise I don't know if I can keep, and I don't even know if it's heard. If House still has a sentience, a soul, it's gone dim and unresponsive.

But I can still feel its own promise, its own accusation, lingering in the dusty air. *Don't make this worth nothing*, it says, and I won't.

I'll find you.

A pin is in one hand, a magnetic destabilizer in the other.

I'll find you.

The cuffs spring free and fall to the ground.

You owe me a better goodbye.

I leap over the mass of canvas, slam open the bay door, burst into the blinding light of the loading dock.

I practically fall off the ramp, and I crash right into my mother.

"Where have you been?" Valyra grabs me by the shoulders and shakes me fiercely, and I'm grateful for it; I can barely hold myself up without the support. Her ivory coat is only half-buttoned and her weapon isn't fastened into its holster properly. "Why are you—" Her wild expression changes shape as she takes in my own clothing, torn yet again, and the way I'm wearing my own blood like a pair of gloves. "The girl. Where is she?"

"She's gone," I gasp, clutching my stomach, not even realizing the implications of what she's saying until I've answered. *The girl.* She knows. She found out somehow. "She went after it. I should have told you everything, I'm so sorry—"

Her eyes blaze, and I know she's going to rage at me for lying to her, tell me how much jeopardy I've placed the crew in.

"Okay," she says, "then we've got no time to lose."

CHAPTER 35

Nym

THE first thing I see is the eels.

They're nothing but long black ribbons draped between the shards of the Ghost Ship's teeth. Their bulbous eyes leer, and their teeth glint, but I touch down in their midst and wait for them to hiss and scatter. It's only when they don't move at all, when their creeping gaze doesn't break, that I see they're all dead.

Dried blood is drawn in streaks across their glistening bodies; discarded organs trail from hide cracked open like a leaking egg. How desperately starving the Shadow must have become to feast on such a rancid offering. How much stronger it must be now.

No matter. The stronger it is, the stronger I will be when I steal its form.

I frown at the hideous carcasses, then whisper a cloak for them until they're not limp corpses, but roots covered in tiny flowers. There is no reason to be careful anymore. There is no more hiding.

I transform the rest of the shrapnel too, growing trees out of metal until the Ghost Ship's mouth is a forest. Branches curve into an arc over my head, turn this ledge into an enchanted doorway to another world. Through the leaves, deteriorating ships sail past, and I can almost imagine they're not deteriorating at all. I can pretend they're every vessel I've ever passed in the night, every port I've ever docked at searching for answers, come back to usher me toward the end.

"Come out," I call out again. "Isn't this what you wanted? To find me? I'm here."

My own voice echoes back. *I'm here. I'm here. I'm here.*

I leap over the edge, painting an illusion behind me.

I think of every flower I've ever seen across the galaxy, of purple oceans crashing against the shore, of ice fortresses that stretched into the clouds. I think of everything that has ever made me happy, and with it, I make the Shadow's lair my own.

I think of my painted starmap, imagining every detail and imperfection, and I cover the ceiling of this terrible ship with it. I hang mirages of glowing lanterns from the gray rafters. I remember every trinket I've collected and the memory I collected along with it, and I bring all of those to life too. Friis, with its gardens grown over with moss, tended by metal giants. Andanere, where the air tasted like frost. Cosalia, and the boy who gave me mushrooms. I breathe color back into graying hulls, I wash away rust, I mend torn sails until they glitter and swell. I will the cyclone churning around me into a carousel of my past with myself at the center.

What else? I wonder, spinning to take in the view. *What else do I want to see one more time?*

But I already know.

Maybe now, maybe with nothing left to lose… maybe I can remember them. I deserve it. I deserve to see the faces of my family again.

But when I call the word forth, something strange happens.

The body is right—periwinkle skin and rippling umbra and arms lined with tiny fins. But when it turns toward me, when I wait for the features that have always eluded me… the only face I can see belongs to a boy with blue eyes and bluer hair.

He extends a hand toward me, and the illusions around me flicker for the first time.

Stay, Aren pleads in my head. *Stay with me.*

I do not feel the first tremors of the earthquake beneath me. I only feel the final convulsion, and then the floor beneath me splinters and bursts.

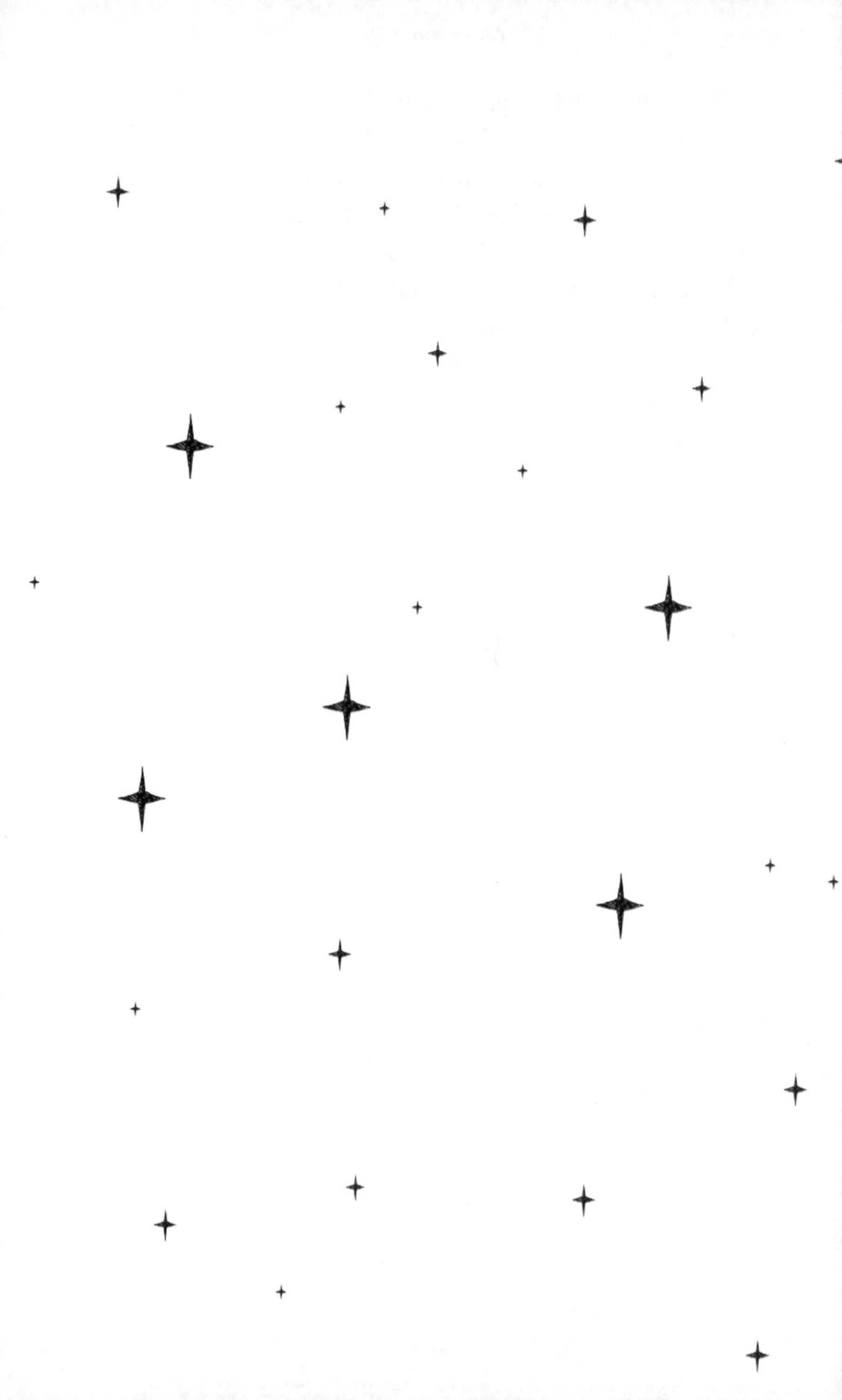

CHAPTER 36

Nym

I stand my ground as the memory of Aren vanishes, sliced through by a tentacle thick enough to drag an entire ship from the sky. The rest of the Shadow rises beneath it, just as bone-white as I remember, but no longer skeletal. Its skin ripples now, as though the souls of the dozens of eels it has devoured in my absence are trapped inside its stomach, straining to be free. And above is the leering, bloodstained mouth, and from inside it leaks a voice, no, a *feeling*. It's—

So happy. So, so happy to have found me.

It's been waiting for me. Craving me.

"I'm not afraid of you anymore," I whisper, and then I lunge.

I'm ready this time. I know what the inside of its head feels like, I know what sort of rabid destruction my thoughts will turn to, and I will not lose control. I stretch my fingers forward, ready to absorb the ghastly shape of it, and—

My arm is wrenched back, something sinuous and invisible wrapped around my wrist.

I strain against it in confusion—there's nothing there, nothing at all, so what has me?—before I realize what's happening. My illusions have coated the ship, giving me courage, but in doing so, they've cloaked all other threats. I banish them all, but it's too late—the prying ribbons of seaweed that once clung to the Ghost Ship's walls have slithered through the graveyard, grown strong and hungry as the Shadow itself.

And they're attacking me.

I claw at the vine around my forearm, but another ensnares my wrist, then a third, then a fourth, until my arms are tattooed with gray-green swirls. I wrench one loose with a snap, but there are too many, and with every inch I free myself there is the rubbery latch of another. "No—*no*—"

A coil winds its way up my back, around my neck, over my mouth.

My scream is trapped in my head, but still I struggle, because it cannot be over this quickly, I cannot have lost so soon. I was supposed to fight it. I was supposed to win. I promised Aren, my family, myself. I *promised*.

The Shadow tilts its monstrous head, then slowly, slowly lowers itself before me. Its dead-branch arms crack away from its body. Its hollow smile peels wide. Wanting me. Hungering for me. So, so happy to have found me.

Please, I think, and I fill my head with thoughts of home, of House, of Aren. I will it to do what it's never done before, and recognize reasons to live. *Please, please.*

The Shadow lifts one cadaverous hand and presses its cold, sharp fingers into my chest.

It opens its mouth.

It *screams.*

Its claws go icy at the tips, colder, colder, until they're the kind of cold that burns like fire. I gasp at the sear, and even though I don't want to look, don't want this to be the last thing I ever see, I look anyway.

I look, and I see the deaths of hundreds of Medyssians

who were lost before me.

The Shadow is sapping the skin from my body; I can see the silvery-lavender haze draining right into its hand. It's feeding on me, *stealing* me—all I can feel is the burn of its hunger as it siphons my essence away. And it screams, screams, screams, nails on metal, strings of an instrument snapping, rusted trap shutting over prey. It does not stop.

Light pours out of me and into it, and I was wrong, I was wrong, I thought I was brave and selfless and strong, but I should never have left Aren. We should have fought together. We might have won.

Now I'll never know.

But then…

Then.

The coil around my waist loses just a breath of its pressure. The ones around my neck and mouth loosen as well, ever so slightly.

The Shadow howls once more.

And I look down and see that the tentacle is receding away from me, back toward its starved body, and—

No.

It isn't.

It's…*fading.*

It loses its solidity entirely; it goes milky and transparent and drops me to the ground. I stare up at it in horror, at all of those tentacles widening, flattening, shrinking at the same time. The lavender stain creeps up the Shadow's body, up its clawed hands, up its leering mouth, which stitches itself closed seamlessly. Its arms are outstretched, its head tilted back in some sort of strange ecstasy.

What's happening to it?

What has it done to *me?*

Suddenly, the silvery light leaps to the Shadow's pointed claws, tracing its protruding veins. Starlight drifts across its skin until it outlines every edge, leaving all the in-between shimmering and ethereal. And the tentacles…

The tentacles complete their painful, writhing conversion. The flat curves join together and explode outward, and when they settle, they're not tentacles at all.

They're *umbra*.

And the creature's chest splits in half, and something else begins to claw its way out. Something silver and gasping, something with opal eyes like mine, fluttering ears like mine, stardust hair like mine.

Halfway out of its mouth, its endless shriek settles into something else. Not a scream. A song. Swirling notes, up and down and never settling. Something else that's mine.

I'm off the ground and floating before I even realize I've moved. The force of the creature's transformation creates a wind that beats against me, but I fight it. It can't be… it can't.

But that's my face. That's my form.

The Shadow is…

The Shadow is…

The Shadow came for them all.

Well. All except one.

The story, *my* story, the one that's guided me across the universe, scrolls desperately through my memory, but something else joins the familiar words. An important thing I lost long before I ever began my desperate search.

A memory about where this story came from.

Another truth I had once known that I locked away deep inside. The creature's luminous hair grows in soft waves, her mouth opens into a half-formed "oh" of disbelief, and I remember.

That story was never about me.

I was never the last Medyssian.

Nym

THIS *is a story about a monster, and a girl who wandered too far. It starts like this.*

Once there were...

No.

That's wrong. My story is different, and always has been, and this was how it started.

Once there was a girl who dreamed of the world above.

Once there was a girl, and she was very young, too young to understand fear or loss or despair. She came from a planet that was beautiful and serene, full of color and life and light. She had lived to see six cycles of a faint, cloudy sun that appeared like a mirage in the sky every day, calling to the girl.

What is it? she would ask. *What's up there?*

Nothing, her sisters would say. She was the youngest of seven. Her sisters were wise and good and would never lie. *Nothing is up there. There is only us.*

But she was curious. Insatiable. She wouldn't stop asking.

Something was calling to her.

Something wanted her to come see.

Finally, the eldest sister took pity on the girl. All others had forgotten the truth, a truth that had been locked away with whispered illusions long ago, but not the eldest. She had a secret she refused to let be ripped from her. She held her youngest sister's hand and asked if she could keep that secret, and she brought her to a cave full of strange objects the girl had never seen before. *From other worlds*, her sister said. *From the universe above.*

I want to see, said the girl. *I knew there was more. I want to see.*

You can't, said her sister, *not ever. Not until it's safe.*

Why? The girl was stubborn, fascinated.

Her sister hesitated. The girl was young, naïve. Her head was too full of fairy tales and dreams. *It is a terrible story.*

Tell me. Tell me the story.

Her sister hesitated again, thinking of the past, of an outside world that had once been warm and inviting but had turned cold and bleak. Of a way she could make her young, naïve sister with her head full of fairy tales understand. Finally, she sighed.

Once, she said, *there were creatures who swam between stars.*

At the end of the story, the sister left the cave, certain she had scared the girl's questions into submission.

The girl stayed behind. She looked at the otherworldly collection surrounding her, and she heard a thousand voices beckoning her up, up, *come away, come see.*

She thought of the darkness her sister had described, of the strange monster they called the Shadow that had been so hungry and cruel that it chased everyone into hiding long before she had ever been born. But mostly, she thought of a universe so big and wondrous that you could spend a million lifetimes traversing it and never reach the end. If there was really a monster up there, how could it ever find one tiny, hidden planet?

She wanted to see it, this universe above. She wanted to know what was on the other side of the barrier.

She decided to swim up and see. Just once. Just for a moment. No one would ever know. One look, and perhaps the endless beckoning would quiet.

So, she did.

She stole an ancient vessel, and she slipped through the atmosphere, and she found the universe splayed out before her in all its glory. She saw a forest of stars in a pastel sky; she saw the bright whorls of galaxies and the shimmering streaks of comets. She heard the voice of space itself singing to her, calling her by name. The ether swept her into its arms, led her in dance. And as she twirled, drifted, laughed, she sighed with content, knowing the memory of her small adventure would be enough to last her until the barrier could open completely.

Perhaps it was mere moments, when she finally turned for home. Perhaps it was more.

But when she turned, Medyssia was gone.

The girl reached out a hand, expecting to see the barrier shimmer to life under her fingertips, and felt nothing.

She called out its name, and the universe was silent.

She searched and searched, roaming the sky, and found no trace.

She was lost. Lost in the world she had thought she'd give anything to be part of, helpless as the ever-shifting cosmos continued to sweep her away. And when the storm came, when it tossed her like a bottle into the maw of the universe, she could not stop it.

I'll come back, she cried out to her family. *I'll find you. I'll find you.*

And as she wandered, she began to tell herself a story, so she would not forget. The only story she knew about the outside world. One that would remind her to be cautious, to stay hidden, to never stop trying to get home.

A story about a monster, and a girl who had wandered too far.

CHAPTER 38

Nym

*I*T *was never me.*

The world is a violet haze. I realize my eyes are blurred with tears and brush them away, and the pale nucleus of that haze becomes a person. This thing I thought was the Shadow… it's a Medyssian. The *real* last Medyssian. Her umbra fans out around her; her eyes are closed. She looks like a sleeping princess waiting to be woken from a curse. The first Medyssian I've seen since… since.

She is the one who was lost. She was the one left behind when the planet was hunted into hiding. I gave myself her story, tricked myself into thinking I was a tragic wanderer, abandoned in the ether. But I am nothing but a restless, foolish child who ran away and regretted it. I remember.

I remember my father's eyes, twinkling like constellations. He taught me to love music; he found it in the whisper of scagrass and the echo of an unexplored cave and the hum of the creatures that burrowed beneath the sand. He would fashion flutes out of shells and play me to sleep, make up stories so fanciful that I'd giggle in fits. And my mother, with hair so long that fish would tangle themselves in the snarls, her umbra constantly stained because she would collect inky little crawlers from the reef and hide them in the folds for me to find. I remember their voices through the windows of the pearly house in the trees, singing for me to *come home, come home* whenever I strayed too close to the surface.

The lost girl, the last Medyssian, coughs.

I float toward her cautiously. No trace of the monster she had been remains. Slowly, her eyes flutter open. Her hands lift to her face, and she turns them from back to palm, examining the smooth, clawless fingers. One drops to her mouth, and a sob chokes out. Then, her gaze shifts to me.

"Auri…" She fights to speak. "You… came back for me."

Auri. *Aurelia.* That was my oldest sister's name. They *knew each other*, the story and the storyteller. "I—I'm not her. I'm Nym." Do I look like them, my forgotten family? Have I been carrying them with me all this time?

"Auri." I have to strain to hear her, so weak from disuse is her voice. "I should have… gone with you. I'm sorry… you were *right…*"

"Right about what?"

"Couldn't become… more than one." Her fingers flex toward her heart. "Went… too far."

"What do you mean, more than one?" I ask, but her Shadow-form flashes before my eyes, and I remember how sickening it was the first time I saw it. Those tentacles, those claws, the maggot-skull. The mouth that seemed to leak poison. All those parts that didn't fit, sewn artlessly into one. "Did you… did you try to transform into more than one creature at once? Is that how you became that—that *thing?*" That's impossible. It ought to have ripped her molecules apart. It *did* rip her apart, in a way, if I understand what she means. Replacing her umbra with one creature's tentacles, her back with another's spine, her teeth with another's fangs. Calling all those monsters of the deep toward her and stealing all of their worst parts. "Why?"

"Wanted to be… terrible enough…" The girl's eyes close as though her own memories are too heavy to contain. "… to scare it away forever."

To scare what away? I'm about to ask, but I know the answer. This story still has a piece missing. The real Shadow, whatever it is—that's what chased her. That's what she tried to become more monstrous than, in order to defend herself. "But why didn't you change back? Why have you been like this since… since…" I can't even remember how long I've been lost. How long must it have been for her, without even her mind to anchor her?

The girl's delicate fingers crawl up her throat and rest in the hollow, to that place where the dustmoth settled when I first saw her. A sad hum grates against her vocal chords. And I understand. I understand and I recoil from it, stomach turning in revulsion. It doesn't make sense. It disobeys physics, logic, reason. But I know why she couldn't change back. That thing I followed—it wasn't the lure of a monster. It was her *voice*, ripped from her throat by something I no longer have a face for, imprisoned in glass, then lost forever. Without it, she was trapped, unable to harness the melody to transform back. If I had not mistakenly set it free, it would be lost to her still.

"The Shadow steals voices." I imagine myself imprisoned in a form that isn't mine eternally, unable to even scream, and flinch away from it. The thought alone is as claustrophobic as one of Aren's starwalking suits. "It stole yours."

And I can see it all. I can see her, years younger, imagining herself into a monster until she forgot she'd ever been anything else. My sister never forgot her friend, though. She turned her into a cautionary tale, preserved her in its lyrics. "And then you were lost."

A tear slips free and curves down her temple. "Lost," she repeats, or maybe mimics. "Lost."

"I thought I was the only one left." I don't mean it to come out as a whimper, but it does. "But then why did you attack us, once your voice had been returned? Why did you…" My words fall away, because no, she didn't attack us, did she? She attacked Aren. The stranger. Never me. "You were trapped for so long, you forgot your own melody. You needed to touch me, so you could remember how to be a Medyssian again."

She turns her head, frowning as though seeing me for the first time. "Auri?" she mumbles. "You came back for me?"

"No, I'm… I'm her sister. I'm Nym." I squeeze her hand. "We'll find Auri, okay? There's this map… it'll lead us home. We'll never be lost again."

"We'll never—" A hoarse, crackling cough tears out of the other girl's dry lips, and it's only when it doesn't stop that I realize it's something resembling laughter. It clears away her throat, relieves her of the rasp that's been hindering her speech. "—we'll never make it," she finishes. "They'll find us again. One already found you."

"Don't say that. Of course, we can—" I pause as her words sink in. "What are you talking about?"

Another sandpaper laugh. "*The Shadow.*"

A chill traces its way down my spine. The unfinished story, the emptiness that demands to be filled. "But if you weren't the Shadow," I whisper, "who is?"

The girl pulls her hand out of my grasp and presses herself away from the floor, long hair trailing.

"You forgot," she says quietly. "You forgot what to run from."

"No, I didn't," I stammer. "Auri told me it's—it's a monster, a great, awful creature who sailed in a beastly ship like this."

"Don't be a child, Aurelia," she hisses. "The Shadow isn't a creature. It's a *symbol.*" And then, worst of worst in a sentence already filled with poison: "That human wears it."

That human. Who… *Aren?*

No. *No.*

Him, the Shadow? Impossible. He is the farthest thing from monstrous. I *know* him. He bears no dark symbol. He—

Ice carves into the base of my own neck as I remember what's carved into *his.*

A tattoo. Two Cs, for the Celestial Company.

Or two crescent moons, overlapping each other. One light, one dark.

One bright, and one… one in shadow.

"You know that's what we called it." The Medyssian girl strains to conjure a smoky mirage in the air between us, and if my own memory isn't enough of a confirmation, there it is. Those two moons. The ones that were everywhere, on Aren's neck, on Cas's wrist, the flags, the sails, the banisters. A hundred moons casting a hundred shadows. "That mark all the hunters wore."

I am unraveling.

The story I took as truth misled me. It was never anything but a tale for a child, because that's what I was. My sister knew I would never understand danger if she presented it to me as it was, so she wrapped it in fantasy. And it still didn't work. I still ran straight toward it. Toward *her.*

The only one that got away from me. I hear Valyra's voice in my head, that hatred and shame in her eyes when she told Aren about the monster that escaped her. *I'll finish what I meant to.* Us. She was talking about us. She's the one who hunted us into extinction and chased us into hiding. She and her loyal crew, her shadows.

"We have to go," I gasp, seizing the other Medyssian's wrist and yanking her up beside me. "I told them—*things*, I didn't know—"

"They're close," the girl says. "We can't escape them, but that boy… he trusts you. I saw it. We can take him and—"

"No." I scan for something, anything that will make this ship fly. I don't care what mark Aren wears. I won't harm him; I won't do whatever she suggests. "We have to—"

A thin, crackling hum, like a harnessed branch of lightning.

A sharp, surprised "oh" from behind me.

A wrist going limp in my grasp.

I turn and catch the lost girl before she crumples, catch her in time to see her eyes go wide and horrified.

A hole runs straight through her chest.

On the other side, the silver-white orb of her heart pulses against the floor.

"No. No, *no*—" She's too heavy to hold. She pulls me down, and I can't look anywhere but the hole, like a bite taken out of her very core, and it's—

—*growing.*

Eating the skin around itself even as I watch.

Without her heart, her body is a black hole. Stardust returning to its place in the universe.

"No—*no*—" I scoop the heart up and clumsily, foolishly hold it to her chest, as though her body will recognize it and take it back, but the flesh fades beneath my fingertips. She's becoming an illusion herself, right before my eyes.

"No, I just found you," I cry as the translucent river of her blood turns my skin glossy. "We have to go home. Auri, remember? She's home, she's waiting for us. Please, *please*—"

"Go… home," the girl echoes, but the light in her eyes

is going dim and her matter is water slipping through my fingers. "*Go home! Go—*"

But before she can say the final word, her mouth becomes ash.

I stare down at my shaking hands. She can't be gone. I never even learned her name. I just held her, and I just found her, and I promised we'd go home, and just like that, she is nothing.

Now, I am the last Medyssian.

My hands clench into fists, and even before I whirl, I know who's waiting behind me, blaster raised.

"*You,*" I hiss, before my rage liquefies into something worse.

Because Captain Valyra is approaching, as I knew she would, but Aren is beside her.

And his is the weapon that is smoking.

CHAPTER 39

Aren

*Y*OU'RE *okay.*

The blaster hums in my hands as I swim against the vacuum, but I barely hear it. I barely hear anything. All I've got is the steady voice in my head, matching time with my heartbeat.

You're okay, you're okay, you're okay.

It's impossible. Unbelievable. The Shadow, that thing we thought would tear the entire *Starsaviour* to pieces, rendered powerless with one shot. I lined the barrel up toward a figure flattened into nothing but iridescent ripples through the light of my specs. I heard the crack, saw the jubilant grin on my mother's face. My third perfect shot, but the victory hardly means anything to me.

Nym's alive. She's okay.

She'll never have to run again; she can go home—

I pull up short before I reach her.

She's not looking at me. She's pressed to the deck of a ship with enough of a gravity core to keep her from drifting, groping desperately like she's searching for something she lost, her umbra pooled around her.

But then her shoulders shift enough for me to see the

umbra isn't just hers.

There's *two* sets under there, but the second fades into nothing as I watch. And above it is the equally vanishing top half of a face the same shade of palest lavender as Nym's.

Before the terrified, wild eyes turn to smoke too, they look just like hers.

My stomach turns in on itself. There was another Medyssian.

That's what I hit.

"You," Nym hisses as she turns, and for a second, her face is full of a hate I didn't know she was capable of.

"I—I didn't—" I don't understand. Where's the Shadow? How is there another Medyssian? Nym was supposed to be the last one. She said she was the last one. "I—"

I…

I *killed* something.

The blaster tumbles from my hands.

"You see? I knew you could do it." My mother's voice cuts through the air beside me, tender and proud. "I knew it was in you."

"No." My tongue is lead. "I didn't mean--"

But before I can finish, Nym lunges.

I turn in time to see her clearing the distance between us, and in that fraction of a moment, she is something else entirely. Her opal eyes are black and her mouth is curled into a snarl; her incisors are thinner and needle-sharp and her fingernails are claws. Just like I am to myself now, she's someone I don't recognize.

And then she's thrown back. The black doesn't leave her eyes and her sharp edges remain, but she lies on the ground in the settling ash of the other Medyssian, something gold pulsing in her neck. I watch it slide up her throat. Into her mouth.

Through her fangs. Out of her body, pale and fluttering like a bird.

"*Nym!*" I skid down to my knees beside her. "No, no, stop—"

She claws at her throat, but it seizes and nothing comes out. Her fingers dig under mine; panic makes her dark eyes spasm. And that *thing*, whatever escaped from her body, lets out a scream in Nym's voice, and it's the worst thing I've ever heard. It rattles my entire head, cuts into my veins, and then I watch as it sucks away from us. Back. Back. A thin flash of light, like a glare through a prism. And it vanishes.

Into the barrel of Valyra's weapon.

"What are you doing?" She ejects one of the compartments on the side of the blaster, and I catch a flash of something opaque and crystalline sliding out into her fist. Nym's hair, colorless as cinder, is a stain pressed to my shirt. I can see her gasping, but no breath comes out. "*What did you do to her?*"

"Weakened it." *Click, click, click,* come the slow boots behind me. "Without illusions, it doesn't know how to attack."

"Don't!" I shout, one arm out wide. "Don't touch her—"

"Aren. Get up. I'll explain everything, but not while you're acting ridiculous. She's not what you think she is."

"*Explain?* I killed someone, I—I—" Blood pounds in my ears; nausea pounds in my stomach. Whatever Valyra's done to Nym, to that other Medyssian, I let this happen. I *helped her.* I'm the monster now, no matter how the rest of this story goes.

I lunge for the cartridge holding Nym's voice, head filled with the roaring of an engine. It's within reach, when something stings at the base of my neck.

"Wha—" I try to clap my hand over it—it feels like the bite of a venomous predator—but my arm refuses to move. Terror washes over me, starting at my neck and working its way down to my ankles, until I realize it's not just terror. It's some sort of immobilizing agent, the kind used on prisoners meant to be taken alive. I don't feel it as I crumple to the ground, every muscle limp; I only see the way my view shifts until all I can see are those tall black boots, stepping over a gauzy purple sea.

No, I try to yell, *let me go,* but my tongue is also a muscle turned against me. I can do nothing but watch Valyra crouch down to my level.

"I was afraid she'd gotten in your head," she murmurs. "Don't worry. I'll fix you."

CHAPTER 40

Aren

I'VE never wanted so badly to be unconscious.

I thought paralyzing me was the worst thing Valyra was going to do, and I was wrong. Worse was when we got back to the ship. Worse was when I was carried somewhere that smelled familiar, like engine fumes and the staleness of metal. And as I stared at a ceiling coated with churning gears and unfinished pipes, desperately trying to remember how long the immobilizer I'd been injected with would last, *that's* when the worst thing happened.

This is going to hurt.

Something cold and hard crammed between my teeth.

I'm so, so sorry, darling. This will fix everything.

And then it was like an exposed wire had been pressed to every nerve ending in my brain.

It feels like sterilization, this torture. It feels like bleach being poured into every corner of my mind. I can't move, can't think, can't escape it.

I don't know how I know, but it's here for Nym. Every scrap of her in my head.

A burst of electricity blinds me, and I see her, only her. Memories as clear as one of her own illusions, forcing themselves into my mind and across this hunter's path without my permission. I'm not allowed to think of anything else. It's dark as pitch, buzzing with static, and then Nym is chaining me to the mast again. Darkness, and then she twirls me in a circle as we dance through space, something distant in her smile. Crying for me to run as she charges toward the Shadow, wreckage crushing down around me.

Don't take them away, I beg as we float before my father's ship, Nym's hand on my shoulder, because that's what I'm most afraid of: that whatever my mother is doing is stealing the memories right out of my head. *Please, don't take her away.*

The hunter stops giving me time to rest. No more brief flashes of darkness between echoes. My eyelids turn to fireworks, Nym and House and swimming through space and the dome of her past and her voice saying my name like an anchor, like a test. And then I see the moment we met: her upside-down, waving gently, asking me if I'm dead.

I cling to that image, knowing it's the last. It's not just about her. I want to believe I would find her again, even if I forgot everything, like there's an invisible string tying us together across space itself. But I don't want to lose how far I've already come. I don't want to go back to who I was before I met her. I can't. *I won't.*

But when the electric sharpness fades from my head like a dial being turned down to zero, every moment is still in place. My ears ring with white noise, but I search frantically through my own history and don't find any holes. I can still trace every second that was ours.

I gasp—in relief, in exhaustion, I don't know. When I try to flex my fingers, they respond too, though the movement is weak and trembling.

I force my head to the side, give myself a different view

than the cogs and gears clicking steadily above me. An entire wall of humming engines and churning mechwork greets me, and beneath that, a jumble of broken machine parts and half-empty vials. Towers of tools, bare lightbulbs, boxes without lids. It looks like a whirlwind has swept through this room, tearing through it and leaving only chaos in its wake, but I suddenly know exactly where I am. My workshop. I'm lying on my own table, and my peripheral vision is full of wires.

"You're awake."

The voice sends a worse electric jolt through me. I strain my neck, millimeter by millimeter, until I see her.

She's draped over a nearby chair, watching me sleep the way she used to when I was a kid. But I don't see a woman who was ever my mother at all anymore. Only a monster.

"Let." My teeth are gritted together so hard I can practically taste blood. "Me. Go."

The monster leans forward, plucks the bit from my mouth. "How are you feeling?"

"Where is she?" I rasp. "What did you do to her?"

She frowns. "The enchantment should have worn off. Your mind should be yours by now."

"What are you talking about?" I drill my fists into the table's surface. I can get up. I have to get up. *Come on—*

"Do you know who you are?" Valyra asks carefully. "Do you know who I am?"

I'd laugh if I wasn't certain it would hurt my ribs. "I'm Aren Vanthal"—I can no longer stand the surname—"and you're the woman who *immobilized and tortured your own son.*"

"Aren, I've gone through that myself. I know it hurts. I told you how sorry I was. But I just saved you, and you will understand that when you decide to listen."

"I have no interest in listening to you, unless you're telling me where she—"

But the last syllable falls off, because the answer is *here.* Nym's here.

She's in a glass column—the one I've been using as a chalkboard for years. Only all my notes have been smeared away, and it's not a glass column at all. It never was. It's a *tank,* completely transparent now that it's illuminated from within. And she's awake, alive, but she's a scrabbling blur, prying desperately at every inch of the walls and floor. She sees me and presses both palms to the glass, screams something shaped like my name. And in the pause, all her blurred edges focus, just as wrong as they were in the moment Valyra stole her voice. Her eyes black, her nails sharp, her skin gray and color-bleached instead of luminous. The ethereal girl from the stars gone, all her light drained away.

It's all my arms can do not to buckle. "What did you do to her?"

"I did nothing."

"Let her go." I snatch as many padded wires as I can reach with one grasp and yank them all loose. "Let her go right now."

"Aren, you need to listen to me." Valyra swoops over and grabs my wrist. "Calm down."

"Don't *touch me.*" I slap her hand away. "Tell me it wasn't you. That monster that hunted Nym's planet into hiding. That faceless thing she's been running from."

Valyra folds her hand back under the crook of her elbow. She says nothing.

"I'm so stupid." I push myself away from her and stagger toward Nym. "They call you *the Shadow,* did you know that? They think you're something so deadly they don't even have a name for it, you—" I can't finish. I know Valyra. Inspiring that much fear will only give her some kind of sick pride.

But—"Is that what I am to you?" she asks, and there's an unexpected confusion in her voice. "You think I just… just picked an entire species at random and hunted them down for no reason? You think I'm nothing but a heartless murderer?"

That sort of plea might have worked on me before, but never again. Of course, that's what she is. They must have gotten in her way somehow, or maybe she wanted to harness their abilities for herself. It doesn't matter. I won't let her manipulate me.

"Tell me how to open it," I snap. There's no mechanism on this thing to break, no console to override. "I don't want to hear anything else you have to say."

"Fine." Valyra's distorted reflection vanishes from the tank, and then the silence is filled with the whirring hum of something mechanical. "Then don't."

I turn in immediate panic, but it's not a new weapon she's pointing at us. It's a holographic protector—the same kind of sphere that powers the training room.

"You don't have to hear me." She sets it down on the floor. "You just have to watch."

A thousand shards of gold erupt from the device.

I put an arm up instinctively, but as the dust settles into place, I see they're nothing but beads of light connected in a pointillist hologram. And though I can still see the outline of the gear-lined chamber, there's an overlay of a ship settled over it. It's not the *Starsaviour*—it's much smaller and plainer, empty of all the noise and color I'm used to. Stars paper the walls; a quiet breeze threads through the threadbare sails. It almost looks like the device I invented myself, to keep watch over the ship. But this one is a captured memory, preserved in a hologram.

"*Mission S14, log one,*" I hear from somewhere I can't see.

"Recording."

"What is this?" I demand.

Valyra doesn't look at me. The hologram lines up with the table, making it look like she's leaning against a phantom staircase. "Just watch."

I tense under the gently swaying ropes. There's nothing *to* watch—I could see the same view from our own top deck.

"It's gonna be okay," I whisper to Nym, though I don't know if she can hear me. Will she even trust me anymore? After what I've done? "I'll get you out."

"Val it's been hours. This is pointless," comes a voice from somewhere I can't see. *"It's not showing tonight. Let's just go back to bed."*

The end of my own sentence trails away. That voice. I've never heard it before, I'm positive, but it triggers something—a memory, maybe. Or just an instinct.

"Will you stop complaining?" A second voice—this one I know. I peer carefully around the tube, and there she is. A copy of my mother, a relic from decades in the past. Her hair is in a complicated braid, and a pale crescent moon charm hangs from a chain around her neck. She's leaning against the central mast, one foot propping her up.

But next to her...

No.

No, it can't be.

A boy who must be barely twenty, with rumpled hair and a sharp jaw and an earring. He's sitting at her feet, legs sprawled, a darker crescent moon caught in the loose threads of his collar. He fiddles absentmindedly with something that looks like a telescope. His fingers are long and fidgety as mine, like he wouldn't know what to do with them if he put the tools down.

"If I stop complaining," he teases, *"I'll die of boredom."*

"Keep it up, Solari, and someone else might kill you first." I'm hardly even listening to her. All I can look at is him. Because it's *him.* One look back at the way my mother's lips have compressed into a hard, flat line confirms it.

My father.

"You did your knots tight, right?"

The boy smirks and tugs at a rope I thought was a belt looped around his waist. *"If you wanted to tie me up, you could have just asked."*

"Shut up." The younger Valyra kicks his leg, then stoops down and snatches the telescope. *"Wait, wait—there it is."*

And I know I'm doing exactly what my mother wants when I turn and look, but I can't help it. This isn't just her memory—it's my dad's. I follow their line of vision, and there's something floating up there, where the walls meet ceiling. As it comes into focus, my heart trips over itself.

It's Nym.

No, it's not. Just another Medyssian who looks eerily similar to her. She bobs in the air the same ethereal way, and her shy smile is the same, and she too looks like she was pieced together out of stray bits of starlight. She giggles and does a loop in midair.

Swimming between stars, curious and happy, just like the story Nym told me.

I turn to see what this means to her. Nym is frozen, her palm pressed to the glass, like she's desperate to reach through the past and swim up to the other Medyssian herself.

"I don't understand," I start, frustrated, but Valyra—the real one, not the memory— shushes me and signals with one finger to turn around.

Then, her eyes still closed, the Medyssian girl from the

past begins to hum. It's the same song I heard when Nym showed me the universe the way she sees it, and I'm flooded with the memory of her head on my shoulder. *Come out, come out, come away.*

Another figure materializes. This one is a man, tall and lanky, with a face brushed with stubble and a shoulder-length crop of blond hair tied with a cord. He's only a few feet away from my parents, but he doesn't seem to notice them. He just leans on the railing, listening to the music.

"Come on," the younger Valyra mutters, eye pressed to the scope. *"Come on, show yourself."*

Solari leans forward. *"Val, shouldn't we at least tell him—"*

"Shut up, I said. You're distracting me."

The Medyssian holds out her arms, and the sailor grins, climbs up to the railing, and begins swimming out toward her. Without meaning to, I see Nym in my window all over again, reaching out her own hand, asking me to trust her.

The Medyssian smiles again, then draws him close, twines her fingers through his hair. The man presses her to his chest, and they glide in a graceful circle, like they're one soul in two bodies. Like they belong together. He spins her, she laughs. She pulls him by the hands, corkscrews around him playfully. His legs hang in limp unison, like he's forgotten he even has legs. Like in his mind, they've been replaced with something else.

And I hate it, hate *her* for even showing me this. It could be a recording of me and Nym ourselves, from just hours ago—but it wasn't like this, whatever this is. It was different. It was special.

The dance has brought the two closer to the ship, and suddenly the sailor's face is in clearer view. He's gone pale bluish-gray, just as I was when Nym turned me Medyssian.

The natural next step in this dance. But then, as they continue turning, the pleasant smile never leaving the Medyssian's face, I see he's not gray with illusion.

He's gray with *ice.*

With asphyxiation.

With death.

He's frozen solid, his eyes locked in an expression of dazed bliss forever. His joints are rigid; when the Medyssian detaches them from her waist, I hear a crack.

He didn't have a tether. He didn't have a starwalking suit or an oxygen tank or whatever it was they used back then. He went out into open space completely exposed.

It was an accident, I think wildly. *A mistake. She didn't know.*

The Medyssian, still singing her gentle lullaby, reaches up and closes the man's eyes, the lashes studded with frost. Her touch trails down his chest almost reverently, and then—

Then her nails turn to daggers. Her eyes go black. Her mouth opens into a cavern of needles.

And she rips the cold heart right out of his chest.

I stagger away from the hologram, fist pressed to my mouth.

"Alright." The younger Valyra snaps the telescope closed. *"Time to go."*

The flat eyes of the Medyssian turn from the dead man's corpse. The heart is clutched in her hands, cradled like a treasure. She cocks her head toward my parents, but for a moment, I forget it's a hologram. For a moment, she's looking right at me, like she can see through time and space and wants to sink her claws into my own heart.

"Run!" shouts Solari, and a knife flashes in his hand, and both their ropes drop to the deck. *"Go!"*

And the Medyssian dives as they run right through me,

dives like it's me she wants and not them. And as she lunges, she once again resembles Nym. Only this time, it's the form trapped behind me, and the attack I saw back on the Ghost Ship—that ruthless, hunted expression in her eyes, the way she bared her knifelike fangs. The way she turned into someone I didn't know.

The Medyssian reaches out, the veins in her clawed hand protruding through skin.

Both Valyras, the real and the memory, scoop the projector up at the same time, and the hologram dissolves.

The light equalizes. The Medyssian, my father, everything—it's all gone. All that's left is me, panting in an empty room. I can't meet my mother's eye, can't turn and face Nym. I'm afraid of what I'll see—something that will tell me she knew all along. That she kept it from me. That she lied.

Quiet footsteps approach, and a hand reaches out to smooth my wayward hair.

"You thought her some ethereal mermaid of old human legend, this creature of yours," Valyra says quietly. "You thought her some little lost girl."

"How do you know they're all like that?" I shoot back, hands curled in fists. "The Medyssians. Maybe that one was a killer, but they might not all have been. Humans—humans have plenty of killers of our own."

"Oh, my darling." Pity tinges my mother's voice. "It wasn't just one. Is that really what you think of me?" Yes. Maybe. I don't know anymore.

"There were legions," she says, and the holographic sphere turns with a cold click. Dust erupts over us again, but this time, it's a tornado. *Click, click, click.* The sphere spins, and with each turn, a new hologram crashes over the one that came before, and I'm in the eye of a storm made of swirling

tentacles that change form as I watch. Medyssians transforming in and out of countless bodies—a flash of wing, of scaly
fins, of black eyes and pale ones. Teeth sharp as needles, nails
that grow into claws. Tentacles. Fangs. Human legs. *Click.*
*"Mission S14, log twelve—" Click. "—log two-four-six—" "—log
one-eight-seven—"*

Click.

Click.

Click.

I see hearts being ripped from bodies, Medyssians shot
down and crumpling to ash, people with vacant smiles clam-
bering up ropes and diving into the ether. And I hear the
melody of the universe underneath it all, those same peaceful
notes, only it doesn't sound warm and inviting anymore.

It couldn't, buried beneath all the screaming.

No. No, this is all wrong. Nym said they were curious
explorers, who just wanted to see the stars.

"Turn it off," I beg. "I don't want—this isn't—"
Click.

The layers upon layers of holographic memories shimmer
away on an invisible wind, until only one is left. A girl with
long, pale hair and an undulating skirt of umbra who turns
toward us, eyes black, and stretches her mouth wide until
tentacles burst out of it like snakes hatching from inside her
stomach, overtaking her in a sea of slithering coils, and then
that's gone too.

"It took years to find them all." Valyra turns the sphere
one last time, and all the light left over suctions back in. "They
were on countless planets, disguising themselves as countless species. Luring people in, singing their hypnotic song.
Gaining their trust, and then killing them, erasing the minds
of any survivors they had no use for, and moving on to the

next world."

The electric hunter in my head, sifting through my memories of Nym. That's what it was doing—making sure I wasn't under that sort of spell.

"But why?" I ask, heart pounding. I'm terrified of the answer, terrified it will be one last thread linking Nym back to this story I don't want to believe in. "What did they want?"

"To collect," my mother says simply, and suddenly I'm the one being held together by threads. "They have to touch their victims if they want to borrow their forms. They steal something out of the heartbeat, mimic it in order to shapeshift temporarily. But if they eat the heart itself, the form is theirs to keep, to use at will."

Collection. All the parts and pieces hanging from Nym's ceiling. Relics from every planet she roamed to. Where did she get them all? Are they not souvenirs, but trophies?

When I finally dare to glance back at her, she looks more ethereal than ever, pearl-gray hair unbridled by gravity and fluttering freely around her. I don't know if I'm expecting her to look caught or guilty or cruel—I don't know anything anymore—but she doesn't. Her eyes are empty black holes, her gently rippling umbra the only part of her that moves. She looks lost, and not just from her home. From the space she occupies, from herself, from me.

"You asked what I did to her." When I try to turn away, my mother holds my shoulders in place. I can't look at anything but Nym, caged, wearing the same body as the Medyssian who killed that sailor. "Don't you see, Aren? *This* is her. This is what she really is. All I did was take away her ability to hide."

I can feel the dull prick of the crystal encasing Nym's voice pressed to my back. I want to not believe it, any of it. I want to look at Valyra and think *liar* as blindingly as I did when I first woke up in here.

Liar, I try in my head, but it's dull and weightless.

"Aren?" Fingers squeeze the bones of my shoulder. "Tell me another word for mermaids, in those old legends."

That other Medyssian—someone Nym could have become in another life—took that man's heart. She coaxed him out and made him feel safe, and then she took his heart. The family Nym misses so much, the ones she convinced me were powerless victims who had to run away from a monster hunting them for no reason. They're—

"Sirens," I whisper.

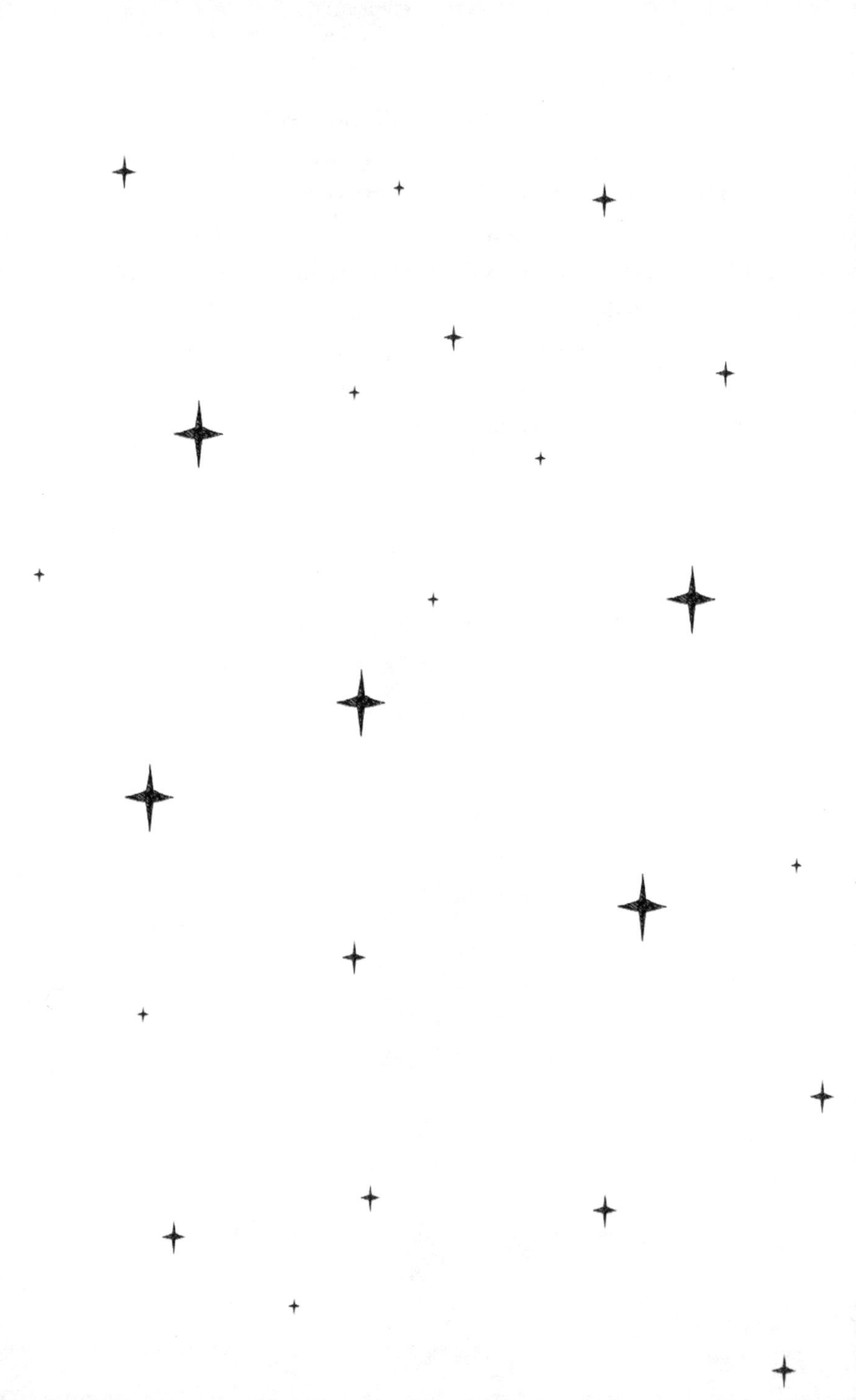

CHAPTER 41

Nym

Lies.

Lies.

This is what monsters do. They don't always creep through the night with tentacles and teeth; I know that now. They can have beautiful faces; they can hunt their prey with words.

Medyssians were not ruthless heart-eaters. I would know. It doesn't matter that I haven't seen another since I was a small girl, doesn't matter that the details of my family are gone. It doesn't matter that I can see the distorted reflection of my own face, a black-irised stranger with hands and teeth and claws that could scoop hearts from flesh so easily and feel nothing. It isn't true. *She* did this. She made me this.

And yet.

The hologram has silenced, but the memory it recreated will not fade. A storm of blood, of deception, of death. Somewhere in my soul, I can feel the same rush of recognition that overtook me when I found the other Medyssian girl and realized I had written over my own history.

Sirens, killers tears away at *explorers, victims.*

"Why did you keep her, then?" Aren's voice is so very far from me, barricaded with glass. "If they're all deadly hunters, why did you put her in a cage instead of—" His fingers flex and his head tilts down as though he can't bear to look at either of us. "—of—of what happened to the other one?"

Valyra purses her lips. Her hand snakes under her collar, and then she draws out a chain until a glass orb settles against her sternum. My blood, silver and almost gaseous, shimmers inside the mechanism.

The first map. She found it.

No. *No.*

She doesn't have to say anything at all. She doesn't have to explain.

I'm finally going home, and I'm leading her and her crew and her cannons with me.

"You're—but I didn't—" Aren's words trip over each other; his legs do the same as he backs away. "How did you know?" he finally settles on, and I realize, too late, something that should have bothered me as soon as I was captured: I was with Aren every moment after he returned to his crew, and he never told his mother about the map, or the lost planet, or who I really was.

Valyra cocks her head, rolls the orb under her fingertips. "Cas and Felix were very worried about you."

The pressure of the glass encasing me seems to multiply.

Cas's cunning smiles, Felix's pleasant questions. Plying me with beautiful things, teasing Aren, making me feel like I could belong here. I trusted Aren's friends because he did, and the entire time I thought they were helping him hide me, like it was some clever game, they were spying. They could not have told her everything—wouldn't have known enough to say the word *Medyssian* or even *shapeshifter,* but they must have learned something, seen me slip somewhere, for her to put the pieces together.

"They told you?" Aren's voice carries all the shock and betrayal mine would if I could speak. "They said—they had no *right*—"

"And you're lucky they did," Valyra snaps. "It's clear the creature was only using you to get this map. Do you suppose she would have devoured your heart before releasing the rest of her planet, or waited until after?"

I would never. I scream with soundless rage and slam my palm against the glass, only realizing when Aren takes a startled leap away that the motion makes me look just as violent and terrible as Valyra wants me to be. I tuck my fist in, but she has already turned him away.

"This is my fault. I should have known there was still a nest out there somewhere, that more than just one Medyssian had escaped. That's two mistakes I've made, and I won't make a third." Valyra's thumb traces the activation trigger. "You said they call me the Shadow. If they really are only in hiding because they're afraid of me, what do you think will happen if I'm no longer around for them to fear, one day?"

I am too aware of every slight movement Aren makes, too desperate to dissect each into something that will let me know he hasn't completely forsaken me yet. But he swallows and looks his mother in the eye, and I cannot find a meaning in it.

"We're going there first," he says tonelessly, no hint of disgust or disbelief.

"Perhaps you'd prefer the alternative," Valyra says softly. "That their hunt begin again. Do you want the full responsibility of defending the universe when that happens?"

Aren says nothing.

"I know how difficult this all must be, how confusing. But this is what I've raised you for." Valyra sighs and smooths Aren's hair behind his ear. "Someday, when I cannot fight anymore, you'll inherit my empire, and you won't just be taking the riches and the power. You'll be taking my enemies, too. Sometimes, just like this, they'll be enemies I thought I'd already defeated. You have to be ready, because they're going to come for you whether you are or not. You understand, don't you?"

I sink to the bottom of the chamber and wish the pressure would crush me completely. I should never have trusted anyone. Everyone will die because of me; Medyssia itself will be burned to its core. No matter what Valyra says, I can't accept that all of them were killers. They do not deserve a slaughter like this.

Aren must know that. His mother made him shoot the girl the Shadow transformed into, but I saw the horror in his eyes. He must know this isn't the only choice.

He'll push her away, snatch the map from her neck, convince her to let Medyssia remain hidden beneath the waves of the ether. He will—

He turns away, closes his eyes. Closes any door left open between us.

"I understand," he says, "I understand everything now," and I shatter.

CHAPTER 42

Aren

THE night goes by in flashes.

There's a crew gathering in the heart of the ship, my mother in the center, her voice magnified and echoing. She tells them how once, there were creatures who roamed feral and free, and now they are back. How she hunted them down and trapped the survivors inside their nest, but then, one escaped. So now, we have to destroy the nest itself before more get out, before a slaughter begins again. How I found a way to lead us straight to it. We'll attack, and then it will be like they never existed—like the one blemish in her reputation never existed, either.

I catch a glimpse of Cas and Felix watching from two decks above me, before they slip away.

The map is sent to the control room, hooked into the navigational system. When it turns on, when the room is bathed in light and a glittering pathway knits itself together out of the clouds, my mother looks at me with an expression I've never seen before.

You had a knack for it after all, she says. Words I've craved since I was old enough to crave anything. *I was wrong to discourage you.*

She brings me to her quarters, unburies blueprints that have been rolled for so long, the yellow edges keep curling. Sketches of massive cannons full of dark matter strong enough to rip away the core of a planet, made of the same material as the weapon I used to kill a single Medyssian.

She doesn't confirm it, but I remember the way my dad's fingers fiddled with tools and wonder if his spirit lives somewhere in this design.

Later, as we walk back to my own quarters, a single set of thoughts echoes in my head. They bury me as I pass crew I've known all my life, hallways I grew up running down.

This is my home. My place in the universe. The only people I can trust.

The Medyssians were all killers and liars, and Nym is just like them. She lied too.

"What are you going to do with her?" I can't help but ask when we reach my room. My carpet is still splotched with discolor—a combination of mud and bathwater that hasn't yet dried. That's right. The Aren who was in here a thousand years ago took a bath and hid a siren. "After, I mean."

Valyra pauses in the door, considers. "Well. She's young. Undeveloped. Powerful. She could be made useful. After enough time in that tank, alone… who knows?"

It's not what I expect her to say, but this wouldn't be the first time my mother found the potential in a killer and shaped them into someone that could serve her. It makes me wonder if there any other prisoners I don't know about concealed somewhere in the ship, being trained into usefulness.

"Until that day comes, however," Valyra says, "under no circumstances are you to go see her, not without my supervision. I won't let her manipulate you again. Promise me, Aren."

Manipulate. I think of Nym drawing me out into space,

filling my head with a false reality. I think of the way she lunged for us when it all fell apart. "I promise," I say, and it's the easiest that saying those words has ever been. "She was never anything but a monster. She means nothing to me."

Even after everything, Valyra's eyes still flick instinctively to my neck. She can't hide the way her brow twitches when I leave my tattoo untouched, and I can't hide the twinge of hurt that she still has to check. But finally, she nods, strokes my hair one last time, and turns to go. Her hand catches in the doorframe before she disappears.

"You do know that I'm proud of you, don't you?" she says. "I admit I was worried for a while, but you… you were trying to fit into your place here the whole time. I see that now." She flashes me a patient half-smile. "After all of this, we have a lot to talk about, I think."

And the door closes, leaving me alone with her pride. The words I've been starving for, finally settling over my chest. *I'm proud of you.* All I've ever wanted.

And I barely hear them, I'm so full of the other mantras that have been settled there instead for the last endless stretch of hours. Since the hologram.

My home. My place. The only people I can trust.

The Medyssians were killers. Nym is a liar. My mother saved me.

I tilt my forehead against the door, listening for the creak of her footsteps.

My home. My crew. My family.

I back away until I reach the corner of my room, one eye still on the door. The loose panel shifts under my fingers.

Liars. Killers.

I can't trust anyone but the Celestial Company.

It's only when the panel clicks shut behind me that I

finally let myself breathe, finally listen to the voice buried underneath. A different truth, hidden under my own kind of illusion.

Because here's the thing: maybe the Medyssians were all killers, and maybe they weren't. I don't know them. Only Nym. And no matter what she or anyone else has done, I won't let her family—or the rest of their planet—be slaughtered.

And I guess Nym taught me one thing, because somehow I was able to look the fiercest woman in the universe in the eye all night and make her think I'd been won to her side without flinching.

The trick to a good lie? You make yourself believe it's the truth.

My feet move automatically through the well-tread tunnels. This is only step one of the plan—I don't know what step two is; only that I have to get Nym out of a cage that doesn't have an opening and send her away with a map that's currently secure in the bridge without anyone realizing. Easy.

I skid to a stop before the grate to my workshop and yank, and my arm nearly rips itself out of its socket.

I stifle my yelp of pain, then scan the hallway, accounting for the familiar network of pipes and the damp smell of steam from the nearby engines. Is this the wrong panel? No, this is it. This is where the panel has always been. I roll out the kink in my shoulder and try again.

The panel rattles and resists.

Locked. It's been sealed shut.

This time, I yell on purpose.

"Careful, star-prince, or you'll draw the whole crew up here."

I wheel, and suddenly everything that's been bottled inside me explodes to the surface. I don't remember deciding to lift my arm, to plant it against Cas's collarbone and slam her against the wall, but that's where we end up.

For one solid second, and then I recognize the familiar prick of a blade against my gut.

"Well," she says, "look who grew some teeth."

"How could you?" I keep her pinned even through the warning bite of metal. "How could you tell her? Do you even know what you've done?"

"Back up, would you? This is my favorite jacket. I'd rather not get blood on it."

"You know, Cas?" I snarl. "At some point you need to figure out that 'knives' isn't a personality."

Her eyes flash. "*Say that again, you—*"

"Enough." Something grabs me by the collar and lifts me away from the dagger. "We don't have time for this."

I writhe, scrabbling to uncurl Felix's fist. "Let *go of me—*"

The fist releases, and I crumple to the floor, panting.

"Calm down." The yellow light of the passageway stains Felix's sharp features green. "Like I said, not much time."

"To what?" I spit out, rubbing the grime from my cheek. "Go running to the captain again? I can't believe you—I thought you were—" I can't find the words. *I thought you were my friends* isn't even right, because maybe they never were. Maybe we just gravitated to each other because we were the only trio our age, and that forced us into some kind of unity. But I thought we at least had an alliance.

"Why?" I demand instead. "What did I ever do to you?"

Cas sheathes her knife. "Typical. Not everything is about you, you know."

"Believe it or not, we're actually here to help," Felix says.

"Yeah. I don't know what a Medaculan is, or whatever, but I don't want Nym hurt. I liked her. She was fun."

"*Medyssian.*" I push myself off the ground, checking my stomach for a reopened wound. "Why would I trust you? You're the ones who told my mother about Nym in the first place. You're the ones who—"

"We didn't know it would go this far!" Cas snaps. "We came back to fix it."

"This *far*? How far was it supposed to go, Cas?"

"Far enough for us to stop being treated like your sidekicks!"

"You—" The accusations die on my tongue. "What? What's that supposed to mean?"

"Don't pretend you don't see it. The captain was in a trio when she started this crew. When she made a name for herself at seventeen. She only adopted us because she wanted you to have the same kind of story."

I gape. "Are you kidding me? She recruited you because you outrank me in every category, Cas. Both of you. Combat, strategy, stealth—am I missing anything? Oh, yeah, you're also not *terrified of space,* as you were nice enough to point out earlier. Don't talk to *me* about sidekicks."

"No one cares!" I can't tell if she's laughing or shrieking. "Nobody notices—not Havelock, not Valyra, not anybody. I slaughter a dozen devouring eels, I target-practice until the targets snap in half, I match everything the rest of the crew can do and more. *She doesn't care.* The only person Valyra cares about improving is you."

"So, what—you got Nym captured for *attention?*"

"*No,* you barnacle-brained, spineless sack of—"

"Cas." Felix sighs and sinks down to a crouch beside me. "We're the only three our age on the entire ship," he says quietly. "We're a unit. We get lumped in with everything you do. It's not your fault, but it's what happens."

"We've been here for six years, Aren. Why are we still in training?" Cas wheels around, and the look on her face scares me for a completely new reason: she looks… vulnerable. Raw. I didn't even know Cas was capable. "You almost destroy the entire ship; we have to help clean it up. You run away; we get sent to the kitchens for not keeping an eye on you. And then you come back, ready to go with another catastrophe, and I just thought—" She drags her fingers into the weaving of her braid. "I don't know. I thought if we figured out what you were doing and turned you in ourselves, Valyra'd finally separate us. Let us go on real missions instead of waiting around for you. Finally remember what she saw in us in the first place."

The ship's anti-grav seems to disconnect from my vital organs. All my fight floods away.

"I—" I swallow. All this time, I thought they were untouchable, effortless, the prodigies that would replace me as soon as I slipped too far. Have they really been struggling for her approval the same way I've been? How? They're like her already, without even trying. Cas's skill with a blade, her shrewdness, her determination. Felix's discerning eye and his smooth, intimidating drawl. "I didn't know."

Felix leans against the blocked panel. "And if you had, what would you have done differently?"

"I mean, come on, Aren," Cas says. "Do you even want to be captain?"

A thin spark of understanding illuminates everything else. "Do you?"

Both her knife and her hands finally sheath deep in her pockets. She looks away, a hard, defiant line where her mouth should be. "Well. Wouldn't you, if you were me?"

I glance at Felix. "You too?"

"Oh, no. No interest in leading." He props one foot against

the wall. "Very interested in the compensation for being sent on missions, though. Would love to get some one day. But since we're probably going to get punished for not stopping you from letting Nym escape, we might as well deserve it for once."

"I won't let you get punished. I'll… I'll…" I'll what? I wait for my nerves to twinge with panic. Because here it is, this thing I've always been afraid of: that someone would look me in the eye and tell me I'm not worthy. My plan was to make Nym's escape look like a system malfunction, but I see now that that would be the first truly cowardly thing I've ever done. Who would I be if I owned up to it, left as nothing but the captain's disinherited, disgraced son? A cabin boy? A servant? No one. I'll be no one.

Is Nym worth it? I start to ask myself, but it's not the right question. I don't *want* that to be the question. It means me saving her is contingent on her innocence, and it's not.

Am I *worth it?* That's the question that actually matters. Is my belief that this is wrong, all wrong, worth sacrificing every stitch that binds me into my place in this world?

Yes. The simplicity of it should scare me, but it doesn't. It's the truth. I don't want to grow into the kind of person who gets to judge whether or not an entire planet deserves to be massacred. If that's what being Valyra's heir was going to turn me into, then I don't want it anyway.

"I'll tell her it was me," I say. "All me. I'll turn myself in, after Nym is free, and I'll tell her to choose you as her successor. I promise."

Cas raises an eyebrow skeptically. "*Can* you even tell her that?"

I nod. "You two were never here," I say without flinching. "I did this all on my own."

Both of them consider my neck, waiting for a twitch, but I don't break eye contact. Finally, Cas reaches a hand down to me.

"I'll start thinking up a new nickname, star-prince."

"Should I start calling you star-princess?"

"I'll kill you."

"I believe it." The motors in my head restart as I climb back to my feet, racing to catch up with the time we've lost. "Okay, so Nym's trapped in some kind of tank—we have to figure out how to get it open. Then get the map away from my mother somehow, and—"

"Please." Cas puts a hand to her temple. "Don't try to scheme. It's not your thing."

I scowl. "I'm sorry, did you already have a plan?"

"Of course. And something even better, I'd imagine." Felix rummages inside his jacket. As soon as I catch the glint of two glittering objects—one spherical glass, one opaque crystalline—my pulse staggers. The map. Nym's voice. "We're still rather good thieves, lest you've forgotten."

"How—how did you—" I cup them in my palms. "I can't believe you got them away from her."

"Well, this one we didn't have to." Felix leans in and adjusts a gear. "This is your second attempt."

This time, the stagger in my heartbeat isn't nearly as pleasant—more like a stone that's been thrown into a set of cogs.

"Felix, it didn't work. It won't—"

"Yeah…" The wince Cas's face settles into is almost apologetic. "About that."

Her nail hooks under the activation switch and flicks.

And light bursts from the map's core.

Impossible. It was broken. We tried it, and it was broken.

"You fixed it?" I gasp.

Felix scratches at his ear. "Well… I don't know if it counts as fixing, seeing as… well, seeing as we're the ones who broke it in the first place."

"You *what?*"

"Tampered with it," Cas says, and this time there's no mistaking whether she's apologetic. "During the ship tour. Sorry. Didn't want the proof getting away before Valyra found out."

I'm going to scream. Nym could have been on her way home by now, if not there already. But it's too late to be furious about how things could have gone differently. All I can do is try to fix them the way they are.

"Forget your plan." I snatch Nym's crystallized voice. "Here's what we're gonna do."

CHAPTER 43

Nym

I have a new collection.

It's a small, ugly collection made up of small, ugly pieces. The blistering skin and broken nails of my fingertips, from searching for cracks in corners that don't exist. The soreness in my knuckles from beating on glass that won't break. And a dull, hollow ache in my heart, because I don't know if there's even any point.

I was afraid she was in your head. Captain Valyra's accusation rings in my ear.

I've always known what I am. Even though I've taken the appearances of hundreds, I've always known exactly what I looked like on the inside. But now even that is a vessel I have no control over.

What else can it be? After all, I followed the same steps the rest of my kind took to lure their prey toward death, on pure instinct. I've been collecting trinkets and talismans from every place I've been, and I'm always insatiable for more. Is this where that hunger comes from? Is it not homesick, but predatory? Would I have grown into a beast, had I kept wandering for long enough?

I don't know anymore. I don't know where the truth is.

I raise my hand to the glass. Gray skin, a cobweb of silver scales trailing back from the wrist. Nails flecked with rust that could so easily be blood. My face, distorted and reversed in the glass, is hollow: hollow eyes, hollow cheeks. Valyra said this was my true form, that the girl I thought I was is just a glamour. I didn't believe her. I wanted to believe she'd stolen the rest of me the way she stole my voice, but maybe even that part is true. I locked so much of myself away—where I came from, how I was lost, what the Shadow really was. The one thing I thought was wholly mine was the melody pulsing under my skin, a home of a body I could always return to no matter where else I wandered. And even that was a lie.

What other truths have I twisted? Maybe these: *I am good. I am kind. I am hopeful.*

I am just a girl who wants to go home.

I never realized what an act of defiance it was, being something good and kind and hopeful, until the tools were destroyed. I should have become something broken and angry long ago. Despair is easier. Despair, and everything that comes with it, have always been easier.

Where would I run to, even if I escaped? Valyra has taken my only way home, and she will destroy it before I can ever hope to stop her. Aren sees only a monster. I myself am now a stranger I will never outrun.

Maybe it makes no difference, whether I am on this side of the tank or the other.

A crash annihilates the ceiling.

I look up. There's a hole halfway up the wall, with two faces and a pair of boots sticking out. Whispered voices made tinny by the glass between us float down.

"Is that the real plan, then? Break my legs with the fall?"

"Thought it opened further down, that's on me."

"Cas!"

"Are you gonna go, or are you gonna yell at me?"

"I'm—" The last word turns into a stifled yelp, and then a blur of white and brown and green comes careening out of the hole. The cot catches most of the impact, but Aren clips the edge and rolls onto the floor with a muffled *thump.*

"Ow," he groans quietly.

My breath catches in my throat. Aren loathes me now, mistrusts me completely—I saw it in his eyes. And with good reason. What is he doing here?

"Move fast." Felix's face materializes next to his twin's. "Once it's triggered, you won't have much time."

Aren rubs the base of his spine. "You're positive you can manage it, right? I don't know if I drew the coiling right—the casing has to be—"

"Please." I can see the way Felix's lip curls from here. "You just focus on your part."

And with that—*clank.* Something heavy closes the gap in the wall, and the scuffle of footsteps trail off, and Aren and I are alone.

"Hi," he says quietly.

I press my fingertips to the glass. *Hi?*

"Are you okay?"

A light flickers in my core. If he truly hated me, he wouldn't care. I nod, even though it couldn't be further from the truth.

He approaches the tank cautiously, then extends his own hand, but right when I think he's going to mirror my touch, he curls it into a fist and taps on the glass. He frowns, then repeats the movement a few inches up, then to the right, half a dozen times, until he's on his toes, craning somewhere over my head toward the top of the tank. I glide up to see what he's looking for, and he taps again. I can't be sure, but the shape of the dull *thunk* might be different.

"It's not level," he mutters. "Pressure imbalance—just needs a focused bit of greater force—" He turns for his worktable, still talking to himself. The names of tools and equipment I don't recognize spill out.

I take my hand away, leaving a frosted imprint that glows faintly and then fades. There can be no mistake. He *is* here to help me. That should be enough, but somehow, it isn't. I still feel so far from everything—from who I am and who my family was and who this person I called my friend sees me as. I test the glass with my finger, watching the way it glazes over and slowly dims.

Why? I write, then knock on the point right after the punctuation.

Aren looks up at the sound. There are already two objects in his hands: one that looks like a vicious sort of hammer, one with a pointed end that appears to be on fire. He squints at the words, turning his head to the side, and I realize they're backward to him. "What language—oh." He looks down as the letters melt away, then angles the fire toward the center of the second tool. "What do you mean, *why?* Because it's wrong. Because I have no interest in being part of a massacre, even if they—even if *you*—" He bites the inside of his cheek, tucking the crucial end of his sentence back inside.

I write again, sure to form the letters in the right direction this time.

Didn't know.

He has to understand. I will make him understand. That this wasn't all a lie, that I wasn't trying to trick him. That when I brought him out into the ether, it was because I truly wanted to show him the song of the universe. Nothing else.

Aren glances back, then shakes his head. "Don't do that. Please."

No. He must know I never wanted to control him, to enchant him. I may have cared about nothing but the map in the beginning, but I found a home even without it. I streak up toward the spot he identified as weak and drive my fist against it, then my shoulder. Words on glass aren't enough. I have to get out, have to tell him.

"Nym! Stop, the noise—" Aren leaps from his chair and rushes for me, flattening his palms against the remainder of my message. "I believe you," he says quietly, urgently. "I believe you if you say you didn't know. But it doesn't matter."

I stop pounding. My arm throbs too much for me to write again, so I plead silently, hoping he'll understand. *Why, then? Why?*

He sighs and retreats back to his desk, then hefts the welded tool. "Fine. You want a list? Number one." He stoops down and rummages in a half-open box. "You could have left me stranded when you found me in the ether, but you didn't." He reemerges, gripping a rope. "Two: You could have let the Shad—I mean, the other Medyssian cat me, but you didn't. Three: You could have let me die of infection after the tentacle incident, but you didn't. Four: You had every chance to rip out my heart, and you didn't. Am I missing anything?"

I inch closer to the glass, watching as he coils the end of the rope around the tool. He keeps saying it doesn't matter, but it must. They're reasons *I'm* clinging to as he lists them—proof that I wasn't a monster even when given the chance. They have to matter. They matter so much to me.

"And none of that makes any difference," he continues, then lifts a strange, metallic sort of wheel onto the worktable and angles the blade of the hammer against its teeth, "because I don't want it to. I don't want to base my trust in you on logic. Isolated incidents I can line up next to each other and analyze.

I trust you because—" He swallows and turns the wheel on, and his voice is replaced by the sparking sound of metal scraping against metal. It's ten agonizing seconds before the tool draws away, its blade filed down to a precise, lethal pincer.

I trust you because…?

He climbs up on his chair, one eye squinted shut to measure the distance, then loops the rope twice over an exposed pipe sagging low from the vaulted ceiling. He catches the end and pulls, and the rope goes taut, hoisting the tool upward. And I finally see what he's doing, what's clutched in the pincer's grasp—a black chrysalis, like the one I found on Cosalia. My voice's prison. He got it back somehow. When it falls, it'll crack right through the top of the glass, shattering it from its weak point out. No, shattering both simultaneously. My voice will be returned.

Hope churns inside me, replaced just as quickly by fear. I am safer to him without it. I am easier to trust without my weapons. What if I enchant him without meaning to? What if something instinctive awakens, and I attack him the way I almost did on the Ghost Ship?

Don't, I cry, the sound sucked back and trapped inside. *Wait—*

But he sees my terror, and all he does is flex his hands around the rope and give me a wry half-smile. "Look. I was drowning before I met you, in every way possible. And since you, I've been able to breathe. I don't care what form you take. I will always know who you are."

He lets the hammer fall, and the world explodes around me.

My prison crashes outward in a hailstorm of glass, and gravity drags me straight to the ground. I lie in the flood, icicle shards pricking at my arms, a warmth like blood coating my neck.

"Are you okay?" Aren rushes over and lifts my back to steady me. "Did I hurt you?"

"Ah—*ah*—" I clap my hand to the warmth in time for a silvery light to fade into nothing. A familiar melody ripples in my ears, in my veins, in my throat until I realize I'm singing it myself. My voice returned, my unmonstrous body restored. Iridescent shades of lavender crawl down my umbra, and the hair falling before my eyes glows faintly. But all I can see are the nails retracting from my fingers and the fangs retreating from my teeth. Masked underneath my magic, just waiting for me to lose control again.

"How could you know?" I whisper. "How could you be so sure I won't hurt you?"

Aren sighs. "All my life I've been afraid," he says, "of the void, of my mother. Of the person I might become. Don't you get it? Nothing could ever make me afraid of you. *Nothing.*"

I am cracked open, caught in a sunbeam through fog. And I know where I've felt this before: when I was lost in my illusions and Aren told me he was *real, I'm real, come back,* and I realize I have no choice but to believe him as fervently as he believes in me. No matter what any other Medyssian may have been, I do not have to be changed. We're the same, aren't we? Haven't I known, since the first time I heard the melody in his veins? I could never be a monster, made from the same stardust as him. He could never be a hunter, his soul a reflection of mine.

"I was the opposite, you know," I say. "I was drifting, and you gave me an anchor."

Aren laughs softly, but there's no happiness in it. "Some kind of fate that we found each other, huh?"

Some kind of fate.

A scream echoes throughout the chamber.

I curl in defense immediately—it sounds like rage, like pain, like death—but then it comes again, and I hear its metallic quality. It's an alarm of some kind, high-pitched and head-splitting.

"I'm going to kill them," Aren breathes. "I told them to wait—"

"What is it?" I ask, clamping my hands over my ears. "Is it her?"

"Um. So. Have I ever told you how most of my inventions don't work?" He leaps to his feet. "I have something of a history with putting holes in the shields."

The crash of something heavy cuts through the alarm.

"Come on!" Aren pulls me toward the line of starlight bleeding through a porthole set high on the wall. But just as we reach the top, something batters the wall. A thin crack splits the top of the sealed door. Dust and splinters explode through.

Aren spins me around, and I suddenly feel the unexpected coarseness of a string around my neck.

"Go," he orders in an undertone as the angry wood drums behind us. "There's gonna be a gap in the shields, starboard side, near the bow. Don't ask."

"No, wait—I have to take House with me." I know now that illusions and memories are two opposing forces in my mind, one constantly devouring the other. If I lose House and all the memories preserved inside, I will forget them once I am back on Medyssia, my entire life before this buried beneath the waves. Aren himself, wiped me from me forever. "Where's House?"

Aren doesn't reply.

"Aren?"

But there's the swift, final tug of a knot, and then Aren leans to open the porthole.

I block his arm after he's pulled the latch. "Valyra? Did she find it? Destroy it?"

"No." he says, voice cracking. "It—it did it to itself, so I could go after you—"

"Did what?" I try to push back, but he lifts me directly into the window's curve. I catch one hand on the upper latch. "I can't leave you both behind. I won't."

"That's not the plan." He flashes me a forced smile. "I mean, one of us has to hide this." And he lifts the object he's tied around my neck.

A glass ball that looks as though it has an entire galaxy trapped inside.

The map.

Home. *I'm going home.*

"Go," he says. There's a loud, final *bang* from beneath us, and an eruption of light from the hallway outside as the door buckles, and a shadow in the frame. "Don't turn it on until you're far away from here, okay? *Go!*"

He pushes me away, and the porthole slams shut between us, and he wheels to face whatever has come for him on the other side.

And I start swimming for the stern the way he's ordered, trying with all my might not to think about how this moment, the one I've dreamed about for as long as I can remember, feels nothing like the way it ought to.

CHAPTER 44

Aren

So much for a distraction. I should have known if anything went wrong, Valyra would come here first.

I've managed to duck inside the towering mechanisms that make up the far wall of the chamber, and now, the gears shielding my face click in steady orbit. Every time they shift, I get a fresh twinge of fear that my next view will be Valyra's face peering in at me. *There you are*, she'll hiss. *Let me fix you.*

"I suppose this is irony," she calls instead, soft voice echoing off brass and bronze. "I'd been hoping you would learn how to lie properly someday."

I suck in a breath and dart a glance toward the lone porthole. No sign of Nym.

"That you would lie to me, of all people, though. That's what I find difficult." Valyra steps lithely over the flooded mirror-glass of the floor, then caresses the holster at her belt. Her gaze curves toward the wall of gears, and as she turns, something hanging from her neck catches the dim light and sparkles. The other map. She's wearing it, clicked off temporarily for safekeeping. She doesn't know there's a second one; she must have assumed Nym would go after the first.

Her finger moves to her temple, and she taps it once,

twice, her head cocked. "She's still in there, isn't she?"

"I'm not under a spell," I say. There's no point in staying silent, not when she's looking right through the cogwork at me. And I let her almost convince me before; I won't let it happen again. "She's not controlling me."

"You should hope she is," Valyra says. "I don't think you want to tell me you're doing this on your own. I don't think you want to betray me like that."

"This isn't a betrayal." My head is full of the sound of gears both external and internal. *The map. I have to get the other map away from her.*

"Of course it's not, darling," she murmurs, the sound like poisoned honey. "You've been possessed."

"I'm not." I inch to my left, away from the sliver of light. "No one's controlling me. I'm just trying to do the right thing."

"So am I."

"You're trying to slaughter an entire planet!"

"I'm trying to protect an entire universe."

A piercing whistle, and then something streaks between two heater tubes, clanging near my ear. She didn't—she wouldn't—

But it's not a bullet buried in the thin cylinder. It's an immobilizer, the same kind she used on me before, and that's somehow worse. She wants to put me under again. Invade my mind until she's certain it belongs to her.

"I'm your son!" I yell furiously, disbelievingly. "I'm your own son!"

"Why do you think I'm doing this?" She's moving now; I can hear the click of boots punctuating her words. "You're the one who put us all in danger. You're the one who lied and hid and shielded a predator who'd happily kill us all."

"She's not dangerous! You know she's not!"

Another shot spears the air above me. I'm already on my hands and knees, scrambling under exposed pipes and valve gears, but I drop to my stomach. How am I supposed to get close enough to take the map without her immobilizing me?

"If anyone else defied me this way, they would be punished. You know that."

"Is that what this is, then?" I pant as I crawl. "Punishment?"

"You don't know what true punishment from me looks like." Her voice is getting closer, closer, closer. "I have given you more second chances than anyone should deserve. Stars help me for giving you another, even now."

"Are you kidding?" I lean on my elbows, gulping for air. "You expect me to believe you're doing this for me?"

"Oh, my darling." Her voice is too close now, impossibly close, and the second after I look up, I scramble backward as fast as I can. Valyra rises right through the space between two cogs, burning eyes and then tense shoulders and then cocked blaster. She steps off the ladder system I was fool enough to invent, and her shadow falls over me. "Everything I've ever done has been for you. Can't you see that?"

I don't think; I don't plan. In the split second where the blaster levels, I yank a wrench from my belt and slash at the nearest pipe as hard as I can, flooding the space between us with steam. I hear Valyra's shot go wide as I stumble to my feet and run, coughing on sweltering air.

"Aren!"

I move without direction, my lenses full of fog. This was a mistake; I should have lunged for her instead. In the eruption of steam, I might have been able to grab the map, but now—

Another *crack* shatters the air, and I stumble as something small and pressurized hits my leg, blocked from reaching skin only by the thick leather of my boot.

"Please—I don't want to hurt you." Her voice cuts through the fog like a searchlight.

I keep crawling, crawling, certain the next pain I feel is going to be either an immobilizer driving itself into my back or my forehead driving itself into a pipe. Hot steam boils my neck, makes my shirt cling to me, erases any sign of light until—

There.

Something pale and bright enough to pierce the haze. I sprint for it and burst out of the cogwork coughing, but as the air clears, I see that the light isn't the lantern I thought I was—it's not even stars or cannonfire or the glow of a warming engine component.

It's a beacon, bright and focused and carving a path through the sky outside the porthole Nym escaped through.

My beacon. Nym at one end, Medyssia at the other. She turned it on too soon.

"There were two."

I wheel, putting the porthole to my back as Valyra steps into the light. She touches the orb around her neck as if checking to make sure it hasn't been stolen. "You made another."

The side of my mouth curves weakly. "Bet you didn't see that coming."

The blaster levels again. Valyra grits her teeth on the other side of it, a wave of hair slipping free of its gold-threaded braiding. "No matter. This ship is going after the Medyssian nest whether you think it's *right* or not, whether we're following this map or the one you gave that creature. Stop this. Stop this insanity, and come back to me."

I take a step back, feeling the cold press of glass against my spine. It's still unlocked from Nym's escape, and the pressure slits the lower edge of it open just enough for me to sense those prying fingers of the ether, the ones that always threatened to drag me out. The beacon teases at the corner of my eye, and as much as it feels like hope, like victory, it feels like defeat now, too. I told her to run farther away before turning it on. What happened to her? Did she get caught?

I can't let this ship follow her home. I have to stop it.

I steal a glance at the orb my mother wears again, the one I know I'll never get away from her, and she curls her fist around it.

"Nowhere else to go, Aren," she warns.

I take a deep breath, flatten my palms. I think of lilac and gold, of whispered melodies, of dancing. "You're miscalculating a lot today," I say.

The porthole wrenches open behind me, and I let space pull me out.

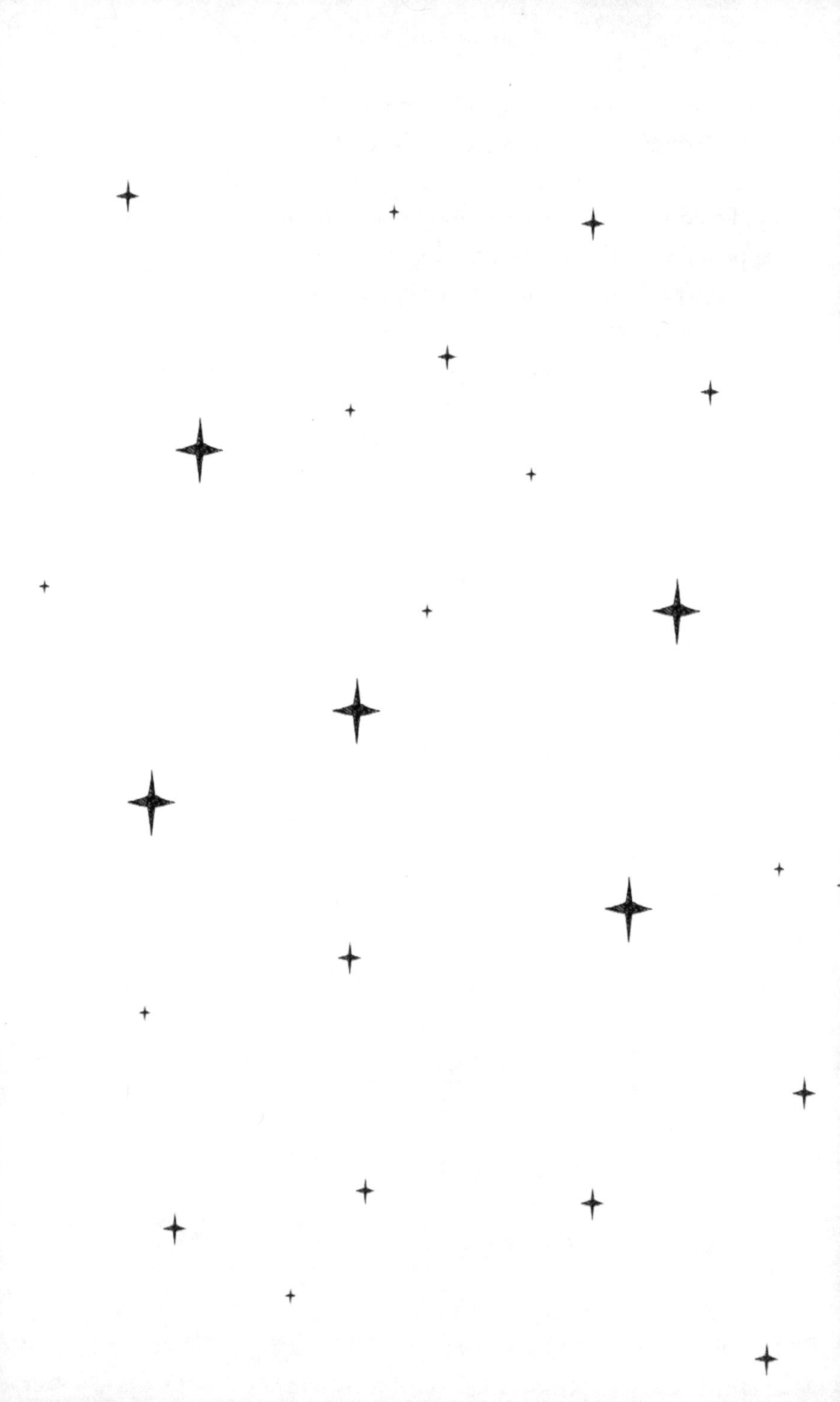

CHAPTER 45

Nym

I shouldn't have turned the beacon on.

It was foolish. Impulsive. I just wanted to see, after everything that has gone wrong, that there was something left to believe in.

And there is. The path home, just as Aren said. I cannot see the end of it, but I can imagine with a fierceness I've never allowed myself before. I can see silver clouds veiling a liquid atmosphere, surrounded by thin, swirling rings. A door that has been locked, finally open. *Come home*, it calls, an inverse to the song that took me away. *Come home.*

I shut my eyes against the desperate pull. I must leave Aren behind forever. I can't leave House, too. So instead of streaking toward the hole in the golden dome as Aren ordered, I race for the belly of the beastly ship that tried to keep us prisoner.

From this angle, its lanterns look like teeth.

The path is frenetic, my umbra billowing and collapsing as I change direction again and again, dodging the sailers that erupt from the underbelly of the ship to confront the shower of fire-touched stones tearing into the atmosphere. Ripples of smoke trail in their wake, and I chase the visible exhale in reverse until I've reached the hold.

There is no need to search for the right bay. The exposed mast runs through the shell of the ship like a broken bone protruding through flesh.

"No… oh, *no*—"

It's worse than anything I imagined, worse than the time I crashed us into a moon years ago, lost in an illusion. I pull myself hand over hand, the song in my veins reduced to numb screams.

There isn't an inch of House that isn't destroyed. Wood that buckles into itself, windows crushed to sand. My collection, years and years of trinkets and treasures and *hope* I'd let become a part of me, in gray ruins across the floor.

I drag my way down the slope of the mast, toward the heart of my ship. My umbra is swallowed by canvas—the paintings I'd turned into my sky, ruined just like everything else—and I sink into it, press my ear to its coarse blanket. "You're not gone. Please, *please*."

The walls pulse with the drone of other engines coming to life, the cry of weaponry, the thunder of boots on metal. *Distraction,* Cas had said, but this sounds more like war, whatever it is. It chokes the sound out of everything, but I can't bring myself to lift away from the canvas, to give up. I've given up so much already.

And then, a weak flutter beneath the floorboards. The barest of creaks in the one rope that hasn't been wrenched from its anchor.

I look desperately up into the cavity. "House?"

Nothing. Nothing and nothing and nothing.

But I felt that solitary flicker. I know something might still be in there, awakened by my presence.

I fly back up the mast until I've reached the gap, then lean out, panting shallowly, to get a better look at the chaos. How much time do I have? How long until I doom us both?

Cannonfire. Alarm bells. The gold-sparking shriek of ice as it collides with the fractured edges of the *Starsaviour's* shields. No Medyssia emerging from the clouds—not yet. I see nothing but a storm of a sky.

No. I see something else.

My breath hitches in my chest. Aren. I see Aren. Out here, out in the ether.

He's ten or fifteen decks above me, no tether, anchored to the side of the ship by his arms alone. I cry his name, and the chaos devours it.

Then, one of those wildly untethered legs rejoins the side of the ship. Then the other. And then he's climbing, one hand over the other, scaling the side of the ship like the ether doesn't exist at all.

He has a plan, I realize, and the gold of the sails providing his backdrop seems to crackle in affirmation. *He has a plan, and this must be part of it.*

I'm about to tear myself away, just as he would order me to, but then the pale silhouette of another face appears in the window he's just emerged from.

The wind takes Valyra's hair in its teeth the moment she steps into the porthole. It's flown loose from its braids, slashing across her face in long, undulating tentacles. Her head tilts up toward Aren, following his path, and now I have to do something—I must, because there's a blaster in her hand and a sword at her hip. The ship is under siege by the ether itself, its captain is out for her own son's blood, and I didn't want this, didn't want *any* of this.

But before I can streak upward, make her choose me instead of Aren, her head turns, and her eyes meet mine. She sees me all on her own. She *sees*.

She pulls herself the rest of the way out of the window, her gaze unbreaking, and I should run, I should fight, but I find myself unable to move. We do nothing but stare at one another.

Then she turns her back, grips the ledge above, and begins climbing after Aren.

CHAPTER 46
Aren

THE top deck greets me with chaos.

Felix has replicated my failed shield-patching device expertly. Too expertly, considering that we've moved way past distraction and far into the realm of actual emergency.

Instead of nine or ten panels missing, there are at least fifty torn out of the shields cloaking the *Starsaviour*. Fifty and growing. The sails scream louder than any alarm, clinging to their masts as the void reaches through the chasm to claw them away. And worse than the vacuum trying to drag bits of the *Starsaviour* out is what it's letting *in*. Stray meteorites plummet toward me like hail; I leap out of the way, and they splinter through the railing. The air crackles with blaster fire, directed at the swarm of deep-space crawlers scuttling down the inside of the shields, impervious to the electric shock. Devouring eels drip in after them like sludge. The smoke that rolls around me is poisoned with the coppery smell of blood, and from every angle there's nothing but shouting, the labored *thwack* of slithering bodies hitting the deck, the sizzle of fired shots getting far too close. Putting another hole in the shields might not have been the best idea, but it's too late for a better one.

I have an even worse one, actually. And I need a sword.

I keep my head down as I race for the foremast, skirting a swarm of gunners firing without abandon in every direction. Something on my right explodes with a contained scream and sets fire to a coil of rope.

A flash of silver spears the air, missing my nose by inches, and buries itself in the wall of the watchtower beside me. It comes to a quivering halt, and I recognize the familiar glimmer of rubies in its handle.

I turn in time to see Cas's grin before she disappears back into the fray, two replacement knives already in her hand.

This works, too.

I jam the knife into my belt, clip my starwalking suit to my ear without even wincing at the bite, then yank one snaking tether free and jam the end into my lower back. Before I even hear the connective snap, I leap for the first foothold in the mast, then the next, then the next. The solar sails shimmer above me.

I hope Cas's knives are as sharp as she claims.

Boom.

A quake tremors through the core of the ship, and the mast vibrates like it wants to uproot itself, but I keep climbing until I make it to rope ladder hanging from the gaff rig. It looms, backlit by orange and red, carving a swaying line up to the apex of the sails. I inhale smoke and cough it back out as I step on the first rung, then lift my other foot and—

And I'm yanked away by the waist, dragged down flat on my back.

"*Stop!*" The shout is viciously distorted through the chaos, but I know the shape of my mother's voice. "*Stop fighting me!*"

"*Let go of me!*" I claw desperately into the side of the beam. I'm not yielding now, not with the sails towering above me to remind me of how close I am and how far I've come. They crackle against a stormy violet sky, and—

The yank at my back falters, and I know it's because Valyra has seen it at the same time I have.

Before, the view was nothing but fire and ash, but now, something else is cutting through the crimson. Blue and iridescent and shimmering. And on the other end of it… on the other end…

A perfect sphere hanging above us, like staring into a sun through a layer of fog. It's not the planet itself, but it might as well be—it's the end of the beacon, washing over and refracting the invisible barrier like waves crashing against an island.

Medyssia.

For a second, I can do nothing but stare at it, even though it's hardly more than a pale shadow in the sky above me… before me… no, almost right in front of me.

We're turning. The *Starsaviour* is adjusting course, inverting itself in a broad loop to follow the path. The chaos isn't enough; someone is still at the helm. We could be there in minutes.

I reach back and wrench the tether free.

The pressure releases. My grip goes slack. *Everything* seems to stop—the pulsing light of Medyssia, the fear in my lungs. Everything except me, because without the tether, I'm weightless and unbound and almost out of reach of gravity. Almost, but not quite.

The ladder tilts toward me, and I lunge for it. One hand, then the other, a scrabbling foot that misses its rung and catches and lifts to the next step, over and over again. I can hear the open, taunting space in the shields peel back even further at the edges, sense the lost planet gleaming somewhere behind it. My pulse is roaring and frantic; if I fall, I'll fall forever, and this time, Nym won't be there to catch me.

Hand over hand, foot over foot, the rope snapping shakily beneath me, until the world is nothing but the shining ripple of solar sails. My unrecognizable face, streaked with ash and blood, refracts from inside them, as though they've bottled me too.

I edge the knife out of my belt, feel the bite where the handle meets blade against my fingertips.

The first slash is harder than I expect.

The sails are thin, but the design is something sturdy and rip-resistant—otherwise, the smallest amount of space debris could damage the ship's trajectory. I lean away from the ropes as far as I dare and hack at the thousands of individual seams, muscles already burning, then pull back. The stiff, reflective edges around the opening flap dismally, but don't tear any further. Again. I have to keep going.

I scramble up another couple of rungs and spear the sail through a second time. I'm so high that the artificial gravity might as well not even exist, and when I relax my grip on the ladder, the riptide of the ether tows me up. The knife arcs along with me, splitting through seams for six—eight—ten feet until the speed of the current becomes too much for me to handle and I have to wrap myself against the ladder again, stomach inverted.

Again. Again.

I reach out and bisect the cut, drawing an X that cuts my reflection into four long, shaky pieces. Just as I wrench the knife out, the ship lurches so heavily that I'm almost thrown. The bow jerks several crucial degrees away from the ethereal pull of Medyssia's barrier, and I hold my breath, waiting for the course to correct.

The sail above me agitates, straining against the mast in strips.

The course doesn't correct. It's working.

I flex my fingers around the hilt and get ready to strike again, only noticing just before metal meets metal that the quadrants of my reflection have doubled. There's eight of me now.

No, that's wrong. Four of the faces trapped in the shattered mirror aren't mine.

I swing around to the back side of the ladder just in time to miss Valyra's lunge.

"Enough, Aren!" Her bellow trails me as I climb the unsteady chain. The ladder tilts sideways; she's severed through the side of it. "*Drop the knife—*"

I can't hang on; the rope swings toward the sails, and I let the momentum throw me onto the upper gaff. The beam catches under my arms, slamming into my stomach, but I manage to kick my way up. I drive the knife through the sail again, hard as I can. "Not until you tell them to stop!"

The turbulence doesn't affect Valyra's balance the way it affected mine. Her hair blows against a smoky wind as the slashed ladder arcs toward me, as she steps out of her one-handed grip and onto the beam. I yank the knife out and take a step backward, feeling around for the edge of the wood underfoot. The tether trailing out of Valyra's waist is a mocking reminder that she will survive a mistake up here, and I will not. The knife held before me is a paper blade compared to hers.

And when she flies at me, I remember something important: my mother is the most feared woman in the universe for a reason.

I knock her first thrust out of the way with an ease that shocks me until I realize it was a feint; her elbow crunches against my cheek while I'm still dodging the sword. Spots cloud my vision; the bones of her wrist twist around my own and *snap*, and the knife jerks free, tossed by our momentum out of the pull of the artificial gravity, then spirals away into the nothing. Her foot hooks around the back of my leg and swipes, and I crash to the beam underneath.

It's only when I'm on my back, dizzy and disoriented after three seconds of combat, that I realize she's been holding back.

"Let me ask you something, Aren," she says calmly, sheathing her sword and replacing it with her blaster. "What are you going to do after you've finished betraying your crew? What then?"

"I'm not betraying anyone." I push myself a few desperate inches away by my elbows, feet fighting against the wood for traction. "You didn't have to go after the Medyssians. You could just leave them alone."

"That isn't what I asked." A dull echo as she cocks the blaster. "I asked what you're going to do next."

Next? After? There is no *next*. Nym has to go home. My mother has to let her. There is nothing beyond that but darkness.

It's only when I'm about to say *I don't know; I don't care* out loud when I realize why that is.

I look up at her, and how every part of her is a weapon turned on me, and I know there will never be any returning from this. We've gone too far.

"I… I can't stay here," I whisper, half-hoping the violent winds twisting through the sails will take the words and hurl them somewhere else. "I don't know how I could."

Valyra's mouth sets; her weapon rises. "You would leave me? You would leave your own mother?"

I thought I was out of fight, but the second the barrel positions itself toward my neck, a spark of terrified adrenaline claws its way back to the surface. "Don't. Please—"

The trigger pulls. I roll out of the way and dive for one of the ropes that hangs like vines from the rigging, and half-slide, half-swing down to the beam below me, barely feeling the burn against my palms or the jolt through my feet as I land.

"I'm not you," I pant. "You chose this. I don't."

A thump of boots on wood somewhere to my right. I back away on instinct, but when Valyra's blaster lowers, her eyes are wide.

"*You* don't get to choose when you leave," she says.

Her blaster moves too fast. I duck away from the shot, and a projectile slams over my left eye instead of my neck. I'm thrown sideways, barely maintaining my foothold on the narrow rig, hand clapped to an impact point that feels like pure, burning, untamed fire. When I pull it away, bracing myself for what has to be fractured pieces of my skull, half a dozen shards of glass lie cupped in my palm. I stare at them in shock, something wet and sticky clouding my vision, before realizing what I'm even holding. My specs. The shot ricocheted off one of the lenses, shattering it. I push the leather straps up with shaking fingers, but the searing pain on the left side of my face remains, and so does the pulsing darkness shrouding my sight.

"So after everything I've done for you, this is how you want it to end," I hear Valyra hiss from somewhere past my shoulder. "You want to turn me into a monster, then run away."

I curl my fist around the largest of the broken shards. My left eye feels as though it's had a sharp, heavy stone forced into it, but I can get a blurry view of Valyra when I blink the blood out of my right. My head is all rattling pain, like a scream's been bottled and trapped inside and is raging to get loose, but I manage to string together the right words. "I didn't have to turn you into anything. How... how can you still think you're the hero, here? *Look* at me—"

"I'm still trying to protect you *from yourself*," she hisses. "But if this is how you want it to be, then so be it. But know this: the story the crew will hear will be mine, not yours, if you leave. I won't have a choice. I'll have to tell them that you—you were weak, and cowardly, and selfish, and that you knew you would never be strong enough to lead them. That in your jealousy of those who were stronger than you, you cast your lot in with that *creature* and tried to destroy the ship itself—tried to destroy everything that reminded you of your own weakness. And that I banished you, as punishment. Because that is what a good leader does, when they're responsible for lives other than their own. They always put their crew before themselves. Is that what you want, Aren?" She's drawn close enough to touch me now, and she does; snatches the heel of my hand away from where it's pressed to my face and clamps her own under my chin, fingers pressing into the bones of my jaw.

"If you make me your villain," she says softly, "I will make you everyone else's."

Another blast from somewhere below shudders through the ship, but I don't feel it. I don't even feel her nails in my skin, the fire in her eyes that would have burned me before, the cut of the glass in my hand or the pain burning behind the eye that can't seem to find the light. I don't feel anything except the hard, piercing rattle of those words as they sear themselves into my head, drowning out anything else. They tangle themselves together; they stitch themselves into something else. And with blood leaking down my face and her final threat hovering in the air between us, I get it. I finally get it.

"He left," I hear myself saying, and as soon as it's said out loud, as soon as that piece is in place, I have to wonder how I went so long without even realizing it belonged there. "He left."

The curve of her eyebrows sharpens. "What?"

"Dad. You didn't banish him. He left us."

"No."

"You did the same thing to him that you're threatening to do to me. He was never a coward. He defied you, and you punished him by writing over his memory."

Her hold tightens. "He *was*," she hisses, but I know enough of lies now to recognize the kind that only become truth through repetition, "*a coward.*"

"No. He didn't run away from the last Medyssian because he was afraid. He let her go on purpose, because he—he knew they weren't all monsters too. Didn't he?" I can't breathe. The accusations must spill out of me on their own, because I know my own lungs can't be working well enough to do it themselves. "That's why you can't let Nym go, isn't it? You can't admit that you were wrong—that if one Medyssian was good, there might have been more, but you killed them all anyway. And you can't accept that. You have to be the hero of the story, no matter the cost."

"I *am the*—" Valyra's jaw goes rigid, and she finally releases me, the vague outline of her head turning away and then back. I'm startled to find her eyes glassy and vulnerable. "Please, Aren. Please don't make me suffer this betrayal twice."

Suffer. All my numb shock drains, replaced with anger.

"*You*, suffer?" I whisper. "Do you know what believing you marooned him has done to me? Do you even care?"

Valyra drags her hand through her hair impatiently. "I know you were afraid of becoming like him. But isn't that still true? He had a choice between himself and his crew, between himself and *us*, and he chose wrong. As you're about to."

"You let me believe you'd abandon me if I couldn't keep up—"

"—you came to that conclusion yourself, I never said I'd—"

"You didn't stop me!" I shout. I can't breathe, can't breathe, *can't breathe.* It's not just my hands trembling in shock; it feels like something is throttling me from inside. Every phobia I've ever had—the ether, the darkness, my own abandonment, my own weakness—exorcising themselves as they finally find their source. "How could you?"

She's close enough for me to feel her breath when she snorts in exasperation. "I don't regret anything I've done to ensure that you stayed here, where you belong," she says. "Is that what you want? For me to regret not wanting you to leave, like he did? Fear can be a good thing, Aren, when it motivates you to be strong, to hang on when letting go would be easier. If you took that motivation and twisted it into something debilitating, that isn't my fault. It's yours."

I take a shallow breath and drag my fist over the rivulets of blood staining my vision red. I could waste a whole lifetime trying to explain to her what she's done, how she let me become so afraid to even exist without her that it almost became irreversible. I could say so many bold, dramatic things. She would deserve it.

I don't do any of that. I don't bother saying anything at all.

Instead, I clench that single shard of glass left in my hand, slash it up in one swift arc, and cut the unguarded chain free from around her neck.

The orb streaks upward, too light to hold onto the feeble gravity when not tied down. Valyra's eyes widen, her hand already lifting to catch the map before it can disappear.

The ship quakes in a way that turns all the previous explosions into tremors, like we've been struck by an entire moon. The rigging beneath me is slammed out from under my feet, and suddenly, there is nothing but sky and space. Me and the orb, both caught in its riptide. I'm too surprised to be scared. It doesn't feel the way it did when I was thrown from my sailer by the eels. There is no drowning realization. My stomach doesn't turn; my heartbeat doesn't rampage. I'm just falling upward. And when I look at Valyra, the last thing I'll see before the universe takes me, she's not looking at me at all. Her eyes are on the map, and she lunges, her own tether anchoring her to safety.

And then—

Then a hand fists at my collar. My ascension jerks to a stop. For a second, both of us just stare at each other, and then we look up and watch as the glass orb spirals away out of reach, nothing but a glittering pinprick rejoining the stars. It's gone. She let it go.

She saved me instead of it.

"You see?" Valyra pants. "I'm not the villain. I'm not."

I clench her wrist and inhale shakily. Her eyes are so wide, so desperate. It's not a question, not a plea or a threat—it's another order. I want it to be true. I want it the way I used to want her approval, the way I used to exist like a plant tilting toward a sun.

I can want it, and still know it's not enough.

"You don't need the map anymore," I say quietly, "do you?"

Her grip tightens. "How dare you."

"Don't." The aching bruise taking over my face pulses dully. "Don't lie to me anymore. Nym's going to beat us there, and you know it. But you found some way to follow her anyway. Is that it?"

Nothing.

"*Tell me.*"

Her mouth flattens. She sighs, looks away from me, runs her tongue over the bottom of her teeth. "Once one of their illusions is broken," she says carefully, "it's broken."

"The barrier." My voice is a stranger, someone calm and impenetrable. It carries no twinge of hurt that I was right, that there was something else. There will always be something else. "It'll shatter if Nym breaches the atmosphere?"

"Until a new illusion can be spun." Valyra tilts her head, following the path splayed before us with her eyes. "I wonder how long that will take them."

Another lie. "You're bluffing," I say, not even bothering to struggle against her grip. To do so would be to let her think she's given me something to fear. "You think it'll make me go after her or something, and then you'll be able to get her back. It won't work. You can't trick me anymore."

"It's not a trick." A quiet voice threads between the sails, out of my view. Soft, musical, sad. "She's right."

CHAPTER 47

Nym

I T's quiet up here, suspended between Aren's universe and mine. It shouldn't be. There's so much noise, so much fire and fury; there's the way Aren and Valyra both breathe shallow and stunned, and the way my heart pounds as though desperate to escape my body. And still, it feels quiet somehow. An ending. A beginning. A place somewhere outside either of the two.

Once an illusion is broken, it's broken.

Aren is all blood and anguish, his left eye swollen shut and streaked with red so dark it's almost black. Glass glitters in his hair, and his body struggles as if at war with itself—torn between fighting the pull of the ether and the stone grip of his mother. And still, he finds a third way to fight.

"Nym—" he says hoarsely, "—no, *no*, get out of here—"

"That's why you went after Aren instead of me." I force myself to ignore him, to speak only to his mother. "You knew if I escaped and went home, you could still follow."

Valyra's beautiful face doesn't shift. I am right, of course I am right.

I turn my head away from them both, toward the brilliant, beckoning path home. It looks like an illusion itself, from here. I look at its intangible atmosphere, and I can see it. Not the planet itself, but the future that waits for me within it. So close. I'm so close.

I'm landing on the surface, the water rippling under my umbra.

I'm soaring through the window in our house in the trees. My parents are sitting there; they've been sitting there for years, waiting, gazing up at the hazy sky.

I was lost, I cry, afraid they won't recognize me. *I was lost, but I found you again.*

And they swoop down, eyes full of shock and love and heartbreak, and hug me so tightly I think I'll burst. *We knew you'd come back. We knew it, we knew it.*

I can see it, I can see it, I'm a breath away.

"And so, here you are," I hear Valyra say from somewhere. "To bargain, or to attack?"

"Neither," Aren answers for me, and his legs kick against the nothingness of the ether. "Nym, what are you *doing?*"

"The only thing," I reply. *So close. I was so close.*

I can almost imagine the me that was first lost from this place, like I could reach through time itself and clasp her hand and tell her we made it back after all, that it took so long, but we are once again standing in the same corner of the shifting universe. One of us is leaving, one of us is arriving.

Once an illusion is broken, it's broken.

So why did the illusion remain when I first left Medyssia? Because I was already inside of it, I suppose. I didn't break a spell; I walked away from one. But if I go back in from the outside… if I look at the cloak of my hidden planet and say *there you are, I see you,* and use this map to lift it and walk through…

My parents. Reunion. *We knew you'd come back, we knew*

you'd come back.

But then, the *Starsaviour,* ripping through the atmosphere behind me before I can find the right people to warn, to put the barrier back in place. Blasts of cannon fire raining down, eating away at the planet until its core turns to ash. Maybe the Medyssians fight back. Maybe their eyes go black and their teeth go sharp like the one in the memory and they attack the Celestial Company, not even bothering to use a song to lure them out, just ripping away at flesh and hearts in the kind of frenzy made even more lethal by withdrawal.

And if I run instead? Take the map, bide my time, wait? Valyra's obsession is fathomless; this I've seen. She will wait and watch forever, as long as needed. I could hide for another ten years, twenty, keeping this map safe, and someone might still be here when I get back.

And as soon as I go through that barrier, blood will come in my wake.

So I don't have a choice, not really.

"I don't understand," I whisper. "You could just let me go. We would disappear again. You could move on."

"You know why I can't do that." Valyra wraps her arm around her tether and glides back to the safety of the rigging until her boots meet beam. She doesn't lower Aren down beside her. She still holds him just far enough away from a foothold that his legs kick and kick and meet nothing. "I showed you what your kind are, what they've done. They've slaughtered too many. They cannot be allowed to exist. But you... *you...*" She tilts her head and looks me up and down so appraisingly that I can feel ice across every inch of my floating umbra. "You may have been born a monster, but you could become something else. I know you saved my son's life. I only caged you because I had to be sure you weren't a threat."

"I don't believe you."

"No? You believe him, though." She shakes Aren gently by the collar. "Did he tell you I was planning on letting you stay here? That you could belong, that you could be honed into something magnificent?"

The glass suddenly feels slick and slippery in my grasp.

Stay here. Aren's voice in my ear, lost in the stars. *Stay with me.*

"You're lying," I whisper. "You don't want to save me. You just want the map."

"Ask him yourself."

Aren's wince rearranges the stream of blood across his face. "Only you would still think that's some kind of prize."

It's not. Of course, it's not. I could never stay with someone like her. And yet, with no options—

My one vision of the future—of going home and then watching home be ravaged—splits against my will. Here with Aren, forever. A universe explored from a different vantage point. A revenge against Valyra that I could let simmer, maybe, until I was strong enough to find its release.

"You must be so tired of running," Valyra murmurs. "Why should you suffer for the rest of your kind's bloodlust?"

Two futures. Both end with my own happiness, one fleeting, one everlasting.

And both end with the rest of my kind dead, turned to ash.

"I will never be what you think I am," I say, and her face hardens. "You would turn me into a monster of your own and call it freedom, and you expect me to thank you for your mercy." Tears cloud my vision, threaten to spill over and choke me from speaking, but I am stronger than them. "I was no one but a lost girl, before you. And you won't let me be that anymore, so now…" I swallow, gripping the orb tighter. It's so small, this thing everyone wants. So fragile. "Now neither of us will ever see Medyssia."

I haven't been around Valyra long, but I find I've seen just enough of her to know what her fear looks like. She's trained it, beaten it into submission, until it takes the same shape wrath would take on anyone else. It's a slant in her brows, a curl of her lip, a fire in her eyes.

"You smash that—" she warns, and her fingers curl deeper into Aren's collar—"and I will only force him to make another one."

"I'll never," Aren spits out. "Do whatever you want to me, I'll never."

I breathe in deep the way I did once long ago, in this very spot. I remember breathing like it would let me take the universe itself into my lungs, so I could carry its color and sound back with me when I slipped under a surface I never found again.

"Make him," I say, and they both turn to look at me. "Make a thousand of them. Fill this ship with orbs. But you won't find Medyssia. Not without my blood."

Valyra sighs with something like pity. "There is nowhere you could go that I will not find you. I hunted you creatures for years. I know your tricks. The only thing that ever kept you safe before was my belief that you didn't exist."

Maybe she's right. Maybe she's not. I ran for many years without her knowing I was even a speck in the cosmos, and I might run for many more even with her trailing me. The story that belonged to the other Medyssian would become mine. *Always behind her, no matter how far she ran. I'll find you. I'll find you.*

"You were right," I say. "I'm so tired of running."

A vacuous roar rips through the sails; Valyra's sword leaps to her free hand. "No—*no!*" Aren shouts, but neither of them is fast enough to stop me.

I grow my fingers into claws. I let my eyes go black and soulless. I become the creature she thinks I am—ruthless, rageful, who feels no pain and fears nothing.

I clench my hand around the orb, and I squeeze.

It cracks in my fist, glass I don't feel driving itself into my skin, and the light home collapses.

The sky goes dim and empty, silver and blue and white melting away into the ether, and I watch it vanish, all of it. The path itself, and the house in the trees, and the image of my family reaching for me from so close, so close, so far.

And then, with a hand still splintered with my last chance at finding home, I reach up, and I rip my own heart out of my chest.

CHAPTER 48

Nym

I feel nothing.

I'm the barest pieces of matter returning to the universe. It feels like transforming, but with no new body waiting on the other side.

I'm turning to stardust; I'm falling into an abyss and floating toward a sky I can't see. And the world is a vacuum, narrowing into one long beam of light. In the periphery are moving forms, slow-motion planets trapped in my orbit. A whirlwind of gold and white, a symphony of screams. They don't exist, and neither will I.

I am gone, I am gone, I am somewhere else.

The beam of light is eclipsed by blue. Blue hair, blue eyes. I can't hear him, I'm too far, but I can read the shape of his mouth. *No*, it says, *no, no, no.*

It pulls me back, just a little. Almost enough. Widens the tunnel enough for me to remember.

The only thing.

This was the only thing, and that's why I'm not afraid.

Can't lose you. That's what he's saying now. *Please.*

Please, I can't lose you.

"I'm not lost." My voice is even farther away than the rest

of me. An odd thing to say, but it feels like the truth, though I can't imagine why.

Maybe I haven't been lost since I first found him, drowning in the stars.

Maybe because he'll be free now, and Medyssia will be safe, though I can't promise that either will be both. And no world where those two things are true could ever, ever feel like losing.

Not lost.

Not lost at all.

But then, with one last dissolving breath, I am.

CHAPTER 49

Aren

THE *Starsaviour* searches for days. Maybe weeks. I don't know.

The damage remains, the shields still in pieces. The bottle containing this ship has been shattered. But still, it roams the sky in meticulous circles, back and forth, back and forth. It sends out every available vessel in the fleet to do the same. It sifts through every inch of space, but space stays empty.

Medyssia is gone.

Without the map, without Nym, there's no trace. The illusion keeping it cloaked is too strong. We could be right on top of it, grazing its atmosphere, with tendrils of seaweed and clouds of fish brushing the wood of the ship, and we wouldn't see a thing.

It's gone, and so is Nym. But one is still safe and alive and out there somewhere, a silent mystery that might never be answered in my lifetime. And the other isn't.

I want to feel hollow. I want to crumble away into nothing the way she did, and I know that if I keep still for even one second, I probably will, so I don't. While everyone is distracted hunting for a planet that doesn't exist, while my mother is busy avoiding me either because she can no longer stand to look at me or because my betrayal's been eclipsed by her own obsession or both, I work.

We've got a lot of equipment on the *Starsaviour*. Lots of replacement parts for ships. Wood, canvas, rope. Gravity cores, oxygen supplements. And even though it would be so much easier to just take any of the other hundred ships in the hold and run, I don't. Doing this one last thing for her is the only thing keeping me going.

I don't know what I'll do after House is fixed. I don't know where we'll go. *I'll figure that out later,* I keep telling myself. *Just weld together one more part. Just tie one more rope. Just replace one more panel.*

It takes longer than it might have before. I have to teach myself to work half in darkness—my left eye, the one pierced through when my specs shattered, stays dim no matter what I do. It takes forever for the swelling to go down enough to even open it, and when I finally do, it's icy blue and refuses to feed me anything but shadow. One eye will always be looking out into the black of the ether.

The days or maybe weeks slide into each other, and I hardly even leave the hold. I sleep in Nym's nest of blankets, trying not to think about how much the dust that still hangs over the floor feels like a ghost. I don't want to talk to anyone. I don't want anyone to talk to me.

It's a strategy that works for days or maybe weeks, until one day, when I'm lying on my back, staring up at the new canvas dome, fresh and bare and untouched by paint, to make sure all the ropes have the right tension, and I hear a creak in the floorboards that doesn't belong to me.

"Hey," I say, tucking my arms under my head. "I told you I'd come back for you."

The floor creaks again. Maybe I'm imagining how aching and accusatory the sound feels, how much it sounds like a question. Maybe I'm imagining the ease with which I can translate the creak into a hum. *Nym? Nym? Nym?*

Maybe it's House's soul returning, or maybe it's just the voice in my own head.

But either way, after that otherworldly creak, I know that I'm done. All the pieces are restored; the ship is ready to fly.

Which means there's only one thing left to do.

I put it off for last because it's not something I can do myself, and it takes days or maybe weeks of not talking to anyone to begrudgingly admit that I'm going to have to talk to one more person before I can finally go. See, I've had an idea. One last paranoia that crept in after spending so much time on House and then realizing I never asked Valyra how she found me after she hauled us in, back when she thought I'd run away. Like I said, I have an idea.

Which is how I end up on a chair in the middle of House with Cas standing behind me like she's cutting my hair, an electro-cautery knife pressed to the base of my neck.

"I'd like to remind you one final time," she says, "for when this inevitably hurts, that this was your idea. You sure you don't want to see an actual surgeon? Bayless could probably give you a telescopic eye like Havelock, too, you know."

"I don't want a telescopic eye. Especially from someone under my mother's command," I say. "And it's gonna hurt no matter what. Just do it."

Cas eases the edge down, and I wince as the heated blade touches skin. "Are you sure you're not acting a little… what's the word I'm looking for?"

I let out an empty laugh. "Irrational?"

"Completely unhinged. I mean, you don't even know if

you're right about this. Besides, even if you are, the captain isn't looking for you, and you've apparently still been on the ship since Ny—since the thing. What makes you think she's gonna look for you if you leave?"

"Not risking it." It's not like I can go ask her whether she's leaving me alone because she doesn't care to find me, still planning on spreading a story about how I was banished, or because she knows for a fact that I'm still on the ship and is waiting for me to crawl back to her apologetic and submissive. And even if it's the former, I can't go with the doubt that she could change her mind someday and try to track me down. It'd be a prickle over my shoulder everywhere I went. No, I need to cut this string.

"*Do* it," I repeat, and she does.

The top layer of skin just below my hairline slices off, and the stab of pain is so sharp and startling that I forget to even scream. In that quick moment before Cas slaps an ice-cold padded bandage over the wound, blocking out the sting, it almost feels good. It's nice to know that I can still feel things.

"Ew." Cas gags and drops the blackened scab of what used to be part of me over my shoulder. Even through the grainy burns, I can just make out the two familiar moons of my former brand. I flick it over, and the outline becomes tangible—not ink after all, not all the way through, but the tiniest and thinnest of wires, curled into those two Cs. A tracking monitor hiding below my skin. Property of the Celestial Company.

Well, not anymore.

I curl my fist around the scab and clench, feel it crumble into dust.

"Huh. Guess you were right." Cas squats beside me and prods the ash with her cauterizer, her mouth curving when she hears another sizzle.

"You probably have them too, you know. You and Felix."
Felix. I should have said goodbye. "Where is he, anyway?"

"Oh." Cas flashes a wry, secretive smile. "Just going over the plans for our first mission."

"Your—what?"

"It's nothing." Cas shrugs in a way that implies the opposite. "Havelock doesn't know we put the top deck under siege, but we made sure she knew how well we defended it. So. No more training."

"That's—" Everything she's ever wanted. I really was holding them back. *I'm happy for you;* that's what I should say. "I don't get it."

Her grin vanishes. "I don't need your approval."

"No, that's not what I meant. I just …" I swallow, searching for the right words. "You shouldn't have to rely on Valyra to get what you want. You're the toughest person I know, and you don't need her. You could start your own crew. Call your own shots."

Cas snorts. "Cute. You think I have the resources to match the Celestial Company on my own? Try again."

"But if you wanted—"

"I don't," she interrupts firmly. "I *like* being here. I like it more than anything in the entire world. I'm smart and I'm indispensable and I'm not afraid of the captain. I choose this." Her thumb presses into the tattoo at her wrist, tracing the curve softly. "Maybe leaving is an escape for you, but for me, it would only feel like giving up."

I nod. I get it. We all have our shadows—the ones we cast, and the ones we stand in. Both of us have been in my mother's for too long, but while I was busy suffocating, she was molding herself to fit. "You'd be a better heir than I ever was. I know that much."

"Well. We'll see." She shoots me a smirk that sends a pang through my heart—it might be the last one I ever get from her. "Hey, be safe out there. There's an endless void of space outside this ship, from what I hear."

"Yeah." I push back the hair that constantly falls over my blind eye now that my specs aren't there to hold it up. "You know, that doesn't scare me so much anymore." I lift myself from my stool, then lift two fingers in salute. "See you around, future captain."

I guess she had one last smirk in her after all.

"Get lost, Aren," she says, flicking my forehead teasingly, and then she slips out of the hold. It's only when she's gone that I realize it's the first time I can remember that she's called me "Aren" and not "star-prince."

It's only when she's gone that I realize there's nothing else left for me to do now, no more tasks to complete before I can leave.

Leave, and figure out exactly what kind of person I am without that title.

I still don't know what that means in terms of a real plan, in terms of where I'm going to go and what I'm going to do. But that doesn't scare me the way it used to. I can't believe I used to think of the world outside the *Starsaviour* as this abyss I was one wrong step away from falling into. I'm going to do what Nym would have done if she'd ever gotten to be completely free: I'm going to go everywhere, see everything, try everything, until maybe one day I finish growing into something fearless.

And I'm going to plant the seeds of a new legend to anyone who will listen—not about hungry sirens who hunted and killed, but about the curious one who turned herself to ash to stop a massacre, who was brave and weird and selfless and proof that other Medyssians were capable of being all those things too. Because she wasn't alone; I know it. She can't have been the only one like her, who truly loved the universe instead of thirsted for it. My mother has spread a story long enough about ruthless creatures desperate for blood, so I will spread one to counter it.

I will—

I will do none of that, because House won't move.

I can hear the hum of its core, and the floor rumbles softly beneath my feet, but when I pull the same cord Nym always did to release it from the hold, the hold remains solidly latched onto us.

"No. No, come on," I beg, because I've been one breath away from breaking down for days, maybe weeks, and if after everything, House is lost too, I won't be able to take it. I pull the lever again, and the canvas moans, but doesn't lift.

I let go and drag my hands through my hair. I can feel it coming, the eruption, and I don't want to take it out on House. "Okay," I finally get out. "Okay, tell me what's broken. Do that wind thing, or something."

A weak moan, and then, like the string of an instrument snapping, the rope nearest the wall suddenly springs free.

"I didn't mean break things yourself," I snap irritably, pushing through neatly stacked boxes to reach the tethering hook. I'm rewarded with another dismal moan, louder this time, and the end of the rope slithers over the railing and off the side of the ship like a skittish animal desperate to get away from me.

I sigh and rest on my elbows. "I get it," I say quietly. "I know you don't want to go without her. I don't, either. But we..." Something stings behind my eyes. *We have to. We don't have a choice.* "I'll look after you. I promise. I don't know if that's worth anything, but I mean it. Okay?"

The rope doesn't move, and nothing else breaks. It's a start, if nothing else.

"Okay," I answer myself, then lean forward to pull the rope back in.

And out of the corner of my good eye, a flash of silver.

My heart stops. I turn toward it desperately, the beginning of her name already jumping to my lips, but when my eye focuses, it isn't her. Of course, it isn't. Just a cluster of stars somewhere outside the ship. There's a hole near the top of the wall, left behind when House ruptured its own mast setting me free.

I guess I'll be looking for her everywhere without meaning to from now on, in every bright twinkle of stardust.

I hang over the railing one moment more, just looking up through that accidental skylight. I can see the shimmering gold glint of the *Starsaviour's* foremost sails from this angle, and a sharp jolt goes through my stomach when I realize I know what part of the ship I'm looking at. It's the place where Nym hovered when she saved me. Exactly where she was when she died. I can practically see her ghost in the emptiness, see the way her eyes glowed and the look on her face when she tricked Valyra. I can see…

No. It can't be.

I'm over the railing and climbing up the rope before I can even make the conscious decision to jump. I don't stop until I'm crouched inside the hole itself, an artificial breeze whistling through my hair. It's even larger than it looked from the ground, an uneven yawn with nothing but open space outside of it. Space, and a crystal-clear view of the foremast. More than enough room.

It can't be.

My hand leaps to my chest, to the string tied under my shirt and the cracked ball of glass hanging from it. The second map is empty and the insides are broken; it'll lead to nowhere, but it was the only thing left of her when she dissolved, so I couldn't let go of it.

Now, I grip it in my fist and feel its coldness bite into my skin. *Feel* it. When Cas called me unhinged before, I wasn't yet, but now I must be. I didn't just see Nym disappear—I felt it. I felt her fall away in my arms. I stole this orb before either the universe or my mother could snatch it away, and I felt that too.

Didn't I?

"You're not real." I close my eyes and imagine that the weight on my chest is gone. "You're not real. This isn't real."

But when I open my eyes, it's still there.

My fingers go slack around the chain. Pathetic. She's gone, and if I keep trying to imagine her back, I'll trap myself in the same desperate dream Nym used to be so afraid of.

The hole is just a hole. It doesn't mean anything.

But for some reason, all I can suddenly hear is Nym. The last thing she said to me. *I'm not lost.*

I take a deep breath. One more try. For her, and for everything she taught me about believing in hidden things.

This time, I keep my eyes open, but I press my hand over my good one, leaving only the obscuring smoke cast by the other. I ignore the map. I just stare fiercely through the murky haze and imagine what Nym might have looked like, lying on her back in the glint of light cast by the faint stars outside, hiding. Creating an illusion powerful and tangible enough to trick Valyra. Me. Herself.

"I see you," I whisper. "I see you."

I drop to a crouch and trail my fingers over the warped

mahogany one millimeter at a time, searching for an invisible veil. The way she must have for all those years, looking for her planet. Two feet of space or two trillion—it doesn't make a difference when you're looking for something that doesn't want to be found. But she must be here, somewhere I can't see, just like Medyssia was. I'm creating my own illusion the way Nym used to, believing in something so hard that it becomes real, and for a minute, inside my own head, it almost is. I can almost see her, her hair like a cloudburst, her tendrils of umbra floating across the ground. Her eyes wide and unseeing, hypnotized by a story. *I am up there, not here. I am disintegrating into nothing. I am nothing. I am nothing.* I can almost see it all.

And then, there's no "almost" anymore.

"Nym?" I breathe, lowering my hand.

Moonlight hair. Umbra cascading over the floor—over my *boot*. Exactly the way I imagined her, like I willed her into existence.

Right down to her eyes. Two twin orbs, unseeing, unfeeling. All the life gone.

Trapped in her own mind, asleep in a window. Lost.

No, not lost, not forever. Because she's here. She's still *here*.

I sink to my knees beside her, afraid to even breathe, like if I move too quickly or touch her at all, she'll dissolve the same way she did before. But she doesn't, not even when I carefully lift her head from the floor.

I brought her back from this before. I can do it again.

"Come back." I feel like screaming, turning my own voice into a knife that'll pierce through the armor locking her away, but I can't produce more than a hoarse whisper. "Come back, come back."

Over and over again, just those two words, like an incantation. So many times that each individual word loses its meaning completely.

"You're not gone," I plead. That's right, that's what worked before. That's how I pulled her out. I had to give her a truth to replace the one that had trapped her. "Medyssia is safe. I'm safe. You're not lost; you're here. Come back."

I imagine I see a flicker somewhere in her hollow eyes, and my heart leaps, but it's a mirage. And I know what desperation is now—I thought I had it before, but this is the real thing, it has to be, because I do the only other thing I can think of.

I lift her hand, and I press it to my chest. Right over my heart. The place where her deepest instinct is supposed to be to destroy me. I hold her there, and I will her to feel a different pull.

"I know you can hear it," I whisper, pressing harder. "You don't get to leave me behind."

I hold her there for seconds that drag into minutes that drag into days maybe weeks. An entire infinity waiting for a sign of movement that isn't just her lethargic pulse under my thumb.

Then, nails press into my skin.

I inhale, sharp and tense. She wouldn't. There is no instinct within her to take my heart. I know her. *I will never be afraid of you,* I said, and this is the proof. I don't tear myself away from her, even as the pointed tips crack the surface.

Come on, Nym. Come back.

But the nails don't puncture. Instead, they... *change.*

The tips shrink, connected to fingers that are slowly staining themselves the same shade as mine, instead of lavender. The first color eats the second like a wave gliding up her arm, over her chest, up to her face. Her hair grows solid, and suddenly I'm not kneeling on umbra anymore, but a skirt. A skirt covering legs.

Human legs.

Because Nym's instinct when presented with a heart isn't to devour it, but to mimic it. It always has been.

It worked. It worked, it worked, she's still in there.

And finally, finally with her hand still pressed tight to my chest, the clouds leave her eyes.

Even then, I'm too scared to speak, because she doesn't blink or sit up or whisper my name or anything that would make sense. She only stares.

"Nym?" I whisper, and I can't decide whether I'm more afraid that she's going to respond like she doesn't know me or the idea that she might never respond again.

Slowly, her eyes slide onto mine.

"You," she says. "You found me."

CHAPTER 50

Nym

I was having a dream.

The dream looked like this: drowning in space, lost, no tether, no voice. Floating into infinity forever and ever, unable to die. I dreamed I was ash, drifting ash, reclaimed by the pull of the universe.

There is nothing outside of this dream. There has never been. There never will be. Only stars and stars and stars and the dust I've become. And yet, suddenly, something has shifted. Something new.

A boy. Swimming through the ether. Ink-blot hair and a scar that runs from his eyebrow through one pale, clouded iris.

He reaches for me.

"Nym?"

"You." I know him, this boy. I know him. "You found me."

His breath catches, and that one small sound is the spark of a match, because all the hazy edges of space around him begin to burn away. The stars that have become my universe shimmer out, then in, and when they return, they're encased by a window. A hole. And the hole is inside of a ship, and I am in that hole, and this boy is beside me, and I *remember*.

I am real. I did not crumble to ash. I am Nym, the last

Medyssian, and I am awake.

Aren. I remember that too. Who he is. What he means to me. "Ar—"

I don't make it to the second syllable. Aren's face illuminates, a moon cycling into the light of a sun, and then he lunges forward. The air bursts from my lungs as he squeezes, tight and fierce and disbelieving, as if desperate to make sure I won't vanish, and we're both too real and solid to doubt whether or not this might be another kind of illusion. Not lost. Not lost at all.

"I've got you," he gasps. "I'm real, I'm here, I've got you."

And I squeeze him back, my anchor, my tether, and feel the last vestiges of my false reality fade away around us. Not lost. Not lost at all.

"You found me," I manage to echo.

"I should have looked harder. Sooner. I thought—" His throat catches, and he draws away, staring at me as though he's forgotten what I look like in the interim. I can see his ice-colored pupil even more clearly now—when I saw him last, it was a river of blood that has since dried up. I reach for the scar without thinking, but he doesn't blink. *Blind.*

"I'm—I'm so sorry."

"Don't. This wasn't your fault." He tilts his head, peers up through his hair. "Making me think you were dead, on the other hand."

I draw back, letting my hand fall. "I thought I could save everything. I… I didn't know how to leave you a sign."

"I think I can forgive you. On one condition." Aren's eyes lower, and I know he's watching the way my heart pulses below my throat, remembering the lie I fed us both. "Promise me you'll never do that again."

Despite myself, my exhale turns into a weak laugh. But

then I look past Aren into the ether, a tideless sea on the other side of the breach, and the smile fades. "And Medyssia? Is it… Did she…?"

Aren shakes his head. "Vanished."

"Vanished." Relief should not taste so bitter. I lift myself all the way up and rest my hand on the curve of the gap in the hold. The shields have not repaired fully, and the ether peeks in between the cracks. An ocean of lilac and silver, the music of the stars calling softly to me even through the cage. And somewhere out there, a planet that might never be found.

"I can never go back, can I?" I ask quietly. "Not while she's still out there searching for it."

Aren is kind enough to not say the truth out loud, but his silence does more than enough. No, I cannot go back. The planet will once again sleep as if enchanted.

Then again, never is a terribly long time.

Long and uncharted, and I have no idea what lies at the end of it. The universe is ever-shifting, ever-changing, and so are the creatures that live within it. Valyra is only one such creature. Perhaps she will change too.

Perhaps it isn't a false hope to replace *never* with *someday*.

And in all of that uncharted space between those tentative boundaries, there is so much. So much I haven't seen yet, so much I wanted to see again. The universe doesn't have to be a prison or a desert this time, trapping me inside it or forcing me to wander. It can be what it is—nothing more or less than an infinite expanse full of beauty and wonder and magic that doesn't belong to me yet.

For now, that is more than enough.

Through the stillness, a quiet whine calls to me, and for the first time, I turn and see what fills the hold behind us.

A silvery balloon held taut with ropes that strain against

their weights. A basket that isn't in shambles at all, but polished and clean. Shiny objects glint from the corners; a joyful whine ripples from under the floorboards.

"House," I barely manage to say, and my heart races and my clouded mind clears. "Oh, *House*."

I seize Aren's wrist and fall back into my true form and *dive*, dragging us straight down, catching him before he falls. I pull us clumsily over the side and into the basket, and I haven't cried yet, but I might now.

He brought my home back to me, just like he brought me back, again and again. And he's even turned it into something far stronger and more beautiful than it was before it was destroyed. My treasures wink above me, returned to their strings; my plants drape neatly from shelves; the mast is papered with drawings. I thought there would be nothing left at all, but he somehow found all the broken pieces and fixed them anyway.

"You—you did this?" I breathe, turning in a stunned circle. "You saved it all?"

Aren scratches his wrist, and I notice for the first time how raw and paint-stained his palms are, as though House itself has bled into his skin. "I couldn't leave you both behind, could I?"

House's canopy sighs, the sound like summer wind dancing beneath a tent. A rope snags free and weaves around my shoulder.

"I know," I laugh, wrapping my arms around the mast and looking up. "I missed you too. I missed you so much."

But as my gaze reaches the apex of the balloon, I'm startled to find one change to the House I know: there's nothing but a bare white canopy where my skymap once hung. Untouched, unpainted. My breath catches.

"Ah… I'm sorry." Aren ruffles his hair. "It—it was the only

thing I couldn't save."

I shake my head. He's misunderstood. "I don't need it anymore." My hand seeks his; our fingers pull together. "We'll make a new one."

Aren tilts his head back to match me, then nudges his shoulder against mine. "So, where should we go first?"

I've never been less sure. That has never made me feel less adrift. I turn to look at them, this new home I somehow found when I wasn't searching for it. A basket full of memories, a canopy full of promise. A boy who is kind and true and brave enough to face the unknown no matter what waits for us within it.

"Everywhere," I say. "Anywhere that calls to us."

And as we set House free from the hold underneath a blank sky, I know without question that both *never* and *someday* might be terrifying and bittersweet and daunting, but it can also look like this: a second chance, a starting over. An unexplored universe singing to me, and I am no longer lost in it.

I will never be lost again.

One Last Story

Once there was a creature who swam between stars.

But now there are two.

What do they look like? No one knows. Or rather, no one can agree. To some, they have vibrant scales or wings or ears shaped like daggers; sometimes they have two eyes and sometimes they have six. Sometimes their lower halves taper into fins. Oddly, they always seem to look like whoever happens to be telling their story.

They tell their own story too, the strange kind that's so unbelievable that it just might be true. About a lost planet enchanted by a powerful spell, full of magical creatures who used to swim through the stars too, but are now gone.

Of how one day, maybe, they'll come back.

The two, one boy and one girl, tell this story. They stay for a day, a week, a season. And then, when it's time, they vanish quietly into the sky, in a balloon half-painted over with colors and trinkets, half-bare and waiting for treasures to come. Seeking out their next adventure, wherever it calls to them. Curious, and happy, and free.

But the story stays behind.

Stories always do.

And in its wake comes a ship.

This ship is not gray or haunted, not glittering or majestic. It has no teeth. Its sails are faded, its hull scratched and worn. It has sailed through the years and through the sky for longer than it can remember, hunting, searching for an elusive creature lost long ago. And now, it follows the trail of this story like a distant light at the end of a once-endless cave.

And within the ship, a man with eyes that twinkle like constellations. A woman with hair long enough to ensnare fish in its tangled curls. Their daughters—the eldest of whom has never stopped regretting not holding her tongue when her youngest sister begged for a story about the world above.

The universe swallowed something precious of theirs. It swept her away like a bottle in a storm. And when the universe laughed at them, taunted them, refused to give her back, they did what they must, though the outside world was cold and cruel and filled with monsters. They let the storm take them too.

They have been looking for their lost girl since the stars first stole her away.

I'll find you, they have called into the night with no answer, through the empty years and the emptier sky. But now, there is finally a melody calling back to them. A story about a girl and a boy and a forgotten planet, seeds of a story planted to root and grow into a path. And when the night goes warm and still, they peer through the clouds and imagine they see the faint

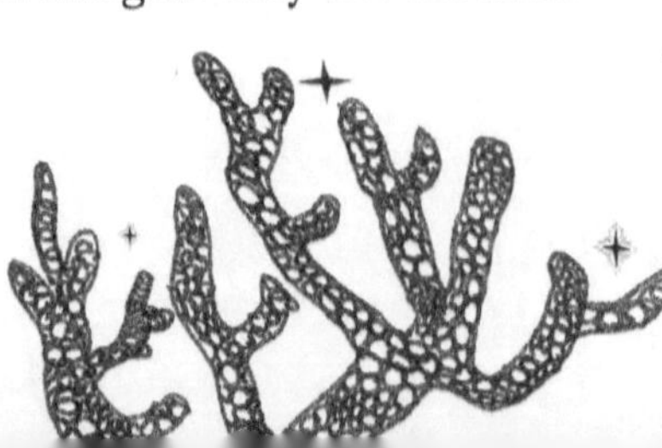

outline of a balloon floating in the distance. They imagine their daughter is safe inside, alive and happy and protected by someone who doesn't fear the depths of space or the monsters that lurk inside it, still waiting for them.

I never stopped looking, they promise, no matter how far behind they fall, no matter how often the light guiding their way might flicker. *And I never will. I'll find you someday, someday soon.*

I'll find you.

THE END

ACKNOWLEDGEMENTS

IF IT TAKES a village to publish a book, this one took an entire planet. I will never have enough words to thank the many friends who read and believed in this book throughout its journey, including: Mahaillie Griffith, Emma Lord, Mike Lasagna, Daniel McCook, Sarah Mills, Joanna Ruth Meyer, Daniel Posada, Breanna Ciccone-Posada, Ashley Poston, Cody Roeker, Ashley Schumacher, Rachel Strolle, Duy Truong, and Lexi Vaughan. Extra-special shoutout to my writing group: Ciara Bagnasco, Brittany Evans, Paige Lavoie, and Aly Mierzejewski. From Zoom sprints to Disney Resort writing dates to the countless "my brain has stopped working, can you fix this plot point" texts, I don't know and do not wish to know what sort of writer I would be without your friendship and support. I adore you. Also, Paige, don't go anywhere, I'm not done with you yet.

My sword, my kingdom, and whatever else you want to Kelsey Soderstrom (@toughtink) for creating the cover art of my dreams and Rena Violet (@violet.book.design) for the beautiful interiors and formatting. My other sword and kingdom to Morgan Germain (@jjgg_art), Daniel McCook, and Sarah Mills for making one of my most persistent daydreams about this book—an animated Disney-style version of the prologue—come to life. And all my gratitude to Lee O'Brien, whose sharp and insightful editorial eye took this story to new heights.

All good productions need a good Craft Services—I'm lucky to have found the best source of friendship and fuel in Book + Bottle. Dom, Andi, and the rest of the gang, thank you for all the oat milk lattes and encouragement while I juggled editing this book with studying for the Bar, which is still a thing I can't believe I thought was a good idea. You are the very best second home in all of St. Pete, and possibly all of Florida.

I simply must acknowledge the significant creative influences that bled into this book: thanks to SVRCINA, for the song *Astronomical,* from which the idea for this story was first born; Demi Chen (@demi.draws), whose beautiful and ethereal moon jellyfish mermaids inspired the design of Nym and the other Medyssians; and James Newton Howard, Really Slow Motion, and Joel McNeely for providing the majority of my writing soundtrack. And can I thank Treasure Planet? Thanks, Treasure Planet. Thanks, Ron Clements and John Musker. The world wasn't ready for your genius.

Now back to Paige. Oh, Paige. My fellow space girl, my sister by choice, my beloved friend of almost ten (!!!) years now—there is no universe where this book existed without you. You are part of every tentpole of this story's creation— that walk to Stardust where I first told you I'd had an idea about a boy drowning in space and the girl who rescues him;

that "research" trip to Kennedy Space Center to learn about physics we promptly refused to implement (all that matters is There Was Only Space Pod); all those days sitting on opposite ends of the same table, writing about earnest, anxious, hopeful kids trying to find their place in the stars (I firmly believe Aren and Nym have linked up with Susie, Eugene, and the rest of the *Dear Galaxy* gang by now, by the way, and you know Aren is losing his mind over that flying car). I love you infinitely. Let's keep going on adventures forever.

Finally, of course, thank you to my family. I have never had to wonder whether you supported or understood the author part of my life, and it's the greatest gift I'll ever have. Thank you Dad for the late-night texts demanding the next chapter; thank you Mom for crying at Home Depot when I told you how the book ends and offering up your Cricut services for marketing at every turn; thank you Morgan for sending me every song you came across that might fit my Spotify playlist; thank you all for always believing in me. Finally, to Aunt Diane and Grandma—I hope I've made you proud too. I think you would have liked this one.

TAYLOR SIMONDS is a Central-Florida based writer of
sci-fi/fantasy and speculative fiction, including her debut,
COLLATERAL DAMAGE. An escapee of Walt Disney
World Entertainment, Taylor holds a bachelor's degree in
marketing from the University of Central Florida and a
Juris Doctor from Stetson University College of Law. She
will see you in court.

9 798218 376895